ZOMBIE, INDIANA

A Novel

Scott Kenemore

TALOS PRESS

Talos Press books may be purchased in bulk at special discounts for sales promotion, corporate gifts, fund-raising, or educational purposes. Special editions can also be created to specifications. For details, contact the Special Sales Department, Talos Press, 307 West 36th Street, 11th Floor, New York, NY 10018 or info@skyhorsepublishing.com.

Talos Press is an imprint of Skyhorse Publishing, Inc.®, a Delaware corporation.

Visit our website at www.skyhorsepublishing.com.

10 9 8 7 6 5 4 3 2 1

Library of Congress Cataloging-in-Publication Data

Kenemore, Scott.
Zombie, Indiana : a novel / Scott Kenemore.
pages cm
ISBN 978-1-940456-00-3 (pbk.: alk. paper)   1.   Zombies—Fiction.
2. Missing persons—Fiction. 3. Indiana—Fiction. I. Title.
PS3611.E545Z65 2014
813'.6—dc23

                          2014000506

Cover photo credit Thinkstock.com

Ebook ISBN: 978-1-940456-03-4

Printed in the United States of America

Dedicated to the memory of Mr. Greg Foote

"You cannot kill it, it is dead; at the same time it lives.
It lives with a sinister life bestowed on it by Infinity."

Victor Hugo,
Ninety-Three

"Have we a chance when the dead rise and dance?
Have we the time for the final romance?"

Motörhead,
"Terminal Show"

"We have not attained an ideal condition."

Benjamin Harrison,
Inaugural Address,
March 4, 1889

1

"A New Indiana."

The governor looked at the campaign banner on the wall of his office—the banner that was now almost eight years old.

In the quiet at the end of the workday, he found it pleasant to stop and consider all of the progress that had been made since his first weeks in office. He looked out of his window, out to the Soldiers and Sailors Monument a block and a half away. The three-hundred-foot column that marked the center of Indianapolis looked glorious in the late afternoon sun.

A New Indiana. Good Christ. They had almost done it. They were almost there.

If any state had changed during the governor's relatively short lifetime, it was his. He was only fifty, young for a governor nearing the end of two terms. But when he thought about how much the state had changed, he felt older. So much older.

Governor Hank Burleson could remember the bad old days. He certainly could. The seventies. The eighties. Downtown Indianapolis so dangerous you got in and out like SEALs on a mission. Burleson could recall going to Pacers games with his dad—back when the coaches wore plaid, and the ball was red, white, and blue—and good Lord, after the game was over, you more or less ran for your car. Now it was different. Now people came downtown and lingered. Spent money. It was safe. There were museums, and a mall, and an honest-to-God canal, and it was all—all of it—walkable.

The state had no debt and no pensions to pay. It had no ties to any entity with financial problems. It had the highest credit rating the agencies could give you. Indiana was growing like gangbusters.

The governor reclined on the brown leather couch usually reserved for visiting dignitaries (if you wanted to call state senators "dignitaries"). He smoked a Cuban cigar. You could get them in the Hoosier State now. Not legally, of course. But still . . . you could get a lot of things in Indiana these days.

Other states had done it fast, Burleson reckoned. Fast, sure. Fast had its merits. Everybody liked fast. But Indiana was going to do it *right*.

On the far side of Burleson's office was a map of the U.S.A. He puffed on his cigar and stared hard at the other states that made up the American Midwest. These were the competition. The enemy. And soon, Burleson thought, they would be the *vanquished* enemy.

The governor let his eyes wander across the map.

Up above was Michigan. That was a gimmie. It was moldering. Rotting from the inside out. The population shrinking. Detroit already bankrupt—a cadaver on a slab. The auto industry half-gone, and those losses weren't coming back. On the Internet there were satellite pictures of Detroit from the 1960s compared with satellite pictures from today. You could actually see the wilderness taking over again. All that concrete grey turning back to green. They were done up there. Done.

The governor cast his gaze westward, to Illinois. It would topple next, with Chicago serving as the weight to send it careening down into the abyss. High taxes. Highly paid teachers and police.

And yet a city full of delinquents with low test scores and 550 murders a year. Illinois's credit rating was now the worst in the nation. Even worse than California's. The population wasn't growing as it once had, either. It hadn't been the "Second City" since 1980, and Houston would soon overtake it to claim the number-three spot. Illinois was on the way down. On the way to irrelevancy. On the way to the trash heap. Burleson knew that the fall of Illinois would be the sweetest of all. He could not wait to savor it. He could not wait for Chicago to become the next Detroit.

And on the other side of the friendly Hoosier pylon? Ohio! Mighty Ohio. Stalwart. Friendly. And yet . . . it simply could not make up its mind. What did Ohio want to be, exactly? It didn't know. It couldn't tell you. In a way, this indecisiveness was quaint. It was like a little America. It had something for everyone. Half liberal, half conservative. Half urban, half rural. Black and white and Latino and everything else now. And all those different forces pushing every which way. And not a damn thing getting done. Cleveland in decline. Columbus still a glorified college town. And Cincinnati had gone whole-hog insane and built itself a creationist museum. (Was there any coming back from such a thing? The governor thought not.)

Out west—*way* out west—was Iowa. "Idiots Out Walking Around" was what *that* stood for. Burleson believed you couldn't hold Iowa to the same standard as a regular state. That was just mean. Criticizing Iowa was like criticizing the relative at Thanksgiving dinner who'd flunked out of school in eighth grade but still liked to call you "stupid" after a couple of beers. ("*Really*, Uncle Larry? *I'm* stupid? *I'm* the stupid one at this table?") Iowa had always been farmland, Burleson thought. John Deere and the Iowa Writers' Workshop weren't ever going to change that. Not by a damn shot. Also, it was boring there. So boring you'd just shudder. (Burleson had once heard that if you got some bad news from your doctor—only a few months to live, say—you should just move out to Iowa . . . because every day there felt like a goddamn eternity.)

Down below—the impaled victim of Indiana's pointy end—was Kentucky. And Kentucky was content just to be Kentucky. It was like Indiana in so many ways, Burleson considered, yet fundamentally without ambition. They have the Derby. We have the 500. Fine. They have Ashley Judd, and we have John Mellencamp. Fine. But when they'd started making Louisville Sluggers across the border in Indiana in the 1970s, something had been lost. It was a small thing, sure. But symbolic. The day tradition and heritage had been outsourced. Ever since learning that, Burleson had never regarded Kentucky as anything of a threat to the Hoosier State's coming dominance.

Then, finally, up to Wisconsin. Idiot Cheeseheads to the last. They had selected a cow for the image on the reverse side of their state quarter. That had given Burleson a deep sense of satisfaction. That told you everything you needed to know. A cow. There was nothing to fear from these gentle bovines. There never had been.

No. It was the twenty-first century, and it was going to be the century of the Hoosier.

It was almost a nonsense word, "Hoosier." Where had it come from? Nobody knew. There were theories, sure. Pioneers shouting, "Who's there?" Combatants arguing about "whose ear" would be torn off. A contractor named Hoosier who'd built the bridge over the Ohio River. (Could it be that simple? That banal?) Some used the term disapprovingly. Some even used it as an insult. That would not last long, Burleson reckoned. Not by a damn sight.

Soon they would come to envy it. Or *fear* it . . .

Indiana was a state that worked. That was honest. That was clean. Not technically, of course. Not by some sort of "science standard." But it looked clean. It looked beautiful. Landscaping and such. Landscaping everywhere. And fields that were green. Big beautiful fields where pesticides killed the insects almost the moment they touched down on the cornstalks.

Businesses were knocking down the door to get in. To be a part of it. Lately, Indiana had gotten brazen about poaching companies from other states. Burleson was behind this in no small way. Every time Illinois or Ohio passed another tax increase, billboards went up in Chicago and Cleveland. They said things like: "Come on *IN*: for lower taxes, business, and housing costs" or "Illinoyed by high taxes?" and had a big ol' picture of Indiana right below it. Hell, they'd put one up in Times Square in New York City, just to see what would happen. Burleson loved these billboards with a deep, abiding passion. He had helped design many of them personally. But the billboards only opened the door. It was up to him to get the business owners inside and seal the deal.

Burleson's pitch was simple: Indiana is the best place because you can come here and do whatever you want.

First of all, you could hire and fire workers at will. They'd made sure of that in the last legislative session. A few strokes of a pen, and the unions had been effectively castrated. That was the word Burleson liked to use whenever he made presentations. "Castrated." It had a real impact, that word. Every business owner—every male one, anyway—winced when he heard it . . . but then smiled from ear to ear. (The unions might still be walking around with their junk, sure . . . but it couldn't *do* anything anymore.) This right-to-work legislation was important to Burleson. It showed that Hoosiers had learned from the lessons that had brought down Detroit and would soon doom Chicago.

You could also come to Indiana and find high-tech workers, if that was what you wanted. Engineers from Purdue and Rose-Hulman. Top-of-their-field eggheads from IU or Notre Dame or Ball State. Indiana had some crazy-bright people. Crazy-bright. Kids who'd taken *all* the STEM classes, and then some. They were here and ready to work for you, yeah.

But *also* . . .

Also . . . in Indiana you could count on finding totally uneducated people happy to work in your plant or factory for a subsistence wage. We had that as well. Oh boy, did we have that. Less than a quarter of Hoosiers had any kind of college degree. Outside of the cities and centers of learning were plenty of farm towns where almost nobody went to school, and those folks were hungry for jobs and thankful for anything you wanted to offer.

What else, what else . . .?

Environmental laws. Can't forget those. Well, maybe you can. Because it seems like we do. Indiana had the least stringent environmental laws in the Midwest. Nationally, experts agreed that only West Virginia's regulations were more permissive. You want to come here and pollute Indiana's soil? We got you covered. The water? Go for it! Did you know that the tiny slice of the Hoosier State that touched Lake Michigan dumped more mercury into the lake than all the other states combined? And according to the EPA, no state released more toxic chemicals into its own waterways than Indiana. But what about the air? People forget about the air. But you can pollute that too! (Last time Burleson had checked, the American Lung Association said that four cities in Indiana had "problematic smog." Smog! In Indiana! Who knew?!) And if you *still* weren't sure that your company was going to be able to keep it up to code, there were *always* special exceptions to be granted to friends of the governor. Usually after a campaign contribution or two.

Finally—and perhaps most wonderfully, thought Burleson—you could come here and not be flummoxed by the culture. Indiana was nice! Hoosiers were nice! They went to church. They weren't going to be all up in your face with the artsy stuff. Yeah, it was a "northern" state. It had been in the Union during the Civil War. But, c'mon . . . *C'monnnnnn* . . . This is you and me talkin', here. Let's be frank. Let's be real. In the early twentieth century, over a quarter million Hoosiers had belonged to the KKK. That's one out of every six people in the state. By 1925, most of the elected government—including the governor—were *openly* Klan members. That was no longer the case, of course. The codified, formalized hostility had gradually faded away. But there was still that underlying feeling that this was not the place to be *too* artsy. Or gay. Or different. Or weird.

More than anything, Governor Burleson found *this* the most wonderful thing about his state. This stern, head-shaking sense of "Nope, we don't put up with *that* here," which some Hoosiers could telegraph without saying a single word! It kept things orderly better than any social program ever could. Cheaper, too.

You see—Burleson would announce to the cornered business executive—Hoosiers were *self-regulating*. It was in their DNA to do the things businesses wanted them to do. To *be* the way that businesses wanted them to be. We're already like that. Being that way is what we Hoosiers know.

Yep. All things considered, selling the Hoosier State was not the hardest job Governor Burleson had ever had.

These days, however, jobs were increasingly on his mind. Maybe not "jobs" plural, but *a* job. *His* job. The one he had was about to run out. Governors were limited to two consecutive terms. He'd considered a run for the senate, sure, but no way was he going to risk getting into a race while some Tea Partier could still jump in and fuck everything up for everybody. (Poor Dick Lugar. May he rest in peace.) Still, there were other employment options until a run for Congress looked more reasonable. There was consulting. Boards of directors of corporations were already calling. Dan Quayle had been in touch personally about a possible opening at a friend's firm. And then all manner of colleges and universities across the Hoosier State had invited him to join their political science faculties as a well-paid "guest lecturer."

There would be no shortage of sinecures to hold him over, the governor knew. He would have his choices out in the private sector. But Christ, thought Burleson. Christ, it would be hard to be out of the game, even for a little while. He loved the game. Loved it so much. It was who he was.

Still, you did what you had to do, especially when prospects for a congressional run looked shaky. So he would bide his time. Yes, he would.

Even the brightest star, Burleson considered, was entitled to an occasional eclipse. And that was him. The Hoosier State's brightest political star.

★★★

Burleson finished his cigar and dropped the butt in his ashtray. When he was satisfied that the majority of the smoke had drifted out his window, he stood on a chair and reactivated the small white smoke detector affixed to the ceiling.

Halfway through this task, his desk phone rang, unexpected and loud. The governor started and his knees went shaky. The chair underneath him quivered crazily . . . but did not quite topple.

Burleson regained his footing and took a deep breath.

Wouldn't that have been something? Weeks from finishing up his term, and the governor of Indiana dies of an unexplained fall inside his own damn office.

In a trice, Burleson pictured it all. The flags at half-staff on the capitol building. The elegant state funeral. The casket on display underneath a marble rotunda, his wife and daughter weeping respectfully beside it. The unsuccessful push to have

I-465 named after him. (A building at his college would eventu-ally get the honor.) He could see it all, clear as day.

Fuck that.

Burleson leapt off the chair with the vim of a younger man and landed on the carpeted floor with a muffled thud. He still had lots of life left in him. Maybe another fifty years. Really, he assured himself, he was just getting started.

So . . . who the hell was calling during cigar time? His recep-tionist had been given explicit instructions that *nothing short of hell or high water should ever interrupt cigar time.*

The governor strode to the telephone and put the receiver to his ear.

"Yes," he said sternly.

The voice that came back was that of his chief of staff. The man sounded terrified.

"Governor," he said. "We may have a problem . . ."

2

Indianapolis Metro Police Special Sergeant James Nolan knew that once he pulled his squad car underneath I-456—and Massachusetts Avenue became Pendleton Pike—he would be out of the Eastern District's jurisdiction. Technically, this was no longer even Indianapolis. It was Lawrence.

But just as virtually nobody who lived in the city made that distinction, Nolan knew that neither did his informants.

Nolan pulled his car under 465 and into the parking lot of the fast food restaurant just beyond. Seated on the curb directly in front of the establishment were two girls in their late teens eating fried chicken out of a greasy sack and maybe waiting for a ride. Also seated with them, though clearly unwelcome, was Nathan Dazey.

Nolan killed the engine and ducked a little as he hoisted his six-foot-nine frame out of the squad car. The young women looked at one another and giggled as he approached.

When Dazey saw the plainclothes policeman he positively beamed.

"Hey, how's it hanging?" Dazey called brightly. "Ladies, this tall drink of water is my good friend James. Me and him go back a ways. We sure do."

This was true.

Nolan had gotten to know Dazey ten years ago when the IMPD was just the IPD, and when Pendleton Pike was still part of the beat for Eastern District narcotics officers. Dazey was a handsome, spry drug addict with almost no compunction or loyalty. As soon as he'd arrived on the scene, IPD officers had found him a valuable resource for meeting arrest quotas and—occasionally—for learning where there were bigger fish to fry. Dazey was usually willing to say where he'd made his last buy when push came to shove. For twenty dollars and a sandwich, he would tell you anything you wanted to know.

Sometimes Dazey left the Eastern District for a while, drifting around the city. He had a rotation of rough neighborhoods. Places with no-name used car lots, strip clubs, cheap motels, and pawn shops. Dazey's idea of time well spent was to pull some kind of small-time job—stick up somebody after they used the ATM, say—and then use the money to hole up in a sleazebag motel for a week with a bunch of dope and a girl or two. As near as Nolan could tell, Dazey had never had a permanent address in his adult life.

The problem for Dazey was that Indianapolis was changing. There were fewer and fewer neighborhoods where he could go unnoticed. Fewer places where people with his proclivities could be out in the open. And he was sitting in one of them right now. Ten years ago, maybe he'd have been okay along Pendleton Pike. Twenty years? Definitely.

But today?

Times had changed.

Nolan reckoned that he and Dazey were about the same age, but Christ, Dazey looked ten years older. He *acted* older too. Though there were still signs of an innate natural cleverness, his brain was beginning to addle from the drugs. He had the permanent grey-brown shade of speed use under his eyes, and his frame was wiry and bedraggled in a way you just didn't come back from. Dazey also wore a brown, stubbly beard that came up nearly to his eyes. This might have once appeared rugged or even handsome. But now, in his premature dotage, it made him look even more like a beat-up Muppet.

"This guy giving you any trouble, girls?" Nolan asked.

They smiled but did not reply.

"That's harsh, man," Dazey protested. "*Haaaarsh.* You don't have to be that way, man."

"Why don't you let me give you a lift, Nathan?" the policeman asked, not waiting for the young women to respond. "It's free of charge. Anywhere on the east side. Your choice."

Nolan understood the value of putting a favor in the "favor bank" with a useful informant, even one as grizzled and hoary as Dazey. (Maybe *especially* with one like that.) He also understood that Dazey's welcome at this location was a short hair away from running out entirely.

"I don't *have* to," Dazey asserted, looking up at Nolan. "I mean . . . yeah, I'll take a ride. That sounds good. But I don't *have* to. Just so that's clear. I'll take it 'cause we're friends."

Dazey collected himself and strode toward the passenger door of the squad car.

"Try again," Nolan said.

"Oh come on, man," Dazey protested. "Come *on.*"

Dazey hazarded a look back at the two girls on the curb. They were still looking at the tall officer, and not at him.

"In the back," Nolan said, stepping over and opening the rear door.

Dazey frowned and shuffled inside.

"You don't need to tell me to watch my head," the addict insisted. "You ain't arrestin' me."

"Of course not," Nolan said. "You're my guest."

Nolan shut the back door and prepared to climb into the driver's seat of the cruiser.

"Hey officer," one of the girls called. "Do I know you from somewhere?"

Nolan stopped and smiled. He didn't know her from Eve.

"Yeah," said the other girl, as if on the cusp of remembering. "Were you maybe on television or something? Like, back in the day?"

It seemed impossible to Nolan that they should know. At the height of his fame, these girls would have been around five years old. Then again, this was Indiana. Some things they never forgot here. Some things were sacred.

"You ladies keep it safe," Nolan responded with smile. He climbed back inside his cruiser and shut the door.

He turned on the engine, and Dazey started in.

"Daaaamn, champ," the addict called from the back seat. "That was a close one."

"It was," Nolan agreed, pulling out of the parking lot. "By the way, where are we going? And remember, I said *east side*."

"Just a ways down Pendleton," Dazey replied. "Just a bit east of here. You know . . . a bit."

Nolan suspected there was no specific destination in Dazey's mind.

"Now, if it were me . . ." Dazey continued, returning to the topic at hand. "If it were *me*? Sheeeeeet. I'd be dropping it myself. Telling people every time I got a call. Every time I got a kitten out of a tree. I'd let people know exactly who I was. That'd get you mad-laid, son. In this town? Mad-laid."

Nolan, who was recently divorced, considered this for a moment.

Then his cell phone rang.

"You go ahead and take that," the addict said, as if his benison were required.

Nolan smiled, pressed the talk button on his phone, and said hello. Then he listened quietly to an intense, rattled voice on the other end. A few moments later, he turned on his bar lights and pulled a U-turn into the oncoming lane. Dazey was momentarily rocked against the side of the squad car.

"Day-um," the addict protested. "What's got into you, buddy?"

"Change of plans," Nolan said, putting down his cell. "I've got to let you out right here . . . unless you want to head south with me. And I mean *south*. I could drop you off in Bloomington, if you like."

Dazey scratched his hairy chin and thought.

"Naw," he determined. "College girls are too snooty. Think they know every damn thing. You best leave me right here."

Nolan pulled over and opened the rear door.

"Be *good*, Nathan," Nolan said, wagging his finger in the scruffy man's face. "*Good*."

"Always am," the addict said, smiling through yellowed teeth.

Nolan hopped back in his cruiser and pulled away. Dazey, inherently suspicious, wondered if this might be some sort of a ruse. Yet the cruiser disappeared into traffic and stayed disappeared. Dazey decided he had been genuinely abandoned.

He relaxed and surveyed his surroundings. By chance, Nolan had dropped him almost directly across the road from the fast food restaurant where the two girls still sat.

Unable to believe his luck, Dazey jaywalked through the oncoming cars and caught up to the girls just as they were finishing their chicken.

"What'd I tell you?" Dazey called as he loped closer. "Me and him go way back."

"So wait," one of the girls said. "Was that really . . ."

"James Nolan?" Dazey said with a smile. "Yes it was."

"Omigod," said the other girl. "I *so* thought it was! And he's a *cop* now?"

"Sure is," said Dazey.

Feeling that his fortunes were improving by the moment, Dazey sat back down next to the girls.

"And he's not just any kind of cop. My man James is a 'Special Sergeant.' Does stuff for the highest-ups in the city. The mayor. The secretary of state. The damn governor hisself."

"Oh, wow," one of the girls said, seemingly without irony.

"Yes . . . yes, indeedy," Dazey said, rubbing his chin as he sized up his odds.

The girls leaned closer.

"Listen . . ." Dazey cooed conspiratorially. "You girls wanna come get high with me, and I'll tell you all about him? I'm only offering because y'all seem like cool chicks. I don't tell just *anybody* what I know about James Nolan . . ."

The young women looked at him, then at one another. Both hesitated, waiting for the other to speak first.

Dazey liked his chances.

3

Kesha Washington, aged fifteen, sat in the back of the metal row-boat and tried not to think about how badly she had to pee. Everyone on the tiny, overcrowded vessel was uncomfortable, but Kesha's seat in the extreme rear—which made extending her legs even slightly a near impossibility—seemed like the worst of the bunch. They were really packed in. Twenty-five high school sophomores, two teachers, and one boring park ranger . . . all in three cramped rowboats.

The boats were on a river—perhaps eight feet across—over two hundred feet below the earth's surface in a network of caverns beneath southern Indiana. The air smelled like an aquarium that had gone unattended, and where half the fish were dead. Lights had been affixed to the odd stalactite or stalagmite every fifty feet or so, but it was still very dark. Mostly the group relied on the single beam cast by the park ranger's flashlight. Beneath their boats, the water was filled with horrible, wriggly things, like blind cave-fish and crawfish. The tiny creatures were bone-white and shimmered translucently whenever the flashlight caught them.

Ahead of Kesha's group were two other identical groups, also crammed into three boats apiece. The entire sophomore class was required to attend this tour. Seventy-five students in all.

The park ranger had just finished a lecture about the ice age that had formed the caverns over two million years ago. (He had already covered the difference between stalactites and stalagmites, and the kinds of fossilized remains—mostly black bear and bison—you could count on finding inside the caves.) The final part of the tour, he'd said, would involve the deeper areas that had been used by Native Americans for over four thousand years.

Now, however, there was a lull in the educational narration as the ranger stopped to futz with his walkie-talkie.

"I hear they're canceling this trip next year," Gillian whispered into Kesha's ear. Gillian was the daughter of a dentist and one of Kesha's best friends. She was smashed next to Kesha in the ass-end of the boat.

"Oh yeah?" Kesha whispered.

"Yeah," Gillian confirmed. "We're the last class that has to do this. Like, ever. Enough people finally complained."

Kesha nodded. She knew that by "people," Gillian meant "parents." And that these parents had complained only because their sons and daughters had insisted they do so.

This flow of procedure did not seem normal or natural to Kesha. Precisely for this reason, she understood that it must indeed be so.

This school—Indianapolis's most expensive private high school—was very different from the public institutions in which Kesha had spent her first thirteen years. But she was learning its rules quickly. Kesha was one of two sophomores on full scholarship, and one of only three black students in the entire high school. The private college preparatory academy was as exclusive as it was small. Her classmates included the Hoosier versions of Carnegies and Rockefellers. The grandsons of pharmaceutical magnates, already being groomed to helm the empire. Kids whose parents owned half the car dealerships in the state. The boy whose father owned the local concert amphitheater where all the biggest touring acts played. The sons and daughters of professional athletes . . . or of the people who owned the teams.

For most of her freshman year, Kesha had absorbed the actions and attitudes of her classmates with a bewilderment that came close to paralyzing. Now, in her sophomore year, she was beginning to understand how it all worked. She was beginning to understand a lot of things. Primarily, that her classmates and their parents used money as a lubricant to smooth over the bumps and rough patches in life. It was their snail-slime. The thing that kept them moving forward. Did something look like it was going to hurt? Money would smooth it over. Take away the pointy bits. Make everything "not a big deal." Having trouble keeping your kid's grades up? Money could hire private tutors with Ivy League degrees. It could pay for SAT prep and practice tests. It could pay for doctors who understood that their primary function was to provide as much Adderall and Ritalin as a parent deemed necessary. (During Kesha's freshman year, an investigative reporter for the *Indianapolis Star* had attempted to learn what percentage of the exclusive school's student body was taking ADD meds. Less than two days into his investigation, the reporter was called off his story by the paper's senior editor. A week later, he was quietly demoted.)

Kesha found that money meant walking around in a world cushioned from any real consequence. Little things that worried Kesha did not even pop up on the radar of her schoolmates. If Kesha—who, at fifteen, had a learner's permit to drive—crashed her car into the garden gnome on her neighbor's lawn, it would be a big deal. Her father would have to pay for the gnome, and that might mean the family going without something. However, if one of Kesha's peers drove over a garden gnome, everyone involved would have a laugh, the parents would buy the neighbor ten new gnomes and a case of Omaha Steaks to say sorry, and it would be a cute story.

Yet amid and among this absurdity—Kesha's parents had *assured* her—this school was, somehow, the best place in the state of Indiana for her to be. The place where she could get ahead. Where she could be part of the "good life."

Whatever that meant.

So what if the school was snooty, and far from her house, and sort of sounded like "rotted crap" spelled backwards? This was where she should *want* to be. These strange, moneyed social mores should be her mores. These attitudes should become her attitudes.

Lately it had not been quite so paralyzing, but instead left Kesha with the feeling of being an imposter. Of being a snail that made no snail-slime. Of someone whose mistakes might still have consequences.

"Okay, okay," said the park ranger, gesturing with his flashlight to quiet the students. "Apparently we're having trouble with the walkie-talkies. While we wait for them to come back on, we're going to do something called 'cave thunder.' It's a bit of a tradition here. Our first step will be to turn out all the lights."

The park ranger's tone said that he expected this to captivate his audience.

Kesha and Gillian exchanged the same weary glance. Kesha shifted in her seat and tried to ease her bladder. The park ranger pulled a small keypad from his pocket. Moments later, the permanent lighting affixed to the walls flickered and went out. The ranger's flashlight was now the only source of illumination. Moments later, that was also gone.

The students fell silent, but not completely. The odd titter or guffaw still echoed through the cave. The park ranger cleared his throat. Both teachers whispered for the students to quiet down. Soon, there was only the sound of the boats sloshing together in the water.

"Now then," the ranger continued. "This is cave thunder. There's no trick to it. I'm just going to hit the side of the boat as hard as I can with my flashlight."

Again, the ranger paused to let the awesome coolness of this sink in. In the darkness, Kesha rolled her eyes.

"I want you to listen to the sound as it echoes down all twelve miles of cavern," said the ranger. "If you have sensitive ears, you might want to cover them."

Kesha stuck her fingers in her ears.

A moment later, the ranger pounded hard on the side of the metal boat. The resulting noise was indeed like a cannon's discharge. Every student, except for Kesha, jumped a little. The powerful blow echoed again and again. Kesha pictured the sound waves finding their way into every crevice and cranny of the cavern walls. It was several moments before they died away completely. When they did, the park ranger struck the side of the boat once again. Then once more.

"This is so . . . *stupid*," Gillian whispered in the silence after the third "cave thunder."

"Yeah," Kesha managed. "Totally."

The ranger struck the boat a fourth time.

"Like, how are we supposed to feel?" Gillian said under cover of the dying echoes. "Impressed? Scared?"

"I think they must be going for 'educated,'" Kesha said. "Though I don't know what loud noise in a cave teaches us. Do you feel any smarter?"

"No," Gillian said, giggling. "This is ridiculous. It's so unfair that we have to be the last ones to get subjected to it."

That gave Kesha a thought.

"Maybe he's trying extra hard," Kesha whispered. "Like, he wants to win our business back by impressing the teachers. Maybe cave thunder is the special bonus."

"Right, can you imagine?" Gillian said. "I wonder if . . ."

Kesha's friend put her comment on hold, waiting for the next bout of cave thunder to cover it. It did not come. Instead, the silence was broken by the shrill voice of a teacher, one boat over.

"Excuse me, *who* is rocking the boat?"

The disdain and humorlessness in Mrs. Klumper's voice was even more pronounced than usual. Kesha surmised in a moment that the round matron could not swim, and was secretly terrified to be in this situation.

"Whoever is rocking the boat, please stop it right now; this is not funny!" Klumper insisted.

Kesha could see nothing. It was the darkest darkness possible.

She could, however, hear a lapping sound slowly increasing in frequency. Someone was, indeed, rocking the boat just ahead of hers.

"What? I'm not!" one of the students cried.

"Jesus," said another.

"Fucking *stop it*; that's not funny!" cried another still.

"Language," boomed Mr. Pierce, the attendant adult in Kesha's boat.

Then a loud "Jesus Christ!" echoed throughout the caverns. This one came from Mrs. Klumper herself. A moment later, Kesha heard a splash as 229 pounds of social studies teacher hit the water.

People began to scream outright. There was another splash. Then another. Then sounds of people flailing in the water. In the amplified confines of the cavern, the din was near to deafening. Kesha—very alarmed—again thrust her fingers into her ears. In the lead boat, the park ranger fumbled for his flashlight and turned it on.

In the resulting, spastic beam, Kesha watched the boat ahead of hers overturn and the remaining passengers tumble into the river. Then the first boat—the one containing the park ranger—also began to rock. Kesha could not have sworn to it, but it seemed a long white hand—so white it was nearly pale blue—extended from the water and lighted on the ranger's shoulder. Startled, the ranger reached for his keypad controlling the permanent lights. He pulled it out of his pocket, looked over his shoulder, and screamed. The handheld device fell to the floor of the rowboat, which was promptly overturned. All aboard tumbled into the underground river. The ranger's flashlight sank into the murky depths that were now full of blind fish and flailing, confused high school students.

Screaming. Screaming everywhere. Every person seemed to be shouting and alarmed. Kesha tried to think of what to do. It was almost impossible. She couldn't plan, only react. The water beneath them had not looked deep, but was it deep enough that you could drown? Kesha could swim, but was no great shakes at it. Could her classmates swim? Her teachers? As the lone flashlight beam fell away beneath the water, her last images were of a sea of flailing hands and screaming faces. Soon, the inevitable began to occur. Kesha's own boat began to sway violently as the terrified, thrashing teens grasped for anything that might keep them above the water.

Kesha wondered: How far away was the next trio of boats? Why did they not turn on the lights? Couldn't they hear that this was no cave thunder, but nearly thirty people calling for help? Her terror was so stark that she hardly registered the awful smell that began to reach her nostrils. A stench had invaded the tight cavern air, like a horrible combination of seafood and excrement and old rotted meat. Beneath her alarm and her own screaming, Kesha realized that the smell was growing stronger.

Moments later, something brushed against the side of her face. It was wet and cold. It did not feel like any part of Gillian, or any other student, yet the horrible rubbery touch of it seemed somehow vaguely familiar.

Then the boat beneath Kesha rocked violently, and she was cast into the chilly water below with the others.

4

Indiana state troopers Leonard and Southerly stood at the mouth of the cavern and waited. A few paces off from them stood three worried park rangers and a school bus driver. Every one of them stared down the empty gravel road leading up to the cavern. There was a parking lot and a small ranger station next to the cavern opening, but little else to see. The park rangers took turns speaking into a walkie-talkie that never spoke back.

"What the hell's a special sergeant anyway?" Trooper Leonard asked his partner. "Special sergeant. 'SS.' That sounds like some Aryan Brotherhood shit to me. Straight-up Nazi."

"I don't think so," replied Southerly.

"No?" wondered Leonard. "Because it sounds right to me."

Southerly sighed. "That's because you're a goddamn fool who never knows when to keep his mouth shut," he said.

Leonard wished to give the impression of remaining unbowed, and so merely spat beside his shoe.

"What I heard . . . 'special sergeant' means that he reports exterior to IMPD," Southerly continued, his gaze never shifting from the empty road. "Don't get me wrong. This guy reports to *somebody*. But it ain't the police commissioner."

"No?" wondered Leonard, genuinely doubtful.

"No," assured Southerly. "Somebody else. Somebody big, though. You can put your money on *that*."

Southerly then risked a meaningful glance over toward the empty school bus. With tinted windows. And velveteen bucket seats. And hydraulics that raised and lowered the bus whenever the students climbed aboard. He lingered just long enough for Leonard to get the idea.

"Why of course . . ." Leonard said. "Those fancy private schools up in Indy got all sorts of rich people's kids. *Powerful* people's kids. It could be any one of them. Or *all* of them. The mayor. The governor. The coach of the damn Colts."

"Mmm hmm," Southerly agreed evenly. "Could be those. Could be. *Also* could be the CEO of about ten corporations with names you never heard of, but which own cigarette companies and coal mines and oil wells. That's where my money'd be, if we were takin' bets."

"We're . . . we're *not* taking bets though, are we?" Leonard asked nervously.

Southerly sighed. He did not move his eyes from the road.

As if in acknowledgement of this remarkable feat of self-control, Southerly was rewarded with the sound of approaching tires on the gravel drive. Seconds later, he saw a plume of dust wafting through the trees. Then the IMPD squad car came into view.

The state troopers waved once, and the IMPD car pulled to a stop in front of them. A mountain of a man got out. Tall with broad shoulders and a helluva lot of muscle. He wore black sunglasses that completely obscured his eyes.

"Damn," Leonard whispered. "This guy's a special something-or-other, all right . . ."

Southerly frowned at Leonard and approached the newcomer.

"You Sergeant Nolan?" Southerly asked.

The sergeant nodded.

"I'm Southerly. This is Trooper Leonard."

"Good to meet you," Nolan said. "Who can give me a sit rep?"

"I 'spect I can," Southerly said. He motioned for the park rangers and the bus driver to join them.

"All I've been told is that some high school students are two hours late coming back from a cave tour," Nolan added as the other men approached.

"Nothing like this has ever happened before!" gushed one of the park rangers. Nolan saw tears in the man's eyes. Honest-to-God tears. He looked ready to start bawling.

Nolan placed a reassuring hand on the ranger's shoulder.

"Here's the timeline," said Southerly, producing a reporter's notepad. "At two in the afternoon, the kids enter the caves. Seventy-five kids in all. They're in three groups of twenty-five. Each group has a park ranger and couple of teachers. They're in boats. The groups are spaced far enough apart that they can't see or hear one another, but they have special radios that work in the caverns."

"But the radios aren't working!" another of the park rangers interjected.

Nolan calmly nodded to signal that this had registered.

"Yeah," Southerly continued. "So the tour was supposed to be over by three-thirty or four. They do a circuit of sorts—the underground river has a pathway that runs in a loop—and end up at the same place they begin. At about three-thirty, the rangers up top noted that the radios had stopped working. Regular cell phones don't work in the cave, either. Then two different pairs of rangers went in to see what was wrong. That was at about four and four-thirty, respectively. They haven't come back either."

"Are there other exits?" Nolan asked, adjusting his sunglasses in the late afternoon glare.

"Dozens . . . maybe hundreds," one of the excited rangers burbled. "This countryside is dotted with little crawlspaces that lead down into the caverns. Indians used them for thousands of years. Moonshiners back in the day. Satanist cults in the 1970s. Meth gangs now."

"That's true," said Southerly. "We find a few bodies in the caves every year. There are probably more that we *don't* find."

Nolan nearly wondered aloud why they let children go inside them at all. Instead, he nodded seriously. Nolan already knew that these caves had an extensive history.

"Could the rangers have taken the students out through one of the *other* entrances?" Nolan asked. "Like, maybe a kid got hurt and they had to evacuate him?"

The rangers were already shaking their heads.

"That wouldn't make sense," a ranger answered. "We have protocols in place for emergencies. They haven't been followed. And the ranger *definitely* would have radioed."

"I think it's terrorism!" another ranger interjected hysterically. "People want to kidnap the children of all these rich people from Indy. Hold them for ransom. And they've got a thousand possible escape routes after we send in the ransom money. It's perfect. It's like out of an action movie or something. You could get away with it so easily!"

"Thought about this some, have you?" Nolan asked with a grin.

The smile was not returned. The rangers regarded the IMPD officer with solemn faces.

"Are you even taking this seriously?!" one ranger barked. His expression had changed from sad to furious. He was at least a head and a half shorter than Nolan, but looked ready to throw a punch.

Nolan adjusted his sunglasses again and stared down at the man for a long time.

"I'm here because there's a *chance* that you will still have your jobs tomorrow," Nolan said. "A *chance*."

He paused to let this sink in.

"I'm here because there's a *chance* that we're going to be able to figure out whatever's wrong, fix it, and haul these kids back home before anybody in Indy has too much of a hissy fit. As I see it, there's still a good shot this'll turn out to be nothing. Hell, one day it could be a funny story that gets told by park rangers. 'That time those high school kids came through and two boats broke at the same time and it took *three hours* just to get them tied together and hauled out of there.' That sort of thing. Do you understand me?"

The rangers said nothing.

They did not know—*could* not know—the false alarms that Nolan had handled in his nearly ten years with the department. His special assignments that at the time had seemed of unimaginable importance, but had later turned out to be little more than misunderstandings. Blips on the radar. A kid runs away from home for a couple of days after a family fight. A wife decides to spend some time at her sister's while telling nobody. A mistress makes some threats while hopped up on vodka and pills.

These all turned out to be fixable. To be nothing, ultimately. But because of the people involved—because of their power and connections—Nolan had been called in to make it all better. And he almost always had. So far, he was batting damn near a thousand.

And so it had become his title within the department. Special Sergeant. High-ups in the state and city government had let the police commissioner know that Nolan could have his day-to-day duties in narcotics, sure, but it would be nice to have him available whenever he was needed.

"Now, it could be that something is *really* wrong down there," Nolan continued. "I sure hope it's not, but that *is* a possibility. So here's what we're going to do. You're going to give me a boat and a radio, and I'm going to go down and find out what's going on. If it's serious, we will handle it. But if a kid just had an asthma attack and freaked everybody out, and then a boat tipped over . . . well, we'll deal with that too. And then I'll buy everybody standing here their first beers. Sound okay?"

There were general nods of agreement.

One of the rangers handed Nolan a radio, and they tried it out.

"This works fine," Nolan said. "I can hear you clear as day."

"Yeah," said the ranger. "We don't know why the others aren't coming back from down in the cave. Let me get you a fresh battery, just in case."

As the ranger trotted over to the small log cabin that served as the ranger station, the bus driver approached Nolan from behind.

"This ain't the place or time," the driver began. "But could I . . . uh . . . get an autograph? My wife's a big fan of yours."

"Later," said Nolan. "When I finish up here. How about that?"

The bus driver nodded respectfully and backed away.

Moments later, laden with a radio and two backup batteries, Nolan followed one of the rangers and both state troopers down into the cave. Nolan removed his sunglasses as they traversed the lighted staircase that took them nearly two hundred feet beneath the earth. The smell of water and rock assaulted Nolan. He began ducking to avoid the low ceilings. At one point, the lights along the walkway around them flickered.

"That reminds me; I need a flashlight," Nolan said.

The ranger handed over a heavy black Maglite.

"That'll do," Nolan said, thrusting it into his pocket.

"There are mounted lights every fifty feet along the cave walls," the ranger informed him. "But we sometimes turn them off to do cave thunder—this thing where we bang on the side of the boat."

"What about off the path of the tour?" Nolan asked. "Like if some kids go exploring in the side caves? The tributaries and such? Any lights there?"

The ranger shook his head no. The electric lights were only on the main boat path.

Moments later, the staircase they traversed terminated at a small jetty where the cave's visitors were normally loaded into rowboats. Huge CFL bulbs cast their grim light down from fixtures mounted to the roof of the cave. Though there were tie-ups for many different boats, only one metal vessel remained.

"We started the day with twelve boats," the ranger explained. "The tour groups took nine—three groups with three boats apiece—and then the rangers who went in after them must have taken the other two."

"Let's check the radios again," Nolan said. He called for the rangers left topside to pick up. They did so immediately.

"Works fine," Nolan concluded brightly.

The ranger looked up into Nolan's face and shook his head. His expression said that nothing was fine. That seventy-five school kids and several adults were missing in a subterranean river deep under the ground.

Nolan's good humor remained intact.

"We're gonna get to the bottom of this," Nolan told the ranger. "You just mark my words."

"You'll want to start in that direction," the ranger said dutifully, indicating a beckoning waterway with a shaky index finger. "The tours begin there, and then circle around. You keep following the lights, and you'll end up right back here again."

Nolan walked down the jetty and eased himself into the remaining rowboat. It was made for two to row at once, but it was obvious that Nolan would have no problem handling both oars. The ranger untied the boat and kicked it away from the mooring.

"If I'm not back in one hour, call 911," Nolan said.

He began to row away. The ranger and the state troopers watched the boat glide around a large stalagmite and into the silent darkness beyond.

"I sure hope he's right," said Southerly.

"About what, exactly?" Leonard asked.

Southerly waved his hand across the entire cavern like a wizard casting a spell.

★★★

The state troopers and the park ranger climbed back up the long rock staircase to the mouth of the cave. All three were wheezing by the halfway point. Soon the cool underground air gave way to a warm fall wind. They neared the top of the staircase and looked out of the mouth of the cave. The early evening sun now cast a beautiful glow on the trees, just beginning their change from green to ocher and fiery red. It was the time of day that moviemakers called the magic hour, when the entire expanse before you seemed to resonate with sunlight.

And nobody was there.

Their cars were there. The fancy school bus was there. The little ranger station was there. But there were no people. Nothing stirred.

The three men looked around, then at one another.

The ranger turned and called to the ranger station: "Hello? Fellas? Marty, you there?"

There was no response.

Leonard looked at Southerly and said, "Now what in the world? Where did everybody—"

Before he could finish his sentence, both men fell silent at the sound of an explosion several miles away.

"What in the hell was that?" Leonard shrieked.

The men turned in the direction of the noise. Far in the distance, a plume of black smoke was already curling into the air.

"I don't know—maybe the power station?—but I'll tell you what it means," Southerly said. "Any ideas you had about not working a triple shift today are damn-straight over. I hope you got your sleep last night."

Leonard, who had actually been looking forward to sleeping off an eight-beer hangover as soon as possible, swallowed hard.

"What's that?" the park ranger shouted. He was not looking at the plume of black smoke rising into the distant sky. Instead, his trembling finger pointed to the trees beyond the parking lot.

The troopers turned and saw a quick flicker of denim disappear into the foliage.

"Was that . . . the bus driver?" Leonard asked.

Southerly nodded. It *was* the bus driver. Running like hell into the forest. Why? Running *to* something? Or *away*?

Southerly's police radio barked to life. The first calls had already come in. An explosion at the power plant. All available units to respond.

The trooper didn't move.

"You gonna answer that?" Leonard asked, looking at his partner.

Very slowly, Southerly reached for his hip and turned off his radio. Then he carefully drew his gun.

"What's going on here?" asked the ranger.

Southerly nodded toward the tiny ranger station.

"Jesus," said Leonard, drawing his sidearm as well.

"What?" asked the ranger, still confused.

The troopers said nothing. The ranger kept looking around. After a moment, he saw it. A long, wet smear of blood down the side of the wooden ranger station.

"I think you should get back into the cave," Southerly said without taking his eyes off the building.

"The cave?" the ranger responded. "Near a hundred people are missing in there!"

"Friend," Southerly said, his gaze intensifying. "I don't think it's any safer up here. If you're smart, you'll take my advice. I think you can tell I'm not fuckin' around."

The ranger nodded and crept back to the mouth of the cavern.

Southerly took three steps toward the ranger station and stopped.

"Somebody inside," he said softly to his partner, then raised his voice. "Come on out! Indiana State Police! Come out of there!"

A figure began to emerge. Because it wore the uniform of an EMT, both troopers were momentarily confused. Had someone already responded to an accident here at the entrance? There was no ambulance or emergency vehicle that they could see.

The figure lingered in the doorway of the cabin. It was a woman. She was Caucasian, with long black hair that fell just past her shoulders and ruddy red cheeks as though she'd been exerting herself. (Had she been tending to an injured person, perhaps?) Her eyes, though, were all wrong. A strange, milky whiteness clouded both pupils like an impossibly advanced cataract. Perhaps in this connection, she seemed not to see. She sniffed the air like a blind dog. A thin sliver of red drool trickled down from her mouth. Her head lolled back and forth as though she was exhausted . . . or maybe drunk on the job.

"Hello?" called Trooper Southerly, the confidence draining from his voice. "Ma'am, do you need a hand?"

The woman did not respond.

Southerly's mind raced. How had she gotten out here? What was wrong with her eyes? How could someone be an EMT if they couldn't see?

Then the woman took another stumbling step out into the early evening sunlight, and the men realized that there was something beside her. She was dragging a dead park ranger, wounded about the head. He looked scalped, and part of his skull had caved in. The woman had stuck two fingers into this hole in his head, and was using it to drag him.

"What the—" Leonard began to say.

"Put your hands up!" shouted Southerly. "Put your hands up right now!"

Nothing happened. The woman teetered forward, still holding the park ranger by his head. Suddenly, the ranger's body shook. His whole length trembled as though he were freezing cold. His legs spasmed wildly. It was almost—both troopers realized—as if he were not quite dead.

The sight was too much for Leonard, who screamed and squeezed his trigger twice. Despite his hangover, his aim was true. The EMT's shirt puffed out as the rounds careened into her chest.

She teetered slightly, but did not fall. Her expression never changed. An awkward beat passed. Then she took another lumbering step.

Southerly shouted: "Vest! Vest!"

Yet even as the words escaped his throat—already dry and metallic with terror—he knew that this was not right. That no bulletproof vest could account for this woman's reaction to being shot two times. (Or, more accurately, for her *lack* of reaction.) There was a wrongness here that was pervasive and deep and felt like a blind EMT dragging a flailing park ranger by a hole in his head might be only the tip of the iceberg.

Both troopers adjusted their aim and prepared to fire again.

★★★

Back inside the caverns, James Nolan rowed along a subterranean river that smelled like water and lichen and cave moss. The permanent lights—the ones affixed to the cave wall at regular intervals—provided just enough illumination to keep it creepy. The rock formations beside Nolan cast long, dark shadows that seemed occasionally to move. His oars played tricks with the reflections on the surface of the water.

Nolan remembered his own tour of these caves as a Cub Scout, back in the late 1980s. Maybe not these exact caves, but definitely ones that looked—and smelled, and felt—pretty much the same. There were caverns like this all over the southern part of the state, and who knows how many generations of Hoosier youngsters had been subjected to educational trips through them? How had it become such a tradition? Nolan was sure that he didn't know.

"Hello! Anybody there?" Nolan called as his oars dipped again and again into the night-black water. Along most stretches of the waterway, Nolan could see no more than twenty feet ahead; the twists and turns of the cave kept anything in the distance a complete mystery. Yet Nolan still felt confident that he was *not* rowing into a nest of kidnappers or terrorists. The most likely scenario, he imagined, would involve some students who had decided to take off exploring down a side passage and gotten lost, cave tour be damned. (Rich kids were like that, Nolan reasoned. Thought there never were any damn consequences.) Teachers and park rangers were probably at this very moment frantically exploring every nook and cranny looking for the errant teens—who, Nolan felt sure, would afterward avoid any substantive form of punishment.

Nolan rowed at a good clip, but did not think to check his watch. Because of this, he had no real sense of how much time had passed when he heard—or *thought* he heard—the distant report of firearms being discharged back at the mouth of the cave.

Nolan dropped his oars and cupped his ear to the sound. It came twice more. Then once again . . . what sounded a whole lot like an Indiana state trooper's 9mm Glock 17 being fired just a few paces past the cave entrance. Nolan waited and listened. No further shots came. The only sound was the water lapping against the sides of the metal rowboat.

Nolan took out his radio.

"Hello!" he called. "This is Sergeant Nolan. You guys okay up there? I thought I heard shots."

He waited a moment.

"Hello?"

Only static came back.

Ever the optimist, Nolan took out his cell phone on the off-chance it might work. The screen said "No Service" and showed zero bars.

For the first time since he'd arrived, Nolan became slightly concerned that something might actually be wrong. He produced his own sidearm and placed it on the seat beside him. Then he snatched up the oars and began rowing once more.

He reached a bend in the waterway where the nearest lighting fixture had obviously gone out. Or been extinguished. He rowed closer to it, and closer still. The area beyond the light was a new level of blackness—subterranean blackness—that he had seldom seen.

Then something in the water. Something floating at the edge of the space where the lights refused to shine.

Nolan put his hand on his gun.

To the untrained eye, the mystery item might have momentarily looked like old clothes bobbing in the water. An errant sweatshirt. A discarded pair of jeans. But Nolan had seen enough floaters to recognize one on sight. This was an older, heavier woman in a white sweater. Her grey hair was pulled back into a bun, and most of her scalp had been torn away. She was unquestionably dead.

Silently, Nolan's boat drifted toward the body. With his free hand, he found his Maglite and turned it on. Parting the blackness before him, the flashlight revealed a scene of utter destruction.

Detritus floated everywhere. Bits of torn clothing, backpacks, and purses bobbed up and down noiselessly. A couple of sweaters and sweatshirts had stayed whole, but most had been reduced to shreds. Above these scatterings, three overturned metal boats floated silently in the water. There were also bodies. Lots and lots of bodies. Most of them, Nolan noted in horror, did not appear quite fully grown.

It was one of the school groups, he realized. And it had been ripped apart.

Nolan carefully rowed into the shredded remains of the field trip until he was surrounded on all sides by the debris. A severed hand bumped against the side of his boat with a soft *clunk*. An iPad floated past in a rubber case that was apparently buoyant. Nolan's flashlight probed from body to body, watching for any twitch that might betray a sign of life. He saw nothing. The carnage appeared complete. Some bodies merely looked drowned, but most bore evidence of having had their flesh hacked or ripped apart. Alarmingly, there were also bite marks. Indentations clearly caused by human teeth, especially around the heads and faces.

Nolan rowed nearer to the three overturned tour boats. A bloody handprint was smeared down the nearest. Nolan used his oar to right it.

Instead of finding survivors hiding underneath, there was only a severed arm. It was covered with translucent crawfish, feasting on the gore. Disgusted, Nolan smacked the arm with his oar, and the tiny beasts scuttled back beneath the water.

Working methodically and carefully, Nolan overturned the two remaining boats. More body parts. No survivors.

In a fool's errand, Nolan tried his radio once more. He kept his voice low.

"Hello. Hello. Can anyone hear me? This is James Nolan. Come back. Anybody?"

No response.

Nolan set down his flashlight, ran his fingers through his hair, and took a very deep breath. He tried not to think about what this meant. He tried not to picture himself in front of a review board, explaining what procedures he had followed . . . or failed to follow.

"How did you know that no one was still alive when you left the cave?"

"How could you have been *certain* that there were not students who still needed your help?"

"Did you check *everyone*?"

Nolan had seen these kinds of questions kill careers. He tried to block them from his mind.

He also tried not to think about the teenaged corpses all around him, or to imagine what had done this to them. It was unfathomable. Sickening.

There was only one course of action, and Nolan knew it. Row like hell back to the dock. Get to where cell phones and radios worked, and call in the goddamn Marines. Call in everybody you possibly could. Turn this whole cave into a crime scene.

This would be national news, Nolan knew. Hell, international. Seventy-five dead teenagers? No question. Everybody would come calling. All sorts of media. The President of the United States would issue a comment on the tragedy. It was the kind of story that would linger. That would get made into TV movies. That would spawn generations of urban legends and conspiracy theories.

Nolan wondered what could have possibly done this. Bears? A murderous gang? A particularly energetic psycho killer? Whatever the ultimate cause, it was going to be a black eye for everyone involved. No police officer associated with this was going to be remembered for anything else. This was going to define careers.

Nolan gripped the oars and took his first powerful stroke back toward the jetty. He knew he had to get help, and get it now. He rowed like an automaton, not allowing himself to think about the cavern around him that had suddenly become a slaughterhouse.

Then, from somewhere even deeper in the cave's ebon folds, Nolan heard a single high-pitched scream.

He stopped rowing.

It came again. Piercing. Reverberating across the walls of the cave. It projected true, animal terror. Yet it was undoubtedly human.

Nolan turned his boat around, and with a few sure strokes sent himself careening past the floating bodies and into the all-consuming darkness beyond. The river curved. Nolan steered quietly with one oar. With his other hand, he held his firearm at the ready.

He listened for the scream to come again.

It did not. Instead, he heard a scuttling, like a huge insect clattering against the rocks ahead. Nolan piloted his boat toward the odd noise. He did not know what to expect, but understood that once he betrayed himself, he might have only an instant to act. Whomever or whatever lurked beyond would know he was there the moment he used his flashlight.

The scuttling got louder. Nolan waited for the scream again—hoped for it, in fact—but nothing came.

Soon the scuttling was close, so close he felt sure he could reach out and touch it with an oar.

Nolan took a very silent, very deep breath. He balanced himself in the seat of the boat. Then he brought up the Maglite and turned it on.

In the brilliant white beam, the police sergeant beheld a sight beyond understanding. In a crawlspace to the side of the cave—just above the waterline—a pink Hello Kitty backpack, held by an unseen person, was being used to block the entrance to a tiny nook in the cave. Outside the nook was a jet-black human skeleton missing its legs. It was held together by a thick dark *material* that might have been mud . . . or rotted, water-logged tendons. And it was moving. It scrambled against the rocky floor, aware and alive. Its thin, inky fingers explored the face of the backpack, looking for a way past. Its rotted nose sniffed the air. It had no eyes.

Suddenly, a female voice came from beyond the backpack. "Hello?"

Whoever it was, she had noticed the flashlight.

The skeleton-thing rocked on the bottom of its ribcage, gal-vanized by the sound. (Though Nolan saw no ears, apparently it could hear.)

The voice came again: "Hello?"

The backpack lowered for a moment, and Nolan saw a scared-looking girl. She was black, with short dark hair and big, Disney-princess eyes. She winced at the light from the Maglite. Then she saw the teetering skeleton, released another shriek, and quickly raised the backpack again.

Nolan hefted his double-action Ruger and drew a bead on the skeleton's forehead.

"Hey," Nolan called. "Hey, you. Behind the backpack. Hold your ears. *Put your fingers in your ears right now!* Do you understand me?"

After a moment, Nolan saw the backpack adjust itself as the young lady complied.

Nolan steadied his weapon and pulled the trigger.

5

In the wet, claustrophobic expanse around her, the report seemed more like an explosion than a gunshot. Even with her fingers stuffed hard into her ears, the pain in Kesha's eardrums was palpable. Yet in the silence that followed, the clicking of the scum-covered skeleton seemed to have stopped. She risked lowering the backpack.

In the space beyond, Kesha saw a brilliant flashlight beam and a man in a boat. A *giant* of a man. (Probably a man, anyway. His voice had sounded masculine. With the beam in her eyes, it was hard to discern much more than an outline.)

Directly in front of her, the horrible thing lay silent and immobile against the cavern floor. It looked even more disturbing than Kesha had imagined it would. A human skeleton covered in sickly dark goo, it was legless and appeared held together only by the thinnest sinews. Its long fingernails were like the alien legs of an arthropod. Its fleshless mouth presented a horrible rictus of tobacco-stained teeth. And now, the back of its skull had been blown apart by a bullet.

Kesha eased her way out of the nook. Her legs were cramped and her stomach felt sick from adrenaline, but there seemed to be no permanent damage. She raised one hand to shield her eyes from the flashlight's glare. The tall, hulking man carefully stepped off his rowboat and onto the ledge beside her. He lowered the flashlight, and the illumination became less overpowering.

The stranger, indeed male, was probably in his mid-thirties. He had short brown hair and playfully arching eyebrows. He smiled down at Kesha and proceeded to confidently prod the skeleton-thing with his foot. The creature did not respond.

"Did it hurt you?" the man asked.

Kesha inspected herself and found several scrapes and bruises, but nothing was broken. She shook her head no.

"I think I'm okay."

"It's like some kind of insect, almost," the man observed, giving the thing a second prod.

Kesha nodded.

"Was this the only one?" the man asked.

"No, there were a lot of them," Kesha replied softly, her voice hoarse from screaming. "I don't know where they all went, but there were a lot."

"What happened?" the man asked. His voice was calm and kind.

"I couldn't really see when it started," Kesha said. "They turned off the lights to do cave thunder—the ranger did—so it was dark. Then something started rocking the boats. We thought it was a kid playing a joke. But then the boats turned over. Then things—like *this*—started coming out of the water, scratching and biting us. I saw them opening people's heads. A lot of us got pulled under."

The tall man nodded thoughtfully.

"Is anybody else from my class alive, do you think?" Kesha asked.

The man looked downcast.

"From your group, I think not," he said.

"Oh," Kesha said in a small voice.

"Yeah," the man replied.

"But there are two other groups!" Kesha said hopefully. "They were ahead of us on the tour."

"Yes," the man said carefully. "I don't know about them yet."

"My name's Kesha Washington," she said. "I'm a sophomore. Maybe you already know that. Maybe . . ."

She trailed off. Just stopped talking. Nolan had seen this kind of shock before. The kind where people simply "turn off" mid-sentence.

He did not press her for anything further.

"My name's James Nolan. I'm a police officer from Indianapolis. I'm going to get you out of here. We're going to get in this boat, and then I'm going to take you back to the entrance of the cave. Does that sound okay?"

Kesha managed a nod.

Together, they got into the boat.

Nolan rowed.

After just a few strokes, they could see artificial light ahead of them, coming from one of the permanent fixtures. Soon after, Kesha began to see things floating in the water.

"Look!" Kesha said, pointing to the bobbing detritus.

"Yeah . . . you don't need to see this stuff," Nolan told her. "It's what's left of your tour group. Maybe just close your eyes and I'll tell you when we're past?"

"No," Kesha insisted. "I mean, look to the right. Over there, next to where the boats are . . ."

Nolan stopped rowing and trained his flashlight in the direction indicated. Something was indeed thrashing about in the water ahead. The movements were stiff and strange. No part of it seemed human.

"It's more of those *things*," Kesha whispered.

The boat drifted closer. Nolan saw that she was right.

Seven or eight bodies in various states of decay walked or stumbled to one side of the river. Some were little more than skeletons covered in black-green rot. Others, however, were disturbingly whole. These wore clothes, had hair and teeth, and managed to look almost alive. Yet it was clear to Nolan that they were not. An alien undeath possessed them. Whatever powered their limbs, it was not a heart and lungs. They jerked in short bursts of enthusiasm, like alligators signaling their presence.

Kesha saw that some of the teenaged corpses in the water were also beginning to twitch. One kicked its foot rhythmically, like a drummer tapping out a beat. Another rolled its eyes as though looking for something with manic intensity. Yet another opened and closed its puckered lips like a half-hearted impersonation of a fish.

"We shouldn't go this way!" Kesha insisted.

Some of the jerking, gibbering things in the water heard this. They began, very slowly, to move in the direction of her voice.

"These things can tip over a boat," Kesha continued, growing frantic. "That's how they did it before. They can turn us right over. Please, let's turn around!"

Nolan reversed the oars until the vessel ceased its progress.

A moment later, a slime-covered forehead emerged from the water not ten feet away from them. It gently drifted closer to their boat.

"I'm inclined to agree," Nolan said, and began rowing again in earnest. As Kesha looked on, another corpse head rose from the nearby water, and then another.

"Oh damn, get us out of here," Kesha cried. Yet even as she said this, she shuddered at the knowledge that the only option was to go deeper into the caves.

Nolan cleared the floating foreheads, turned the boat around, and rowed with all his might into the darkness.

"Take my flashlight," Nolan called to her. "Shine it ahead and be our headlights. I can't see where I'm going."

Kesha carefully took the Maglite from Nolan and shone the beam over his massive shoulder.

"Hang on to me," Nolan said, feeling the girl's unsteadiness in the boat next to him. "Physically grab me."

Kesha put her free arm around the giant policeman's chest.

They edged deeper and deeper into the night-dark cave.

★★★

"So . . . where's everybody else?" Kesha whispered. "You said you're with the police. Where are the *other* police? Police always come in groups. At least in my neighborhood . . ."

Kesha's eyebrows knit as she thought for a moment.

"Do you even have a badge?"

Nolan smiled.

They had drifted into the darkness for several minutes, powered by Nolan's mighty rowing. There was no indication that the horrible animated bodies had followed them. Even so, Kesha used the flashlight to regularly probe the sides of the boat, wary of a sneak attack. (The things had come from beside and below. Would they next drop from the ceiling? Kesha would not have been surprised.)

"I just saved you from a crawlspace in the wall," Nolan said. "Do you really need me to stop rowing and fish out a badge? 'Cause I will."

"Oh," Kesha said. "I guess not."

"The other police should be here very soon," Nolan explained. "Radios and phones don't work down here, so all anybody knew was that your school group was two hours late getting back. I'm the guy they send when they want to keep things from turning into something big. But I think this *is* something big. When they don't hear back from me . . . let's just say the cavalry should be riding in very shortly."

"You mean you're *it*?" Kesha asked, hardly able to believe her ears. "There are no other police here? It's just . . . *you*?"

Nolan had received more stinging assessments in his ten years on the force, but this one still made him smile.

"There are some state troopers back at the entrance," he told her.

"Well that's good, at least," Kesha said after a moment's consideration.

Nolan continued to propel the boat forward, aiming to stay in the center of the subterranean river where he guessed the water would be deepest. Kesha shone the light in a search pattern that became regular—up in front, then down the sides. Before long, both of them detected institutional lighting up ahead.

"Finally," Nolan said in relief.

"Maybe the other group's up there?" Kesha wondered.

"Maybe," said Nolan. "But maybe not. And I'm concerned we could run into more of those things when we find the group."

"Do you know what they are?" Kesha asked. "Those things, I mean . . ."

Some deeper part of her understood that there was no answer to this question. Those things had been impossible. Living impossibilities. Dead bodies rising from out of the water. They should not have been able to move, much less ravenously attack people. And yet they had.

"Some weird stuff happens down in these caves," Nolan returned evenly, his eyes fixed on the water ahead. "A lot of criminal activity. In the seventies, people used to pray to the devil down here. Have ceremonies. That might sound far-fetched, but you can Google it."

"Are you saying this has something to do with *religion*?" Kesha asked, as if such a conclusion were exasperatingly ridiculous.

Nolan shook his head.

"Do I know *exactly* what that thing was that pinned you in the corner? No. But I know that when I shot it in the head, it stopped moving. So now I know that much. See what I mean?"

The way ahead of them grew brighter as they approached the lights. The underground river also grew, expanding out to about twelve feet wide. They reached the permanent lighting fixture, and found they could see yet another down the corridor beyond it. Then, after about twenty yards more, they encountered the remains of the second tour group.

Three capsized boats floated aimlessly in the widened canal, as did about thirty bodies. Most were face-down, but a few corpses rested on their backs. Those in the latter category displayed the grim, empty faces of the dead, troubling to behold. Many of the bodies bore wounds to the head. More than one had a skull that had been completely bashed in, and the contents apparently removed. It was startling to be able to see inside the floating heads. (It was startling enough for Nolan, who had not known these people personally. He wondered what it was like for the girl.)

The only sound was the splash of Nolan's oars in the water as he navigated between the bodies.

"Normally, I would tell you to look away," Nolan said. "But please don't, okay? Your eyes are too valuable right now. I need you to look for anything that moves. Any sign of those things. You've got to help me keep us safe."

"Okay," Kesha replied. Her voice was strained as she took in the decimation of her classmates.

"Do you see anybody who looks alive?" Nolan asked.

Kesha shook her head no.

"We need to check underneath those boats," Nolan said.

"What?" Kesha shot back. "No! Why?"

"People could be hiding under them. Hiding from these things and breathing the air inside. I can't risk leaving behind someone who's still alive."

Terrified, Kesha looked on as Nolan steered them toward the nearest overturned boat. As Kesha swiveled her neck all around, looking for any movement in the water, Nolan leaned over the side and flipped the boat.

Underneath was nothing.

Kesha felt herself exhale.

"Okay," said Nolan. "One down."

He eyed the next overturned boat, and steered through the floating human offal until they floated next to it.

This time, Nolan used an oar to lift it. Again, nothing.

"One to go," he said.

Nolan rowed until they were adjacent to the final boat.

"It's on your side," he said to Kesha. "Do you want to do it?"

Kesha reached over and pushed up the lip of the rowboat using the Maglite. Nolan watched, his hand on his weapon.

The boat overturned to reveal a screaming girl underneath. Except she made no noise at all. It was one of Kesha's classmates, clad in a red dress with a floral print. Her eyes bulged like a frog's, and her mouth was open as if in perpetual shriek. But there was no sound. After a moment, it was clear that there was also no breathing. The girl was frozen that way, in death, perhaps exactly as she had died.

"My God," Kesha said. "How can she even be like that? *How can she even be like that?!*"

Nolan had seen bodies do strange things.

"Let's let her be," he said. Kesha nodded and lowered the boat until it covered the girl once more.

With several powerful strokes, Nolan propelled them down the river, once more leaving the floating dead behind.

★★★

"There's one more group . . . but they're going to all have been killed too, right?" Kesha said. "So why are we even doing this? We shouldn't be going after dead people. We should be finding a way out!"

"Not necessarily," Nolan replied.

"But . . ." Kesha began to object.

"You'd be surprised what can happen in a crisis situation," Nolan said. "Even if they were attacked, some could still be alive. They might also just be lost, or trapped. Or hiding, like you were. They could be confused as to why they haven't heard from the other groups, and just waiting to be rescued. They might not even know about what's happening."

"They might *all be dead*," Kesha said.

"You weren't dead," Nolan pointed out.

Kesha had no answer for this.

After some time, they did arrive at another scene of carnage and confusion.

At first glance, it looked just like the others. The water ahead was littered with torn fabric. Dead bodies bobbed up and down. Bags and backpacks floated beside them.

"See? I damn told you so," Kesha said.

Yet there was one crucial difference. It took them both a moment to notice it.

Instead of three overturned boats, only two were upended. The third had remained upright, and apparently been piloted onto a ledge at the edge of the water, directly underneath a fixed light. Also underneath the light was what looked like an emergency station fixed to the cave wall, with a life preserver, a telephone, and a first aid kit. The phone had been torn out of its socket, and the first aid kit had had its contents strewn everywhere.

"Shine the light there," said Nolan, gesturing to the back of the ledge.

Kesha lifted the Maglite and explored a shadowy area covered by a pair of dripping stalactites. Past these shadows, the cave wall formed a large hole that went deeper into darkness. Nolan rowed closer.

"Keep shining the light," he said. "Don't stop."

Nolan felt for his gun.

They floated closer, and the shadowy area became more discernibly a passageway.

Nolan docked next to the other boat, jumped out into the knee-deep water, and pulled their metal vessel up onto the ledge. There was a loud grating as the hull scraped on the sheer rock below. Nolan nodded to Kesha. She exited the boat after a couple of awkward stumbles and joined him.

"Can I have the flashlight, please?" Nolan said.

"Yeah," Kesha said. "What's going on?"

"I think there's a tunnel there," Nolan said, inspecting the area with his bright beam. "I think some of your schoolmates might have gone down it. We need to check it out."

Kesha's eyes widened a little.

"You want to go explore that hole?"

"Could be a way out," Nolan said, extending his free arm to steady Kesha as she slipped again on the slick rock. "I think it's our best option right now. I have no idea how far we are from the dock, but it could be miles. And if we don't help these people now, we might not get another chance for hours."

Kesha scanned the water where so many of her classmates floated. It was a good number, but was it twenty-five? When she tried to do a quick count, she thought it seemed more like fifteen. Twenty at the most.

Kesha looked over at Nolan, who held the flashlight in one hand and his gun in the other. He examined the ripped-out telephone and first-aid equipment, seeming to discover nothing of value. Then he turned his attention back to the tunnel.

"Yes . . ." Nolan said, almost to himself. "I think one of the boats landed safely after the attack happened. The kids got out, and this is where they went. We *have* to go after them."

Nolan began walking into the dark, unlit passageway. Kesha reluctantly followed.

"Look here," Nolan said after just a few paces. He bent and picked something up, shone the flashlight on it. It was a woman's sandal.

"We don't need to call in a detective to figure this out," Nolan said, tossing the shoe to Kesha.

She caught it. Kesha tried to remember if anybody she knew wore this style and brand.

"C'mon," Nolan urged. "I can smell fresh air! This must take us topside."

Kesha took another look back at the bodies in the water, then disappeared into the passageway after the hulking policeman.

It got really small, really fast.

Nolan had to duck, and then bend his knees, and then angle himself forward like a hunchback. Even with these efforts, the ceiling managed to smack against his head every few steps. Kesha, who was shorter, had an easier time.

Nolan had no compass and was completely disoriented. Where would this tunnel take them? They might end up back at the parking lot, or more likely come out in the middle of nowhere. There was no way to know, at least not at the moment.

After five minutes of plodding, Nolan saw a prone figure on the tunnel floor ahead. He froze in his tracks and fixed the flashlight beam upon it. Kesha poked her head around Nolan's armpit and together they took a look.

A girl lay crumpled on the cavern floor. She wore a yellow sweatshirt stained red with blood. Her long blonde hair was sopping wet. She was mottled all over with a wet black ooze that made Nolan think of the sludge that had held together the skeleton pinning Kesha.

"That's Martha McCranner," Kesha said. "Her dad owns a chain of supermarkets."

They stepped closer.

"Martha?" Kesha tried. "Martha?"

There was no response. Nolan could only see one side of the girl's face, but she did not appear to be alive. Nolan awkwardly dropped to one knee—steadying himself in the tight space against the cavern wall—and placed his hand on the girl's throat. Nothing. No pulse and no breath. For a final acid test, he lifted her eyelid and ran his fingernail over her unseeing eyeball. Kesha winced and looked away. The girl on the floor did not respond.

"She's gone," Nolan said. "Were you two friends?"

"Not really," said Kesha. "She was one of the popular girls."

"Oh yeah?" Nolan said cheerily, rising to his feet and hitting his head once more on the roof of the passage.

"Yeah," Kesha said. "She was in the cliques with those fancy girls. The rich ones, I mean. But all the girls at my school are rich girls compared to me."

"But even *within* that," Nolan said with a smile. "You're saying she was with the richest and most popular . . . of the rich and popular girls?"

Kesha nodded.

"Yeah," Kesha said. "But the big three are named Sara and Tara and Madison. Madison's the queen bee. She's the governor's daughter. The one they all cluster around."

"So . . . this girl on the ground was friends with Madison Burleson?" Nolan said. His tone indicated that this information might be important.

"Yeah," Kesha said, wondering why the police officer had suddenly perked up.

"And they were in the same boat together?"

"I mean . . . probably?" Kesha said with a shrug.

Nolan shone the flashlight back down the tunnel.

"Let's keep going," he said.

They left Martha McCranner there on the ground.

★★★

The passageway got even narrower. Despite being fairly fit, Nolan often had to suck in his gut and turn sideways just to squeeze through. In one of these tight spots, Nolan noticed fresh blood smeared on the rocks next to them.

"Other people were here," Nolan said, pointing the stains out to Kesha. "This is just a couple of hours old."

"I wonder how many survivors there are," she said as Nolan probed the bloody smear with his finger. "And if they have a flashlight."

"Hmm," said Nolan pensively. "I don't know. I'd hate to do this in the dark."

"The smell is even stronger now," Kesha said. "I can smell the outside, I mean."

Nolan nodded. He could smell it too.

"Yes, I think we're getting close."

Nolan guessed that they were, in fact, *very* close to the surface. What he did not know was what kind of openings there might be, and if he would be able to fit his six-foot-nine frame through them. Or even if Kesha would fit.

They continued into the cavernous dark. Soon there was no longer any doubt. Nolan felt warm wind on his face and could smell fresh leaves as though he were in the middle of a forest. A few paces after that, and they saw daylight up ahead. The sun had not yet set.

"Omigod, we're actually going to make it," Kesha said quietly. "I thought I was going to die down here. I was so absolutely sure."

Nolan only nodded.

The pair crept on through the narrow cavern until they saw the opening in full. Nolan checked his watch. He had been below less than two hours.

The exit to the cave was not a clear hole in a sheer rock face, but rather a dim opening set back into the side of a hill. The mouth of the cave was overgrown with weeds and bushes. Rusted beer cans, broken bottles, and cigarette butts littered the area. The pair picked their way through this detritus with little difficulty and gratefully stepped out into the dying sunlight.

In front of them was a small clearing. Thick rows of trees edged it on all sides. Nolan had no idea where he was.

To one side of the clearing were two figures, one hunched over the other. Nolan squinted, trying to understand what he was seeing. Then Kesha screamed.

At this, the hunching figure jerked upwards and Nolan got a good look. It was a middle-aged man, rail-thin like a meth addict. He wore blue jeans and an ancient black T-shirt with HENRY LEE SUMMER emblazoned across the front. His face was white as a sheet. Blood and gore dripped from his masticating maw. Even in the dying light, Nolan could see that this man was not alive in any conventional sense.

In a trice, Nolan's weapon was out. With his other hand, he brought the flashlight up and shone it in the man's face. He quickly wished he hadn't. The man's eyes were milky white and his lips had gone black with rot. Translucent maggots shimmered all across the surface of his skin like a wriggling force field.

Nolan dipped his flashlight beam down to the body on the ground. It was obviously dead. Most of the head had been torn away. Eaten. It was hard to determine back from front.

"Another one," Kesha whispered.

"Yeah," Nolan said reluctantly. "It sure is."

Both Nolan and Kesha had hoped that the horrors of this day might somehow be confined to the caverns. In this zombie's rotting countenance, both their hopes were dashed.

The emaciated figure rose to its feet and took one shambling step toward Nolan. It walked unsteadily, like someone very drunk or very sick or possibly both. Its eyes, likely unseeing, rolled crazily in their sockets. Yet somehow the thing knew where to go. It hobbled closer, and closer still.

Nolan saw no reason to let the tension build. He took several steps forward, pulled his gun level with the zombie's head, and pulled the trigger. The thing's forehead opened up like a fleshy firework—spitting brains wildly out the back. It fell over quite unceremoniously, sideways, hitting the clearing floor with an audible thud.

Nolan walked over to the corpse that had been its dinner. This one wore designer jeans with expensive-looking stitching on the pockets. It had, or had once had, long hair . . . which was now strewn all about the body. The face was virtually impossible to discern.

"Allison Duprix," Kesha pronounced. "I can tell from her clothes."

Nolan looked at her in surprise, then turned back to the corpse he'd just shot. He bent down and peered intently into what was left of its rotting face. He looked for any clue. Any sign at all. What was this guy's story? What on earth was happening?

A single writhing maggot stood upright on the corpse's nose for a moment. It wiggled back and forth, as if taunting him. Whatever it knew, it would keep secret. There was nothing more for Nolan to learn.

"Do you think it followed them out of the caves?" Kesha said.

"I hope so," Nolan said, "but I'm worried it didn't."

"Huh?" Kesha said.

"I'm worried that this is not confined to the caves," Nolan said, pacing around the clearing as he looked for other clues. "Did you see how slowly that thing moved? How could it catch up to them here, twenty paces outside of the cave?"

"Maybe Allison was hurt," Kesha offered.

"Yeah, maybe," Nolan said. "I see some defensive wounds on her hands . . . There's nothing that should make her *that* slow."

"Maybe it snuck up on her?" Kesha tried.

"Yeah, I think it did," Nolan said. "But not from behind. Look. Imagine this . . . You come out of the caves like we just did. You're scared. You want to get away. What do you see? Where do you go?"

Kesha stood at the mouth of the cave and looked around the clearing in the waning sunlight.

"I think over there," Kesha said, pointing past her prone (or possibly supine) classmate. "It looks the most like a trail."

"I agree," said Nolan. "So you start to walk that way, and then—boo!—captain cataract steps out from these bushes and takes a bite of your forehead."

Kesha tried to imagine it. Pretty soon she was nodding.

"So what do the others do, assuming there *are* others?" Nolan asked. "Your friend is getting eaten alive, so where do you run?"

Kesha slowly turned in a circle, tracing every fold of the surrounding foliage.

"There," she eventually declared, pointing to a dark opening in the tree line where heavy branches kept out nearly all of the sunlight.

Nolan probed the opening with his flashlight. Then he said, "I think you're right."

Nolan walked over to the dark, shadowy fold. He carefully avoided touching the nearby branches, as if disturbing them might erase some important evidence. Kesha watched curiously. After a few moments, Nolan cried, "Aha! Come and look at this."

Kesha carefully approached his position. She followed the flashlight beam as he trained it on the leafy ground. A fold of yellow leaves was smeared with ocher.

"That's blood," Nolan declared. "At least one is still alive. Probably more. And this is damn-straight where they headed."

"Are we going to follow them?" Kesha asked.

"*I* am," Nolan told her. "But first we're going to get *you* to a safe place."

Nolan produced his smart phone and began pressing buttons. It had no service. Frustrated, he tried the phone's mapping application—at least he would know where he was—but that didn't respond either. Neither did his search engine, which loaded and loaded but never launched. With growing frustration, Nolan put his cell away and instead tried the park ranger radio. The line crackled, but nobody came back. Nolan surveyed the darkening sky. He saw no manmade lights in any direction.

"Do you have a phone?" he asked Kesha desperately.

She patted her pockets and shook her head.

"It fell out when I was in the water," she said. "My dad's gonna kill me."

"I think your dad will be happy that you're alive, and not care about your phone," Nolan told her. "But damn. We need to figure out where we are."

"Do you have a compass?" Kesha tried.

Nolan smiled at the quaintness of this idea and said, "No. But the sun sets in the west."

"The way *they* went," Kesha pointed out. "The people from my class. The survivors."

"Yes," Nolan agreed absently. If only there were some way for him to tell in which direction the caverns had taken them. The way had snaked and twisted so many times, Nolan didn't even dare to guess. The parking lot and ranger station could be just a few paces through the trees . . . or several miles away.

"Do you hear that?" Kesha asked.

"What?" Nolan said, his hand flying to his weapon. He hadn't heard a thing.

"In the distance . . ." Kesha said. "It sounds like a tornado siren."

Nolan went motionless and listened. She was right. There it was.

"And do you smell that?" Kesha said.

This time Nolan nodded right away. He did. Something burning. Something industrial. Something with a biting, chemical stench. The kind of air pollution that, even in Indiana, you couldn't get away with for very long.

"What is it?" Kesha asked.

"I don't know, but something's not right," Nolan said. "Something's *definitely* not right."

"What are we going to do?" Kesha pressed.

For the first time, Nolan detected something close to hysteria in the girl's voice. With each question that he could not answer, it seemed to grow a little more.

"I don't know exactly where we are, but we can't have gone that far," Nolan said, trying to sound like a calm policeman. "At this point, one direction is as good as another. We're bound to run into people soon. I'm not worried about that. But somebody from your school group is alive and bleeding. I think it makes sense for us to follow them. If they run into civilization first, that's great. If they don't, maybe we can catch up to them and help."

Kesha started nodding slowly. A plan was a plan. A plan made you feel like you were taking steps to solve things. Even if, really, you were just picking a direction in the middle of a forest and praying.

"Okay," Kesha said. "Let's just get somewhere before the sun goes down. I don't want to be out here in the dark."

"You're a city girl, huh?" Nolan said, the smile returning to his face.

"Um . . . definitely yes," Kesha returned.

"Gotcha," said Nolan. "We'll see what we can do."

They set off together into the steadily darkening wood.

6

Although an Italian leather chair had been positioned at the head of the table, Governor Hank Burleson was too nervous to do anything but stand.

How had this happened? How had things gone from zero to absolute monkeyshit in just a few short hours? Why could no one tell him that? Why could no one tell him *anything*?

Cell phones were down. Landlines were starting to fail—you'd occasionally get through to someone, and then static would cut you off. Power outages were rolling across the state. And, most alarmingly, there was chaos in the streets.

What *kind* of chaos? Of that, people were less sure. . . .

Was it rioting? It sure *looked* like rioting. People were running about and screaming. But what was there to riot about? There had been no controversial courtroom verdict. No political rally. No sports victory. No, there had been nothing of the kind. So why were people acting so crazy?

Was it a terrorist attack? Burleson had been in Manhattan on 9/11 attending a political conference. He remembered the running to and fro. The stunned office workers parading up Broadway as they walked home to the Bronx. The general alarm and confusion. But 9/11 had had a clear inciting event. There had been no grand explosion in Indianapolis. All tall buildings were present and accounted for. And yet the chaos was upon them.

That morning, the citizens had risen as on any other day. They had commuted to their jobs, taken lunch breaks and smoke breaks, and settled in for the long commute home on I-465. But now in the early evening, these same citizens were running around as though the city were under siege. Some were openly carrying guns. Why? *Why???*

The governor could not bring himself to sit still until he had answers.

Burleson's chief of staff was a man named Doug Huggins. Even-tempered and unsmiling, Huggins could usually explain current events and their implications for the governor in a clear, concise way. Huggins was a wiry man in early middle age with curly brown hair and tiny Benjamin Franklin glasses that always seemed in danger of falling off the end of his nose. For the governor, these glasses symbolized the precarious unpleasantness of dealing with Huggins in general. Just as the glasses were always in danger of falling, even on the sunniest of days, there was always the danger of Huggins walking into his office with word of some new problem or dilemma looming on the horizon. And while the governor may not have always liked the information Huggins brought, he could at least count on Huggins to *have* it. On this day, however, the chief of staff was uncharacteristically tight-lipped.

In addition to Huggins and Governor Burleson, there were five other staffers in the conference room in the basement of the capitol building. At least another five came and went in a constant stream. The large television affixed to the wall had been turned to the local Fox affiliate, which had broken in over regular programming. Two other TVs had been wheeled into the conference room. They also played, albeit with the volume muted, different local news broadcasts.

The uncharacteristically silent Huggins circled around the chaos that had enveloped the *de facto* war room. The governor decided he looked like a man with money on a horse. A horse that might be struggling just to stay out of last place.

When he could bear it no longer, the governor waved his hand to get Huggins's attention as though signaling for a waiter.

"Can we go over the facts again?" the governor asked. "I want to keep them straight. This stuff on the TV . . . it all looks like chaos. And these reporters are just guessing. What do we know for sure?"

Huggins acknowledged the request by smiling to himself. Burleson hated when Huggins smiled. The glasses dangled indefinitely.

"What we know for *sure*?" Huggins answered rhetorically. "We know for sure that there are reports of rioting and violence across the city. We know that in the last three hours, the IMPD have received the number of calls that they would otherwise receive in a month."

"What about the rest of the country?" Burleson pressed. "Chicago, Cleveland, Detroit? Anything?"

Huggins shook his head and shrugged.

"Damn it all," Burleson cried.

He had always hoped that Hoosier exceptionalism would keep his state safe from any disaster that befell the entire Midwest. Back in the 1960s, when Martin Luther King had been assassinated, Indiana was the only state where there had not been rioting in the major cities. Thus, Burleson believed, there was precedent for his conviction that Hoosiers would behave differently in times of crisis.

Huggins continued.

"We know that every IMPD officer, firefighter, and emergency services worker has been called up, and that people are asking us where the Army troops are. . . ."

Huggins let this hang, almost like a question.

Burleson had called up the Indiana National Guard about an hour prior, but asking the regular army to send tanks rolling down Keystone and Meridian felt like too much. Especially when the nature of this rioting was still so intangible; he still could not, in good conscience, have told anyone what the fuck was going on in his state. What if it turned out to be nothing? What if this was some small misunderstanding that just *seemed* like rioting? What happened to the political prospects of a governor who cried wolf like that?

"No," Burleson said, waving his hand to dismiss the idea. "I'll tell you what I told Washington, D.C. an hour ago. I haven't seen anything yet—*anything*—to make me think we can't handle this on our own."

"Mmm," Huggins said neutrally.

Burleson turned and regarded the local television newscast for a moment. They'd cut to a live-remote news reporter not a hundred yards from the capitol building. The camera showed mostly abandoned city streets. The few pedestrians present rushed to wherever they were going with their heads down. A police car drove by with its lights flashing.

"We also know—*for sure*—that people are scared," Huggins said as he watched the same screen. "We know that people want answers. They are looking to their elected officials to provide a sense of stability. To let them know the problem is being addressed. They want to know that—pardon my French, Mister Governor—shit is getting handled."

The governor also waved this away, as if it did not answer his question.

"How about what we *don't* know?" Burleson asked.

"What we don't know?" Huggins repeated. "That's just about everything. What do you mean, Governor?"

"I mean, what do we need to know in order to solve this? What are we trying to find out that puts us one iota closer to *fixing this*? What are we waiting on?"

The governor was breathing hard.

"Well . . ." Huggins began, running his fingers through his increasingly sweaty forelocks. "We don't know *why* people are rioting. Or being violent. Or doing . . . whatever it is they're doing. Is this an insurrection? Terrorists? Communists? Some kind of group from the Internet?"

Burleson was not impressed.

"What do *you* think, Huggins?" the governor asked.

Huggins ran his hand through his hair once more and looked over at the three yapping television screens. One carried a crawl reading "Violence Crisis." Another showed fires burning across a whole section of the city. A south-side working class neighborhood. Half the homes on one block were aflame.

"I think that TV news is not always where you learn what's going on," said Huggins.

"What the hell does that mean?" the governor responded.

Huggins picked up one of the laptops on the conference table.

"For the last couple of hours, reports have been circulating on the Internet of dead bodies coming back to life all across the state," Huggins said. "Bodies coming back to life and *eating people.*"

Burleson suddenly wanted to rip those tiny glasses off of Huggins's nose and crush them in his fist. He found the strength to resist this impulse. For the moment.

"There are videos," Huggins continued. "They're a little grainy and shot on cell phones, but they seem to show dead bodies getting up and walking around."

Huggins turned around the laptop so the governor could see the screen.

The video that played had been uploaded in the last ninety minutes, but already had over 50,000 views. It was shaky, obviously shot by an amateur. The description merely said "Indianapolis, Castleton, 4:30 p.m." and bore that day's date. The video showed the interior of a modest home, and focused particularly on the doorway to the home's exterior. Walking through that doorway—but momentarily blocked by a screen door—was a man who was obviously dead.

The man was white, maybe six-foot-two, and in his mid-thirties. He had short hair and his face held a cheerful smile. He wore slacks and a T-shirt that said BORN TO CODE. It was a little hard to read the shirt, however, because what looked like a railroad tie was sticking out of the bottom of his stomach.

Each time the thing moved forward to enter the house, he was stopped by the tie pushing against the screen door. Though seemingly stymied, the man's face showed only a genial bemusement. Then the camera zoomed closer. The thing's mouth was constantly moving, though it was not forming words. A red drool could be seen on its teeth. It growled like a dog.

"It looks like Andy," a voice said from just out of the frame. A child's voice.

"Shhhh," someone else said.

There were evidently a number of people behind the camera operator, watching this spectacle.

"Get away from there," another voice called.

The camera operator did the opposite.

The camera moved forward until it nearly touched the screen door. The thing outside looked up. It was clearly *aware* of the people on the other side. Its gesticulations became more animated. It mustered itself into a new assault against the door with a long, hard slam. It did not make progress, but the railroad tie was pushed farther into its stomach . . . and farther out of its back.

"Oh my God!" someone called from inside the house.

"That *is* Andy, isn't it?" the child's voice cried again.

The thing backed up a few steps and made another lumbering run toward the door. The result was the same. The railroad tie continued to make progress.

Suddenly, a girl of no more than six or seven ran forward into the frame. She cried, "It's Andy!" and gripped the knob of the screen door.

A voice offstage cried, "Charlotte, no!"

But it was too late.

The small girl turned the handle and threw the door wide. The impaled man took a step inside the house, looking around dumbly. The young girl remained where she was, staring up expectantly into the thing's face. An instant later, it lunged forward and descended on her. The audio erupted into shrieks. The person holding the camera dropped it to the floor. The video stopped.

"That's just one," Huggins said as the screen went black. "Seems like more are being uploaded every few minutes. I haven't had time to keep up."

Burleson remained absolutely motionless for a moment.

Then he reached over—delicately, slowly—and slapped Huggins once across the face.

Though few had the temerity to hazard a look, everyone working in the conference room froze for a second as the sound of palm-on-cheek ricocheted off the marbled walls.

Then it was back to business, as if the blow had never happened.

"This is serious, Huggins. *Serious.* I'm not paying you to look at Internet videos like a teenager. Not at this particular moment in time. No sir! Do you understand me, Huggins?! Not right now! I'm depending on you to be sensible, Huggins! I need your help. . . ."

"I do understand, sir," Huggins said, retrieving his glasses from the floor. "But these videos . . . They're being uploaded from all over the area."

"It's a *prank*," the governor insisted, raising his hand. "People taking advantage of the chaos outside to pull a prank. How in the Sam Hill do you not see that, son? It is a goddamn. . ."

Only the approach of the mayor of Indianapolis prevented his chief of staff from receiving a second blow.

The familiar *click* of her high heels preceded the mayor by several seconds, giving the governor the time he needed to compose himself.

"Kelly, how are you?" Burleson boomed as she strode into the room.

The mayor—whose office in the City-County Building was about six blocks from the state capitol—was accompanied by a pair of staffers and two security officers with holsters on their belts. All of them had the same no-nonsense look.

Personally, Burleson had never known quite what to make of the mayor. Though they were members of the same political party—hell, they attended the same church—Burleson had difficulty relating to anybody who had come into politics *reluctantly*. And that was the mayor's whole spiel. The reluctant politician. Except maybe it wasn't even a spiel. From all appearances—when it came to Mayor Kelly Brown—it might just be the real thing. Sure, Burleson thought, the whole "working mom reluctantly runs for school board, reluctantly runs for city council, reluctantly runs for mayor . . ." It *could* happen. It was a nice political story to tell, sure. And Kelly gave quite a stump-speech. It chronicled the way that her modest wish—any parent's wish, really—to improve the safety of her community for her children had led to the difficult decision to seek ever-higher public office in order to create positive change. It was a hell of a speech. No doubt about that. It had just the right mix of "Aw, shucks" humility, Hoosier pragmatism, and spirited pride in the community—with just a sprinkle of soccer mom thrown in for good measure.

It was so good that Burleson thought it might actually be true. And that, for him, was the confusing part.

How do you not *know* you want to be mayor? How do you not wake up every morning since you were a kid *wanting* the power and prestige that came along with elected office? And why, on God's green earth, would you wait for other people in the community to "insist" that you run?

Burleson would not have said that women, generally, were a mystery to him—but he'd have gladly granted that Mayor Brown was. He just couldn't relate to anybody, male or female, who didn't *want*.

"Hank, what's this I hear about you turning away federal troops?" the mayor said, speaking as if calm discourse required great self-control. "Please tell me there's been some sort of mistake. We need all the help we can get."

She might have been a mother chiding a son fresh from detention.

"Kelly, I can assure you . . . when it comes to the point that Indiana actually *needs* federal assistance, I'll be the first one to make the call," the governor began.

"Omigod," the mayor sputtered. "It's true! You actually did it. You *actually* told them not to send help."

The governor bristled.

"Soldiers in our streets—with machine guns and grenades?—that's not help," Burleson replied sharply. "That's a PR disaster. Please try to think about the future, Kelly. People will remember what Indiana does here. You want us to be like New Orleans after Hurricane Katrina? People thinking we're a third-world country? Have half our population evacuated to Houston, or wherever?"

The mayor cast a long, meaningful look of disappointment across the conference table.

"Hank, what the hell is going on?" she said. "You're not telling me something. You *know* something."

"No secrets, hon," the governor said brightly. "I know as much as you do."

"Then why did you say no?" the mayor replied, telegraphing genuine concern. (This too—Burleson marveled—appeared to be no act.) "People are running wild. I heard gunshots a block from my office!"

"Gunshots downtown?" the governor replied skeptically. "I'll bet it was a car backfiring."

"Cars don't backfire anymore," the mayor shot back. "It's not 1970, Hank."

The mayor turned as though she would now depart. Burleson relaxed and finally slumped into his leather chair. Then the mayor wheeled back around on a pointed heel.

"And I will tell you something, Mister Governor," said the mayor. "You're right about one thing. People will remember this. *Voters* will remember. And I will be good-God-damned if I will stand by and say that I agreed with this decision. Do you hear me, Hank? I will not do it."

The governor smiled. The girl had a political bone in her body after all.

"I hear you, Kelly," Burleson said. "Loud and clear."

The lights in the windowless conference room flickered. The TVs momentarily lost power. Everyone looked at one another.

"I want updates," the mayor said, heading toward the door again. "Regular updates. You keep me in the loop, Hank Burleson. If the phones stay down, you send a damn foot messenger to my door. Got it?"

Burleson nodded and watched the mayor depart. Then he took a very deep breath.

"Governor . . ." Huggins said.

Burleson took a second deep breath.

"Governor . . ." his chief of staff called again.

"*What,* Huggins?" Burleson said.

"Look at the TV," Huggins said soberly, extending his finger toward the screen.

After a third sigh, the governor turned and regarded the glowing television. The screen showed a familiar news reporter holding a microphone. He was standing outside a museum where a traveling exhibit was on display—real, preserved human bodies, reduced to muscle and sinew and posed in a variety of educational positions. As the reporter looked on, museum-goers ran screaming from the institution's regal copper doors. Burleson could not hear the narration, but the reporter appeared confused. Then something emerged from the museum that was not a patron, but one of the embalmed, skinless bodies. It walked slowly and dragged a large plastic cube behind it, to which its foot had been affixed. After a few moments, it sighted the reporter and began to lope closer. The camera operator backed away. Then suddenly the feed went black.

"So?" Huggins replied. "What do you think? That's not the Internet. That's a museum just a few blocks away from where we're sitting."

"Just . . ." Burleson began, wagging his finger in the air. Huggins recoiled in anticipation of another smack.

"Just let me think," the governor managed.

A uniformed police officer entered the conference room and looked around hesitantly. He was very young;—probably fresh from the academy.

"Governor Burleson?" the policeman said.

Burleson saw the officer and smiled.

"Some good news, I hope?" the governor said.

The policeman nodded.

"Your wife is inside the capitol, governor," the policeman said. "We've taken the precaution of creating a secure perimeter, and assigning her a permanent security escort. Since the phones are going down, they sent me to tell you personally."

The governor stood.

"My wife?" he boomed. "My *wife*? You came here to tell me about my wife? Tell me, did you bring her tennis coach inside the capitol too? What about her therapist? Or her nutritionist? Does *he* get a goddamned security escort?"

Confused, the young police officer shook his head and slowly began to back away from the conference table.

"I gave the police *one* request, and—as I recall—that was several hours before this bullshit even got going," Burleson growled.

"Yes, I'm sorry, sir," the policeman managed.

"Now I want you to go back to whoever the fuck you report to and tell them I only want to know two goddamn things: Where the hell is James Nolan, and *where the hell is my daughter?*"

7

Kesha stayed close to Nolan as he conducted her through the indention in the underbrush that might, very charitably, have been called a trail. They chased the sunset, but already most of the illumination came from Nolan's flashlight. Everything felt wrong. Everything felt strange. Even the early fall leaves around them smelled different than they should have, as though their normally pleasant scent concealed something wrong and awful.

After twenty minutes of walking, they found an empty vest.

"This belong to any of your friends?" Nolan asked.

"Not everyone in my class is my friend," Kesha said. "But yes. I wonder why she dropped it."

"Moving fast, sweaty, not really thinking . . ." Nolan said. "Makes sense to me. Who does it belong to?"

Nolan turned the vest over in his hands. It looked expensive. He had never heard of the designer.

"It's not Madison, if that's what you're wondering," Kesha said.

"Oh," said Nolan. He let the garment fall back to the ground and continued down the trail.

"Can I ask why you're so interested in her?" Kesha asked. "It's because she's the governor's daughter, right?"

"You're a smart young lady," Nolan pronounced. "Yes. I work for the governor. He and I are old friends, you might say. Sometimes I do special favors for him."

"What kind of favors?" Kesha asked.

"Not interesting stuff," Nolan said, smiling. "Boring adult stuff."

"Does the governor know about these . . . *things*?"

"Not that I know of," Nolan said. "All they told me was that his daughter's field trip had lasted a couple of hours longer than it should've. See what I mean about boring?"

"Yeah, I guess," Kesha said. "Even if you don't find Madison, I'm glad you're here. But I also hope you do find her."

"Yeah," Nolan said. "I do, too. But my number-one priority is to get you home safe, if I didn't make that clear. Did I make that clear?"

Kesha nodded.

"All right then," Nolan said. "So where do you live?"

"Just southwest of downtown," Kesha answered. "Where they're redeveloping?"

"Sure," said Nolan. "I know it."

"I live with my dad," Kesha said.

"Uh huh, and what does he do?"

"He's the editor of the *Indianapolis Recorder*. The African American newspaper?"

"Wow, the editor," Nolan said. "That's like the top guy, right?"

"The publisher is the top guy," Kesha said. "My dad reminds me of that whenever he can't afford to buy me something."

"Ha," said Nolan. "That's a good one."

"You got kids?" Kesha asked.

Nolan shook his head.

"No, I don't," he said. "I was married for a while, but it didn't work out."

Kesha said nothing.

"Look," Nolan said. "I think the forest ends up ahead."

It was now almost completely dark. The Maglite's beam showed Nolan that the trees surrounding them were near to terminating. Terminating into what, he was not yet sure.

Nolan pressed forward cautiously. After a few moments, they stepped out of the woods and into a farmer's field full of soybeans. The plants were healthy and green and ready to be harvested. Nolan could now see the sky. It revealed a nearly cloudless night. The moon was full and bright. Nolan turned off his flashlight to conserve the battery.

The soybean field was several hundred yards wide and at least two hundred yards across. The woods rose at its edges. There was no artificial light anywhere. No headlights from cars. No residential lighting.

Because of this darkness, it took a full minute for Nolan to see the tiny farmhouse on the far side of the field. It had filthy glass windows with thick curtains. It was old and didn't look structurally sound. The grounds around it had not been tended for years.

"See that little house?" Nolan asked.

"Yeah," Kesha said.

"Maybe they'll have a phone."

Kesha nodded hesitantly.

"You okay?" he asked, this time more quietly.

Again, just a nod. Then a shrug.

Nolan turned to Kesha and flashed an expression that said this was not a time for subtlety. Out with it, girl.

"I just . . ." Kesha began. "It looks scary, is all."

Nolan smiled. He did not disagree.

"Maybe you don't get out of the city much?" Nolan said.

"I told you I'm a city girl," Kesha said.

"Well, I grew up in a house like that," Nolan told her, and began to stride across the soybean field.

Kesha trailed after him.

★★★

Nolan kept an eye out for any sign of Kesha's schoolmates having also crossed the soybean field—another dropped item of clothing, or perhaps an errant iPhone. He saw nothing. Nolan knew, however, that if the teenagers had emerged from the woods here, they would have done exactly what he and Kesha were doing; they would have made straight for the only sign of civilization.

When Kesha and Nolan were about fifty yards away from the tiny home, the moon came out from behind a cloud. In the increased light, Nolan suddenly made out a clump of clothing on the ground about ten paces beyond the front door. He knew, of course, that it was not a clump of clothing.

"Whoa there," Nolan said, putting a hand on Kesha's shoulder.

"What?" the girl said, startled. She looked around for a sign of danger.

"Change of plans," Nolan said. "I'm going to go knock on the door, and you're going to stay over here."

"Okay . . ." Kesha said, sounding confused.

"I just want to be careful," Nolan told her. "We don't know these people. If it looks good to me, I'll call you over. If anything seems weird, just run back into the woods."

"I thought you said this was safe," Kesha said, sitting down cross-legged on a soybean plant.

"I said I grew up in a place like this," Nolan corrected her. "Safe is another matter entirely."

Nolan crossed the rest of the field by himself and strode to the door of the ramshackle farmhouse. It had once been painted light blue or gray, but years of neglect had allowed the natural wood color to seep back through. It felt like a place where any pretense of hospitality had long since been abandoned. Where you're not worried about neighbors stopping by. Or maybe you just don't give a fuck when they do.

Nolan's eyes trained on the dirt-encrusted windows. There was suddenly light and movement from inside. The particular kind of illumination was dim and hard to place. After a moment, Nolan realized that it was candles.

He hazarded a quick investigation of the clump on the ground. It was the body of a very old Amish man. Nolan turned on his flashlight, aware, now, that he was being watched from the house. The Amish man was embalmed. The eyes and mouth had been sewn shut. The fingers and fingernails were full of tiny pine splinters. The corpse had a bullet hole from a .22 in its forehead, and two others in its chest. They looked recent.

"Hello there!" Nolan called to the house. "Anybody home?"

Nolan kept his hands in plain sight, and turned so that the bulge of his sidearm beneath his clothes would be less visible.

The door of the farmhouse opened with a squeak, and an elderly man in a plaid shirt and suspenders emerged. Behind him stood a woman about the same age. She was holding a candle in one hand, and a rifle in the other. It took Nolan a few moments to realize that the man was completely blind.

"How y'all doin'?" Nolan said in his friendliest country accent.

There was an almost tangible silence as the couple considered their response. Would it be friendly or hostile? (Nolan did not think the elderly woman would be quick on the draw. He let his free hand hover closer to his own weapon, just in case. If it came down to guns, Nolan liked his chances.)

"Yes?" the old man said, turning his head toward Nolan. His voice was feeble and ancient, like a tight cord dragging across old wood.

"Hello," Nolan said slowly. "I was wondering if I could come in and use your telephone. There's been an accident in the caves. A group of high school students was attacked. I need to call 911."

"Phone's not workin'," the man said. "Power's out, too."

"Ahh," Nolan said in genuine dejection, supposing that a charged-up laptop with WiFi was probably also off the menu. "Is there another house around that we could try? One of the students is with me. I need to get her to her parents, you see."

Nolan instantly regretted the choice of words, as it was clear the man saw nothing.

"It's the end times," the man stated, as if Nolan had asked for another subject to discuss.

"Is that right?" Nolan said cautiously.

The woman behind the old man nodded in agreement. Yet as she stared hard into Nolan's face, he saw a sudden twinge of recognition. The old woman's heavy lids began to lift, and her eyes went round and wide.

"Oh my sweet Jesus!" the woman softly declaimed. "I know who you are!"

She pushed past her husband and set down the rifle. The husband teetered for a moment, but found his balance. The old man opened his mouth to object, but then thought better of complaining and kept silent. It was apparent to Nolan that this happened with some regularity.

"Oh, these are times of portent indeed!" the woman cried. She stood next to Nolan. Her neck craned until she was looking straight up into his face.

"Whazzat?" the blind man asked, sniffing the air.

"Why, this pilgrim at our door is James Nolan!" the elderly woman cried. "Please, come inside. Join us. You look weary."

"Thank you for the invitation, but we've really got to get to a place where . . ." Nolan began.

Then he thought about Kesha.

The girl was probably exhausted from the ordeal in the cave. Her clothes were still wet, and she likely had not eaten for eight hours. Who was he to deny her a rest?

"Please, I insist that you join us," the woman said.

"Who?" sputtered the old man.

"James Nolan!" the woman repeated loudly and slowly. "You remember him. From the TV."

The old man continued to sniff the air.

"I guess we can come in for a second," Nolan said. The woman smiled from ear to ear.

Nolan turned and waved to the quiet spot in the field where Kesha was hunkered down.

"Kesha!" he called. "Come on over."

A few moments later, a figure moved above a soybean plant. Kesha began to approach the house.

Nolan turned back to the old woman. Her gaze went from Nolan to Kesha and back again. Her smile turned to a cautious frown.

"What happened with this guy?" Nolan said, motioning to the Amish man with his foot. "Looks like one tough customer."

"The dead are coming back to life!" the woman replied, the smile returning to her face. "The end times! Didn't you read your Scripture? But of course you did! A nice young man like you has got to be familiar with the ways of the Lord."

Kesha drew closer. She smiled at Nolan cautiously. He returned what he hoped was a reassuring glance.

"That thing came to our door with the fury of a demon!" the old woman explained, looking down at the dispatched corpse with an almost tangible enthusiasm. "A thing that shouldn't be alive . . . but was! I didn't know if my squirrel gun would put him down, but it did . . . with the help of the Lord. I shot him twice, and it didn't do a thing. I saw those bullets go right into his heart, and he was still slobberin'. Moaning like an old ghost. But then I said a prayer . . . and *then* I pulled the trigger again. That was the one that put him away."

The woman indicated the headshot with a bony finger. Nolan nodded seriously.

The old woman gazed up from her handiwork and looked hard at the teenage girl.

"Hi," Kesha said.

"Mmm," the woman said. Her utterance was like a senator voting present.

"Whose 'ere?" stammered the old man, blinking his blind eyes.

"This is Kesha Washington, a high school student from Indy," Nolan said.

"Indy?" the old woman said, cocking her ear.

"We're both from there," Nolan said. "Her class was underground in the caves when these things started coming up. Things like the Amish man."

"Who is it?" the old man wondered aloud, loping closer.

"A girl from Indianapolis," the woman said loudly. "A little . . . Daughter of Shem."

Nolan and Kesha exchanged an uneasy glance.

"How would you all like to come inside and have a nice ham sandwich?" the old woman asked.

"That would be okay, I think," Nolan said, looking to Kesha. "Right? We could both probably stand to eat. Then we keep going to find a phone?"

Kesha nodded. There was a longing in her eyes, probably for rest and food.

"Okay then," Nolan said. "You folks lead the way."

They stepped over the Amish man and into the darkened farmhouse.

★★★

Nolan and Kesha sat at the small kitchen table and ate sandwiches. The house smelled like hay and artificial air freshener. There were newspapers in the corners and dishes in the sink. The sandwiches tasted delicious.

Kesha felt better the moment white bread, ham, and mustard hit her stomach. She stopped at two out of a sense of propriety. She could have eaten five or six of them.

"James Nolan, in *our* house," the old woman said as they finished their repast. "I've got a magazine with your face on it around here somewhere. Newspapers too. I certainly do. Oh my, oh my! These are times of portent indeed. The people from my magazines coming knocking at my door!"

"Yes . . ." Nolan said uneasily. "Now, we really need to find a phone. Or a place where we can get cell service. Or the Internet. Anything, really, that will let us get in touch with people in Indianapolis."

"Times like these, why would you care about something like *that*?" the old man said. "You should be talkin' to the Lord. Thinkin' about your soul."

"We're heading over to the church," the old woman said. "We were almost out the door when you walked up. I imagine that's where others will head if they've already realized what we have. We were going to take the truck. It's out back."

Nolan nodded evenly.

"I expect there would be room for the two of you," the old woman said.

"That's kind of you," Nolan said. "I think that would be perfect."

Kesha could tell that Nolan's mind was not on religious matters, but on finding civilization as quickly as possible.

"This is no time for anyone to be alone outside," the woman said. She took the sandwich plates and put them delicately in the sink. They went *clink-clink-clink* as they settled on top of others already there.

Kesha and Nolan drained their tall glasses of Cola-Cola and ice cubes, and then stood up to signal they were finished. The old woman agreed that it was time to go. Nolan convinced her to leave her rifle behind.

They went outside. Nolan and Kesha watched as the old man—despite his handicap—locked up the house. They circled around the side of the house, where a 1988 Toyota pickup truck was resting underneath a weeping willow. The old woman helped her husband into the passenger seat, then indicated that Kesha and Nolan ought to get in back. Nolan climbed in first and then helped Kesha up. The truck bed was wet and full of old leaves and smelled a like a dog. Kesha stuck her head over the side to minimize the odor.

The Toyota roared to life and pulled away down a crunchy gravel drive that led into the trees. The way was dark, and the headlights on the old pickup had clearly dimmed over the years. But the old woman seemed to know the way, anticipating each turn before it came.

Eventually, the trees gave way, and the gravel drive merged with a paved road. The truck picked up speed. They began to pass new fields of cultivated crops. For the first time since entering the caves with her class, Kesha felt herself beginning to relax.

The food in her stomach helped, but something about the familiar lull of automobile travel seemed to be the central factor. She had been plunged into a nightmare cavern of murder and walking corpses and what had seemed like certain death. Now she was being carried back to civilization. Back, eventually, to a city. And there was a huge policeman with a gun right next to her in the truck bed. That helped, too.

Kesha relaxed and allowed her eyes to wander over the green fields.

That was when she saw it.

"Omigod," she said loud enough for Nolan to hear. "I think I just saw some of the kids from my class."

"What?" Nolan said. "Where?"

Kesha pointed across a half-harvested field of feed corn.

"There," she said. "At the far side, I saw . . . I don't know. It looked like people running into the woods."

Nolan took a long look but did not respond. Then he banged hard on the back of the cab.

"Stop the truck!" Nolan called, and banged again. A few moments later, the wheezing Toyota pulled to the side of the road.

Nolan jumped down from the bed and walked to the driver's side window.

"I have to go look in that cornfield," Nolan told the old woman. "Please take Kesha somewhere safe."

"No," Kesha called, alarmed. "I'm going with you."

She jumped down from the truck as if her life depended on it, taking her place beside the tall police officer.

"You don't have to come with me," Nolan said, turning to her. "These folks can take you to a town where there will be other people; where you can find a phone and call your dad. Think about it."

Kesha adamantly shook her head no.

"Okay then," Nolan said.

"What's this about . . .?" the old woman asked from the front seat. She seemed only vaguely aware of what was happening.

"Thanks for your help," Nolan said. Then he took Kesha's hand and they raced off into the field.

★★★

They had not gone more than fifty feet when Kesha tripped. Nolan helped her right herself.

"You got to watch how you walk," Nolan said. "You can get your feet hooked real easy. Try to take bigger steps."

"Yeah," Kesha said. "Okay."

Halfway across the field, Nolan began shouting hello. Kesha joined him. There was no response. When they had nearly traversed the entire field, Nolan stopped and put up his hand. Kesha became still. For a moment, all they could hear was their own breathing.

"Do you see anything, hear anything?" Nolan asked, shining the flashlight into the woods ahead. "What color were their clothes?"

"I saw a pink jacket . . . I think," Kesha said.

"They need to hear your voice, not mine," Nolan told her. "They don't know me. They're running because they're scared. Their phones don't work. They don't know where they are."

"And they're a bunch of spoiled brats who have everything handed to them all day," Kesha said. "Which makes them really ill-fucking-suited to this situation."

Nolan raised an eyebrow and smiled.

"What?" Kesha said, smiling back. "Whose feelings am I gonna hurt?"

Nolan laughed a little.

"I think we've been following them," Nolan said. "I think they came out of the forest like we did, and then saw that house with the dead Amish man in front of it. But then they just kept running."

"Those people were not cool," Kesha said, feeling bolder. "What was up with that 'Daughter of Shem' stuff?"

"I think the scientific term is 'racism,'" Nolan said with a smile. "But you'd be surprised how folks act in a crisis. I mean, when their whole world is changing."

"What does that mean?" Kesha said, crossing her arms.

"What if they were usually *more* racist than that?" Nolan said. "I have a feeling those folks were on their best behavior just now. Thinking of their souls, and all."

"Ugh," said Kesha.

Nolan merely shrugged.

They pressed on.

At the edge of the cornfield was a tall hill silhouetted against the moonlit sky. Aside from an ancient, half-collapsed barn, there was no sign of humanity.

"Do you think they went up that hill?" Kesha asked.

"I don't know," said Nolan, his eyes intently scanning the horizon for any sign of movement.

"Maybe if we go up there, we'll have a better view?" Kesha offered the suggestion like a question.

Nolan stopped his frenetic visual search.

"Yeah," he said. "Good idea. I don't know if they would have made for the top of the hill—if their goal is *not* to be seen, which I think it is—but I agree with you; maybe we'll be able to see them better."

They began the trek toward the hill. Soon the grass at their legs was nearly knee-high, and nighttime insects chirped and whizzed in their faces.

From somewhere in the back of his memory, Nolan recalled that Indiana was full of mounds built by Indians. They were not burial mounds. *That* was the creepy thing. Burial mounds, Nolan could understand. Just a Native American mausoleum then, right? Everybody buried their dead. But the fact that, thousands of years ago, the people who had lived on this land had gone to great effort and expense to move and shape giant mounds of earth for some *other*, unknown reason? That was what sometimes gave Nolan the willies.

He swallowed hard and hoped that the hill before them was naturally occurring.

The ground began to tilt upwards beneath their feet. The insect buzzing intensified.

"So, I have a question," Kesha said.

"Uh huh," Nolan responded. "Hit me with it, as they say."

"Did those people back there *know* you?" Kesha asked. "I mean, they did. They knew you. How?"

Nolan swallowed hard. He knew what was coming, and it never got easier. Even in the middle of a zombie-filled blackout, on a remote hill in southern Indiana, with only one person asking—it never got any easier.

"Are you, like, famous or something?" Kesha pressed. They were starting up the incline now. Kesha was a little out of breath.

"I used to play some college basketball," Nolan answered. "Some people still recognize me from that, I guess."

"Waaaaait . . ." Kesha said. "Are you *the guy from Ball State*? The one who had the car accident?"

Nolan took a deep breath that had nothing to do with the incline underfoot.

"Yeah," Nolan managed. "That's me."

"I remember hearing people talk about you!" Kesha quipped cheerily.

Then her tone turned respectful and somber.

"I . . . I'm sorry for what happened to you," she added. "It sounds like a real sad story."

Nolan was taken aback. For a quick moment, his eyes scanned the tops of their sockets as he thought about how to respond.

"I don't know if it was sad, exactly," Nolan huffed as the incline further steepened. "I feel pretty lucky that I got to play D-1 ball at all. Most people never even get the chance."

Kesha looked up at Nolan. She tried to recall the snatches of information she'd heard about this man who was suddenly a celebrity. She remembered articles in newspapers that had mentioned him, and the references that sportscasters had dropped. (References that had eluded Kesha entirely at the time . . . and she'd had to Google to understand.)

Bit by bit, Kesha began to pull it all together in her mind.

James Nolan had first risen to attention as an Indiana high school basketball standout back in the 1990s. He was from some flyspeck town out in the sticks—a place with no real basketball tradition. It took everybody by surprise when his team started doing well in the state tournaments. After a hit-or-miss freshman season, Nolan had led his team to the state finals three years in a row. The final year, they won. The sports pages loved it. It was like something out of the movie *Hoosiers*.

There was a lot of speculation as to whether or not Nolan would leave the state for college—he must have had scholarship offers from all across the country—and locals were overjoyed when he chose to stay home and play for Ball State. Nolan was the starting small forward for the Cardinals his freshman year. He was everything coaches loved. A team player who made those around him better. A hard worker. A soft-spoken, good-looking kid who didn't have an ego and didn't say stupid things in press interviews. And each year, he got better.

During Nolan's sophomore year, Ball State went to the NCAA Tournament for just the fourth time in the school's history. His junior year, Ball State made the tournament again, and surpassed all expectations by advancing to the Elite Eight. And Nolan's senior year?

That, Kesha recalled, had been the doozy . . .

It would be an understatement to say that folks were excited to see what would happen during Nolan's senior season. Was this going to be *the* year? Would the NCAA Championship finally come back home to the state that loved basketball more than any other? It was exciting to think about. The air was thick with promise. Even fans fiercely loyal to Purdue or IU would stop and acknowledge that something special was going on over at Ball State. You didn't have to be a Cardinals fan to want to root for Jimmy Nolan. He was the kind of guy Hoosiers could get behind. Handsome, honest, clean-cut as his crew-cut, a great white hope if there ever was one.

And, look, he wasn't going to be the next Michael Jordan, all right? *Nobody* thought that. Hell, he wasn't even going to be the next Reggie Miller. But he had a shot at doing the best that a farm kid from rural Indiana could do these days. He could win an NCAA Championship with an in-state team, and go on to be a bencher in the NBA for a couple of years. Then, after riding the pines in the big leagues for a while, he could return home as a conquering hero. Be a big man in Indianapolis. Hell, a big man anyplace in the state. He could be a coach. Probably a college head coach right off the bat. Or go into business. Any company would be proud to have him as a "senior manager in training." They could use him in their TV commercials. Or what about politics? Who wouldn't want to have James Nolan as their state representative? Or their city's mayor? Or maybe even something bigger . . . but whatever he chose, James Nolan would be beloved by Hoosiers forevermore. He would be a living reminder that it was possible. That the Hoosier dream could still come true.

All this was to be James Nolan's.

And then the accident.

The accident—Kesha now remembered—*that* was what had interested the adults around her so much. That was where they always dropped their voices when they talked about James Nolan in public. The accident told Kesha a lot about how things worked in the big dirty world . . . .

In the fall of his senior year at Ball State, Nolan had been one of four students coming back to Muncie from a party over in Anderson. It was two in the morning, and they were driving in a brand-new convertible. Everybody in the car was blind drunk. When the convertible ran into a thick-trunked sycamore near campus, it was going over sixty miles an hour with the top down. All four were thrown from the wreck. Police arrived ten minutes later. One student was dead. The remaining three—including Nolan—were seriously injured.

Exactly what had happened was not clear. The only thing upon which the police, the school, and the mayor of Muncie were in total agreement was that James Nolan had *not* been the one driving. This was articulated from the start in one voice, and repeated again and again in all official statements and press releases.

But they protested a little *too* much . . . or so the national media thought. And thus it had begun. The investigative newspaper reports. The magazine cover stories. The TV specials. The Internet gossip. Was the NCAA coddling its star athletes yet again? Were college ballers now so untouchable as to be literally above the law? Would universities, municipalities, and law enforcement agencies collude to ensure that sports stars got away with crimes?

In the end, there was an investigation and an inquest, but very little was established. Nobody had seen the four students driving on the road that night. Nobody at the party could recall who had climbed behind the driver's seat when the four had left, and no security camera had caught them stopping for burgers and fries on the drive back to Muncie. Even the students themselves had no clear memories. Ultimately, the driver of the car was never determined. The surviving students, including Nolan, would pay fines and do community service.

It was also the end of the road for Nolan's basketball career. (And, it seemed, for the Ball State Cardinals—at least for a while— who finished that year 9–21 without Nolan, and didn't even make the NIT.) After three operations over eight months, Nolan was able to walk normally again. He might even play basketball, they told him. Not competitively, of course. That was over for good. But backyard hoops with friends might be possible.

After a few intense weeks of coverage, the crash had gradually faded from the national news. Then from the sporting news. Then, even from the local news. Nolan had quietly completed his degree and left Ball State for parts unknown.

Yet now those parts *were* known, at least to Kesha. Somehow, James Nolan was the police officer who had rescued her from a cave full of walking dead people, and who would not rest until he had found the governor's daughter.

"Sorry," Kesha said quietly. "I didn't mean to bring it up. I just couldn't figure out how that woman knew you."

"No harm done," Nolan replied. "If you want to ask me any questions, I don't mind answering. I think a lot of people want to ask about my basketball days, but they don't. Then they just assume things."

"Okay," Kesha said. "Then why did you become a police officer . . . you know, after everything?"

"I like helping people, I guess," he told her. "I figured I had to have some kind of job. See, the whole thing with basketball was really . . ."

And the tall man simply trailed off.

For a moment, Kesha thought she had upset him. (Perhaps she should not have taken him up on the offer to ask questions.) Then she looked and saw what had stopped Nolan's words. They were now cresting the top of the hill, and they could see the landscape beyond. Being a full foot taller, Nolan saw it first.

In the valley below them was a country fair. It had a very modest Ferris wheel, and a few other smaller rides. There was a long row of carnival games, and food vendors, too. There were also pens full of hay where prize farm animals were being displayed.

And it was in chaos. Utter chaos. The power was apparently out, and the rides had gone dark. People were running to and fro. Parents were calling for their children, and farmers were trying to load bleating farm animals into trailers. The only light came from the headlights of cars and trucks . . . and there were *lots and lots* of cars and trucks. A giant parking lot sat next to the fairground. There were so many white and red headlights. People were driving right into the carnival . . . looking for loved ones or God-knew-what.

Some fairgoers were trapped at the top of the Ferris wheel. A worker below was trying to rotate the wheel with a giant metal pike. The passengers seemed very alarmed, though the drop to the ground was not particularly severe.

There was an urgency as if a tornado were on the way. But the night sky was clear and still. Why such alarm? Why such madness? All that had happened—Kesha reflected—was that the power had failed.

No.

In a trice, Kesha knew the missing element. In the beams thrown by an F-150, Kesha saw a cadaverous body teeter into view. Dripping matter oozed from its empty eye sockets. Its teeth were black as tar. Something that might have once been a nose was hanging down the side of its face. The fingernails at the ends of its hands had rotted into talons. The thing stumbled forward, gnashing its ebon teeth and howling like an animal.

Then another. A rotund man in overalls wandered into the same set of headlights. He was barefoot, and most of his skin had rotted off. His face was a horrid mask of death, but this one's eyes still shone in their sockets. It was horrible to see them fix upon a terrified fairgoer, and then watch as the thing loped in that direction. It didn't move quickly, however. That was the only consolation. (This man could not have moved swiftly in life, and in death was now even further handicapped . . .) The portly zombie swung its arms to and fro, and clacked a set of square Teddy Roosevelt teeth in anticipation. A trickle of red adorned its mouth, indicating that, despite its lack of speed, it had already found at least one human who was even slower. The thing had fed.

"What is *this*?" Kesha asked.

"Maybe, um . . ." Nolan said, baffled by the chaotic sight. "It's a little late in the year for a fair. Could be a 4-H get together. You don't see a police officer down there anywhere, do you? Anyone with a radio?"

"I don't know," Kesha said. "But I see those things. They're stumbling around in the shadows on the edges of the carnival."

"Yeah," Nolan said in a disappointed tone. "I see them, too."

A car successfully pulled away from the carnival lot. It sped off down the road leading out of the valley. It was going fast—far too fast, Kesha thought—and a few moments later there was a thunderous *crash* as the car swerved to avoid something and then struck a tree head-on. The headlights blinked once, and then went out. It was as if the vehicle had suddenly disappeared into the darkness.

"Let's see what we can do for these people," Nolan said. He began jogging down the hill toward the madness below.

"Um . . . okay," Kesha said, trailing after him.

"Stay close and be careful," Nolan added.

He didn't have to tell her twice.

By the time Nolan reached the bottom of the hill, he'd already heard what he was dreading: gunshots rising amid the fray. With so many people running hither and thither, it would be all too easy for someone to get struck by a stray.

Nolan made for the Ferris wheel first. The operator was still doing his best to rotate it with the long metal pole. The cars were small, only two occupants each, but many were nervous and rocking back and forth in alarm. With no hesitation, Nolan jumped and gripped the base of a car that dangled above his head. (Kesha was astonished at his vertical. The policeman must have jumped three feet or more.) Nolan hung from the bottom of the Ferris wheel car, letting his own weight pull it closer to the ground. The entire wheel rotated. The couple inside the car understood what he was doing. After a few moments, they risked a jump—plummeting awkwardly and landing on top of one another. Nolan released his grip on the car and stooped to help them up. Kesha lent a hand. Then Nolan jumped again and gripped the next car.

"Never seen anything like this," called the ride operator. He still struggled to guide the wheel with his pole, though it was clear Nolan was doing most of the work. He had a pack of Winstons in the pocket of his blue janitor jumpsuit, and a lived-in face that looked like it could tell some tales.

"What happened here?" Nolan shouted as he struggled to pull down the next car. From his hanging position, he hazarded another glance around the darkened midway. There were no walking dead in the immediate area, but it was clear that people were now avoiding certain parts of the fairground. The zombies in the shadows were gaining ground.

"Power went out a few minutes ago," the ride operator shouted as he strained to move the cars. "We're ready for that, o' course. Got generators. But then these strange people—covered in mud and look like they's dead—come on out of everywhere. Start chasing people and nobody knows why. Then we lose our generators for some damn reason. Then . . . well, you got this."

"Understood," Nolan said as he helped the next pair of Ferris wheel riders to the ground. "Do you know where we are?"

"Huh?" said the operator. He looked Nolan up and down to make sure he'd heard right.

"Where *are* we?" Nolan shouted as he jumped again to grip the next hanging car. Only one more contained riders—a couple of petrified-looking teenagers, obviously on a date.

"We're not really anywhere," the operator said. "This late in the season . . . this is what you'd call a 'secondary market' for us."

"You must know something," Nolan insisted as he dangled. "Come on! We're in southern Indiana. *Where* in southern Indiana?"

"Uh, we passed Oakland City on the way in," the operator said. "I think that'd make us . . . east of there?"

Nolan had never heard of Oakland City.

The two men combined their efforts to rotate the Ferris wheel a final time. The teenage couple above them leapt to the ground. Nolan released his mighty grip and landed back on his feet.

"Thank you, mister," the young woman said as she fled into the night. Her suitor wordlessly adjusted his baseball cap and followed after.

"Jesus Christ!" the ride operator suddenly cried, his eyes going wide.

"What?" Nolan said.

The operator did not immediately answer. Nolan drew his Ruger and spun around to see whatever he was missing.

"You . . . you're James Nolan!" the operator said.

Nolan exhaled, shook his head, and put his gun back into its holster. Then he turned back to the ride operator.

"Yes. You got me."

The emergency at the Ferris wheel now corrected, Nolan turned his attention to the remainder of the carnival. The chaos seemed to have abated slightly. More people had made it to their cars and trucks and were pulling away into the darkness. Some clogged the road headed north out of the valley, but others took off willy-nilly—careening into the moonlit fields and whatever lay beyond. Those with four-wheel drive had an easier time of it. The hills gradually became pocked with the red and white lights of stranded cars never meant for off-roading. The drivers usually abandoned these vehicles and fled on foot.

There was a frightening crash on the far side of the carnival. A trailer that sold cotton candy had been turned on its side. Nolan had trouble seeing exactly what had happened, but there were several shadowy presences lurking beside it.

"Stay here," Nolan barked to Kesha. Then he bounded toward the overturned trailer.

Kesha considered obeying this command for about half a second, and then followed Nolan's trail through the darkened maze of rides.

They passed a Scrambler, an Alpine Slide, and a Tilt-A-Whirl—then found themselves astride an empty midway where unattended ball- and ring-toss games sat quietly in the darkness. Giant winnable stuffed animals swayed softly in the breeze at the tops of the booths. Hurdling past a Guess-Your-Weight machine, Nolan looked over his shoulder and saw Kesha running after him. He frowned and slowed to let her catch up.

A man in short pants and a straw hat came sprinting out of the darkness. He did not speak or stop, but his eyes comported the entirety of "Don't go in *that* direction."

Nolan and Kesha continued on.

The overturned cotton candy trailer was covered in gaily-colored flags, bunting, and laminated pictures that showed the treats it sold. Three silhouetted figures stumbled soporifically beside it, looking for a way in. Their heads and limbs lolled as if they were exhausted. At the same time, their night-dark mouths masticated with a horrible ferocity.

"Help," a male voice cried from inside the overturned trailer. "Help me, mister! I got hot oil on me."

He had seen Nolan. Somehow, through the darkened side window, the man inside the trailer could look out.

Nolan wheeled on his heels, looking for anything that might solve this problem. There was nobody else in this section of the fairground to assist him in righting the trailer. A cart serving elephant ears and another advertising sno-cones stood dark and empty. A broken Whack-A-Mole machine rested against an empty tent. That was all.

Forty feet away, a car suddenly turned on its high beams. Nolan was not blinded, but the figures of the three undead became less distinct. Despite this, Nolan could tell that they had already lost interest in the man in the trailer. They were now shambling in his direction.

"Fuck it," Nolan said quietly, producing his Ruger.

With the gun in one hand and his flashlight in the other, Nolan approached the first shuffling corpse. It had inky green-black skin. The remains of a T-shirt showing the faces of two radio DJs had fused with the flesh of its upper body, forming a disturbing mix of cloth and plasma. The thing had powerful-looking limbs, but moved them slowly and carefully, as if this required great exertion. Nolan didn't yet know the implications of being bitten or scratched by one of these things—besides, probably, a horrible infection—but he didn't want to find out. At the same time, he could not risk discharging his weapon at this distance and hitting a panicked fairgoer.

Nolan leaned in to the zombie, lighting up its horrible, dripping face with the Maglite. He brought his gun up to the thing's mouth like a dentist aiming to do a field extraction. The thing bared its teeth and hissed. Then, in a sudden motion, Nolan jammed the gun up inside its mouth. Nolan squinted his eyes shut and pulled the trigger, and the top of the thing's head exploded.

The report of his weapon was nearly lost amid the surrounding chaos, but a couple of people in the distance screamed. The undead man went weak in the knees and fell to the ground. Nolan's weapon and forearm were instantly covered in a gauntlet of gore.

"Jesus!" Kesha called. "That might not be safe to do. What if you get that stuff in your mouth?"

"Stuff" was hardly adequate, but Nolan understood what she meant. He wiped his gun and hand against the side of his shirt—then regretted the decision. The horrible smell of rotting flesh immediately attached to his clothing.

"Try getting behind them," Kesha cried. "You could shoot them in the *back* of the head."

Nolan narrowed his eyes as if to say 'Oh, have *you* done this before?'

"Here, I'll distract it," Kesha added.

Though she looked terrified, the girl edged her way to the overturned trailer and picked up a box of wooden cotton candy sticks. She ripped the box open and began to throw handfuls of sticks into the face of the nearest stumbling zombie.

The reaction was instantaneous. The thing growled and lunged in her direction. Nolan saw that this would indeed give him the opening he needed. He leapt to the direct rear of the zombie and angled so his bullet would travel away from Kesha. Then he pulled the trigger.

The thing's forehead exploded out, resulting in a shower of brain-grey matter. There was an audible *slurp* as the contents of the zombie's forehead hit the ground like a thrown cup of water. Then there was a louder *slump* as its rotting body fell to the earth.

"Good work," Nolan said to Kesha. "Do it again."

Kesha steeled herself and eased toward the remaining zombie, a heavy woman in a floral-print dress, now caked in mud. Most of her nose had rotted away, and her scalp was hanging heavily to one side of her skull like a wig gone askew.

"Roarrr!" Kesha screamed like a battle cry, and threw a handful of sticks in the round woman's face. The zombie took two lumbering steps toward Kesha, walking with heavy feet as though its legs were stuck in a bog. Kesha threw another handful of sticks, and then another.

The box in her hands was empty. Kesha threw the box. The thing stepped closer still . . .

A moment later, Nolan's gun thundered and the zombie fell back, arms outstretched—motionless—to the earth below.

Nolan used his flashlight to probe each of the zombies, ensuring they no longer possessed whatever force made them move. Then he motioned for Kesha to help him with the trailer. They heaved once, but it was clear they hadn't the strength to move it.

"Can you get out?" Nolan shouted into the window that had formerly been used to sell treats, but now constituted part of the roof.

"I'm burned on my leg," a voice called back. "Hot oil burned me, mister."

With some effort, Nolan climbed to the top of the trailer and looked down into the gaping window. Inside was a teenager in an apron with a thin beard and a buzz cut. He was wedged awkwardly between a fridge, fryer, and cotton candy machine. Syrup and oil had indeed been splattered on his side. For many would-be rescuers, the man would be beyond assisting, but Nolan had a longer wingspan than most.

As the young man looked on with a mix of hope and incredulity, Nolan lay flat on the trailer and reached his enormous arms inside. Nolan gripped the man under his left armpit and began to pull him up. The man was slippery with oil, but Nolan gradually made progress.

"Ugh," the man complained as he was lifted.

"Help me," Nolan said as he strained. "You have to help. Use your legs."

The man scrabbled against the slick metal walls like a rodent struggling to get out of a trap. Nolan could see that one of the machines had him partially pinned.

"Here," Kesha said.

Suddenly, she was next to Nolan on the top of the over-turned trailer, reaching down into the opening alongside him. Kesha gripped the young man's other arm, and together they pulled him out.

They paused for a moment on top of the trailer, exhausted.

"You're strong for a . . ." Nolan said, then raised a finger to say "wait" as he struggled to catch his breath.

"Strong *for a girl,* you were gonna say?" Kesha shot back, also breathing hard.

Nolan, still panting, shook his head no.

"I was going to say *for a teenager,*" he told her. "But that's not even true. You're just plain strong."

"Ha!" Kesha said with a smile. "I do track and field."

"I believe it," Nolan said.

"Oooogh," the young man said, looking around the nearly abandoned carnival. "I feel horrible. What's happening? What is this?"

"The short version is zombies," Nolan said. "Actually, that might be the long version too. Dead people who eat people are coming out of the ground. Been that way for at least the past few hours."

"Oh," the young man said. "Great."

"Hey guys . . ." Kesha began, more than a touch of alarm in her voice.

"What?" Nolan said.

"Look."

Kesha extended her hand toward the nearest edge of the carnival grounds. Nolan looked and saw nine or ten of the slow, stuporous bodies edging toward them.

"How can there be so *many*?" Kesha whispered.

Nolan opened his mouth to speak, but nothing came out. He thought about it.

How many unsolved murders were there every year? And how many cases where people disappear and the body is never found? All those people who you hope are living in another state or somewhere overseas. What if they're right here, just a few inches underneath the ground? Dumped into shallow ponds and thrown into caves. Buried in an unmarked location with no coffin to prevent a reanimated body from clawing its way back up through the earth.

Sure, not *that* many people a year go missing. But add them all up, year after year, and then set them all loose again, all at once? Yeah, it would look a lot like this, Nolan decided.

"We need to get down from this trailer," Nolan cried.

"What?" the carnival vendor said in alarm. "Are you crazy? Down there with *them*?"

"You want to get surrounded?" Nolan asked, sliding his bulk to the edge. "These things are slow, but they can also be strong. It only took three to overturn your trailer."

"Ehh, this trailer was wobbly anyway," the young vendor said. "Even so, I don't want them on all sides of me," Nolan said. "What's more, I'm about out of bullets."

Nolan slid off the edge of the trailer with Kesha following soon after. Then he and Kesha helped the vendor descend as gingerly as they could. It looked to Nolan like the young man had some first-degree burns, but would probably be fine after a little aloe vera.

Kesha shrieked and began pointing. Nolan turned and saw a man with rotting flesh emerging from the shadows, mere inches away. How had he gotten so close, so quietly? The man's arms extended as if he were fumbling for a light-switch cord in a dark room. His teeth were audibly gnashing. Nolan's reflexes took over; he kicked the thing in the center of the chest as hard as he could. It staggered backwards, giving Nolan just enough time to draw his Ruger. Nolan took aim and shot the zombie in the forehead.

"Damn things are sneaky," the carnival vendor said as the undead man fell to the ground.

Nolan frowned and replaced his weapon.

"Now we're down to *bullet*," he said. "Singular."

A horrible chorus of moans arose from the far side of the trailer. The things were still coming.

"Here, follow me," the vendor said. He took off at a jog, wincing each time he stepped with his burned leg. He led them back through the maze of rides, attractions, and animal stalls at the center of the fair.

"Where are we going, kid?" Nolan asked.

"Somewhere with a *door*," the man replied.

Moments later, the trio stopped in front of a small white trailer at the edge of the carnival near the parking lot. It was unmarked, and had only two small windows. The young vendor tried the door, but found it locked.

"Sheree!" he called, banging on the side. "Sheree, it's me, Steven! Open up!"

The young man began to fumble with a set of keys. Nolan looked around the dark midway, behind and beside them. There was movement in the shadows nearby. What might be man and might be zombie was impossible to tell. The abandoned carnival rides creaked in the wind. Almost all of the carnival patrons had now escaped. Even so, in the distance Nolan could still hear revving engines and voices raised in alarm.

The door to the trailer opened, and all three of them rushed inside. The young vendor—Steven—shut the door hard behind them and stood with his back against it.

The tiny interior smelled like a dorm room where laundry had not been done for the better part of a semester. It was dark. Nolan could see clothes, food, cookware, books, and toiletries scattered across every surface. There was hardly room for anybody to move. Nolan had to stoop to avoid hitting his head.

It was difficult to see Sheree—the woman who had opened the door for them. As Nolan waited for his eyes to fully adjust, he watched her come into view piece by piece. She had long hair and glasses, and held a rifle in the crook of her arm. On top she wore a light pink sweatshirt—worn and comfortable looking—

and had blue "mom jeans" on beneath. Nolan guessed from her voice that she was in late middle age.

"Steven," Sheree cried. "Where on earth were you? Why didn't you come? I was worried sick."

"Mama, those things . . . they turned over the cotton candy trailer," Steven said. "I got burned on my leg. Then these folks pulled me out."

"Are you all right?" Sheree asked, quite alarmed. She bent and attempted to inspect her son's leg in the darkness.

Steven nodded and said, "I'm okay. It doesn't hurt so bad now."

"Looks like he just got a little singed," Nolan told her. "You got some of that green stuff for sunburns?"

Sheree did not respond to the giant, crouching man, and instead continued inspecting her son.

"Steven . . ." Sheree eventually said. "You're going to be fine. Now tell me again, who are these folks?"

"Well," Steven began. "I don't rightly . . ."

"I'm a police officer from Indianapolis. My name is James. This is my friend Kesha. She's a high school student. Also from Indy. Her whole class—or *almost* her whole class—got eaten by these things a few hours ago. We're trying to get to a phone."

Sheree nodded grimly.

"Phones have been down for the last few hours," she said. "Not that I expected much service out here."

"What are those things?" Steven asked.

Nobody tried to answer this question. There was silence in the trailer. They heard a few shouts in the distance, and then a smattering of gunfire. The report from the weapons echoed back and forth across the valley.

"We met some people who thought it was the end of the world," Kesha said. "That it was the dead coming back to life, like in the Bible."

Sheree scratched her head and said, "No, it's not that. If it were the end of the world, I'd know."

Kesha wrinkled her nose. Nolan laughed audibly.

"Mama is a little what you might call . . . 'gifted,'" Steven said. "Sees things before they happen, time to time."

"I knew something was coming," Sheree said, now looking away from her son. "I didn't want to worry you with it, Steven. But I saw the end of this job for us. I thought you were just going to do something to get us fired. I knew I couldn't stop it, so I didn't say anything. Now it looks like we're out of work for a whole different reason . . ."

"Work is not the first thing on my mind right now," Steven said, reclining into the tiny lower bunk where he slept.

"Those things pushed over your cotton candy trailer," Nolan said. "I don't want to wait for them to come and tip this, too."

"I told you, there was something wrong with that trailer," Steven said from his bunk. "They won't be able to tip this. At least I don't think they will."

Sheree joined her son on his bed and helped him remove his trousers. Even though it was dark, Kesha was embarrassed and turned toward the wall.

"Ouch," Steven said. "Oh, damn, that hurts."

"That oil got you good, didn't it?" Sheree said. "It doesn't look like it broke the skin. You just sit there and let me put some bandages on."

While Sheree ministered to her son, Nolan looked out the two small windows. He saw almost nothing. One by one, the remaining headlights faded into the distance or simply turned off. The carnival outside became different shades of black and grey cut through by occasional shafts of moonlight.

"Okay, young lady," Sheree said. "You can turn back around."

Kesha turned and saw Sheree delicately helping Steven back into his trousers.

"Do you see any more of them?" Steven asked.

"No," said Nolan. "There's nothing."

They waited. The noises in the background became less distinct. The shooting ceased nearly altogether. An engine rose and fell in the distance.

"There's room to sit over here," Sheree said to Kesha. "Steven can scoot over. We don't bite."

"Thank you," Kesha said, and crossed the little trailer to sit down next to them.

Nolan stayed by the window, stayed standing.

"How long have you folks been on the road?" Nolan asked, still looking out the window.

"This is near-on the end of our season," Sheree said. "Some carnivals power on through until Halloween, but not us. Not Carrothers Brothers. That's the name of the company, though there ain't been any Carrothers in twenty years."

"Where are you based?" Nolan asked.

"People come to work here from all over," Sheree answered. "The carnival's based in Denver. We live just outside of Cedar Rapids, though."

"Not Hoosiers then?" Nolan said. "And you don't recognize me?"

Both Steven and Sheree shook their heads no.

"God, that's a nice feeling," Nolan said. He looked at Kesha and smiled. She had never seen him look so genuinely pleased. Outside, in the far, far distance, a single firearm sounded. It made Nolan think of the rifle he'd seen in Sheree's hands.

"Do you have many rounds for that rifle?" Nolan asked Sheree. "I only have one bullet left."

"Yes, there's a whole box under the bed," Sheree said.

"Good," Nolan told her. "I have a feeling you may need them."

Kesha detected furtive, furry movement in the shadows. A moment later, something ran across her toes.

"Eee!" Kesha said, lifting her feet.

"Don't mind Furbus," Sheree whispered. "Just a cat. A fat, spoiled one."

"She's usually friendly," Steven added. "I think she's frightened tonight. Cats can tell when something's up. Sometimes animals know things."

Kesha nodded, wondering if zombies ate cats. She didn't think they did. Kesha decided that being a cat in a zombie outbreak might not be so terribly bad. She looked over to Nolan, who remained by the door.

"What do we do now?" Kesha asked.

Nolan took another look out the window, rubbed his face, and blinked like a drunk man trying to sober up.

"For a while . . . just this," he said.

8

If asked outright, Kesha would have declared her falling asleep to be a physical impossibility. Thus, her experience of surprise on waking from a deep doze was not inconsiderable. The mother and son—Sheree and Steven—were still next to her on the little bed. They nestled together, snoring lightly. Nolan was still leaning against the door. His eyes were heavy, but open. Outside, the earliest blue light of dawn had begun to creep over the horizon.

"Hey, sleepyhead," Nolan whispered.

Kesha stood and joined Nolan by the door.

"I didn't mean to nod off," she said. "What's happening?"

Nolan shook his head.

"Nothing; it's quiet," Nolan said. His voice was shaky. It might only be his having stayed up all night, but Kesha wondered if there were something amiss.

"Is everything alright?" Kesha asked.

Nolan pursed his lip and said, "Relatively speaking, I suppose."

Kesha looked at the sleeping mother and son. It made her long for her father with an unexpected intensity.

"Is it safe out there, do you think?" Kesha asked. She risked a peek through the dusty pane. Beyond she saw only the empty carnival grounds. No people. No zombies.

"I haven't seen any more of those things, if that's what you mean," Nolan said.

Kesha relaxed a little. But Nolan's face fell.

"There are other things I haven't seen," Nolan told her. "I haven't seen any survivors from the carnival. I haven't seen police, or fire, or emergency vehicles. I haven't seen airplanes or helicopters. My cell phone still has no service. And I don't think the power has come back on."

Nolan steadied himself against the door.

Kesha wrinkled her nose to ask why this upset him so.

"I guess I was hoping that this—whatever it is—was something isolated. Maybe just down in those caves, or in the fields right around them. But I think this is everywhere."

"Are you going to go back to Indianapolis?" Kesha asked. "Back to the governor?"

"What am I gonna tell him that he doesn't already know?" Nolan said, shaking his head. "That there are zombies eating people all over his state? I think he knows that already. If he doesn't, he's no kind of governor."

"Oh," Kesha said. "So what are you thinking, then?"

Nolan shifted uncomfortably and did not look directly at Kesha as he spoke.

"You're a little young for this, but because of these circumstances, I'm going to talk to you like an adult for a moment. Okay? But please understand, I'm only doing this because of . . . the circumstances."

Kesha was a little confused, but nodded yes.

"So . . ." Nolan began. "The governor has a hunting cabin in this part of the state. It's over near Bedford. He doesn't use it for hunting, though. He uses it to spend time with women who are not his wife. Do you understand?"

Kesha nodded quickly to indicate that she did.

"I think the governor is not as good at keeping it a secret as he thinks he is," Nolan said. "For example, I know from people on his security detail that his wife is aware. Most of the people who work with him know too. I just can't help but wonder if his daughter might also have gotten wind."

"Yeah, she knows," Kesha said without thinking.

"Oh?" Nolan asked with genuine curiosity. "Does she talk about it at school or something?"

Kesha shook her head.

"No, but . . . parents always think kids aren't going to know about things like that. But we always know. Always."

Nolan smiled.

"Well, there you go," he said. "Anyhow, I think that the governor's daughter—Madison—might try to head for that cabin. It's what I might do if I were her. I don't know if she knows the way, but it's the best lead I've got. I don't want to go back to Indy empty-handed, and I sure as hell don't want to go back without having looked first."

"How will you do it?" Kesha asked.

Nolan pointed out the window.

"Try to find a car that still works. It looks like there's a bunch still out there. Maybe I'll find a map in one of 'em, or else hope that the GPS on my phone comes back online. I don't spend too much time in this part of the state. But hell, maybe there will be road signs. Bedford's small, but it's not that small."

Kesha nodded.

"You want to come on a little recon mission with me?" Nolan said, indicating the trailer door with a bob of his head. "We can let these folks sleep a while longer. They look like they need it."

"Should I take the rifle?" Kesha asked.

"No," Nolan whispered. "That's theirs. I expect taking another person's firearm is going to be a pretty touchy subject from here on out. Besides, I've still got *one* bullet left, remember?"

He smiled broadly. Kesha nodded to say that she would go. Nolan carefully opened the trailer door.

Outside, dawn was breaking over what remained of the fair. There were empty animal pens and overturned fences, quiet midway rides, and vacant booths. Nothing moved. Were others holed up inside the trailers too, or had everyone evacuated— literally headed for the hills? To Kesha, it felt like the latter. The place looked utterly abandoned.

They crept toward the parking lot at the end of the mid- way. The cars on the Ferris wheel gave a two-syllable *cre-eak* whenever the wind blew. The sky was pristine and bright. It looked like it was going to be another cloudless day. The kind of weather that made people from Indy drive down to this part of the state to look at the leaves. But something told Kesha that people were going to be staying in their houses with the doors locked and the shutters closed for the foreseeable future.

"Do you think this is happening all over the state?" Kesha whispered as they stalked past an empty row of smelly Port-A- Johns. "Or what about all over the country? All over the world?"

"I don't know enough to guess," Nolan told her. "But I'll bet we find out soon."

They crept silently past an abandoned tent selling caramelized popcorn. The tent flaps were billowing in the warm morning wind. There was a loud *clank* as something inside the tent fell over. Kesha nearly jumped out of her shoes. Nolan put his hand on Kesha's shoulder to steady her. Then he produced his weapon, ready to use his remaining bullet if necessary. Nolan edged forward and looked into the tent. It contained a lone doe feasting on scattered caramel corn.

"It's just a deer," Nolan whispered.

Kesha crept forward and risked a glance. The deer looked up as if to acknowledge them, then returned to its morning repast.

"Aww, it's pretty," Kesha said.

They continued across the carnival until they reached the parking area. From this new perspective, they could see a wide swath of the countryside, and the chaos created by people rushing to flee the carnival. Nolan saw at least ten cars that had been crashed and abandoned at various points along the road. A trailer containing pigs had been left behind; its porcine inhabitants still alive and bleating. The area was also covered with things that people had dropped in the course of their retreats. It made the field beyond the carnival look like the aftermath of an outdoor rock and roll show, before the cleaning crew had had a chance to step in. Clothing, food, bottles, picnic baskets, and backpacks were littered all around.

Kesha craned her neck and tried to take in the entire expanse. She saw nothing that looked like a human or a zombie. She saw no movement other than the tall grass bobbing in the wind.

"Keep an eye out," Nolan said, and jogged over to the cluster of remaining vehicles. Kesha watched as he tried handles, reached through open windows, and searched glove boxes and visors for keys.

Then, on a distant hill, Kesha saw a classmate of hers. Melanie Adams.

The girl's clothing appeared to be torn, and her hair was streaked with what looked, from a distance, like mud and dirt. She stumbled forward slowly, moving determinedly, as though near exhaustion. The expression on her face was completely flat. It said that she didn't care anymore. That she could take it or leave it.

"Aha!"

Kesha heard Nolan's cry and swiveled back to the parking area. The policeman was sitting behind the wheel of a Jeep Wrangler. Kesha heard the jingling of keys. Moments later, the engine *vroomed* to life. Nolan smacked the steering wheel with pleasure.

Kesha jogged over.

"And it's even got a full tank of gas," Nolan beamed down from the driver's seat.

"I see a girl from my class on the other side of the valley," Kesha said. "I think she might be a zombie."

Nolan's expression grew serious.

"Get in," he said.

Kesha climbed into the passenger seat. It smelled like pine-scented air freshener and cigarette smoke. Nolan put the Jeep into drive, and they trundled toward the hill in the distance.

It was bumpy. The Jeep was old, and the shocks clearly weren't what they once had been. Nolan slowed down considerably as they entered the grassy field beyond the carnival.

"Who's the girl?" he asked.

"Melanie Adams," Kesha said. "She's standing over on that hillside."

"I see her," Nolan said, swerving to avoid an abandoned Chevy van.

"She's friends with Madison," Kesha said. "Not in the inner circle, but close."

Nolan nodded silently, his eyes fixed like a laser on the girl in the distance.

When they were halfway across the valley floor—halfway to where Melanie stood—the girl in the distance suddenly fell down and disappeared into the grass.

"Oh shit," cried Nolan. "Where did she go? I lost her."

"I've got my eyes trained on the spot," Kesha said. "Just keep going."

Nolan drove to the base of the hill. He turned off the Jeep and put the keys in his pocket. They got out and began walking up the hillside.

Nolan drew his gun.

They soon came upon the girl. She had fallen onto her side, and lay with her eyes closed. Her head had been grievously injured. Her long blonde hair was caked in dried blood. But unless it was a trick of the wind, she appeared to be breathing.

"Melanie?" Nolan called out. "Melanie, can you hear me?"

The girl rolled a few inches. Then she opened her eyes and looked up.

Her eyes lingered on Nolan. Her face showed only pain and confusion. Then she noticed Kesha standing beside him.

"Kesha . . ." the injured girl whispered. Her voice was so weak and soft—almost lost entirely on the warm wind—it made Kesha think of a dying bird.

Kesha kneeled beside her wounded classmate. From this perspective, Kesha could see that Melanie's head had been hacked open, as if with a giant blade. She thought maybe she could see a bump that was the top of Melanie's brain.

"What happened?" Kesha asked.

Melanie started to cry.

"I'm so sorry, Kesha," Melanie said. "I'm sorry we weren't nicer to you. I'm sorry we never invited you to parties. I'm sorry we ignored you. I'm so, so sorry."

Kesha looked up at the horizon for a moment, confused.

"I . . . I don't care about any of that," Kesha said. "It doesn't matter now."

"It wasn't because you were black," the injured girl continued. "It's important you know that. It was *never* because you were black . . . it was because you were poor. And also the new girl. Most of us . . . we had known each other since we were little. But you? You were new and didn't fit in. And you were from the poor part of town. But those were the *only* reasons we were mean to you."

"It's okay," Kesha said absently. "Honestly, I don't care."

Melanie began struggling to breathe in a way that had nothing to do with her sobs. Kesha experienced the sobering realization that this girl had only moments to live.

"My friend here is a policeman. He's looking for Madison and anybody else from our class who might still be alive. Do you know where Madison is?"

Melanie continued breathing hard, and looked over at the big policeman.

"No," she said. "We all got separated after the cave. We met some people. Some of us wanted to go with them—*I* did—but she didn't. I should have stayed with her. The people we went with . . . they were *bad* people."

Nolan nodded. Kesha found her own eyes were welling with tears, and intentionally looked away.

"They were stupid rednecks," Melanie said, now obviously struggling to keep her eyes open. "Goddamn . . . stupid . . . downstate . . . rednecksssssss . . ."

With this final sickly hiss of distaste, the girl in the designer jeans ceased to breathe.

Kesha turned so that Nolan could not see her crying.

Nolan knelt down to inspect the body. Finding no signs of life, he placed his arm reassuringly around Kesha.

"It's stupid," Kesha said to him, trying not to blubber. "I didn't even *like* Melanie. She was a jerk to everybody. I shouldn't even be sad."

"It's okay," said Nolan. "However you feel, it's okay."

Kesha stayed like that for a few minutes, with Nolan's arm around her.

"Are we just going to leave her in the grass?" Kesha asked as they walked back to the Jeep.

"It's not safe to bury her right now," Nolan replied. "I don't know what makes a dead body come back to life as one of those *things*—or how long it takes for that to happen—but I don't want to find out while we're moving her into a grave. Imagine if she rears up and bites off your finger."

Kesha shrugged to acknowledge that this was, in fact, a reasonable concern.

They climbed into the Jeep and rode back across the bumpy field toward the carnival.

"What are we going to do now?" Kesha asked.

"*I'm* going to head for Bedford and find that cabin."

Kesha did not like Nolan's use of emphasis.

"I talked with that woman—Sheree—a little bit while you were asleep," Nolan continued. "She seems like a good person. It sounded like it would be all right if you stayed with them for a little while."

"What?" Kesha said. "No. That's . . . I want to get back to Indianapolis. I have to find my dad. Not stay here."

"Look," Nolan began. All at once, his tone had shifted in a way that said he wasn't going to be a nice, cool, friendly policeman (who was maybe even a little bit handsome)—he was going to turn into a shitty adult, just like all the others in Kesha's life.

"I want to keep you as safe as possible," Nolan continued. "After our little walk around, I'm more convinced that this fairground might be one of the better options for that. It's down in a valley, and you can see people coming at a distance. They've got a trailer that locks and some food. Did you think about that? I don't think grocery stores are going to be open today."

"No," Kesha said defiantly. "I'm not staying here with these people. You can't make me. I can steal a car and drive back to Indy myself."

"Yes," Nolan said, clearly perturbed. "You certainly can. You can also end up like your school friend back there, with a goddamn machete wound in your skull. Listen, Kesha, there are a lot of people in this world who are basically good. I think Sheree and her son might be some of them. But there are a lot of people who would use a disaster like this to do whatever they wanted, *to* whoever they wanted. For most of my years as a police officer, I've worked narcotics. You wanna talk about not giving a fuck . . . I've dealt with people who *did not give a fuck*—not about what they were doing to their bodies, not about what they were doing to other people's bodies, or to other people's children's bodies. A whole lot of folks out there are living just for today, and I don't mean that in a good way. Until this—whatever 'this' is—blows over or calms down or whatever the fuck, it's not safe for you to be running around. I'm a police officer with a gun, and I don't feel fucking safe. But a fifteen-year-old high school kid with no map and no gun who doesn't even have a proper driver's license?"

There was a pause as Nolan used all of his concentration to avoid a shallow ditch.

"I wouldn't wish that on my enemy right now," he concluded.

"Okay, fine," Kesha said, staring straight ahead into the windshield.

"And I'm sorry for cursing so much," Nolan said. "I don't usually. It's just . . . *this*."

"Yeah," Kesha said, looking at the wrecked, abandoned cars on the other side of the window. "Tell me about it. Fucking *this*."

They arrived back at the carnival grounds, and Nolan pulled the Jeep all the way up to the door of Sheree's trailer. It was now no longer dawn, but full-on morning. The sun inched its way higher into the completely cloudless sky. Steven was standing in front of the trailer, limping a little on his burned leg. He waved as they pulled up. Sheree was standing to the side of her trailer talking to a tubby man in a green baseball cap whom they had not seen before.

Nolan and Kesha got out of the Jeep and walked over.

"You wasn't kidding!" the large man said in a thick Southern accent. "Jimmy Nolan in the flesh!"

"Hi," Nolan said, and looked to Sheree.

"This is Walter," Sheree said. "Part of the crew."

"Can I shake your hand?" Walter wondered. "Big basketball fan."

Nolan extended his hand, aware that it was still caked in dried zombie-goo. Walter gripped it and pumped hard without a second thought.

"Yeah," Nolan said to Sheree. "I guessed some of your folks might trickle back in when dawn broke. Is Walter the only one so far?"

"Yes," Sheree said. "I'm surprised there aren't more. There are twenty of us who travel full-time with the carnival."

"Welp . . . give it some time," Nolan said. "Maybe more will come over the course of the day."

"I ran and hid in some corn when I saw those things," Walter announced. "Then I climbed a tree. Stayed up there pert all night."

"I'm going to run a little errand in this Jeep," Nolan informed Sheree. "I told Kesha what we talked about. She's going to stay here with you. I'll be back soon, if I'm able."

"That's just fine," Sheree said.

Sheree walked to a table near her trailer and picked up a paper sack. She brought it over to Nolan. The wind hit it from behind, and Nolan's stomach grumbled.

"It's just carnival food—hot dogs and fried dough—but it ought to get you through the morning," she said.

"Thank you," Nolan said, accepting the sack. He could hardly wait to dig in.

Steven limped up beside them.

"And here," Steven said. "You also ought to have this."

He handed Nolan a wrinkled road atlas.

"We never know when our GPS is gonna go out—usually, it's at the worst possible time—so we keep a few of these around."

"Perfect," Nolan said, accepting the atlas with his free hand. "This is just what I need."

Steven turned and looked out at the wreck-encrusted road out of the valley.

"I keep waiting for the cavalry to come rolling in, you know?" the young man said. "That . . . or for the power to come back on. This is just . . . I don't know. I keep thinking: 'They'll have it fixed in the next hour. Okay, they'll have it fixed in the *next* hour.' But they don't. This is the longest blackout ever. It's like they just don't care."

"Yeah . . ." Nolan replied pensively. "I don't know if there's even a 'they' right now, if you follow me."

Steven nodded grimly.

"But if I find any answers, you'll be the first to know," Nolan added.

He opened the atlas and flipped to the pages marked with Is.

"Here we go," Nolan said to Steven. "We're somewhere east of Oakland City?"

"That's right," Steven replied.

"I'm guessing that'd put us around here," Nolan said, touching a spot of farmland in the southwest quadrant of the map. "That makes it maybe 60 or 70 miles to Bedford."

Nolan looked over to Kesha, who was eating a cold hot dog.

"With the roads messed up, I'm guessing it will take me at least an hour and a half to get where I'm going," Nolan said. "If I don't find anything, I'll head straight back. You could see me again in three hours."

Kesha nodded, restored by the hot dog, but still uneasy.

"Here," Nolan said, handing Kesha a business card from his back pocket. "That's got my cell on it. The moment the phones go back up, you give me a call. Got it?"

"Yeah," Kesha said.

"And if I can't come back here, I'll try to send word somehow," Nolan said.

Kesha did not reply.

Nolan walked to the Jeep and climbed inside. He started the engine and waved once. Sheree, Steven, and the fat man—Walter—waved back. Kesha only looked on with an uneasy frown. Nolan put the Jeep into drive, headed through the parking lot and down the road leading away from the carnival, and into whatever world might exist beyond.

9

Ellard van Zanten's full title was assistant director of communications for the Indiana governor's office. A relatively recent graduate of Indiana University, van Zanten was originally from Holland but had shown great interest in—and aptitude for—American politics. During Burleson's re-election campaign, van Zanten had managed the governor's social media presence and spoken to groups of young voters on the governor's behalf. Burleson liked the athletic, perpetually smiling Dutchman, and had made him a full-time member of his administration soon after the election.

And though the word "assistant" was embedded right there in his title, van Zanten was starting to get the feeling that he might have just received a battlefield promotion.

As dawn broke over the capital building, Governor Burleson sat at the head of the conference table in his war room. He sat unmoving. Both hands on the table. Eyes staring straight ahead. (Presumably, the governor viewed one of the three television screens, or twice as many computer monitors, arrayed throughout the busy room. Screens and monitors that were now entirely filled with static and test patterns, or "no service" messages. Still, to van Zanten, it seemed Burleson's eyes stared into cosmic distances far beyond the four walls of the Indiana State Capitol. The governor was not "zoned out." His brain was working, always working. If van Zanten knew anything about the man who ran this state, it was that he *never* stopped thinking.)

In the fourteen or so hours since the outbreak, almost none of the governor's regular staff had reported for duty. With telephones now completely down and power out in most of the city—the capitol, a rare exception, had generators—there was no way of contacting the staff, short of sending police cars to their homes . . . which, in fact, was what Burleson had ordered done. The problem was that most of Burleson's staff were not in their homes. They had fled the city entirely, taking their families with them. Van Zanten ran through the list in his head.

Director of operations? Gone. Chief counsel? Gone. That community-liaison manager lady, whatever the fuck her title was? Gone. Even the lieutenant governor had failed to show up. Certainly, van Zanten's boss, the director of communications, had not been seen since five o'clock the day before.

As van Zanten looked around the room, he realized with mounting terror that he and Doug Huggins—the governor's chief of staff—were probably the two highest-ranking members of state government in the building . . . behind only Burleson himself. The few employees who otherwise remained were all secretaries, IT staff, security guards, and interns.

It was a time of great mystery and confusion, but a few facts had begun to solidify among the stream of more and more unbelievable news that flowed in every hour. Van Zanten tried to put together a timeline in his mind . . .

Early the previous evening, reports of an unexplainable uptick in violent acts had washed over the city. Mobs had formed in the streets, and people were brandishing weapons openly. Nobody knew why. A few hours later, this became tentative—then *definitely*—linked to reports of dead bodies getting up and eating people. The people in the streets with guns and clubs weren't just attacking each other—though some of them were *definitely* doing that—they were defending themselves against these walking dead men . . . which, incidentally, it seemed you could not "kill" unless you had destroyed their heads or punctured their brains. And speaking of brains, it seemed eating the brains of the living was the ultimate goal of these things. To achieve this end, they would bite and scratch and claw like wild animals. They could not be reasoned with. They could not speak. They could only kill.

That was where knowledge ended, and speculation began.

The duration—if, indeed, an end was in the cards—was the central matter of conjecture. Would this insanity soon pass? Would the dead fall motionless back to the earth after a few hours or days? Or . . . was this the new normal? Was the land forevermore to crawl and lurch with zombies?

It was this last idea that seemed to stymie van Zanten, Huggins, and even Governor Burleson. After all, they had plans and procedures in place for emergencies—natural disasters, terrorist attacks, and so forth. Oh boy, did they have those. The last three administrations couldn't wait to get that gold star, A-plus rating for terrorism readiness. (They could even claim to be anti-terrorism leaders, in a way. The Indy 500 was the largest single-day sporting event in the world—almost half a million people came—and it had never been attacked by a terrorist. So that meant they were doing something right, right?)

But this was different. This was one of the few things the United States no longer worried about: an invasion.

Coming, as he did, from the Netherlands, van Zanten found it difficult to imagine a country that believed it could not be invaded. His own homeland had been sacked by everyone from the Romans to the Nazis. Of course invasions happened. Of course they did. You prepared for them like you prepared for anything else.

But not here, apparently. Not in the Midwestern United States. Not until now.

There was nothing in the playbook for this. Americans were *not* prepared. Maybe nobody was.

Van Zanten was exhausted. He'd been on a date at a café in Broad Ripple when the shit had started to hit the fan. He'd kissed his girl goodnight and caught a cab to the capitol as fast as he could. But he also knew that crisis bred opportunity. Maybe even for assistant directors of communication . . .

10

The governor was snapped out of his early-morning meditation by the only member of his press team who had bothered to show up. It was that kid—what was his name?—van Zanten. The tall one, from Europe. Belgian, or something. The good-looking one who made all the college girls want to come out and vote the Burleson ticket.

The governor did not enjoy being disturbed when he was deep in thought.

"In my opinion, we need to make some sort of statement," the tall foreigner was saying. He smiled brightly across the conference table and nodded, as if agreeing with his own idea. Maybe that was a European thing, Burleson thought.

Burleson's eyes did not stir from their fixed position.

"When I want *your* opinion, I'll choke you to death and guess," Burleson responded flatly.

Van Zanten realized this was probably not hyperbole. The Dutchman's face fell.

"Now go get me a cup of coffee," Burleson said. "Heavy cream. Three sugars."

The young man nodded and quickly backed out of the room.

"He might have a point," Doug Huggins whispered when van Zanten was beyond earshot. Huggins had not left the governor's side for the past twelve hours, not even to use the bathroom.

The governor looked at his chief of staff with a stern disappointment.

"I expect that from a kid . . . but not from you," Burleson said. "You know what the procedure is now, Huggins. You told me yourself."

The governor gestured to the emergency satellite phone resting on the conference table in front of him. It was enormous and looked very old—from the 1990s or earlier. It was physically dusty. It had sat in a storeroom in the capitol basement for who knew how many administrations, until a terrified secretary had dug it up and brought it to Burleson a few minutes after the phones and Internet had failed completely.

This overgrown piece of metal and plastic was the last and best hope issued by the Feds for just such a disaster. Instructions on what to do—and, indeed, on who was running the country—would presumably emerge from this device as soon as the federal government got its act together. That was the official story, anyway. Now it seemed laughable—laughable and terrifying—that such an ancient and poorly-maintained piece of equipment was all that stood between Indiana's total disconnection from the larger world. Only the single glowing LED light on the side of the phone gave any indication that it was even operational.

"We can wait for them to call from anywhere," Huggins said to the governor. "Theoretically, that phone will work in any conditions."

"Theoretically?" the governor replied. "I'm not interested in theories right now."

"We really should think about a press conference," Huggins pressed. "Our young Dutch friend is too timid to say it, but people remember political appearances during times of crisis. People remember Giuliani after 9/11. People remember Churchill walking the streets of London after it was blitzed. But people only remember those things because they were *captured by a camera*."

Burleson nodded.

"What the people think still matters, Governor. You want to rule whatever is left of Indiana after this, don't you?"

The governor had to admit that he did.

"So we need to start thinking along those lines," Huggins said.

"And maybe . . ." Burleson replied, brightening visibly for the first time in hours. "Maybe this constitutes extenuating circumstances . . . that override traditional restrictions on things like term limits."

Huggins nodded, pleased to watch the governor's soul catching fire.

"People will remember what you did here," Huggins said. "People at the national level will remember. But they have to *see* it first."

The use of opaque terms like "national level" was the only way Governor Burleson would consent to talk about his ultimate goal, which was, of course, the presidency. The impact of his actions at a "national level" was a delicate subject, but always on his mind. Burleson wanted it so badly that he couldn't think about it for more than a few moments. Like watching your team shoot those final two free throws that would decide the championship. It was just too much. Yes, there it was, behind all that he said and did. The ultimate prize. A Hoosier had not been president for over a hundred years. Perhaps Burleson was the one to make it happen once again.

A terrified Ellard van Zanten reentered the conference room with a small, Styrofoam cup containing old, burnt coffee. He set it gingerly on the table in front of the governor.

"Remember the Gulf oil spill in 2010?" Huggins continued. "Or the Exxon Valdez back in the 80s? When you think of those disasters, what do you think of? What did the cameras show? They showed boats and cleanup crews on the water almost immediately. Do you think those ships were *actually cleaning anything*? Of course not! Not the first ones. They were window dressing. They were there for show. It was weeks before the proper cleaning equipment actually arrived. But people didn't see that. When citizens turned on their TVs, it looked like the oil companies were responding quickly."

Burleson did not like it when oil companies were bad-mouthed in his presence (which, it seemed, Huggins had just come precariously close to doing). Still, he saw that his chief of staff might have a point.

"Something for the media?" the governor said.

He turned to look at Huggins and dipped his chin, as if examining him over the tops of invisible eyeglasses.

"It's definitely an idea," Huggins explained. "And it doesn't matter if people see it right away. We record it—create that digital asset—and then people will see it *eventually*. They'll know what you were doing when the outbreak started. We create a record for when the power comes back on."

The governor was silent for a moment.

"We should include the mayor," he finally pronounced. "Do we know where she is?"

"Still in the City-County Building, I expect," Huggins said. "Ellard's been out more than I have."

They looked down the table to the tall, nervous Dutchman.

"I . . . yes . . ." van Zanten began, looking around, trying to think. "I've heard from IMPD officers that she is still in the Green Zone."

Police and Indiana National Guard troops had worked overnight to create a barricaded area containing the government buildings in downtown Indianapolis, blocking off streets and erecting barriers to funnel traffic away from the heart of the city. (Not that there was much. For the moment, the downtown streets were quiet and bare.)

"As far as a press conference . . . I've seen a couple of reporters, but they come and go," van Zanten added.

"Explain that," the governor said, taking a tiny sip of his awful coffee. "What do you mean?"

"I think with the local news outlets, it's—erm—sort of like here," van Zanten stammered. "They are running on generator power that they don't like to expend. And that many personnel are missing. Then some who *are* present leave to go home to their families."

The governor winced at the mention of family. There was still no word from his man Nolan. Still nothing about his daughter. Yet the governor had faith. If Nolan could not do it, then it could not be done. He shook off the thought and turned back to the matter at hand.

"That's not a problem," Huggins said. "We have our own camera equipment. We can shoot the video ourselves, and then take it over to the networks. You've got a nice new digital camera in the communications office, right, Ellard?"

"Absolutely," the Dutchman agreed.

"See, we can take care of it," Huggins said, "we'll create our own movie that lets the national audience see what you're doing. The networks can run it the moment the power comes back on."

The governor smiled, but cautiously. Mostly this was because, deep down, he knew that he had done almost nothing worth recording in the hours since the start of the outbreak.

There had been a bit of talk—when the existence of the zombies had become absolutely incontrovertible—of sending what remained of the IMPD to keep watch over the city's cemeteries and graveyards. They'd had a meeting about it and looked at maps. However, the few officers sent ahead to investigate had reported counterintuitive findings. Namely, that cemeteries were not the problem areas. Only a few of the walking corpses had found the strength to escape their coffins and dig through six feet of dirt. Most mausoleums were locked up tight, leaving the reanimated bodies to stagger around harmlessly inside. Even the funeral homes were mostly locked. The problem, it turned out, were all of the bodies that had been disposed of through *extralegal* channels. Bodies dumped by criminals. Bodies buried by meth gangs in shallow graves in cornfields. Bodies of people who had fallen down wells or into sewer drains. *These* were the ones who were coming out to roam the streets in search of brains. And they were all over the city, not centralized. There was almost no way to predict where the next one would pop up.

Thus, the governor had scrapped his plan to guard the cemeteries. Aside from giving his cursory blessing to the creation of the Green Zone, he had issued no other substantive order for the duration of the night.

"I'm not talking about *specifics*," Huggins said, seeing the governor's hesitation. "We're not going to give *specifics* in this video. No, no, no. I'm envisioning something where people simply see that you are here. That you're in control. You're walking the streets of the city. You aren't waiting for the federal government to tell you what you need to do. You're out there being a leader."

Burleson, Huggins, and van Zanten all looked at the large satellite phone for the smallest fraction of a second.

"I like it," the governor finally said. "I like it *a lot*. How do we make it happen?"

Huggins stood up and stretched.

"Okay," Huggins said. "I'll spend the next few minutes crafting some remarks for you and the mayor to read. Van Zanten? Go get the camera and anything else that might be useful. Mister Governor, I'm thinking a jacket with no tie. Maybe khakis or even jeans."

Burleson kept several changes of clothing upstairs in his office.

"We meet back here in twenty minutes?" Huggins said.

The men nodded in agreement, and each went to his task.

Burleson rose to his feet and finished the tiny cup of coffee. Then he placed the large satellite phone in his pocket—so heavy it pulled his blazer to one side—and trudged to the elevator. Moments later, he stood in front of the comically tall, yet venerable wooden doors—flanked by rows of flags—that constituted the entrance to his office.

He ached all over from lack of sleep and even felt slightly lightheaded. Yet in the governor's breast there burned a hot, intoxicating spark of excitement usually reserved for election cycles. This was it, he realized, as he locked the door, pulled the shade, and began to don an ancient pair of Wranglers. This was the application for his next job. This *was* the campaign.

Yes.

He would lead Indiana through its darkest moment. He would do it without any help. And he would do it right now.

Minutes later, with the sun grandly lighting the Soldiers and Sailors Monument at the end of the street, the governor stepped out onto the front steps of the capitol building. He was flanked by Huggins and van Zanten, and also by six uniformed IMPD officers.

One look at the sky, and he knew it was going to be a beautiful day. The air had that wonderful early-fall smell that made the governor think of high school football two-a-days, meaty cookouts, and long road trips with the windows down. It was a glorious, invigorating thing. Not quite the equivalent of a good night's sleep, but the governor would take it.

They descended the stone steps of the capitol, passing statues of Civil War soldiers holding ancient rifles and bayonets. These unmoving works of bronze were flanked by SWAT teams—quite alive and real—draped in jet-black body armor. They parted ranks for the governor and his team.

"Has there been any action inside the Green Zone?" Burleson asked the senior-looking member of the SWAT team.

"We put down one of those things at about two in the morning, before the barricades were finished," the officer answered stoically. "No trouble since then."

"Good," the governor beamed.

"We're headed over to the City-County Building," Huggins interjected.

"Sure thing," the SWAT leader said, fingering his sniper rifle. "We can cover you for most of the way. Until the monument, at least."

The governor and his party reached the street in front of the capitol. Huggins began to organize his players like a movie director on a set.

"Okay . . . van Zanten, start filming," Huggins barked. "Turn on the camera and leave it on. Do it this moment."

"Now?" the tall Dutchman said, fumbling with the tiny device. "Um, okay . . . we are now filming. This is going be very DOGME 95."

"Very *what*?" the governor asked with a frown.

"It doesn't matter," Huggins told him. "I want to capture everything, not just the governor reading his statement. We want to show him walking through the streets. Surveying the city. We'll edit it all later, and keep only what we want to show the public."

Burleson nodded, apparently satisfied, but still narrowed his eyes at van Zanten one last time.

The Dutchman peed a little.

"Of course we'll want you out front, Mister Governor, in the center of the shot," Huggins continued, still directing. "I'm going to walk with you, but off to the side. Van Zanten, you stay close to us, but not too close. And make sure you get some shots of our surroundings. We need to show the emergency vehicles. The equipment. The point is to make it clear that things are being done. Look at all of this equipment; it's doing something. Got it? Now, officers . . ."

Huggins turned to the six uniformed police.

"Sad to say, this is not your big Hollywood moment. I need you to stay at least ten paces behind our cameraman, understand? *You* are not in the shot."

The police collectively retreated a few paces. They looked bemused by this attempt at choreography.

"All right, good," Huggins declared, surveying the scene. "Now, Mister Governor, if you'd allow me . . ."

Huggins untucked the governor's shirt from his blue jeans and rolled up the sleeves of the governor's jacket. Then he tussled Burleson's usually immaculate hair. It made the governor look five years older, true, but it also removed the patina of preparation. Now he looked like a man who had been up all night, working. (On solutions, no doubt, for his beloved state.)

"What in the Sam Hill is this?" Burleson said, wrinkling his nose to show he was uncomfortable with the new hairdo.

"Trust me," Huggins said. "Okay, van Zanten . . . you're rolling?"

"I am, I am!" the Dutchman insisted, and pointed to the little red "record" light on the camera.

"Crouch a little as you shoot," Huggins told him. "You're so tall; we don't want the governor looking short."

The Dutchman dutifully crouched down until he stood beneath the governor. He gave Huggins a thumbs-up from behind the lens.

It was time to begin.

The governor set off down the street toward the City-County Building. After just a few steps, the governor hit his stride. Why, this was no different from a campaign commercial. He had done dozens of those. This was the same deal. (What did they always say to him? "Just have fun with it!")

Burleson could feel that this was going to be big. This would be what he'd be remembered for. *These* moments. People all over the country would see the governor braving the streets. Commanding his troops like a general. Making things right again.

His courage would stand as an example to Hoosiers everywhere. No . . . as an example to the entire nation.

"Mister Governor," Huggins called—he was using his "onstage" voice; the one he used at press conferences when he told reporters no more questions. "Can you tell everyone a little bit about where we are and what we're doing?"

The governor nodded. His voice dropped into an affable Hoosier twang.

"Lessee . . . it's coming up on eight in the morning, and we're here in downtown Indianapolis," the governor said. "It's been a long night, but we're making progress. I'm proud of the job that everyone is doing. I don't think anybody here has slept a wink, but I haven't heard a single complaint. I think all of us are just as committed to digging out."

Huggins, though generally pleased with this opening, winced a little at this final phrase. Was a zombie outbreak like a snowstorm from which you dug out? Would Hoosiers see it that way? Maybe it was. Maybe in a few days the zombies would be removed like so much snow, and commerce, government, and everything else would begin to function again. Huggins found himself hoping that this was the case, and not just for continuity. . . .

"At this moment, we're headed from the capitol over to the City-County Building to check on the city government," the governor continued. "I'm excited to work with the mayor personally on a solution. That is . . . we *are* working together. Why, the mayor and I spoke just last night, at the beginning of this emergency. We're continuing now to collaborate despite the . . . difficulties that have arisen."

Huggins liked "difficulties." It spoke to the zombies without using the z-word. Very clever. On a good day, the governor still had a little magic in him. (Huggins remembered what he had seen in this man so many years ago. Why he had selected Burleson as the horse on which to bet his career. The charisma. The on-camera magnetism. The whip-smart intelligence.)

Governor Burleson made this nod to zombies more explicit by winking at the camera.

Huggins liked it. Huggins liked it a lot.

"We're also doing our best to move resources around where they can do the most good," the governor continued, the bullshit beginning to flow more easily. "We've got an award-winning emergency management team in this city. Groups come from all over the world to learn from us, in particular how we handle the 500. And now all these people are working as hard as they can. But as you see, we've had to close the center of the city for security reasons. We're still without electricity, but, uh, I've been assured that the folks over at Indiana Power and Light are doing everything they can to get the grid up as quickly as possible. My office is working closely with them."

This was just a boldfaced lie. The governor had not heard from IPL at all. Since the power had died, there had been nothing but total silence.

They neared the Soldiers and Sailors Monument and the giant traffic circle that flowed around it. Huggins motioned for van Zanten to move the camera lower still. He wanted people to see the towering monument in the background as the governor sallied forth on his quest. They could make stills from these shots, and send them around to the newspapers, too. There would be no question about where Governor Burleson had been during the outbreak. (What was *your* governor doing during the first moments of the crisis? You don't really know? That's funny, 'cause ours was *right here*, in the very heart of the city!)

The governor rounded the circle and continued east down Market Street toward the City-County Building. Before he could make much progress, a uniformed police officer coming

the other way ran up and asked what was happening. An anxiety
in the policeman's eyes said *please, somebody, anybody, be in charge.*

"We're here to connect with the mayor . . ." Burleson told
the policeman. He turned and smiled into the camera.

The policeman said okay and ran back toward the City-
County Building. Burleson and his entourage continued along at a
leisurely pace. The businesses and tall office buildings surrounding
them were shuttered and dark. Nobody had had to tell employees
not to come in today. The governor had never seen the heart of
the city so reduced. None of them had. Somehow, more than
just commerce had stopped. It—whatever *it* was—went deeper.
It was as if the city's very soul had departed, at least temporarily.

A few moments later, Burleson saw a trio emerge from the
City-County Building. It was the mayor, flanked by two police.
She was still wearing her heels, and her suit still looked more or
less immaculate. Only the heavy circles under her eyes betrayed
that she—like Burleson—had been awake all night.

Huggins looked back at van Zanten, and gave an expression
intended to comport that he should not fail to document this
meeting. Van Zanten gave another thumbs up and continued to
shoot.

The *click-click-click* of the mayor's shoes became audible.
Moments later they heard her voice.

"Hank?" she called.

"Kelly!" the governor shot back jovially. "What's going on?
Tell me something I don't know."

The mayor cocked her head to the side like a momentarily confused canine. She stopped and surveyed the governor,

his chief of staff, and the cameraman capturing it all. Then she motioned for her security detail to wait behind.

"Hank . . . what is all this?" the mayor asked as she crept closer. "Do you know what kind of help we can expect in the next twenty-four hours? What have you heard from the Feds?"

Huggins winced. The F-word. No matter. It could be edited out in post-production.

The governor reached the mayor and they awkwardly shook hands.

"Is this a *media* crew?" the mayor asked, motioning at the camera. "Why is there a *media* crew here?"

"Why, no," Burleson said. "You remember my chief of staff, Doug Huggins? This was his idea. That we document this. Could be important to posterity. Historical. He thinks so, anyway."

Huggins liked this. The governor as the reluctant star of their production. Good. Yes. God, the man could think on his feet.

"Hank, where is the Army?" Mayor Brown continued. "Not the National Guard . . . the *army* Army. And have you heard from Homeland Security? Have you let them know how bad things are here?"

"We're waiting for that call," Burleson answered. He took out the satellite phone and held it up—to the mayor, and then also to the camera.

"The situation is developing, yes . . . but things seem to be under control," Burleson continued. "My concern at this point is for the rest of the state. We need to replicate the success we've created here in Indy."

"The success . . .?" the mayor wondered.

Huggins stepped in to redirect the conversation.

"Madam Mayor, we were thinking maybe some shots of you and the governor in front of the City-County Building, for starters?" Huggins said. "Then I've prepared some remarks for you and the governor to read. I think Monument Circle would be a fine backdrop."

"What?" the mayor asked, still obviously confused as to the nature of their project.

"We need to let people know what we're doing, Kelly," Burleson said.

"Hank, what *are* we doing?" the mayor asked emphatically. "What are *you* doing? I've been working all night trying to communicate with anyone I can. Indiana Power and Light. Emergency services. The city shelters. We're sending runners, out there, outside of this 'Green Zone.' And they're not all coming back. Hank, do you know what's happening? Have you *seen* the rest of the city—how it is now? Because my people have, Hank. And it's falling apart."

Huggins frowned. This entire section would need to be left on the cutting room floor.

"Madam Mayor," Huggins entreated, this time adjusting his expectations. "We were hoping at least to get some shots of you and the governor conferring. We wouldn't even need to use the audio. Just something we could put on the websites to let people know you are working on the situation. Could you stand to face the camera a little more?"

The mayor looked at the governor in disgust.

"Really, Hank?" she asked. "*Really?*"

The governor went silent.

"Send somebody over when you have some *real* news," the mayor said.

She turned around and headed back toward the City-County Building.

Burleson was at a loss. He looked over to Huggins. Huggins frumped one side of his face as if to say, "Well, what can you do?" Both men stood quietly, trying to figure out what their next step should be.

Then van Zanten—still behind his camera—called, "Uh, guys . . . "

The governor turned and saw the tall Dutchman pointing back toward the mayor. Burleson did a one-eighty. At first, he discerned nothing out of the ordinary. The mayor, still look-ing very annoyed, was headed back toward her security detail. (She was walking a bit slowly, Burleson noted, no doubt a consequence of having not slept.)

"The green dumpster on the right," van Zanten called.

The governor looked. There was indeed a cluster of green trash bins at the side of an alley near the mayor. Lurking between the bins was a humanoid figure. The governor watched as it slowly loped out into the morning sunlight.

It was a woman—maybe early thirties—in a black dress and high-heeled shoes. She had glistening, almost seductive eyes, and these were framed by bright purple eyelash extensions. She had perfect teeth and round cheeks that dimpled when she smiled. She was smiling right now. The governor didn't like the way she was smiling. He didn't like it at all. (Something was not all together *there*. It was the smile of someone who did not fully appreciate that a zombie outbreak was underway. It was the smile of someone under the sway of a religious delusion or a powerful mania. The governor had seen it on the mentally ill, and, occasionally, on those in the pew or pulpit. Even under the best conditions, the governor was rarely able to restrain himself from smacking a person bearing this expression. And these were not the best conditions.)

With no explanation to his staff, the governor took off at a jog toward the smiling woman. How nice it would be to cuff someone like that across the face. How cathartic after such a night as he had had! Some people were in need of a good smacking. The governor knew this if he knew anything. Who was this woman and what did she think she was doing? Sneaking around downtown when no upstanding person should be out and about. . . . Wearing decadent purple eyelash extensions, like she was at a goddamn New York City disco in the middle of the night, and not on the honest, hardworking streets of Indianapolis at eight in the morning!

The mayor heard the governor's jog and turned to see what was the matter.

"You need something else, Hank?" she called.

The governor gave her an expression that said: "Don't even worry about it." And pointed to the cluster of green dumpsters.

The confused mayor saw the woman in black, and looked back and forth between her and the governor.

Then, suddenly, the expression of decadent nightclub-patron fell away, and the strange woman opened her mouth to release an inhuman howl. She arched her back like a beast, raised her long fingernails like claws, and fell upon the mayor.

Luckily, the governor was already in mid-slap.

Burleson brought the ridge of his hand down hard across the woman's face. Her head snapped sharply to the side, giving the governor, for the first time, a look at the back of her head. Which was not there. Despite her immaculate clothing and makeup, the back of the woman's skull was half-destroyed. The flesh was bashed in, and the bone had been crushed. Likely, she had been the victim of a fall, perhaps from a trendy rooftop lounge onto the distant concrete below.

Instantly, the governor understood: One of those things. No longer a "who" or a "whom" . . . but an "it." A zombie.

The thing staggered only for a moment under the governor's blow. Then it released a second howl and lunged again at the mayor, who screamed and fell to the concrete. The thing jumped on top of her, teeth gnashing and nails scraping. Security teams from both sides began sprinting toward the mayor, but it was clear that vital seconds would pass before she could be reached. One officer raised his gun, but found no shot to take.

Burleson moved without thinking. He was a broad-shouldered man, and had been fairly athletic in his day. Wrestling had been his sport, and you never forgot the moves. They came to him now without being consciously called.

The governor dove forward and knocked the gnashing thing off of the mayor, who was still screaming and flailing. The governor leapt and fell on the zombie from behind, placing it in a full Nelson hold. (This hold was banned in competition—both high school and intercollegiate—but the governor didn't see any referees standing nearby. What he *did* see was a monster that wanted to eat the highest municipal officer in the city.)

The governor felt his fingers interlace behind the zombie's neck. The undead woman bucked powerfully in the governor's grip. It was strong—not supernaturally so, but it was giving all it had. Disconcertingly, the governor found himself vulnerable to the thing's long fingernails, which began to dig at his sport coat, scratching for his ribs underneath.

The governor rose to his feet, pulling the thing up and away from the mayor. Still wincing at the attacks to his midsection, he forcefully walked the zombie over to the wall of the nearest building. (He looked like a rookie policeman struggling to detain his first unruly suspect.) A comic book store occupied the street-level storefront nearby. With a cardboard Superman and Batman looking on from the window, the governor forced the zombie forward against the stone wall of the building, and proceeded to bash out what was left of its brains.

CRACK! CRACK! CRACK!

Again and again, the governor brought the thing's head down hard against the stone wall. His jacket was soon flecked with blood spatter. After five or six blows, the thing stopped digging for his ribs. After a few more, it collapsed completely in his arms.

The governor gave it one more smash for good measure, and then dropped the motionless corpse to the sidewalk below. It hit the ground and rolled over once, revealing a forehead quite caved in, and a face now unrecognizable.

A fake purple eyelash had attached itself to the front of the governor's jacket. He ticked it away with his middle finger as though it were an insect. It spun through the air and drifted quietly to the ground.

Burleson helped the mayor back to her feet. She looked quite stunned. It had all happened so quickly! Uniformed police arrived from both sides of the street. Some secured the elected officials, while others poured several rounds of ammo into the unmoving zombie.

The governor brushed away his security as if to say, "No, I'm all right." He patted his ribs where the zombie had clawed at him. There would be some bruises in a few hours, he decided, but nothing had broken the skin. Even the jacket itself was not beyond repair. Not too bad, all things considered.

Van Zanten stood at a distance and continued to film. Huggins stood with him. Both men were smiling from ear to ear. Huggins actually looked as though he were fighting the urge to start jumping up and down and cheering. Burleson met the eyes of his chief of staff, and began to understand.

Yes, he thought. This would do.

It might not be Birch Bayh rescuing Ted Kennedy from a burning airplane, but as acts of heroism by Hoosier elected officials went, it was pretty darn good. Saving the mayor of Indianapolis from being eaten by a zombie? Yeah. That would do *nicely*.

A few feet away, the governor heard his chief of staff address the cameraman.

"You can stop filming, van Zanten," he said. "I think we've got what we came for."

"Yeah," van Zanten said, lowering the camera. "I think so, too."

With the camera off, Burleson felt himself relax. He walked over to the mayor, who was still being tended to by police.

"You okay, Kelly?" he asked.

She appeared ruffled and scratched, but otherwise fine.

"I think so," she said as a female police officer brushed away dust and blood from her suit. "Thanks for that, Hank."

"Yalp," the governor responded.

Their summit apparently over, he turned and began a leisurely stroll back toward the marble capitol building.

This was something. In the space of an hour, he had gone from a do-nothing (waiting for a call from the Federal government like a teenager waiting for a date to the prom) to a take-charge hero who was physically protecting the women of his state—well, one woman, technically . . . but an important one!—on the mean streets of Naptown. That was going to be the impression, anyway. And that was what counted. Governor Burleson knew that in minutes, Huggins and van Zanten would have that footage edited and uploaded to every news website that still existed.

All in all, a solid morning's work.

The governor felt he more than deserved a reward. If only it were possible. (Though, alas, in *these* circumstances, it was not.) Still, in his mind, the governor momentarily allowed himself to drift down to his "happy place." The place he went to reward himself for having done something really important . . .

That quaint, secluded cabin in the woods, an hour or so south of the city.

11

Nolan parked his Jeep in front of the cabin and killed the engine. Several years had elapsed since his last visit—and *that* had been in the dead of night—yet he felt reasonably certain that this was indeed the correct location. Set back in the woods southwest of Bedford, near the White River, down a long gravel road—the place was a "cabin" in only the loosest sense of the word. Many families did not have houses this nice, or spacious. But the Lincoln-log theme to the construction—and the stained, unpainted pine exterior—seemed to make clear that the notion of "cabin" was being, if not fastidiously upheld, at least invoked.

Nolan got out of the Jeep. It was now practically midmorning. It had taken him just under two hours to navigate the country roads—paved, but usually without painted center lines—leading from the carnival to the governor's not-so-secret cabin in the woods. The journey had been more difficult than Nolan had expected. This was not because his atlas had been inadequate, or because there were not road signs at regular intervals. Rather, Nolan had had difficulty because the landscape around him was so utterly changed.

It seemed every hundred yards or so there was a new sign of *wrongness*. A new sign that the hours of darkness just preceding had not passed peacefully across the countryside. Wrecked cars and trucks were a regular feature along all the roads. Most of them appeared to have been headed south—away from Indy. (But going where, exactly, Nolan had wondered? If you kept driving, you just hit other cities. Louisville. Nashville. St. Louis. Wherever you fled in this country, you were fleeing "to" just as surely as you were fleeing "from." Maybe the gamble everyone was willing to take was that there weren't zombies in other places, or that it would be "not so bad" in another environment.)

Some of the wrecked cars had occupants inside that were obviously dead. Nolan had stopped counting bodies when he got to twenty.

It was also clear that many fires had been set overnight. Few were blazing now, but many still emitted the thick smoke of a slow-smoldering flame. The smell was horrible. Some things you wanted to smell burning in early fall in southern Indiana. Leaves. Charcoal. Bonfires. These, though, were not those things. This was plasterboard and metal and rubber and gasoline. This was a house fire combined with a chemical plant fire combined with whatever else was handy. These were not the things that burned during an overnight snuggle in a sleeping bag after a few brewski's. These were things that burned only in times of crisis and disaster.

The roads Nolan took usually abutted cornfields or undeveloped land, but occasionally there were houses set back a few hundred feet—often with large, immaculately cared-for lawns. Occasionally, Nolan would round a bend or crest a hill and come upon a small house that had been completely looted. Possessions would be dragged halfway into the yard and then just abandoned. Bed frames and couches sticking out of windows or jamming doorways. Once, Nolan saw a yard that looked as though a whirlwind had simply blown all of the clutter outside of the house; the carefully trimmed lawn was completely covered with paper plates, blankets, clothing, and appliances.

Twice he saw zombies.

One was an armless man in blue jeans and a blaze-orange vest. He staggered in a pigpen just visible at the edge of a farm. The pigs were nowhere to be seen, but they had eaten away the flesh on his arms, and some of the flesh on his face. He now walked dumbly into a fence, unable to undo the latch that would allow him to escape.

The other sighting was a pair of the things, way out in the center of a cornfield. Both were caked in mud from head to toe. They moved like ancient arthritics, so frail it seemed the taller cornstalks might prove too much for them.

Yet the most awful encounter of his journey had involved two living men walking along the side of the road. They had worn overalls and baseball caps, and neither could have been over twenty. One carried a burlap sack over his back. The other held plastic grocery bags filled with God-knew-what. Both of them shouldered rifles. They were smiling. Chatting as they strolled. And before Nolan had so much as waved hello, one of the men had leveled his rife and taken a shot at the Jeep.

The bullet had gone wide, and Nolan stepped on the gas and shot past without incident. But Nolan had been able to see the expression on the shooter's face. Nolan was already haunted by it. The man's face said that this—shooting at the Jeep—had been something perfunctory, like swatting a fly or casting a fishing line. It meant nothing. These two men could have been walking to a bar or a football game, or just going home for the night. But instead they were shooting at people in cars. And maybe worse. And it was no big deal.

Why?

With increasing uneasiness, Nolan had decided that the correct question might be: "Why not?"

Now, sitting in front of the governor's $150,000 "cabin," Nolan felt relieved to see something even vaguely normal and familiar. Something that, at least from first appearances, had not been corrupted by the wave of violence and chaos that had settled over the countryside.

Yet.

The cabin's recently washed windows were unbroken and dark. Nothing stirred inside. There were no cars in the drive, but—if Nolan's hunch was right—the governor's daughter would have come on foot. (And even if she had walked all night, she would not have arrived much before him. She would be terrified and—moreover—exhausted. If she *was* in this cabin, she was locked in a back bedroom somewhere, fast asleep.)

Nolan was no longer hungry. The carnival hot dogs were not sitting well in his stomach, but they had done the trick. Still belching a little, he got out of the Jeep and crept up the stone walkway to the door of the cabin. An ADT security sticker was boldly affixed to the front window, and there was a keypad next to the door. Nolan doubted the system would be operational during an extended power failure. (And if it *was*, he was willing to bet the PIN code would be the same as for the governor's mansion, which he knew by heart.) Nolan prepared to punch the numbers into the beige keypad, just for the hell of it. Then he looked more closely and saw that the door was ajar.

Nolan frowned. He looked around for any other clues. There were no signs of illegal entry. No broken glass. No trauma to the lock. No nothing. Perhaps Madison had gained access to the cabin and simply failed to close the door behind her.

"Hello!" Nolan called, cupping his hands to his mouth. "Madison, are you in there? This is Sergeant Nolan; I work for your father . . . Hello?!"

He waited for a response. Nothing came.

Nolan kicked the door open—not hard—and peered inside.

The cabin looked as it always did—which was to say, immaculate and ready for a photo shoot with *Indianapolis Monthly*. There was the beautiful, unused fireplace and hearth. To one side a deluxe kitchen, its granite countertops and Sub-Zero appliances freshly dusted. Even the floor looked recently swept. Nolan stepped inside and smelled potpourri-scented air freshener.

Then the butt of a shotgun hit him hard on the side of the head, and he went careening to the floor.

Nolan's head swam. There was pain. It took Nolan a moment to understand where he was and what had just happened. It was like suddenly waking from a dream into a horrible reality where your cheek feels like it's on fire and you're seeing stars.

Nolan knew it would be a few seconds at least before he could right himself and go for his gun. He just had time to think, "Well . . . if they want me dead, I'm dead."

Nolan waited, wondering if these would be his final thoughts.

The barrel of a shotgun pressed against his forehead. Hard.

"Where is he?" a voice asked urgently.

Nolan hesitated and tried to think: "Where is who?"

It was surreal. Nolan felt as though none of this was actually happening.

"Where is the governor?" the voice said again.

"I . . . I . . ." Nolan began to push himself up off of the floor. "I assume back in Indianapolis, where he lives."

"Why are you here?" the voice said. "What are you doing?"

"I'm looking for Madison," Nolan said. "His kid."

Somewhere in the back of his mind, Nolan could feel himself hoping that bringing up children might awaken some empathy in the assailant.

Nolan rose to his knees.

"Whoa there," said the voice. The shotgun barrel pressed harder against the side of Nolan's forehead.

Nolan stuck his arms out to the side and raised his hands to indicate surrender. Then he risked a glance at his assailant.

The man holding the gun couldn't have been more than five-foot-ten with shoes on. Wasn't too broad in the shoulders, either. He was wearing gloves and a ski mask, and clearly had a pair of Coke-bottle glasses on underneath. His upper lip was covered by a thick mustache.

Were it not for the shotgun, Nolan would have already had this guy down and cuffed. But a shotgun was a shotgun was a shotgun. In his ten years on the force, Nolan had known men who'd failed to appreciate the immutable nature of facts like these. Those men usually didn't last very long.

"I'm a police officer," Nolan said, trying to speak calmly and clearly. "My name is James Nolan. I work for the IMPD. I came downstate last night because some kids in a school group got trapped in a cave."

The masked man reacted, leaning in close.

"What?" he barked intensely. "What do you know about that?"

Nolan looked back and forth quickly. Why did his assailant care?

"Some kids from a private school up in Indy came down to tour the caverns. Then they didn't come out. Nobody knew what was happening. The governor's daughter was in the group, so his people called me. I drove down and tried to find out what was going on. It was zombies, of course. We just hadn't seen them yet. I went into the cave and found zombies and a lot of dead kids . . . but a few had escaped. I found one girl in the cave who was still alive. She and I went to try to find other survivors. The governor's daughter survived, but I don't know where she went. I thought she might have come here."

"There are kids still alive?" the man asked. The hostility was draining from his voice. It was replaced by a vulnerability Nolan had heard before, usually in persons confronting family tragedy.

"Yeah," Nolan said. "We think a small group of them. Madison, and maybe a few of her friends. And then the girl I found down in the caves, Kesha Washington is her name."

The man's eyes went wide, an effect greatly magnified by the thick lenses in front of them. He stepped back from Nolan, lowered the shotgun, and removed the ski mask.

"My name is Drextel Washington," said the bookish, unassuming, accountant-like African American man underneath. "Kesha is my daughter."

★★★

The two men sat at the kitchen table and drank coffee with lots of cream and sugar. Nolan held a kitchen towel to the rapidly swelling side of his face. Drextel talked, and Nolan listened.

"When I realized what was happening, I drove down to try to find her. It was a nightmare, as you might imagine. The highways were clogged. People running everywhere, hoping there would be another place—anyplace—without zombies. I think people from the country ran to the city, and people from the city ran to the country. Then they realized both were just as bad. Anyhow, I knew some back roads. I got down there pretty fast. It turned out I wasn't the only parent from Kesha's class with that idea. There ended up being a group of us. What we found wasn't encouraging. An abandoned school bus. A handful of dead bodies, some of them park rangers. Lots of blood. A couple of parents got brave and went down into the cave with flashlights. A few minutes later, we heard screams, and they didn't come out again.

"As far as I know, some of the parents might still be there, sitting at the mouth of that cave. Sleeping in their BMWs and Mercedes. I don't know. It was a bad scene. People weeping and screaming. Nobody could reach anybody on the phone back in Indy. Everybody was really beside themselves."

Nolan nodded. He could imagine it. A lot of entitled parents used to getting *exactly* what they wanted all the time. They sure weren't going to get it last night. There were precious few favors you could call in during a zombie outbreak, especially when the phones you did the calling with were dead.

Drextel continued his tale.

"With those things walking around, I didn't give high school students down in a cave much of a chance. God help me, I assumed my daughter was dead—that they *all* were. Once that idea began to take hold in my brain, the only thing I could think about was the man who had ruined my life. I knew that he was probably back up in Indy, surrounded by police. But then I got to thinking . . . What if he had run away, like most people did? What if he just put his assistants in charge and high-tailed it? I might do that, if I was a cowardly governor. I might want to get the hell out of Dodge. And where would a fleeing governor go? I thought it might be to his cabin. I decided that if I was going to get eaten by zombies anyway, I had some unfinished business with Hank Burleson first."

Nolan nodded and took a sip of coffee. His face hurt like the dickens. The cabin's medicine cabinet had nothing stronger than aspirin, and his kitchen towel soaked in cool water wasn't doing much.

"How did you even know about this place?" Nolan asked. "It's supposed to be a secret. And what have you got against the governor? What did he do to you?"

"The answer is one and the same," Drextel said soberly. A sad grimace came across his face. He struggled to push it away.

Nolan reckoned that nobody was exactly suited to a zombie outbreak, but this man seemed especially *ill*-suited. He seemed gentle. Naturally timid. Bookish. The kind of person who, when he was feeling particularly extroverted, might look at *your* shoes when he talked to you.

"Do you know Angelica Burnett?" Drextel asked. "If you work for the city, you might've heard of her. She's on the city council? Represents the eleventh district? She was in the news a few years back over that parking meter schedule controversy. Good-lookin' lady."

Nolan shook his head and said, "No, I don't. Sorry."

"She's Kesha's mother and my ex-wife," Drextel said. "We divorced a couple of years ago. I found out she'd been 'carrying on,' as they say, with the governor. He would meet her right here, in this cabin. I tailed her down to Bedford a couple of times after some friends tipped me off. I wanted to see it with my own eyes. And I did. Sometimes, the governor would spend the whole damn weekend with my wife. They were brazen about it, both of them. When I confronted her, she basically told me I was being uptight. That it wasn't a big deal. That I didn't know how the world really worked. I said that she was married . . . and she said so was the governor.

"I wouldn't have cared so much if she'd fallen in love with him. At least I don't think I would have cared. But it wasn't that. It was just like, 'Oh, you want a career in politics in this town? We should hang out more.' It was banal. Like they were just playing golf together. She wanted me to accept it, and I didn't. So we got divorced. She left. I haven't spoken with her for a while. She's supposed to get Kesha on the weekends, but she's always too busy."

Nolan took another sip of his coffee and thought.

"If you were mad, it seems to me that you could have ruined her . . . and the governor," Nolan said evenly. "Kesha said you run a newspaper, right?"

"Yeah . . . " Drextel said hesitantly. "Let's just say my paper isn't exactly the *Indianapolis Star*. It would have been my word against theirs. Maybe if I'd taken pictures of them together in the cabin, which I didn't . . . maybe that would have done it. I loved Angelica. I *still* sort of love her. I get this feeling that one day she'll wise up and apologize, and it will be like it was before. Her and me and Kesha. We had some good times together, you know? Back in the day? I didn't want to ruin her. I still don't."

"But you came down here to see if you could blow the governor's brains out?" Nolan asked.

"I don't know," Drextel managed. "I only grabbed the shotgun because of the zombies. I don't know if it even works. I haven't fired it in years. But . . . but . . . I felt like this man had taken everything from me. I was furious . . . I wasn't thinking straight . . . Well, maybe I *was* going to kill him . . . just a little bit."

Nolan shrugged as if to say that these things happened. Especially to priapic narcissists like Hank Burleson.

"I'm sorry about your head—really, I am—but can we get to where Kesha is?" Drextel asked. "I won't be able to think straight until I see her again."

Nolan agreed that they should move out. They did a quick sweep of the cabin, but found no sign of Madison or anyone else.

Nolan still felt like she would try to come here—like his hunch wasn't wrong. But at the same time, he knew how badly Kesha wanted to see her father—and vice versa. He couldn't in good conscience delay that.

He considered leaving a note for Madison, but what would it say? With the lines of communication down, what could he reasonably tell her to do? Stay here and wait? For what? Nolan could not guarantee when or if he would ever be back. There was also a chance that a bad person could see the note and then lie in wait for her, just as Drextel Washington had lain in wait for him.

In the end, Nolan simply turned off the battery-powered coffeemaker and locked the door behind them. Drextel pulled an aging Honda Accord from its hiding spot behind the cabin and followed Nolan's Jeep. It would be at least an hour before they made it back to the fairground. With all the busted and abandoned cars on the road, Nolan knew it would probably take much longer. . . .

12

Kesha sat in a collapsible lawn chair outside of the Hipwells' trailer. Furbus the cat, who had taken a liking to Kesha, rested in her lap and allowed itself to be petted. Now and then, the expansive feline offered fitful purrs.

"Looks like you got a friend," Steven said from next to her. He was helping his mother pick up the area around the carnival workers' housing. Trash was scattered all across the grass. How much was the usual result of a fair—and how much a consequence of the zombie attack—Kesha didn't know, but there were food wrappers and paper scraps everywhere. Steven had a dowel with a nail on the end of it that he used to expertly spear the scraps. He had evidently done this before.

"I can't believe she doesn't run off," Kesha said. "Furbus, I mean."

"She knows to stick around," Steven said. "Now and then she'll slink off and come back with a baby bird or some setch, but mostly she stays put."

"Are you ever afraid you're going to leave her behind, like when you move on to the next town?" Kesha asked.

"Oh, it's happened," Steven said. "She always finds her way to wherever we are. You'd be surprised what cats can do."

Kesha could not quite believe this.

"What?" she said. "Furbus just shows up in another town?"

"Yep," said Steven. "It's amazing."

Then he winked at her.

Kesha looked back and forth, unsure what to think.

Steven disappeared to spear more trash around the side of the trailer. His mother approached from the other direction.

"Don't you go believin' my son for one moment," Sheree said. "He'd lose his damn mind if we forgot that fat cat even once. Loves the thing."

Kesha smiled and continued to stroke the feline's dark fur, warm in the mid-morning sunlight.

A few moments later, Steven came around the other side of the trailer with several new scraps impaled on his dowel.

"Think that's about got it, Mom," he said, flicking the paper into a round metal trash bin. "I was thinking that next maybe somebody ought to go collect all those cars."

"And I suppose that somebody is you, huh?" Sheree asked, a skeptical hand on her hip.

"What if people come back and they want their cars?" Steven said. "We could organize them. Put them back in the parking lot in an orderly way. In nice rows."

He gestured to the fields and hills beyond the carnival mid-way where dozens of vehicles had been wrecked, abandoned, or—more frequently—wrecked and then abandoned.

"Hmmm," Sheree said, surveying the scene with a hand raised to shade her eyes from the sun. "It *would* be good to clear up the road. But it looks dangerous. Some of those cars are not safe. And what if some of those *things* come back?"

"Mom, they're slow," Steven assured her. "And anyhow, it's day-time. We could see them coming. All those cars out there are in the middle of empty fields. No way those things could sneak up on us."

Sheree scratched her shoulder, considering.

"Kesha," Sheree said. "You want to go with Steven? Keep him company? Keep him *safe*?"

Kesha had not been expecting this, and shifted awkwardly in her seat. This displeased Furbus, who dug in her claws just enough to say, "Watch it!"

"Umm, okay," Kesha managed. "I only have a learner's permit, though. I don't have a full license yet. I'm just fifteen."

Sheree and her son looked at one another for a moment, smiling. Then Steven full-on laughed. Then his mom did too.

"What?" Kesha said. "I don't get it."

"It's just . . ." Sheree began. "I don't think that they're going to be checking *anybody's* driver's license for a while . . . That's sweet though, that you're so . . . what's the word . . . conscientious."

Kesha blushed.

"C'mon," Steven said to her. "We can start with the ones along the road. We'll move them back into the parking lot. Then we can do the ones out in the field."

"That sounds okay," Kesha allowed. She stood slowly, allowing Furbus time to sense the inevitable and slide reluctantly into the grass at her feet.

"Don't go too far," Sheree called as the two made their way toward the road leading away from the valley.

Steven waved his hand in the air once to acknowledge he'd heard her, then smiled to Kesha. She smiled back.

★★★

The dirt crunched under Kesha's shoes as they walked to the nearest target, an aged Ford Aerostar with tinted windows.

"This is better than sitting and waiting," Steven said. "I don't know about you, but I couldn't just do nothing while this is going on."

Kesha nodded. She felt the same way.

"Yeah. It feels good to move."

"This was definitely not what I saw myself doing this morning," Steven said.

"Tell me about it," Kesha said. "Usually this time of day I'm sitting in Algebra II, bored out of my skull. I don't even know if my school still exists now. If it does, it doesn't have a sophomore class anymore."

"I'd be a junior, I think," Steven said. "If I was in normal school, that is."

"Does your mom just home-school you?" Kesha said.

Steven looked away, bashful.

"Something like that," he said.

They arrived at the Aerostar. The windows were down and getting inside was not a problem, but the keys were nowhere to be found. The van was in park, and the parking brake was on. They gave the interior a cursory search, but discovered little more than fast food wrappers and a small fire extinguisher.

"Should we take this?" Kesha wondered, holding up the extinguisher.

Steven looked at it and shrugged. Were they merely storing things for the owners, or was the real plan to start foraging and stockpiling? Neither Kesha nor Steven knew.

For the moment, Kesha replaced the fire extinguisher and they continued down the road toward the next vehicle.

Kesha found herself intrigued by Steven. "Attracted" was definitely *not* the word. Not yet. But he was so different from the boys she knew from her private school—or, for that matter, the boys at her public junior high on the south side of Indianapolis. This boy was friendly, disarming, and somehow mysterious. Kesha felt there was more to him than there was to most his age . . .

They had better luck with the next car, a pickup with its keys inside the visor. Kesha sat in the passenger seat as Steven helped the engine roar to life. Then they eased it up the drive and back to the parking lot. Steven put it into park, killed the engine, and left the keys where he had found them.

They exited the truck to find Sheree watching cautiously from the edge of the carnival. She gave them a cautious smirk. Steven smiled, and Kesha waved. Sheree shook her head and turned away. The teens headed back up the road to get another vehicle.

For the better part of an hour, it went on like this. Kesha and Steven moved however many cars they could from along the road. About one in four had keys inside. (An ancient Saturn had the keys still in the ignition, but the battery was dead. Kesha steered while Steven pushed it back to the lot.) Then they started on the cars that had been left out in the field. It was here that they began to discover the bodies.

Some had tumbled to the knee-high grass and lain concealed all evening. Others were inside the cars, often still wearing seat-belts. Some were shot, while others were simply the victims of automobile accidents. Others still were simply dead . . . without a mark on them. Had internal organs given way under the stress of a zombie onslaught? It was beyond Steven's or Kesha's power to know. The bodies were disturbing, and Kesha tried not to look. For the moment, they stuck to the cars that were empty.

Halfway across the field, they found a Chevy Impala that had crashed into a three-foot stump. The stump was thick and more than half-concealed by the grass. It was the kind of thing you would for-sure miss when fleeing from zombies at night through an unfamiliar field. The driver of the car—a portly man with long white hair—had been thrown through the front windshield and impaled on the hood ornament shaped like a fleeing African deer. He had been killed instantly. Yet now, as Kesha and Steven approached, they heard his earthy growl and gnashing teeth. It was all too clear that he had reanimated. He was one of those things now. And all that was keeping him rooted in place was the large hood ornament, lodged between two of his ribs.

"Whoa," Steven said as the attached man came into view.

The zombie spotted the teenagers, and began trying to free himself. It was obvious that he would make no progress.

"That's lucky for us," Kesha said. "Most cars don't even *have* hood ornaments anymore."

"I don't think he can get loose," Steven said. "But we probably shouldn't get too near."

"I'll second that," said Kesha.

"Why don't all of them turn . . . like him?" said Steven. "There were plenty back there that weren't moving. They were just dead. What makes this one so special he comes back?"

Kesha looked once more at the zombie attached to the hood. He looked so much like the other bodies, except he was alive. Kesha had no answers.

Steven conducted them toward the next car, a junky green Toyota Celica. It was resting nose-forward in a ditch. Kesha wondered if it would even run.

Suddenly, Steven said, "Well, would you look at *that* . . ."

Kesha craned her neck up from the Celica, expecting zombies or worse. Steven was grinning and extending his finger toward a clump of trees at the top of the valley. Kesha followed his line of sight. Hidden in the foliage—though just visible from their perspective—was a cherry-red Hummer H2. It was immaculate, not so much as a speck of mud on the tires. And oh, how that surface gleamed in the morning sunshine. Someone had hit it with Turtle Wax the night before.

"Whoa," Kesha said. "Maybe *that* should be the next one we move."

Steven smiled, and they both took off toward the H2 at a jog.

"Have you ever driven something like that?" Kesha asked.

"No, have you?" Steven responded.

Kesha shook her head. Their smiles broadened. They kept running.

"Oh, please have left the keys," Steven sang to himself. "Please, please, oh pretty-please have left the keys . . ."

They drew closer. The wind whipped up and blew the trees around. The sunlight beaming off of the giant SUV began to dance and dazzle, like lights at a disco. The H2 glittered like a prize. More details came into view.

"The window's open!" Kesha announced. "Look! Somebody left the window open!"

The two teenagers exchanged an excited glance and picked up their pace. Soon, they no longer traveled at a jog, but at a full-on sprint. By the time they reached the H2, it had become a race. Steven won, but just narrowly.

"Omigod, this thing looks awesome," Kesha panted as she skidded to a stop in front of the giant machine. She rested her hand on it for a moment. It was warm and inviting.

There seemed to be nobody in the immediate vicinity. Neither were there any signs of a dead person. It was just a pristine H2, left to its own devices. Abandoned without explanation.

Steven headed straight for the driver's side door. The window had been left open. Steven climbed inside. Moments later he emerged with a glistening ring of keys. He held them aloft like a fisherman displaying a champion catch.

"Holy crap!" said Kesha.

"C'mon, get in!" called Steven. "This is going to be awesome."

Kesha jogged over to the passenger side and climbed in. The interior had been kept nearly as immaculate as the exterior. Steven put the key in the ignition, and the great metal beast churned to life. Steven began to edge it backward out of the copse, and down into the grassy valley.

"Omigod, this is so cool!" Kesha said.

In the moment, there was no undead and no uncertainty. There was only a big-ass Hummer and a beautiful wide field in which to drive it.

Steven got the H2 out of the trees and put it in drive. The entire valley lay before them.

"Maybe we don't have to go *straight* back to the parking lot," Steven said, testing the gas pedal. He grinned as the SUV responded.

Kesha, who wanted her own turn to drive, liked where he was going with this.

"Yeah," she said. "Maybe we should take it over the ridge into the next valley. It would probably be safer."

"Oh, absolutely," Steven said with a grin. "For safety's sake. Completely."

With growing excitement, Steven piloted the Hummer to the top of the nearest hill that rimmed the valley. It occurred to Kesha that she had not seen much beyond the carnival fairgrounds for the past twelve hours. Would the world have changed? Would the countryside be engulfed in flame and pestilence?

Yet when the Hummer cleared the hill, they found only another valley beyond them, abutting a thick forest of red cedar. A small lake sat some miles off in the distance.

Steven and Kesha looked at one another. Kesha nodded and held on tight to the side of the Hummer. Then Steven pressed the gas pedal down as far as it would go.

For the better part of an hour, the teenagers took turns careening down the valley walls in the bright red Hummer. Time got away from them as they steered it again and again down the hillside, then used it to explore the surrounding fields. After the first fifteen minutes, Steven let Kesha into the driver's seat. She took to it quickly, the great metal beast responding easily to her commands.

Kesha explored the edges of the wooded area, enjoying the bumpy ride. Near the far edge of the wood, Kesha began to turn the Hummer around—possibly to head back to the carnival grounds, possibly for yet more off-roading—when she saw something that made her pull to a stop, and then put the H2 into reverse.

"What's up?" Steven asked.

Kesha did not speak, but used the button on her door to lower the window.

"Do you see something?" Steven tried again.

Kesha stayed silent as her eyes scanned the quiet forest.

What *had* she seen? Only the quickest flash of red and black. But it was the *kind* of red and black that had caught her attention. It was a special kind—especially the red. A subtle, unique shade of dark crimson that someone, somewhere, had probably tried to copyright. Exactly the kind that pricey, exclusive prep schools might select as their school colors.

"There!" Kesha shouted triumphantly, gesturing out the window.

"What?" Steven said, still not seeing anything.

Kesha pulled the H2 to a halt and climbed out. She left the driver's side door open behind her.

"Kesha?" Steven tried one more time. The girl did not respond. She moved as if possessed . . . her eyes fixed upon the forest, as if afraid to look away.

Steven hopped out of the H2—almost tripping on the running board—and caught up to her.

"What are you on about, girl?" he asked.

This time she answered.

"I thought I saw a gym bag from my school," Kesha said. "I think it's down this way."

"A gym bag?" asked Steven.

"Maybe somebody went this way, into the forest," Kesha said.

Steven nodded and resolved to help her look. It was not a lengthy search.

After no more than two minutes, Steven produced a black and red nylon bag from underneath a thorny bush.

"Aha!" he said brightly. It did not feel as though it contained much. He tossed it to Kesha, who caught it enthusiastically.

"You saw that when you were driving?" Steven added. "Damn, girl. You got good eyes."

Kesha, who had been told this before by countless coaches in a variety of sports, nodded absently and began to inspect the nylon bag.

It was definitely from her high school, but was not monogrammed. Inside was a bunch of trash and what looked like leftovers from lunch. Wrappers from granola bars. Sandwich bags with crumbs. A couple of empty soda cans. And blood.

Steven spotted it first, examining his own hands after tossing the bag to Kesha.

"Yeeash," he said, making a nonsense noise indicating alarm and disgust. "That's bloody."

"Uh huh," Kesha said calmly, looking at the crimson smear down the side. "I saw it, too."

"What do you reckon happened?" Steven asked.

Kesha dumped out the bag to see if anything else was hiding within. There was nothing of value.

"James Nolan and I found a girl from my school—Melanie— in the field over there," Kesha said. "She was hurt and dying. Maybe it was her bag. She could have dropped it when she was confused in the dark. I don't know."

"Someone from your class was here, then?" Steven said. "Maybe it was someone else. Maybe they went into the forest."

"Yeah, maybe," Kesha said, staring deeper into the trees beyond.

Suddenly, a gunshot echoed in the distance. Kesha looked at Steven, alarmed.

"Omigod," she said. "Was that a gun?"

"That's my mama's gun," Steven answered. "I'd recognize it anywhere."

Steven cupped his hands as if impersonating a catcher await- ing a pitch. Kesha fished in her pockets and tossed him the keys. He took off toward the Hummer. Kesha followed, still holding the bloody bag.

"She's probably just using it to get our attention," Kesha said reassuringly as she climbed into the passenger seat. "We've been gone a long time. She wants to know where we are."

"Yeah . . ." Steven said noncommittally, putting the H2 into drive. "But that sure doesn't sound like something Mama would do."

The giant SUV was now two valleys away from the carnival encampment. Steven piloted the Hummer straight through the tall grass and back toward their trailer. Kesha found herself being rocked about and quickly fastened her safety belt.

The windows of the SUV were still open. When they got close to the valley containing the carnival, Kesha thought she heard the gun again.

"Was that . . . ?" Kesha started to say, turning to Steven.

To her surprise, he brought the Hummer to a crawl and then to a stop.

"What're you . . . ?" Kesha tried again.

"Come with me," Steven said, opening the door. "And stay low."

Kesha wrinkled her nose. Though not entirely clear on what was happening, she decided to stick with her new friend. She exited the Hummer and followed Steven as he stalked up the grassy hillside to the lip of the valley. She watched as he stooped down with his hands on his knees. Then he fell forward and began crawling.

Steven looked back, intent that Kesha should do the same. His expression was all business. Wordlessly, Kesha copied him and they crawled until they could look down into the valley. Even before she was able to see a thing, Kesha heard the roar of engines.

Down in the valley below them, a group of people were ransacking the carnival. Some drove cars, while others piloted motorcycles or motorbikes. Some were obviously helping themselves to the automobiles that Steven and Kesha had moved into the lot. The invaders were in no way uniform, save that most of the men wore beards and some form of camouflage. There were perhaps twenty in total. All seemed to carry guns, with the exception of a pair who proudly sported expensive-looking composite bows. About a quarter of them were female. Many of them appeared to be drunk.

In the open field near the carnival, they saw the body of Walter—the large carnival worker who had returned only that morning—face down in the grass. As if to leave no doubt as to the nature of his final seconds, three hunting arrows protruded from different parts of his back.

There was no sign of Steven's mother.

Kesha looked over at Steven and stayed low in the grass. She could tell the young man was torn—wanting to race down the hillside, yet knowing it would mean certain death. Kesha looked back to the chaos below. The looters had overturned some of the carnival carts and were helping themselves to what was left of the food. A few climbed aboard the silent, dark rides. Though on top of the hill and looking down, Kesha's angle of sight was not perfect. There were still many parts of the carnival that they could not see. Where was Sheree?

"What the hell is this?" Steven eventually stammered. "Why would anybody do this?"

Part of Kesha wanted to say: "You tell me. You're the white-boy carnival worker who knows these downstate areas."

Instead, she said, "I don't know. Maybe some people just wanted to ransack a carnival. These look like the kind of people who would want to do that."

"I can't see my mom," Steven managed. "Can you?"

Kesha shook her head.

"What the *fuck* . . . " Steven stammered. He beat his fists against the ground in frustration.

Suddenly, Kesha's eye caught one of the scruffy men below gesturing to his compatriots. A group of them started shielding their eyes from the sun as they pointed to Kesha's position on the hill. Moments later, one of the looters on a motorbike took off across the field towards them.

"Oh shit, they see us!" Kesha said.

Steven continued to survey the scene.

"Come *on*," Kesha urged, rising to her feet. "They have *guns*, Steven. There's a bunch of them. We have to go."

Kesha began tugging Steven by the back of his shirt. After a few seconds he relented and rose. By that time, two motorbikes and one silver RAV4 were headed toward them. Kesha heard the report of a rifle as someone below took a potshot.

"These people . . . they're just killing anyone they can," Steven intoned sorrowfully.

"Come on," Kesha urged.

They scurried back inside the H2.

Steven started up the engine, turned the hulking thing around, and began driving like hell in the opposite direction. The hillside was not made for automobiles, and the jarring bumps came thick and fast. Kesha looked nervously at the side-view mirror.

"We're not going fast enough," she cried. "Those motorbikes were going so much faster than this."

"What do you want me to do?!" Steven yelled at her. The Hummer hit a shallow ditch and bucked violently, as if to put an exclamation mark on his point.

"Omigod, they're going to catch us and shoot us!" Kesha cried.

"I'm going as fast as I can," Steven said. It appeared that he was. The steering wheel seemed just barely within his control. It rolled right and left in his hands like the tiller of a foundering ship.

Kesha took another look back and saw the first motorbike cresting the top of the hill. The driver paused near the spot where she and Steven had been hiding in the grass. Then he spotted the Hummer, narrowed his eyes, and sent his bike shooting down the hillside after them.

"This isn't going to work," Kesha said. "We can't outrun them in this! Oh shit, oh shit, oh shit!"

The Hummer suddenly swerved ten degrees to the left. It was no longer headed for the floor of the valley, but instead the woods where they had found the gym bag. For an instant, Kesha's imagination showed her suicide by car crash—Steven would take both of their lives rather than let the looters catch them.

"What're you doing?" Kesha cried.

"The woods," Steven called. "It's the only thing that will work. Those trees are thick. Old growth. You probably couldn't ride a motorbike in there. If we want to lose them, we have to go into the woods . . . on foot."

In a trice, Kesha understood that Steven was right. It was their only hope. She risked another glance back. The first motorbike was gaining, and the second was just coming over the hill.

Moments later, Steven brought the Hummer to a bruisingly abrupt stop at the edge of the forest. He and Kesha sprang from their seats and headed for the tree line as fast as their legs would carry them. Kesha heard one of the bikers open up with a handgun behind them. One of the rounds went into the Hummer with a noisy *KLANG!* Another knocked loose a bird's nest from a tree, just as Steven and Kesha sprinted past below it.

Inside the trees, branches and nettles began to scratch and sting. Pointy obstructions—easy to avoid when you had a moment to notice them—came too thick and fast to circumvent. Kesha and Steven plowed straight through, their adrenaline such that they hardly felt the scrapes and scratches. Behind them, the motorbike engines roared closer and closer still.

Kesha and Steven nearly became separated when they circumvented different sides of the same enormous maple and Kesha fell into a ditch. After a few steps, Steven became aware that Kesha had disappeared. He stumbled backwards, found her, and helped her to her feet with a powerful yank on her hand.

From that moment on, he did not let go.

13

It had been a fool's errand, the whole thing. Ellard van Zanten knew this, and that made it all the worse.

Editing down the video of Burleson's heroic defense of the mayor had taken only a few minutes. Then it had been uploaded and emailed to every news outlet in the state, and all the national media. But the Internet did not seem to be working normally, and van Zanten was unsure if the emails were going through. Even so, van Zanten had been absolutely giddy to report the video's successful dispersal to his superiors.

It was, however, not enough for Doug Huggins. The chief of staff had expressed skepticism that any of the news outlets would be opening emails from PR distribution lists at this moment.

"So what do we do then?" the governor had wanted to know. Though expressing a concern, he was still obviously in a fine mood. The good feeling from his incident with the mayor had not faded. Instead, it was like a time-release drug. He was going to be cheerful for hours to come.

"Van Zanten could hand-deliver the footage to TV stations around the city," Huggins suggested. "Put it on a zip drive and physically hand it off."

Governor Burleson raised his eyebrows to indicate that it might be a good idea.

"Are you serious?" asked van Zanten.

"WTHR is just up on Tenth Street," Huggins said. "You could do it on foot. Take you twenty minutes, tops. Everybody's power—and their *TVs*—could click back on at any second. When that happens, we want them seeing our footage."

"You know, the more I think about it . . . " Governor Burleson interjected, his good humor making him increasingly ebullient. "The more I think about it . . . the more I think that we should have some kind of event as well. A follow-up to the tape. It could be a rally. Somewhere downtown. I could still give a speech or something."

"That's an excellent idea," Huggins said. "I'll get started on crafting something right away."

The chief of staff turned back to the assistant director of communications.

"As for you, van Zanten," Huggins said, "make some copies and take them to the television stations personally."

"But the zombies!" van Zanten managed.

The governor bristled uncomfortably, as if the junior staffer had used a racial slur.

"If you're concerned about the . . . dangers of the situation, by all means take a police escort," Huggins said in scolding tones. "Now, Mister Governor . . . let's talk a little more about your next move."

Van Zanten backed out of the room and sulked down the corridor to his cubicle. There, he dutifully copied the governor's zombie encounter onto four different thumb drives. One for each local affiliate.

He next walked to the rotunda of the statehouse, because it seemed to have the most police presence. Though now perhaps the third highest-ranking member of Indiana's functioning state government, van Zanten hesitated to interact with the officers who stood milling about or resting beneath the marble columns. He normally never talked to police. He had certainly never ordered one to give him a ride. Eventually, van Zanten summoned the courage to approach a tired-looking veteran with a salt-and-pepper mustache who did not look very threatening.

"Excuse me," van Zanten said to the exhausted officer. "I'm the governor's acting press secretary. He told me to deliver some footage to the local TV stations. It's outside the Green Zone. He said I could get a police escort. Do you know who I should talk to about this?"

The police officer let out what was possibly the longest sigh van Zanten had ever heard. The man had bellows for lungs. Then he stood up from the marble bench where he had been seated and began to walk to the front of the capitol. He turned and motioned for the dumbfounded Dutchman to follow.

Minutes later, van Zanten sat in the passenger seat of a squad car as the very sleepy IMPD officer drove through the improvised checkpoint and out of the Green Zone.

"Let's hit WTHR first," van Zanten said. "On Tenth Street."

The policeman gave a lazy bob of his head that might have been a nod.

The first thing van Zanten noticed outside the Green Zone were the plumes of smoke rising into the air.

There were wrecked and abandoned cars everywhere. There were also bodies. The alarming thing was not their number, but that they had been left where they were, usually on sidewalks or in gutters. (Death happened. People didn't like to think about it, but it was a day-to-day occurrence. People died in automobile accidents all the time. But bodies were something that got *attended to* almost instantly. Frowning, head-shaking crowds formed around them. Emergency vehicles came and took them away with great speed. Firemen used hoses to wash blood off of the pavement. In a matter of minutes, you never would have known that one had been there at all. But now that was not happening. There were bodies here that nobody had bothered to deal with, just lying in the streets. Or walking around.)

As they passed the public library at Meridian and Ninth, the police officer finally said two words to van Zanten.

"Look there."

The Dutchman looked.

A mail carrier—tall, middle aged, and still in his uniform—was shuffling down the sidewalk with an unnatural gait. His eyes had a milky-white sheen. His mouth was caked in red and slashed apart as though he'd French-kissed a running fan. A couple of errant letters were mottled in blood and stuck to the front of his shirt.

"Jesus!" van Zanten said. "You can't let that thing walk down the street!"

"Whaddaya want me to do, arrest it?" the policeman quipped.

"No . . . but . . ." van Zanten tried. "You could pull over and shoot it, right?"

The exhausted officer looked over at van Zanten, then wordlessly tendered his sidearm to the Dutchman.

"What?" van Zanten said, physically squirming away from the gun. "No! *I* don't want to do it!"

The Dutchman had never in his life touched a gun.

The police officer replaced his sidearm and continued driving toward the NBC affiliate.

The squad car stopped in front of the television studio and van Zanten got out. The parking lot was mostly empty, but van Zanten thought he saw movement inside the building. Thus emboldened, he made his way to the front door and tried it.

Locked.

Van Zanten looked back at the squad car. The police officer had already pulled his hat down over his eyes and assumed a sleeping position. Van Zanten sighed. He began knocking as hard as he could on the door.

After what seemed like a full five minutes, there was movement inside. The door was answered by a sweaty, exhausted-looking man in a pit-stained dress shirt. He had short grey hair and a bulbous, W. C. Fields nose. After a good night's sleep and a shower, the man might have passed for fifty. In the unforgiving light of the noonday sun, he looked well past-due for retirement. Van Zanten guessed he was the station director.

"What?" the man snapped.

"I'm from the governor's office," van Zanten explained. "I have some footage for you."

The station director man looked left and right—as if checking for any sign that this might be a ruse—then relented and pulled the Dutchman inside.

"You're from Governor Burleson's office?" the station director asked.

Van Zanten followed him down the darkened corridors leading to the production booth.

"Yes," van Zanten said.

"What is the governor up to?"

"That's, um, what the video is about," van Zanten explained. "He's, you know, liaising with the mayor. Putting up a Green Zone around the capitol. Handling stuff. He's definitely handling stuff."

"Do you have power?" the station director asked. "Do you have phones? We have a generator, but it's not giving enough power to broadcast. The best we can do is update our website, but it's acting futzy too."

They passed an employee lounge with vending machines and a fridge. At one of the tables sat a TV anchor van Zanten recognized from nightly newscasts. With apparently nothing to do, he sat alone playing solitaire. The nearest vending machine had been jimmied open, and a row of empty Diet Cokes sat next to his cards on the table.

"Does the governor know how bad things are?" the station director continued, conducting van Zanten deeper into the station. "Because things are bad. Really bad. And it's not just the zombies, or whatever we're supposed to call them. CNN was saying 'moving cadavers' before they went off the air. Sounds like a PC euphemism to me. Are we trying not to hurt their feelings?"

"Heh," van Zanten laughed.

The station director turned back to him and showed a frown saying no part of this was funny.

"We've been getting reports from all across the state," the station director continued. "People have been coming here all night. On bikes. On foot. They think we can do something. I don't know why. It's you people who are supposed to do something."

"What do they tell you?" van Zanten asked nervously.

They stopped in front of the station director's office. Van Zanten handed him the zip drive.

"There's widespread crime all over the city," the station director explained. "People think there aren't police anymore. People believe it, and it becomes true. Criminals think they can do what they want. People are scared. Nobody knows when the power's going to come back on. The generators at the hospitals weren't built for this. What are all the people on life support supposed to do? And the phones are completely down now, even the landlines. Have you tried to make a call recently? It's like the Middle Ages out there. You want to talk to somebody, you've got to go physically find them. And try not to get shot by a criminal or eaten by zombies in the process."

"Well . . . the movie on this drive should give folks some inspiration," van Zanten said brightly.

"What is the U.S. government saying?" the station director asked. "When did Burleson last talk to the president? When can we expect help?"

"Yeah . . . " van Zanten said as he looked away and scratched the back of his neck. "The governor's examining all appropriate options at this time. If a call from D.C. comes, the governor will make some decisions, I'm sure."

The station director paused. He studied van Zanten's face suspiciously, as if the tall Dutchman's sympathetic eyebrows might conceal a horrible secret.

"Make some decisions?" he said. "What decision is there to make? It's chaos outside. Half my staff is missing or dead. Nobody can tell us if the police force still exists, much less the fire department or the EMTs. A city can't live like this for long, son. We need all the help we can get, and we need it now."

"The governor is doing . . . " Van Zanten stopped short of saying everything. What was the governor doing? Everything that was prudent?

"The governor is doing what he can," van Zanten tried again.

The video downloaded, the station director handed the zip drive back to the tall Dutchman.

"Can you find your way out again?" he asked.

"Uh, sure," van Zanten said, accepting the drive.

The station director looked at van Zanten one last time and shook his head. Then he closed the door to his office and left him standing outside in the hall.

On his way out of the station, van Zanten ran into the idle news anchor again, this time almost physically as he walked down the hall.

"Hey," he said, stopping to shake the anchor's hand. "Ellard van Zanten, with the mayor's communications office? You might know my boss?"

"They're *all dead*," the anchor sputtered, his eyes wide and insane.

"What?" Van Zanten had time to wonder.

"Every reporter we had wanted to do a live remote from the field," the anchor stammered. "Every cameraman wanted to be the first to get B-roll of a walking dead man. I wanted to go, too, but they kept me here. Said they needed at least one talking head sitting in front of the camera. I wanted to go like hell . . . but then I was glad I didn't. *None of them came back.*"

The reporter grabbed the collar of van Zanten's shirt for emphasis.

"*None of them came back!*"

Van Zanten writhed uncomfortably, eventually freeing himself from the anchor's grip. It was deeply disconcerting to hear the familiar, sonorous voice—one that usually shared even, measured words written by another person—reduced to mania and fear.

Van Zanten brushed past him down the hallway. The handsome anchor leaned against a cubicle wall for a moment, and then collapsed to his knees.

"*None of them came back . . .*"

Van Zanten exited the WTHR offices to find that his ride had disappeared. The police car and driver were simply not there. Van Zanten surveyed the sparsely populated parking lot, hoping the policeman had simply moved his car to the shade. Yet he was nowhere to be found. Just gone. And there was no clue left as to what had happened.

Exhausted and confused, van Zanten rubbed his forehead and tried to figure out what to do. He didn't want to go back inside the station and deal with the creepy anchor or the angry director.

At the same time, he wasn't going to walk across Indianapolis to each of the other TV stations. The Fox affiliate was way out in Pike Township, for chrissake . . . No, he couldn't do that.

He would return to the Green Zone on foot, van Zanten determined, and requisition a new driver. That was the only option that made sense. Maybe, on the way back, he would see a police car or National Guard Hummer and be able to flag it down. After all, he was the governor's emissary on important state business. That had to be good for a lift a mile south.

Van Zanten stood on the curb and looked down the length of Meridian Street with great trepidation. It was now his gauntlet to run. In the distance, he could see the Soldiers and Sailors Monument eclipsed on either side by the jutting skyscrapers of the downtown skyline. Beneath it was the Green Zone and relative safety. This normally bustling thoroughfare was quiet, but not completely empty. Every few moments, van Zanten would notice movement in the landscaping. Maybe a person. Maybe an automobile. Maybe . . . something else.

He began heading south along the sidewalk. Despite waves of exhaustion and lightheadedness, he managed a brisk pace. It was positively eerie to see the city's downtown so dark and barren. This was quieter than during holidays, and emptier than during tornado warnings. Still, squint your eyes, and it was easy to imagine that nothing was wrong. The zombies had only come in the last few hours. The trash was still collected. The lawns and bushes were neat and trimmed. Were it not for the plumes of smoke in the sky and intermittent gunshots in the distance, van Zanten might have been able to convince himself that it was a nearly normal day.

Van Zanten crossed Michigan Street. Ahead of him loomed the Indiana War Memorial, an enormous marble temple to the victors of the First World War. It seemed to van Zanten that figures cavorted in the shadows of the great building, yet always scuttled out of sight before he could make sense of what he was seeing. This did not produce any sensation other than sheer alarm. Van Zanten could now clearly see the Green Zone. A military personnel carrier and a set of IMPD squad cars had been parked to cordon off Meridian Street near the circle. Some of the cars even appeared to have live police inside of them. Van Zanten was almost there.

Then the tragedy.

Nothing less than a sewer grate at the Dutchman's feet had been his undoing. Only a block from the beckoning police officers at the cordon, van Zanten had failed entirely to notice the sewer opening set into the curb. From it, a long arm wearing a tattered green jacket had slowly extended. From its sleeve further projected a blue-green hand with long, sharp nails. As van Zanten strode past, the hand reached out and gripped his ankle. More confused than startled, van Zanten looked down in time to see the apparently disembodied arm yank on his leg. The tall Dutchman's feet went out from under him and he fell hard against the concrete. A moment later, the hand was crawling up past his knee like an excited lecher's, grasping for his groin and whatever lay beyond. Van Zanten saw the horrid, rotting hand and tried to roll away. As he did, he risked a quick glance into the sewer opening. Inside was a horrible thing, like half a human face with eyes on stalks. Rot and sewer water had morphed the zombie's face into a fleshy parody of human features. Muscle and bone had mostly washed away, but somehow the glistening, perfect eyes had remained. They projected tenuously on lengths of sinew just above a pair of obscene openings that might once have been a nose and throat. Though the thing no longer had a lower jaw with which to masticate, something in it still bespoke the hunger to put a delicious young Dutchman inside of it.

Before van Zanten could roll away, the thing pulled his leg inside the sewer opening. Van Zanten felt something pierce his flesh. Was it a fingernail? A tooth? Whatever remained of the zombie's jaw? Or was it something else entirely—some bone or cartilage not designed by evolution to pierce or impale, but now repurposed to serve that function?

Whatever it was, it hurt. A lot.

Van Zanten cried out and tugged his leg free. In doing so, he severed most of his pants and tore a furrow of skin from the side of his leg. Blood began to spill from the long gash almost immediately. The pain was incredible. It did not quite seem real. Van Zanten scrambled to his feet. The troops at the entrance to the Green Zone looked at one another. Perhaps, thought van Zanten, they had not grasped the enormity of what was transpiring.

Van Zanten scuttled toward the Green Zone cordon and the confused guards, largely unaware of the trail of blood he left behind him. He ran on adrenaline and fury. Fury at his own inattention, and fury at the guards who had not reacted. Some part of van Zanten knew that these military reservists could not,

practically speaking, have done a thing to help him. Even if a
guardsman had had a sniper rifle loaded and aimed, no one could
have gotten a shot at this zombie, huddled like a hermit crab in
a sewery shell.

Van Zanten neared the edge of the Green Zone cordon, and
one of the guards set down his rifle and came forward to help.
Van Zanten began to feel very, very weak. It became hard to
think, as though his mind had become clouded. Yet it seemed
impossible that a wound to his leg—however deep—might cause
this sudden a retardation of his faculties. Van Zanten's gait slowed
to little more than a crawl. Before long, the solider was nearly
unable to move him.

"I'm Ellard van Zanten," he managed, as the guard motioned
for other sentries to come and assist. "I work for Governor Burleson. I was . . . I was . . ."

And van Zanten collapsed quite completely into the arms of
the soldier.

★★★

Governor Burleson was catnapping in his leather chair inside
the war room when three National Guard soldiers dragged in his
lanky assistant director of communications.

"This one said he was with you?" one of the soldiers said as
van Zanten was deposited into a nearby office chair.

The governor nodded, allowing that this was so.

Almost immediately, van Zanten began bleeding onto the
floor below him. There was also blood coming out of his nose
and mouth.

"Jesus!" said Huggins, still both physically and spiritually at the governor's right hand. "Why didn't you take him to a medic?"

The chief of staff began to move laptops and papers away from the parts of the table where van Zanten's blood might smudge them.

"He said he was with the governor," the solider replied. "The ID in his pocket backed that up."

"Go and get a medic," cried Huggins. "*Now.*"

The three soldiers departed. As if on cue, van Zanten lifted his head slightly and began talking.

"I'm going to die *here*," the Dutchman moaned.

Both Huggins and the governor noted that van Zanten had placed his emphasis on the wrong word.

"Now, now," Huggins assured him. "We've sent for the medic. You're going to be fine. You're a big strong man. What happened? It looks like you just cut your leg. Maybe hurt your nose?"

"Did you get the video to the TV networks?" the governor wanted to know.

Van Zanten nodded. His head lolled back and stayed back. He was looking up at the ceiling.

"One of them," van Zanten croaked. "I got it to one of them."

The governor cast a sideways expression at Huggins to say that this was better than nothing.

"I'm dying," van Zanten continued. "I'm dying *here*. My parents don't even know where this is."

"We . . . " Huggins began awkwardly. "We can get in touch with your parents if anything happens. When the phones come back on."

"They don't even know Indiana," van Zanten lamented. (His eyes were now crossed, and the pool of blood beneath him was growing.) "They know California. Movies. Celebrities. They know Michigan for cars. They know New York for New York City. They know that Texas has cowboys and oil. But people in Holland don't know Indiana. I try to tell them . . . I try to explain to my parents who we are and what we are doing here. I try to tell them what the project is. They are always confused. They always mix us up with Ohio or Iowa or Wisconsin. No, I tell them. No. It's Indiana. *Indiana* . . ."

Huggins wondered if he should stop the young man from speaking; it was now beyond any doubt that van Zanten was legitimately on his way out. Yet no sooner did Huggins open his mouth to do this, than van Zanten went limp and collapsed forward in his chair. His head struck the conference table with an alarmingly powerful *bonk*. Then all was silent.

Huggins looked to the governor, who motioned for some nearby administrative personnel to remove this body from his headquarters.

As they were dragging van Zanten out, Huggins took aside a security guard and told him to put a bullet in van Zanten's brain, just as insurance. The guard nodded and readied his gun.

14

James Nolan and Drextel Washington stood next to one another and looked into what remained of the carnival.

"Was it like this when you left it?" Drextel asked softly.

Nolan shook his head.

Fully half of the carnival attractions had been tipped over. Several had been set on fire. Many of the smaller trailers that served as booths for food vendors were missing entirely (doubtless lost to an enterprising looter driving something big enough to tow). There were fresh bullet holes in the trailers that remained. There was a corpse in the field nearby, with honest-to-God arrows sticking up out of its back. The only movement came from Furbus who sprang between the shadows of the creaking carnival rides.

Nolan produced his Ruger and motioned for Drextel to bring his shotgun to bear.

"What's happening?" Drextel whispered as he followed Nolan. "Where's Kesha?"

"I don't know," Nolan said gruffly. "We're going to find out."

They crept into the fairgrounds. Nothing moved except for the cat in the grass. Still, Nolan had the feeling they were being watched. This feeling was not usually wrong.

Suddenly, a weak voice cried: "Here! Over here!"

Nolan cautiously rounded the side of a large white residential trailer and saw, on the ground quite near him, Sheree Hipwell supine in the grass. Her .22 rifle was just beyond her reach. She had a pair of bullet wounds in her side, and another in her arm. The ground beneath her was stained dark with her own blood.

"I could hear you two a damn mile away," she said.

Nolan smiled. Then frowned. It was clear the woman did not have long to live.

"What happened?" Nolan asked. "Where's Kesha? Where's Steven?"

Sheree looked straight ahead and blinked several times, as if summoning the will to re-live it.

"Bunch of criminals came, wanting to kill us and take whatever they could," Sheree said. "Thank God Steven and Kesha were off somewhere moving cars. I think they had the sense to stay away."

"What happened to Kesha?" Drextel asked. "She's my daughter."

"They were moving cars out in the fields," Sheree reiterated. "Over there."

With what was clearly considerable effort, Sheree bent her arm and pointed out to the far edge of the valley.

"Can I . . . " Nolan began. He was going to ask if he could do anything, but it was painfully obvious that there was nothing he *could* do, other than perhaps make the poor woman comfortable. There were no emergency services to contact, and no phones with which to make the call.

"I could *tell* something was going to happen on this trip," Sheree said. "I knew it was going to be bad. Just didn't know *how* bad. I didn't want to scare Steven, so I sort of didn't give him the full version. When those dead men walked into the carnival last night, I thought, this is it. This is how bad it's going to get. But I was wrong, wasn't I?"

Sheree coughed. Her throat rattled and her chest heaved. It was apparent to all—including her—that these were to be her final moments.

"What should—?" Nolan tried again.

"You should find Steven," Sheree said. "Find Kesha, too, while you're at it. They're onto something, those two. I can tell. Something big. And it concerns you too, James Nolan. It concerns everybody in this whole entire state."

"What?" Nolan said.

"The girl you're trying to find," Sheree said. "Not Kesha. The daughter of the governor . . . *that* girl. It's very important that you find her, James. It's important that she gets back to her dad. It's important to thousands and thousands of people. Do you understand?"

"Not really," Nolan said.

Sheree said nothing else.

It took them both a few moments to realize that she was gone.

Nolan placed Sheree's body on the bed inside her ransacked trailer and shut the door. Then he handed Sheree's .22 rifle and some ammunition to Drextel.

"This is probably better than your shotgun," Nolan said, "which you told me might not even work."

"And this old rifle works?" asked Drextel, accepting the gun.

"It's been recently fired," said Nolan. "So yeah, it works."

The two men returned to the parking lot.

"I think we go in that direction," Nolan said, nodding toward the far lip of the valley where Sheree had gestured. "And I think it might be more sensible to take one car. I have a feeling gas is going to be at a premium for the foreseeable future."

"A lot of the stations back in Indy ran dry just a few hours after the chaos started," Drextel said. "But wait . . . I can't just leave my car out here, can I?"

Nolan raised an eyebrow to indicate that perhaps Drextel had missed a crucial point.

"Are you really attached to that old clunker?" Nolan said, gesturing to Drextel's ride.

Nolan nodded at the rows of empty automobiles stacked next to them in the lot, keys in their ignitions.

Drextel relented, and together they took Nolan's Jeep westward across the valley floor and up over the crest of the hill beyond. After only a few minutes of exploring, they discovered a bright red Hummer parked against the edge of a forested area. The doors had been left open.

"Well, hell," Drextel quipped. "If we're trading up, let's trade for that."

They piloted their Jeep over to the tree line and got out. Nolan explored the driver's side of the Hummer, yet found very little. Drextel took the passenger's side. It took him a few seconds of inspection to ominously intone, "Oh fuck . . . "

"What?" Nolan said.

Drextel reached to the floorboard of the H2 and came back clutching a gym bag smeared with blood.

He handed it to Nolan.

"That's from Kesha's school," Drextel said.

Nolan turned it over in his hands for a long time. Then he held it very still.

"This blood isn't either of theirs," Nolan said. "It's maybe twelve hours old."

Nolan surveyed the Hummer and its exterior. On a whim, he popped the hood and put his hand on the engine. It was still hot.

Next he took a long hard look into the woods.

"It's kind of hard to see," Nolan said to Drextel, "but somebody ran into those woods right there, and fast. Look at the undergrowth right at the edge."

"Are you saying it was them?" Drextel asked.

"I think so."

"What do we do?"

"We go after them," Nolan answered.

"On foot?"

"On foot."

The men walked slowly. The trail of ripped foliage and muddy footprints was not hard to follow, at least not at first. Drextel intermittently cupped his hands to his mouth and bellowed out a few loud cries of "Kesha!" They were not returned.

Nolan, a bit concerned by this, chose to emphasize the bright side.

"We have every reason to think they're still alive," he said as they carefully navigated a row of barbed boxthorn. "They didn't try anything stupid back there in the valley. I'm guessing that was *their* Hummer. They drove it to the woods and ran away, which was the right move."

"Doesn't mean they're safe," Drextel said.

"Well . . . I mean . . . it's the woods, I guess," Nolan said. "There could be cougars, but you hardly see those anymore. Maybe the odd coyote."

"I don't know that boy Kesha's with," Drextel said.

"I met him," Nolan replied. "Seems like a good kid."

"Maybe for you," Drextel said. "Kesha was just learning how to get along at her new school. The last year has been hard for her, but she's done it. She's starting to fit in with those upper-crust people. She also knows the south side of town, where she was raised. Those are her two ecosystems. But this? I'm worried about her. She's only fifteen."

"I think there are actually advantages to this terrain," Nolan said. "It's safer than a city, anyway. The zombies pop up and you've got plenty of directions to go in. Plenty of things to climb."

"I'm worried about the *people*," Drextel said. "This part of the state is tough. Mean. You go more than a mile off the beaten path, you get some rough characters."

Nolan thought about the old couple he and Kesha had met the night before. She had seemed to handle herself just fine.

"I don't think it's as bad as all *that*," Nolan said. "I grew up in a place like this."

"Humph," Drextel said. "You know about Larry Bird, right? I'm guessing you do. I recognize you, by the way. I know who you are, Mister Basketball."

"I get more comparisons to Damon Bailey, actually," Nolan said. "But yeah, I know who Larry Bird is. Of course I do. I watched him when I was a kid."

"Larry's from this part of the state," Drextel said ominously.

Nolan waited for more information.

"Soooo?"

"So?" Drextel returned. "So if you grew up watching him, then you know how that boy played! I can't remember a meaner, more tight-lipped, *tougher* son of a bitch in the NBA. That's a guy who started more fights than people can count, all elbows and fists and teeth when he could get away with it. That's a guy who came home in the off-season and split wood and did farm work . . . for fun. For fun! Can you ever remember Larry Bird smiling? Think about that for a second, big man."

Nolan did.

"I *can* actually . . . but I still take your point," Nolan said. "The times I can remember him smiling were pretty few and far between. And usually it was because a bad thing had happened to somebody on the other team."

Drextel nodded.

"And you remember about how much he loved Boston, the city he played for?" Drextel said.

"How much he . . . " Nolan said, trying to think.

"You don't remember that, do you?" Drextel elaborated. "You don't remember because all he ever talked about was French Lick. Southern Indiana. This was his kind of place. The kind of place where quiet, mean, violent sons of bitches fit right the fuck in."

"I'm guessing you were more of a Magic Johnson guy back in the '80s?" Nolan said.

"Joke all you like," Drextel told him. "You're a tall-ass white boy everybody loves. Kesha is a fifteen-year-old black girl from the south side of the city, who doesn't know a damn thing about this part of the state. Her only exposure to white people comes from the rich ones she goes to class with at her private school. And something tells me they're not around here right now."

Nolan decided just to nod.

"Like I said," Drextel continued, "I'm not worried about the *zombies* . . . this here is *Larry Bird* country. That's what's got me scared."

Moments later, a single gunshot echoed from the distant hills.

Nolan and Drextel looked at one another, and headed deeper into the trees.

15

Kesha stayed a few paces behind Steven as they continued their flight through the woods. The ground beneath them had inclined and declined several times, so that now Kesha reckoned they were maybe in another valley entirely. The air smelled like deep woods, that powerful, raw chlorophyll scent you just didn't get in the forest preserves up in Indianapolis. Buzzing insects popped up in clusters that Kesha did her best to shoo away. Now and then they encountered a tiny creek with small fish you could see in the shallow water. Kesha's shoes were caked in mud.

They no longer counted themselves pursued by the looters, but neither did they choose to slacken their pace. Or risk going back.

Something in Steven's intense marching style made Kesha wonder if he could even stand to go back. He was like a boy leaving home for the first time. Running away. Maybe that's how human brains work, thought Kesha. You see something like your mother and your home getting shot up by criminals, and you just got to start walking. It doesn't matter where.

An hour into their journey, they encountered a living dead man—a hunter dangling from a metal ladder leading precariously up to a tree stand. The hunter's ankle was caught in the rungs of the ladder. Now, as a zombie, he lacked the wits to extricate himself. When Kesha and Steven approached, he began gesticulating and growling wildly, but it was clear he would not free himself anytime soon.

"Look for his gun," Steven said. "Maybe we could use it."

Giving the zombie a wide berth, they scoured the nearby bushes and shrubs, but detected nothing. The zombie growled and swatted the air with his mitts.

"Maybe it's up on that stand . . . up in the tree?" Kesha tried.

"I don't think so," Steven said with a grim shake of his head. "I think somebody else already got it."

Kesha gave the surrounding woods a quick glance, as if there might be another clue to what had happened. She saw nothing. The only movement was the wind in the trees.

"C'mon," said Steven, and they left the dangling zombie where it was. It swung its arms as the teenagers walked away. Blackish drool seeped slowly from its mouth and ran down over its eyes and forehead. It continued to gesticulate long after it had been left alone.

After another hour, Kesha put her hand on Steven's shoulder to halt him.

"What?" the boy said, flinching. His voice was loud and angry.

"I hear water running," Kesha said. "Can you hear it?"

"There are a lot of little creeks around here," Steven said. "So?"

"This sounds bigger," Kesha said. "It sounds almost like a waterfall."

"There could be a little one, I suppose," Steven allowed.

"Let's go see," said Kesha. She shifted their course to the direction of the water. Steven didn't seem to mind Kesha taking the lead, as long as they kept walking.

They soon discovered a small creek, no more than an inch deep and a couple of feet wide. They followed it. The sound of running water got louder. The wind smelled like water, too.

"Yeah, okay," Steven said. "I can hear it now."

They followed the creek up a shallow hill until they stood at the top, looking down into a large clearing. Through the clearing flowed a more substantial creek that did indeed cascade over a series of moss-covered rocks. There was also what appeared to be a cave set into the side of a hill. Kesha opened her mouth to say something, but Steven put up his hand to stay her. Then he pointed down at the mouth of the cave. After a moment, Kesha noticed the barrel of a rifle protruding from it.

"What do we do?" Kesha whispered.

Steven thought for a few seconds, and then answered, "I don't see what we'd gain by going over there. Like, no reason says we have to go *this* way."

Kesha nodded. "Backtrack, then, to where we were?"

"Sounds good," Steven said.

They turned to depart.

Instants later, both of them fell to the leafy ground as a rifle report echoed across the clearing.

"Fuck!" said Steven. "They saw us."

Kesha risked a glance back at the cave. Sure enough, the weapon was now being pointed in their direction. But it was held by a young woman whom Kesha recognized. She was wearing pink shorts and a white top that was smeared with mud and grime. She had shoulder-length brown hair and a brand-new pair of Keds with bright yellow laces. And she looked painfully sunburned.

"Sara!" Kesha cried out.

Kesha's voice echoed across the clearing, like the gunshot before it.

Obviously surprised, the young woman below them hesitated.

"Sara Lindsay!" Kesha cried again. "It's Kesha Washington! Kesha Washington from school!"

The girl with the rifle stood rigid, still unsure.

"Who's that man?" Sara called back. "I saw a strange man!"

Her straining voice betrayed a girl who was exhausted, confused, and very terrified.

"His name is Steven," Kesha called back. "He's friendly. He's been helping me. I'm gonna stand up now. Please don't shoot me . . . "

Kesha rose to her knees, and then to her feet. Some thirty yards away, Sara lowered the gun.

Kesha began to pick her way through the foliage in the direction of the cave.

"C'mon, Steven," she whispered.

Steven stood, but seemed less keen to advance, perhaps because he had been the target.

"What happened to you?" Sara called.

"I got trapped for a while after our boats turned over, but then I made it out," Kesha answered back. "A policeman came and found me."

Sara turned her head and whispered something into the mouth of the cave. Kesha realized that Sara was not alone.

"What happened to *you*?" Kesha asked, now close enough to speak at a more-or-less normal volume.

Sara did not respond. Instead, she stood where she was and looked hopefully into the mouth of the cave. Someone inside said something to Sara, and she nodded. Kesha stepped closer. Moments later, two other girls emerged. One was Tara Welch, another of Kesha's classmates. The other, limping on a broken ankle and supported by Tara, was Madison Burleson, daughter of the governor of Indiana.

Both Sara and Tara closed ranks around Madison. Sara did not raise the rifle, but neither did she set it down.

Though she was injured, exhausted, and starved, it was clear that Madison was still in command of their group.

Kesha and Steven came to a halt in front of them. Kesha looked deep into the eyes of the governor's daughter. Madison stared back, doing her best to betray no weakness, despite the obvious evidence to the contrary.

"Do you have any food?" Madison asked.

Kesha shook her head no. The pained disappointment on the faces of her classmates was almost palpable.

Then Steven said, "I have something, actually."

He reached into the front pocket of his trousers and came up with a mushy, wet, malformed hot dog and bun wrapped in tin foil—leftovers from one of the carnival trucks.

"I grabbed it before we went to move the cars," he explained. "I thought I might get hungry if we stayed out a while. You all can have it though."

Steven handed the mushed-up hot dog to the girls. They quickly broke it into three pieces and consumed it. Kesha noted they made certain that Madison got the biggest piece.

"You have no idea how hungry we are," Sara shared after inhaling her fraction of the hot dog. "We haven't had anything to eat in, like, a day. We've been drinking water from that creek. We all probably have rabies and tapeworms and a million other things now. Does your cell phone work? Our cell phones all don't work."

Kesha shook her head no.

"I lost my phone in the caverns, but nobody's phone works," Kesha said.

Sara looked dejected.

"Have you got anything *else* to eat?" Tara asked hopefully.

Steven shook his head.

"What happened to you guys?" Kesha asked. "I could tell that I wasn't the only one who made it out of the caverns. There were bloodstains leading out and stuff."

"I don't know how many of us got out," Sara said. "We were feeling our way in the dark. Nobody knew what was happening. We were using our cell phone screens for light. It was awful."

Sara looked back at Madison, as if asking permission to divulge something. Kesha already knew what it was going to be. It seemed absurd that they should hesitate to make it official. Even so, the deputies waited until Madison gave the smallest of nods.

"Madison broke her ankle when we were almost outside the cave," Sara said. "There was a wet spot on the ground. All of us were slipping and falling. Tripping over each other. Madison fell really hard."

"We couldn't move fast after that," said Tara, taking up the narrative. "We had to support Madison every step of the way. And we couldn't find any adults who weren't crazy. People had guns and were acting like nut jobs. And we kept running into more of those *things*. We had to spend the night in the forest. We got this gun from a hunter who was dead."

"Yeah," Steven said. "I think we ran into him a ways back."

Madison, supporting herself on Tara, hobbled forward. Slightly restored by her hot dog third, Madison assumed the slow, clear, authoritative cadence of a leader in crisis.

"We have *got* to get back up to Indianapolis," Madison said firmly. "I have to find my father before it's too late."

"That's what I want, too," said Kesha. "I really want to get back to my dad."

Madison shook her head no, and her face said that Kesha had not responded correctly. That Kesha still did not understand.

"My father is going to do something *bad* if I don't reach him soon," Madison said with an eerie certainty. "Something very, *very* bad. He's not a good person."

Kesha had *never* heard Madison talk like this. In a world of upper-crust sensibilities and inherited wealth, ideas like "good" and "bad" were hardly ever mentioned in regard to one's parents. (Someone's father might be behind the discharge of, say, 23.1 parts per trillion of mercury into the waters of Lake Michigan each year. But if this discharge meant that his daughter got a brand new BMW and a sweet sixteen party to rival the ones they showed on MTV? Well then . . . who was to say what was good and what was bad? Certainly—it seemed from the dialogues in the school's cafeteria and along its hallways—not the students at Kesha's school.)

And yet here it was. The word "bad." Applied to her own father. Her father, whose power had fundamentally greased the wheels of Madison's life since the day she was born.

"I don't understand," said Kesha. "What's he going to do? I mean, what *can* he do about zombies? He's the governor."

Kesha said this final sentence quietly. Her father's position was always top of mind when you spoke to Madison, yet also the first thing you remembered never to mention. Now, somehow, all bets were off. When you were in the forest drinking from a stream and eating day-old carny dogs, you said what you had to say.

"He can do something bad," Madison said. "You have to trust me on this, okay? You have to trust me. I've heard him talking about things. Things that scare me to death."

"I still don't understand," Kesha said.

"Look!" Madison cried. "You want to know what's happening? Why the dead people are getting back up? I think my dad knows. I think he . . . "

Madison began to cry.

Despite herself, Kesha was deeply touched. Since they were putting it all on the table, Kesha decided to volunteer something. Something that, just twenty-four hours earlier, she would have been utterly petrified if any of her classmates had discovered.

"Do you know about my mom?" Kesha asked Madison. "Angelica Burnett? She's a member of the city council. She and your dad . . . "

Madison looked up and smiled through her tears.

"No . . . I actually didn't," Madison said. "I sure believe it, though. I know about all the other women. Adults always think we won't find out about stuff like that, but we always do."

"Right?" Kesha said. "How can they think we won't?"

Madison's expression turned sour again.

"My dad has been doing some bad things," Madison continued. "Things I hear him talking about on his cell phone late at night, when he thinks the rest of the house is asleep. The state is sick because of him. Now these zombies are everywhere, and people are doing bad things to each other. And my dad's not going to fix it. Unless we force him to."

Kesha and Steven looked at one another. How could a group of teenagers force the governor of a state to do anything? It seemed a ridiculous notion.

A few moments later, Madison was able to stop crying, and the group began to discuss their next steps.

Kesha told the girls how she had fled from the caverns with the policeman, and then ended up at the carnival in the valley. Then she described how she and Steven had run for their lives the next morning when the carnival had come under attack.

"The carnival sounds good," Tara said. "If we could ever find it again."

"Yes," echoed Sara. "Maybe we should go there. It had hot dogs and cars and people."

"Were you even listening to Kesha?" Madison said. "It got taken over by criminals with guns. You want to go get killed?"

"Maybe the criminals will be gone now," Tara tried. "Like, they've taken what they wanted and left?"

Madison just shook her head.

"I think we should just go north until we find a road," Kesha offered. "Then maybe someone can give us a ride up to Indy."

"Or we can *make* them," Sara said, hoisting the rifle. "This is a matter of, like, state security. The ends will totes justify the means."

"Omigod, totes," Tara added.

"Which way is north though?" Sara asked. "The map on my phone won't work."

"It's that way," Steven said.

"You can just *tell*?" Tara asked skeptically, still unsure of this scruffy outsider with his lower-class accent.

"The sun sets in the west and the moss grows on the north sides of the trees—so *yeah* . . . I can just tell," Steven said.

"Are you able to walk?" Kesha asked Madison. "It doesn't even look like you should be *standing* on that."

Everyone looked down at Madison's ankle, which was swelled to the size of a tennis ball.

"No, I can't really walk," Madison said. "It takes Sara and Tara both to support me, and we have to go really slow."

"That's not going to work," Kesha observed. "Not if we want to get back to Indianapolis any time soon. What about him?"

Steven realized he had been indicated.

"What about me?" asked the lanky teenager.

"Can you carry her?" Kesha asked.

Sara and Tara exchanged a horrified glance. The scion of the Hoosier State—with a backside meant for Mercedes and Lexuses—reduced to using a sweaty carnival worker as her chariot? Had they fallen so far? Had it really come to this?

For her part, Madison seemed more pragmatic.

"Maybe piggyback would work?" the governor's daughter said. "Do you think you could carry me?"

"Only one way to know," Steven said, kneeling down.

Sara and Tara both opened their mouths to object, but nothing came out. What could they say? The queen had selected her steed. There was nothing more to discuss.

Kesha helped Madison hobble over to Steven and swing her legs over his back.

"Here we go," he said. "Hang on tight. One, two, three . . . "

Steven carefully stood.

Madison gave a small whimper of pain as her foot jostled once against Steven's side. After that, she seemed fine.

"Gee," Steven said. "You weigh nothing."

He took turns turning right and left, and then took a few steps forward. If it was uncomfortable for Madison, she did not complain.

"Will that work?" Kesha asked.

"I think it's got to," Madison said.

With no further fanfare, they set off into the woods. Steven and Madison led the way north. Sara and Tara followed like good retainers. Kesha assumed the rear guard.

The trees were still thick with late summer leaves, but look-ing up through the waving branches, Kesha could tell that sun was already past its apex in the sky. From here on out, it would only get darker.

16

"What in the actual *fuck*, Hank?"

The governor chose to forgive his chief of staff for the overly familiar choice of words. The man had had a long day. Both of them had. Hell, when he thought about it, Burleson was surprised they hadn't already snapped at one another. Both men were running on a mix of anxiety, fear, and the piss-poor food from the lunchroom in the basement of the capitol building.

They had been lost—for the past four or five hours—in a sea of piecemeal information that never seemed to stop coming. IMPD officers, capitol security guards—really, anyone who had a badge and a gun and had shown up for work—were being used as messengers to gather information from what remained of the municipal entities throughout the city.

Not knowing was the hardest part for Burleson.

"I feel like Lincoln waiting to hear what was happening at Gettysburg," the governor had remarked.

"At least Lincoln had telegraphs," Huggins had shot back. "We don't even have that."

What came back—when information came back at all—usually wasn't good.

Foremost on the governor's mind was restoring electricity to Indianapolis. According to the reports coming in, the entire state appeared to be blacked out. Not a single city from Gary to Evansville had a working grid. Yet it also appeared that Indy was the area where headway would be the most difficult. Few IPL employees had shown up for work, and the crews they had could not promise any progress in the short term. (Burleson was not surprised. The Great Blackout of 2003—the one that had taken out the entire northeastern United States—had resulted from nothing more than a tree falling on some power lines in Ohio, followed by a few computer glitches at crucial points. Indiana's power grid had never faced a challenge like this. Nobody's had. Walking dead people everywhere—walking into power lines, fouling up machinery, scaring away necessary workers. It was uncharted territory.)

The news was a little better when it came to emergency services. A trickle of firemen, policemen, and EMTs were coming back on the job. Most hospitals were still operating on generators, but those would fail soon. There were also several large fires ranging across the city, and probably others around the state. By messenger, the chief of the fire department had assured Burleson that they would begin putting them out as soon as possible. (The governor noted that no hard-and-fast deadline for this was included.)

A bigger problem was the zombies. Many of the patrolmen sent out as messengers returned with stories beyond crediting. Tales that *had* to be whoppers. Had to be. (Who'd have guessed the police department was so prone to exaggeration?) They told stories of packs of zombies all across the countryside, apparently traveling in large groups. One officer said that hundreds of the undead had emerged from watery graves in Eagle Creek Reservoir, and were now clogging the west side of Interstate 465, making it virtually impassible. Another astounding report—

surely, it could not be true—said that the Brickyard Crossing golf course was full of holes where zombies had burrowed out. The course had apparently been a dumping ground for hit men and gangsters wishing to conceal bodies. Now those bodies, quite unconcealed, spilled out onto the Indianapolis Motor Speedway and stumbled around aimlessly on the track.

Yet the behavior of the ravenous undead was sometimes less troubling than that of the city's criminals. Governor Burleson heard tale after tale of violent robberies and rampages. Of living humans mistaken for zombies (with tragic consequences). Of neighborly grudges and family vendettas settled once and for all . . . now that the law wasn't looking. Of prisons across the state abandoned by their guards when the electric fences had failed, and now in the hands of the inmates.

These and similar reports weighed on Burleson's mind. And on Huggins's, too. You couldn't hear these tales and not wonder. Probably people were exaggerating. Yet even if only one out of ten was true. . . .

For these and other reasons, Burleson forgave his chief of staff.

For the moment.

They were alone in Burleson's office. Burleson had eventually retreated there to smoke a cigar and, if possible, rest his eyes for a moment. He had forgotten his jacket on a chair back in the war room. Huggins noticed this, and had picked it up, intending to bring it up to the governor. It was then that the satellite phone had fallen out of the jacket pocket, and Huggins's jaw had nearly hit the floor.

"You can leave my jacket on the desk," the governor responded coolly, not even lifting his head.

Huggins unceremoniously tossed the governor's jacket on the corner of his desk, but the satellite phone remained in his hands. Both halves of it.

"You took it apart," Huggins said.

This statement was true. Both men knew it. The governor fiddled with his cigar and considered how to respond. After a few awkward seconds, he silently nodded in agreement.

"But we won't know what's going on!" Huggins cried. "The federal government could be trying to contact us this very moment. They might have a cure for the zombies already. Or Army troops could be on the way."

Burleson, who had taken the phone apart just after his successful on-camera defense of Mayor Brown, wrinkled his nose at this final suggestion.

"Answering that phone is tantamount to begging for help," Burleson said, moving the unlit cigar to the corner of his mouth. "I can't allow that to happen. I can't even put myself in a situation where someone can suggest that that *could* have happened."

"But—" Huggins began.

The governor waved both arms wildly, an unusual gesture that Huggins had long ago realized meant Burleson desired complete silence.

"Do you remember the Mike Tyson rape trial that happened here some years back?" the governor asked, lowering his arms and rising to his feet. "You're younger than me, Huggins, but

not that young. It took place in Indianapolis, back in the early
'90s. You couldn't have missed it."

"I . . . sort of remember it, yeah," Huggins answered.

"Do you remember what Tyson said after he was con-
victed?" Burleson asked. "He never admitted to the crime, but
he said his failure had been putting himself in a situation where
he *could* have committed the crime. Taking an eighteen-year-old
beauty pageant contestant back to a hotel room in the middle
of the night, where it would be his word against hers? Even if
nothing went down, that's a situation where something *could*
have happened. If you put yourself in that position—even if you
do nothing wrong—you make yourself vulnerable. For a guy
who got hit in the head for a living, I thought that was a pretty
bright observation."

"So . . . ?" Huggins began. "Why are you bringing this up
now?"

"So, I don't want to put myself in a position where I can
even be *accused* of having asked for help from the federal government of the United States of America!" the governor boomed.

Then he chewed his cigar for a moment, seeming to grow
calmer and more thoughtful.

"Look, between you and me, they're going to send
something eventually. We both know that. We're both adults,
Huggins. It's gonna happen. It might be troops. It might be first
aid kits and FEMA trailers. I don't know the details yet, but
they're gonna send something. And when that happens—when
the grid gets back online and people start asking who did what
during the great zombie blackout—I want people to know that

I didn't ask for help. Indiana didn't ask for help. I want to be able to look at the cameras and say there was no phone call to the Feds begging for troops. I want to say, 'Search through the electronic records for any instance of a phone call between me and the federal government—and you will find *nothing*.' And that will be God's own truth."

"When did you make this decision?" Huggins asked soberly.

Burleson brushed off the question.

"Look, we are going to be *fine*," Burleson told him. "I know what I'm doing here. I know how to play this. Things are going to be up and running again before you know it. When they are, you're going to be damn glad I did this. Search your heart. You know I'm right."

Huggins searched his heart.

"Is there anything else I should know about?" Huggins asked. "I've devoted my professional life to you for over eight years, Hank. I think I deserve to know what's going on."

The governor moved his cigar to the other side of his mouth.

"I sent some people up to Whiting," the governor said quietly. "Couple of squad cars and an armored tank-thing the SWAT team had. I don't know how long it will take them to get there with the roads all crazy, but I said not to dilly-dally. I gave them a message for Burundi Petroleum. Wrote it on official stationery and everything. Told them to be ready for . . . every contingency."

For a long moment, Huggins said nothing. He placed the broken satellite phone on the corner of the governor's desk, and turned to leave the room.

"Thank you for telling me," Huggins said as he walked out the door.

"Close it behind you, would you?" the governor called, preparing to light the cigar.

Huggins did so.

Flanked by the flags that surrounded the governor's office, Huggins felt a tear roll down his cheek. He knew it was only the exhaustion—the chief of staff was not a man readily given to emotion—but it felt real nonetheless.

The governor had sent folks to Whiting.

He had reached out to BP.

The man might just have a soul after all. . . .

17

James Nolan and Drextel Washington crept deeper into the woods. They followed the muddy footprints that were sometimes visible on the dirt paths beneath their feet. The prints did not occur regularly, and did not always look like Kesha's or Steven's, but the two men would take what they could get.

In the early afternoon, they stopped to drink from a creek.

"Look . . . I appreciate your help with Kesha," Drextel said. "I know finding her wasn't your original focus. You were looking for Madison."

"At this point, I'm not convinced the two are exclusive," Nolan said, standing up from his perch next to the creek.

Drextel looked puzzled. Something clearly did not sit right with him.

"It's just . . . why would a guy like you work for a guy like Hank Burleson?" Drextel asked. "You're near to a damn hero in this state. You could work for anybody you wanted."

Nolan sighed.

"Not everybody likes the governor's politics," Nolan said. "I realize that. I'm an adult. Maybe you didn't vote for him. That doesn't mean we have to be enemies."

"Naw," said Drextel, wiping his mouth and standing. "I mean *you* personally. You could work for anybody. Hell, I'd give you a job if you wanted one. First white columnist for the *Indianapolis Recorder*. Why not? It'd open up new circulation markets for us, for sure. Why do *you* stay with the governor?"

Nolan hesitated and shook his head.

"Hank Burleson helped me out back in the day. He was good to me. So I try to be good to him. I like helping people, and he knows that. It's just my personality. This job I have, it puts me in positions where I feel like I can do a lot of good. I like that."

Drextel narrowed his eyes, as if somehow unconvinced.

"Our esteemed governor's had a long career in Indiana politics, as I recall," Drextel said. "Long career . . ."

Nolan knew where this was going.

"Look, you can stop right there," Nolan said, "because the answer is no."

"Hmmm?" said Drextel, feigning innocence.

"*Yes*, when I had my car accident in college—the one that ended my career—Burleson was the mayor of Muncie at the time. *Yes*, he was involved in the investigation afterwards. And *yes*, he was one of the people who argued for leniency. But I don't owe him anything. That's not why I work for him. We just—you know—got to know each other during the whole process. Years later when he found out I'd joined the IPD, we sort of reconnected. That's it."

Drextel looked skeptical.

"That's it, huh?" he asked.

Nolan nodded.

Drextel shrugged as if to say he had heard worse prevarications. Maybe not much worse, but worse.

They went back on the march and followed the creek for about a mile. After that, the worn trail beneath them seemed to veer away, but Nolan stayed with the water. A footprint near the bank had caught his eye. Also, water. Teenagers needed water. So did adults.

After following the creek for a few hundred yards—through a landscape that was often hilly and full of rocky outcroppings that were a challenge to traverse—they sighted a small lean-to. The walls featured haphazard tarpaper and odd scraps of wood and insulation that had been left exposed to the elements. The door was an oblong grate that looked as if it might once have been part of a farm animal's pen. A dilapidated ATV was parked beside it.

"What do you think?" Drextel asked as they observed from behind a hill. "Meth house? Moonshiner's den? Broke-ass hunter's cabin?"

Nolan shook his head. The hovel was upwind, and it sure didn't smell like anybody cooking meth or moonshine. All he could think about was the ATV. They could probably both fit aboard, and it would allow them to navigate the wooded trails at five times their current speed.

Drextel whispered, "Look!"

Nolan did.

A man emerged from the lean-to. He had the slouch and distracted stare of a person who clearly believes himself unobserved. He was in his late 50s or early 60s, and had wild, shoulder length grey-black hair. He wore glasses and was dressed in jeans, a flannel shirt, and a blaze orange vest. He had an unkempt beard that grew wild and uneven across his face. In his hand he carried an oblong case that might have been a fisherman's tackle box.

"What do you think?" Drextel whispered.

"I don't see a gun," Nolan observed. "I think we go say hi."

Nolan stood to his full height, instantly becoming visible. The man in front of the lean-to stopped and eyed him warily. Drextel stood up too. Both men waved. The stranger cautiously set down his case and waved back.

The only sound was the trickling creek.

"Howdy," the stranger called as Nolan and Drextel approached. "Y'all hunters?"

He indicated Drextel's .22 rifle with a nod.

Nolan could tell the man was nervous—and possibly dangerous. Just because he didn't have a visible weapon did not mean he couldn't be concealing one beneath his shirt, just as Nolan himself did.

"Not hunters," Nolan replied as they reached the lean-to. "I'm a police officer. This is Drextel Washington, a newspaper editor. We're looking for Drextel's daughter. She's missing somewhere in these woods. About yea high. Short hair. Big pretty eyes. You seen anybody like that come through?"

"Hmm," the man said, as if not entirely convinced by their story. "I recognize you. You're that ballplayer, right?"

"Yeah," Nolan said. "Used to be. Police officer now."

He fished his shield out of his pocket and perfunctorily held it up.

"Long way from Indianapolis," the stranger observed, eyeing the badge.

Nolan nodded.

"Have you seen anybody come past?" Drextel asked. "My daughter could be with another teenager."

"No," the man said. "Haven't seen anybody. Not for two days."

"Are *you* a hunter?" Nolan asked. He looked at the strange, oblong case the man had set down. The man saw him looking.

"I'm a biologist," the man said. "I teach up at Purdue. Name's Richard Niel."

He extended his hand to both men, and they shook it.

"I study the things that live in the water in this part of the state—in creeks like this one," Richard continued. He opened the case to reveal tiny clear plastic boxes full of field samples.

"Do you, uh, know what's going on?" Drextel asked.

Richard looked back and forth between them and raised his eyebrows. He clearly didn't.

"What do you mean 'going on'?" Richard said.

Drextel and Nolan both sighed.

"Do you have a radio or a cell phone or anything?" Nolan tried.

"I listen to an iPod while I'm working," Richard answered. "And my cell phone's broken, I think. It hasn't worked since yesterday."

"Maybe you should sit down for a second," Nolan said. "There are some things we should probably tell you."

"I'm fine to stand," Richard said—still clearly uncomfortable, still unsure what to make of these strangers.

"Sure . . . stand," Nolan told him. "Either way, you should hear this."

They stayed standing.

18

Kesha kept her body low and hidden as she looked down from the crest of the rock outcropping to the creek below. Her mouth hung open in surprise. Her eyes went back and forth rapidly as she tried to make sense of the scene.

First of all, her father—her father!—was here. Not up in Indianapolis. Not at home, or at the offices of the *Recorder*, or even out somewhere trying to find her mother. Against all reason, he was here, in southern Indiana. Less than a hundred feet away.

And Kesha wanted nothing more than to bound up to him and hug him. To run to him, calling his name, and throw her arms around his middle. To feel her arms around the familiar daddy-contours of his shoulders, his chest, his belly. To smell his cologne that smelled like home—not even like a house, like the *idea* of home. To feel safe and loved and like Dad was there once more.

Not even "like." He would be there. He was. Right there, in the clearing below.

But standing next to him were IMPD Special Sergeant James Nolan and a strange bearded man with a tackle box.

She looked again at her father. He appeared exhausted, and utterly out of his element. He was also holding a gun, which Kesha had never seen him do. He was sweaty. His glasses were fogged from exertion. His spavined frame bore the wear of years spent hunched over typewriters and computers, and a steady diet of crullers and black coffee. This was not a man designed to roam zombie-filled hills with a gun. This was a man built for reclining in leather chairs and examining written copy with a careful eye. (And still Kesha loved him. And still she wanted to be with him in this time of horrible crisis more than anything in the world.)

Kesha turned and looked behind her. There, at the foot of the hill beneath the outcropping, crouched the rest of her group. Sara and Tara relaxed against the same tree. Steven had helped Madison into a seated position atop a mossy log. All four of them looked up expectantly at Kesha. What were the noises that had sounded like conversation? What had the scout seen and heard?

Kesha raised a finger to say they should wait a moment more. She took another long glance down to where her father stood. The three men were talking. Actually, James Nolan was doing most of the talking. He was the concern.

Nolan worked for the governor. That was the one fact that Kesha just couldn't shake.

She'd seen him in action. How he always rushed in to do the right thing without a second thought. And that was what worried her.

In her year-and-change among the children of Hoosier royalty, Kesha had come to understand what the system rewarded. If any single trait was encouraged, it was an alacrity to help. Whatever the task, you showed up and did it with a smile. Whatever the request, a good Hoosier said yes if he possibly could. That was what good Hoosiers did. That was *especially* what good Hoosier athletes did. You did what coach said. Whatever he said. It was no great leap for Kesha to imagine how a man like Nolan might go into the "real world" seeing every authority figure as a coach. And who was a bigger coach than the governor of the entire state?

When coach said hit those free throws, or block that shot, or find my daughter—you just did it. There was no reward for stopping and thinking. For wondering if it was the right thing to do. There was only the task at hand. The play. The score.

Nolan was brave, and Nolan was doing what he thought was right. No question. But he was a good servant. That's what he was at the end of the day. A servant. And who did he serve? Governor Hank Burleson.

Nolan was like the clean-cut athletic boys who sat next to her in homeroom and dreamed of basketball scholarships and big futures and rising just as high as their parents had, or even higher. And no part of that ever involved questioning the coach about the play he had just called. To the contrary, such a thing would be a horrifying heresy to those boys.

Was Nolan looking for Madison because he had her best interests in mind? It was possible, sure. Anything was possible these days. The ravenous dead walking the countryside proved that. But it seemed infinitely *more* possible that Nolan was looking for Madison because her father had told him to. And that was that, was that, was that. He had thought about it no further.

Nolan was also a charmer. Kesha knew that once Madison looked up into his big, brown eyes, it would all be over. She would be seduced by his fame and his smile and his big safe shoulders, and he'd whisk her away to wherever the governor had told him to take her. But where was that? To a safe house up in Indy? Into some kind of rich-people perimeter surrounded by security guards with zombie-killing rocket launchers?

Sure, maybe.

But could it also be something darker?

Madison had said she knew secrets . . . secrets about what the governor was doing. Secrets that meant he had to be stopped.

And would they stop him? Could they?

With increasing alarm, Kesha realized that if Madison met James Nolan—here, now, like this—they would probably never know.

In a world of zombies and murder, it was not beyond conceiving that the governor might have anyone with purposes contrary to his own put out of the picture. Even his own daughter. Even permanently.

When the lights were out all across the state, and no one was looking, what would a man like that do?

Kesha put a finger to her lips and crept back down the hillside. The other teens huddled around, waiting for the verdict.

"Some hunters," Kesha whispered. "They don't look friendly. Lots of guns. I think we should go around."

The group nodded seriously. Tara and Sara cast worried glances up to the top of the outcropping.

"We can backtrack through that thicket; connect with the creek somewhere further north," Steven suggested.

"Yeah," Kesha said. "That's a good idea."

As silently as he could, Steven took a knee and let Madison climb back on his shoulders. Then they set off into the woods. The sunlight twinkled through the trees, dappling their bodies as they moved.

Kesha looked back once and said a silent prayer for her father's safety. Then she followed Steven and the others back into the underbrush.

19

A knock at the door roused Hank Burleson from his late afternoon slumber. He opened his eyes slowly. His mouth was dry. He could not remember being so tired.

He was lying on the couch in his office. He was on his back, looking up at the ceiling.

For a few sweet moments, he wondered if it had all been a dream. The zombies. The loss of power. The chaos in the streets. . . .

He stared up at the ceiling. His eyes lit on the smoke alarm. Hope! Its electronic light still blinked intermittently. Full of life. Full of power. Power that—the governor remembered an instant later—came from a nine-volt battery, and not from the grid.

With considerable effort, Burleson sat up and surveyed the rest of the room. His office was without power. Outside his window, an eerie dimness pervaded. The streets were empty, save for National Guard troops and police. Only the odd passing headlight brought illumination to the shadows cast by the capitol. Not a single electric light shone inside his office . . . save the tiny one, straight above, on the smoke alarm.

The knock came again.

"Yes, Huggins," the governor called irritably.

It wasn't Huggins. The door opened to reveal a scared-looking security guard who couldn't have been more than twenty. The governor found it hard to believe a boy this fresh-faced was allowed to carry a gun. Yet there it was, in the holster at his side.

"Mister Huggins was called away," the guard said sheepishly. "But he said I should tell you if anyone from Burundi Petroleum showed up."

"BP!" the governor said brightly, jolting up from the couch as if the two letters had galvanized him. "Ah, yes, send him right in. Or her. Whoever it is."

"Yessir," said the guard, exiting directly.

The governor rubbed the sleep from his eyes and tucked his shirt back into his pants. Then he plopped down in the chair behind his desk and tried to look gubernatorial. Soon, he heard loud, confident footsteps coming down the hallway. Moments later, three tall men strode into his office. Two were BP private security, their body armor festooned with the garish yellow-green Burundi Petroleum logo. The other one looked entirely different, and it was clear that he was there to do the talking.

He was a towering man of indeterminate age (Burleson would have guessed forty-five, if pressed), wearing gigantic boots, mud-stained khakis, and a golf shirt with a tiny "BP" on the left breast. An Indiana Jones-style fedora sat atop his head, the brim pushed back. He had not one, but two scars—one on his left cheek, and one running down the center of his forehead.

Burleson understood right away that this was one of BP's fixers. Oil companies did business in places all over the world. Some of them were nice, reasonable places that had things like democratic elections and fair trials. But others were . . . not. It was into this latter environment that BP sent men like *this*. (Burleson could picture him riding in the back of Jeeps down muddy roads, on his way to make deals for oil rights with warlords, pirates, or members of the armed opposition.)

"Mister Governor," the man said in greeting. "I'm John Dawkins from BP. I'm here to talk about Eventuality Receivable Nineteen."

He exuded a confidence that Burleson knew well—that of a man who understands his wishes are backed by unimaginably large sums of money.

"Shut the door," Burleson said gruffly.

Nobody moved.

"Please?" the governor tried.

Still nothing. After a beat, Dawkins gave an almost imperceptible nod, at which point one of his guards pulled the enormous wooden door closed behind them.

Burleson was not an easily intimidated man, but at that moment—with these three large men from BP in front of his desk—he would have liked to have had his own fixer in the room. James Nolan was taller than all three of these jokers. Bigger, too. And probably faster with a gun.

"Mister Governor, as you must already know, events in the last twenty-four hours meet the qualification threshold for ER-19," Dawkins said from beneath his scars and fedora.

Burleson nodded. He respected big companies for the way they pushed people around and made money hand over fist . . . but he could have done without the corporate doublespeak. (Who were they trying to impress with it, each other?)

"I'll say they meet the goddamn qualifications," Burleson said, hoping to make clear that he was a plain-spoken sort of man.

"You know, when we had that briefing back in the day . . . eight years ago now . . . you all made it sound like—what did you call it?—'reanimation of fast-twitch muscle in necrotic tissue' was just one of a *bunch* of possible side effects. You sort of snuck it in there, didn't you? It did this. It did that. Gee willikers, what *didn't* it do? You probably thought I wouldn't even notice—and *if* I noticed it, that I wouldn't remember . . . but I *did* notice . . . and I sure as hell *do* remember."

Dawkins smiled at Burleson by quickly lifting the corners of his mouth and lowering them again. It was intended to impart a shared understanding, but only for a moment—the equivalent of a wink, Burleson gathered, but with the plausible deniability of having technically been a smile. Burleson wondered: Upon how many banana republic dictators had he honed this exact expression?

"So you were telling the truth . . . in your way," Burleson continued. "Hell, I'm not mad. I respect you for it! I just hope you were telling the truth about the rest of it. About the antidote and such . . ."

Dawkins flashed the mouth-corner smile once again.

"Well then," Burleson said. "Just tell me what the fuck we do next."

"I take it the federal government has *not* been involved?" Dawkins asked.

"You take it correctly," Burleson returned. "I've disconnected the damn satellite phone. There's no way they *can* be involved, that I know of. Unless you guys are in the mood for a road trip out to D.C."

"I will trust that you are telling the truth," Dawkins said. "You will recall that that qualification was necessary to comport with our resolution to move forward."

"Yes, yes, fine," Burleson said, waving his hand back and forth as though the corporate jargon were smoke he could disperse.

One of the private security handed Dawkins a heavy black briefcase. Dawkins set it on the governor's desk—quite as if the desk were his own—and opened it.

"We are ready to begin the resolution phase of ER-19," Dawkins said as he produced several manuscript-length documents from the briefcase. "Distribution of the phytochemicals. We simply need your signature on these documents in order to begin."

Good Christ, Burleson thought. Even at a time like this, lawyers still ruled the world.

Dawkins flipped to the back of one of the manuscripts and pointed at a dotted line. Then he took the governor's own pen from his chestnut and leather pen holder and offered it to him. The governor leaned in to take a closer look.

"Nobody said I needed to sign anything for this to happen," Burleson said. "Should I go and fetch my attorney?"

In point of fact, Burleson was ready to sign anything put in front of him, with or without counsel. (He had no idea where his lawyer was, but sincerely hoped the man was dead.) However, Burleson knew the value of being difficult when dealing with an entity that wanted you to do something expeditiously.

"This simply says that you are authorizing us to release several thousand tons of phytochemicals into Indiana's waterways, and into Lake Michigan. And that this authorization has *nothing* to do with the current . . . breach of ER-19 threshold."

"Which of course it does," Burleson said.

Dawkins flashed the little smile again.

The governor took the pen from Dawkins and intentionally doddered like a nonagenarian before the book-length document. With great dramatic skill, he moved his shaking pen down until it almost touched the page . . . then abruptly pulled it back.

Dawkins winced.

"How is your intelligence regarding the radius of the . . . breach of ER-19 such-and-such?" Burleson asked.

"The radius?" Dawkins asked.

"What I want to know is how widespread this is," Burleson told him. "That's what no one can tell me. Is it just *my* state? Just the Midwest? Or has the whole damn world gone sick with zombies? You're about the wealthiest company on the planet. I imagine you have communications when the grid goes down. . . ."

Dawkins said nothing. Did nothing.

"Well?" asked the governor, drawing his pen even further back from the page.

Dawkins stared at him hard. Then looked around the room. Then at the door behind them. Then back at the governor.

Burleson realized that Dawkins was probably considering whether or not to kill him. It would not be difficult. Do it silently, and Dawkins and his two guards could be out of the capitol building before any of the exhausted, underpaid police and National Guard knew what was going on. (The governor's signature could, of course, always be forged at a later date.)

"I mean, I'll sign it, sure," Burleson said, hurriedly returning the pen to the extremely long document and giving it his John Hancock. "There. There you go. I just wondered how much you could tell me."

The governor smiled at Dawkins, who promptly placed two more copies of the enormous document in front of him.

"It's just, as you can see, we're a bit limited right now," Burleson said, signing the other copies. "Generator's used up. No phones. And it's going to start getting dark again soon. All our intelligence comes from firsthand reports."

The final copy signed, Dawkins placed two of the enormous manuscripts back into the briefcase and handed it to his security escort. The third copy he left on Burleson's desk.

"It's been a difficult time for all of us," Dawkins allowed with a sympathetic frown.

Then he was done. It was over. He'd gotten what he came for. Burleson could see it in his eyes.

Dawkins nodded to his escorts and they began to exit Burleson's office.

"What . . . ?" Burleson managed, surprised. "So . . . are you just . . . ?"

"Thank you," Dawkins said perfunctorily, without turning his head.

"When will I hear from you?" Burleson called as they paraded underneath his doorway. "What happens next?"

"Thank you . . . " the BP official called again, waving his hand in the air without turning around.

And then they were gone.

Burleson stood behind his desk, confused, panting.

That was really it. They had come and gone in a matter of seconds, and he had learned . . . not a damn thing. The impressive legal document was the only evidence their visit had even happened. It sat like a fat cancer on the edge of his desk.

Burleson glared at the offensive thing for a long moment, then brushed it into the trash with a powerful swipe of his arm.

To do whatever BP wanted—whenever they wanted it—was one thing. Hell, that was what Indiana governors *did*! But to threaten him inside his own damn office? That was too much!

Where was *his* muscle? *His* brawn? Burleson imagined James Nolan head butting the BP fixer and knocking out the security buffoons with swift punches before they even knew what was happening. That would show them. That was what should have happened!

The more he thought about how he'd just been treated, the more blinded with fury the governor became.

James Nolan—that fuck!—*Where on earth was he?*

20

Though he had initially resolved to stand, Purdue biology professor Richard Niel found himself leaning against a tree by the end of Nolan's tale. (This was not necessarily due to the content of what Nolan had had to say; the day had been hot and Richard was already beat when the two strange men had showed up.) He kept his eyes locked on Nolan's, though, and nodded periodically to show he was following the narrative.

When Nolan finished, there was a long silence. Richard had not interrupted him, or asked for clarification at any point. The biologist looked down at his own shoes, and then down at the tackle box full of water samples.

"I suppose you're looking for some kind of verdict from me?" Richard said. "Well . . . what would *you* say if two strangers with guns showed up at *your* place and started talking about zombies?"

An awkward beat passed.

"I'd say that anybody who just wanted my ATV could come up with a much more believable story than that," Nolan replied.

"It's true," Drextel added. "This sounds crazy, because we're telling the truth. You can go all detective on us, if you think we're lying. Separate us. Ask us questions about the tiniest details of our story. Our answers are going to line up."

Nolan, who had questioned suspects before, smiled at the notion. He also reflected that it was not a bad idea.

"Then here's my question . . . " the biologist said, absently stroking his beard. "And I don't care who answers; I'm asking you both. If you're telling the truth—if this *is* happening—then is it just here, or is it all around the world?"

Drextel shook his head. Nolan swallowed hard.

"That's the million-dollar question," Nolan said. "I haven't met anybody who knows."

"It could just be the Midwest," Drextel ruminated. "It could just be Indy and the southern part of the state, actually. Those are the only places we've been."

The biologist looked the two outsiders up and down for a long moment.

"Okay," he said. "I'll be good God-damned . . . but I think I believe you."

Drextel and Nolan smiled.

"What did it?" Nolan asked.

The biologist bit his lip underneath his wild beard. Then he looked left. Nolan and Drextel followed his gaze. There was only the burbling creek that ran beside his makeshift hut.

"I've been studying these waterways for most of my life," the biologist said. "I didn't start with that, of course. No kid wants to study water. I wanted to study fish. These amazing little creatures that live in their own little world—right next to ours, but so different—you know? But when you start studying fish in Indiana, you start noticing all the shit—for lack of a better word—that contaminates the waterways. After that, you can't in good conscience spend your time looking at anything else. I realized early in my career that instead of studying trout and bass and sunfish,

I was actually gonna be looking at parts-per-million of mercury, polychlorinated biphenyls, and about twenty different kinds of pesticide.

"I could throw statistics at you, sure. What percentage of our waterways have stressors and pollutants above the national mean. It's a lot, but you wouldn't care. Nobody in this state seems to. Our goddamn politicians . . . this governor we have now . . . there's no way to say it, other than they pimp the state out. That's what they do. They say to these polluters: 'Doesn't Indiana look nice? Isn't she just the prettiest little thing you ever laid eyes on? Well, if you come here and open a factory, we'll let you do anything you want to her. And I mean *anything*. Nobody will be watching.'"

Nolan had heard a few folks—most of them political opponents—characterize his boss as a pimp or a hustler before. Usually it happened during the election debates. Nolan crossed his arms to show he was not entirely receptive to the idea, but still kept an even smile on his face.

"This goes beyond politics, though," the biologist quickly added. "No political party has been able to keep our water clean. And now there's this new *stuff* in it . . . and no, I'm not avoiding a 'science term' because you two don't have PhDs. I'm calling it 'stuff' because *I don't know what the fuck it is*. Nobody does. I mean . . . I know it's a suspended solid. I know that sometimes it acts like mercury and sometimes it acts like ammonia and sometimes it acts like arsenic. But I've seen it do things. Things that made me get my eyes checked, and then my head examined. Things that made me think a graduate student was playing a practical joke on me by sabotaging a brand-new electron micro-scope display. This stuff in our water . . . what it does . . . you won't even believe me."

Drextel took a step forward and raised his hand to interject.

"All due respect, Professor . . . after what we've seen in the past twenty-four hours, I'd say we're liable to believe quite a lot."

Richard Niel nodded. For a moment, he looked straight ahead, staring at nothing. His eyes wandered randomly. He was remembering.

Nolan had seen this look before, usually on the faces of witnesses asked to recall the details of a horrible crime. Whatever was coming next, Nolan realized it would be bad.

"It reanimates dead tissue," the biologist finally said. "Not often. Not reliably. But sometimes. Now that in itself is not as earth-shattering as you'd think. Throw some fresh-skinned frogs' legs into salt, and you'll see something much more dramatic. A lot of our bodies are just chemical reactions. Nerve impulses. You connect a corpse to an electric wire, and it'll damn-sure dance for a while. But *this* stuff. This is operating on a whole other level. A *cellular* one."

"And it's behind the zombies?" Nolan asked.

The biologist continued to stare straight ahead. He stroked his beard, trying to think.

"It's possible," the biologist said. "What I've observed has just been in the lab. I've seen human skin cells twitch—cells that were in a freezer for twenty years. I've seen a human heart beat once—like an engine unsuccessfully trying to turn over—and then fall silent. I've watched isolated cardiac muscle expand and contract, and I didn't know why. But this . . . what you're saying . . . this is a whole new ballgame."

The biologist wiped his brow.

"Sometimes chemicals can slowly build up in waterways, and you only see evidence way off in the outliers—a cancer cluster here or there—until one day, boom! It reaches a critical mass. Overnight evidence is everywhere, and you can't believe you didn't see it before."

"Or see it walking around and eating people," Drextel added.

The biologist nodded seriously.

"So anyway . . . you can use my ATV, if you think it will help you find those kids. I'll be okay where I am. I've got a gun inside the hut, and some camping supplies."

"Thank you," Nolan said.

"But if you two are somehow bullshitting me, I will hunt you down and cut off your balls," he added. "Got it? Don't think I won't, just because I'm a scientist."

"Yeah, okay," Nolan said. "Got it."

A few minutes later, Nolan and Drextel were cruising across the forest floor on a bright-blue Yamaha ATV. The biologist had pointed them in the direction of the nearest highway, but for the moment they both wanted to stay inside the trees. Something told both of them that Steven and Kesha—and possibly Madison Burleson—were still to be found within these leafy folds.

As he gripped the ATV's handles and steered around tree trunks and fallen logs, Nolan found it tempting to allow his mind to wander away from where he was. The woods had an intoxicatingly alien smell, so different from the city parks he was used to. Not only were there virtually no other humans around, there were no *signs* of humans. No noise. No litter. No smoke or exhaust, except from his own ATV. In this arboreal strangeness, he felt disconnected from reality.

The shadows drew long and Nolan stopped to look at the sky. Hard as it was to believe, the sun was starting to set. It had been twenty-four hours—more or less—since the outbreak had begun. Twenty-four hours, and Nolan knew almost as little as he did when he'd first seen that mess of bone and sinew scrabbling against Kesha Washington's backpack in the cave. Twenty-four hours felt like a long time not to learn anything new. A long time to wonder.

Where was the government? Where was the Army? Where was the goddamn cell service and electricity?

And where was the governor's daughter?

In his ten years of service to the department and the governor, this was probably Nolan's only categorical failure. No one would blame him, of course. These were the most extenuating circumstances he could envision. Even so, it gnawed at the back of his brain. He had not found the governor's daughter. He still did not know if she was even alive.

In the dying light, it was harder to look for clues—for footprints or other signs that the teenagers might have passed this way. Yet something in his gut told Nolan not to pack it up and head back to Indy quite yet.

Once, it seemed to Nolan that he heard gunshots in the distance, and he stopped and turned off the vehicle to listen.

He and Drextel cupped their ears and surveyed the shady trees around them, but heard nothing more.

"I'd hate to run into somebody who wasn't friendly," Drextel said. "Too easy for them to hear us coming in this."

Nolan agreed, increasingly aware that they were potentially the hunted as well as the hunters. The ATV was loud, and also left them sitting exposed.

Soon, the trees around them became noticeably smaller. They were more like saplings, and could be crushed easily under the ATV's powerful tires. Nolan understood that they had probably reached the western edge of the woods.

Ahead of them, the tiny trees fell away entirely. Nolan and Drextel could see a road and fields of waving cornstalks beyond. Nolan looked back once at Drextel, whose expression indicated that he had no better idea.

Nolan piloted them out of the trees. The two men found themselves staring at a small cultivated clearing between the woods and the highway. It was a little campsite, with three picnic tables and two filthy grills. The grass had been mown—not recently, but at one point.

Two of the picnic tables were empty, but atop the third were the remains of a human being. Legs, a glistening ribcage, and a skeletonized face were all visible in the dying light. Blood had poured through the slats of the table, and now soaked into the ground beneath. Around the table hunkered five shadowy figures—zombies—themselves in various states of dismemberment and decay. Two of them looked at Nolan as he parked the ATV some thirty yards away. The other three remained focused on the feast spread out before them.

"What the hell is this?" Drextel asked, awkwardly dismounting behind Nolan. He raised Sheree Hipwell's .22, just in case the assembled undead should make a charge.

Nolan also got off of the ATV and stretched his legs. He took a long look at the cornfield beyond, and only then surveyed the grisly scene upon the picnic table. Something in his policeman's instincts told him that there was more to this than met the eye.

"Five zombies and a dead guy," Nolan said. "Or gal. But the way the body is sitting there on that picnic table. The zombies didn't do that. It's like it's been laid out on purpose."

"Like for . . . a picnic?" Drextel asked.

Nolan nodded yes.

The two zombies that had noticed the newcomers began to take a few steps toward the ATV.

"You want me to take these guys out?" Drextel asked.

Nolan scanned the cornfields once more. The stalks whispered in the late summer wind. Insects buzzed and flitted.

"I wouldn't like to make our presence known more than we need to," Nolan said.

Drextel lowered the weapon.

"Okay," Drextel said with a shrug. "But they're coming over now. You see that."

"Yes. I also think we can easily outrun them."

Drextel looked at the ATV and nodded, but Nolan had been thinking of running on foot. The hand of the gas gauge on the Yamaha was just above the "E."

As Nolan watched the waving corn and thought about what to do next, he heard a strange sound in the distance. A low metallic burbling, Nolan first imagined it might be gunshots or cannons. Then the sound moved closer and became more distinct. Motorcycle engines. Lots and lots of motorcycle engines. A convoy. A gang.

"Motorcycles?" Drextel asked, cupping an ear.

"Yeah," Nolan said. "A bunch, too. Coming up fast."

"What do you want to do?" Drextel asked.

Nolan hesitated, something he rarely did. The cornstalks and trees affected the noise in strange ways. The engines seemed to go from distant to just-behind-the-next-row-of-corn and back again. It was hard to tell exactly from what direction they were approaching.

Then, all at once, the bikers were there.

A hard-looking bunch, they appeared suddenly at the end of the gravel road. They wore black jackets full of patches and brain-bucket helmets with chinstraps. Most of the men had facial hair. They all carried weapons. One had a shotgun strapped over his shoulder like it was a backpack. Perhaps twenty-five in all, they rode slowly, surveying the sides of the road as they went. It was clear they were looking for something. Or someone.

Nolan quickly realized there was no time left to hide.

"*I'd lower that rifle!*" he shouted to Drextel over the roar of the engines. He made a hand-lowering motion. Drextel eventually got the idea.

Nolan stood up straight as the bikers approached. There were more than a few bike gangs in Indianapolis. In his time working narcotics, Nolan had crossed paths with most of them. Some were criminal assholes, sure, but some could surprise you and be downright friendly. Nolan had a feeling that his own celebrity status likely colored the positive reactions he often got. Bikers who remembered his time playing ball often wanted to be "down" with him. Get their picture taken and such. (Once, off the clock, Nolan had accepted an invitation to follow a group back to their clubhouse for drinks. Aside from signing a basketball and doing several rounds of shots, Nolan had almost no remaining memories of that evening.)

This gang, however, he did not recognize. Nolan looked in vain for a familiar patch or insignia.

The bikers slowed as the feasting zombies came into view. Then they slowed more when they saw Nolan and Drextel. A few brandished their guns. Others simply telegraphed icy stares from above their wild mustaches.

The lead biker—a huge, round man with fat fingers full of rings—raised a hand and pulled to a stop in front of Nolan. The bikers behind him followed suit. For a moment, they did not turn off their bikes. The noise was deafening. (From the corner of his eye, Nolan saw that Drextel had dropped his rifle entirely and had put his fingers in his ears.) The bikers appeared to be a hard bunch, but Nolan saw recognition on more than a few faces as they looked him over. Eventually, the lead biker killed his engine and stepped off his hog. The others copied him.

The round leader walked past Nolan as if he weren't there. He examined the remains of the corpse on the picnic table, along with the attendant zombies. Then, after a few moments, he went back to Nolan.

"What part did you all have in this?" the biker asked, gesturing to the table.

"We just got here," Nolan said, indicating the ATV. "We're looking for some teenage kids who got lost."

"Yeah, you are," the biker said, as if he did not quite believe it. "That was our man, on the table. He got took last night."

"Do you know who did it?" Nolan asked.

The biker looked up into Nolan's face and grinned.

"We might have some idea," the biker answered.

Another member of the bike gang approached. He had a thick grey beard and an almost unbelievably large forehead.

"I know you," Forehead said to Nolan. "The college boy. The one who got drunk and crashed his car and killed a guy."

Nolan understood that this hectoring was a test. It was also a show of power. In days like these, the checks and balances that might have kept a bunch of bikers from acting like a real gang were long gone. They knew it too. A whiskered geezer with an enormous brow could be the most powerful man on the scene if he was part of an armed group.

"That's what they tell me," Nolan replied evenly. "Some people, anyway."

Forehead smiled confidently.

Someone fired a handgun. Then another. Nolan turned and saw dismounted bikers pointing their guns at the zombies who surrounded the picnic table. They opened up on the zombies like it was target practice. Nolan didn't think they were shooting to kill. (They had to know by now that a headshot was required.) They were shooting for the hell of it. They made the zombies twist and dance and, eventually, fall under a hail of bullets. The bikers continued to shoot the zombies even as they writhed on the ground. One biker took a fireman's axe off the back of his bike and descended on the prone undead with a murderous fury. It seemed cathartic. These men—and a few women, too—had tensions that needed releasing.

"Where you all coming from?" Nolan asked.

"We're headed north," the round leader said, not really answering the question. "You should be too, if you've got any sense, basketball man."

"Oh, really?" Nolan said.

The biker gestured to the carnage over at the picnic table.

"Them things. They's joining into big groups. The whole damn south of the state is lousy with 'em. Seen whole fields full. Eat up small towns all at once."

"Where are you headed, north?" Nolan asked.

The biker did not immediately respond. Forehead crept over and whispered into his ear. The bikers looked at one another and smiled. Then they looked back up at Nolan.

"Headed up to Indy," said the leader of the biker gang.

"Oh yeah?" said Nolan.

"Yeah," the biker said. "And guess what?"

"What?" Nolan asked warily.

"You're coming with us."

21

Kesha, Steven, Madison, Sara, and Tara emerged from the twilit woods just as the sun was beginning to disappear from the horizon. Darkness was only minutes away, but, for the moment, the sunset lit up the western half of the sky like a brilliant trail of neon lava. The way before them opened onto cornfields with a small white farmhouse just beyond. The house did not appear inhabited.

The teenagers paused for a moment, considering what to do.

"You want to just go up and ring the doorbell?" Kesha asked.

Madison did not immediately answer. Sara and Tara exchanged a look of grave concern.

"I should go," Steven volunteered.

"What?" Kesha asked. "Just because you're a boy?"

He shook his head.

"There's no nice way to say this, so I'm just gonna say it," Steven answered. "I'm the only one here who doesn't sound like a city slicker."

Kesha smiled. The rest of the girls did not disagree.

"But maybe you should keep that hunting rifle handy," Steven added. "Kind of cover me, yeah?"

Tara, who was holding the weapon, nodded seriously.

With the girls waiting at the edge of the woods, Steven carefully approached the farmhouse and knocked on the front door. There was no response. The house stayed dark.

Steven tried the handle and found that the door opened easily. Kesha watched as he called "Hello!" Nobody answered. Steven disappeared into the house, then reappeared moments later. He motioned for the girls to join him.

With considerable effort, they helped Madison cross the field and make her way to the farmhouse door.

"Nobody inside," Steven announced. "The fridge is full, though. Might as well have at it. Everything inside is gonna go bad anyway."

This was what they wanted to hear.

The girls unceremoniously deposited Madison in Steven's arms, then made a mad dash for the kitchen.

"Oof," Madison said as the handoff was made.

"Almost there," Steven said to her. "I'll help you the rest of the way."

Tara and Sara raided the simple but fully stocked fridge. Kesha made for a jar of cookies next to the kitchen sink.

"Omigod," said Sara, drinking straight from a container of lukewarm orange juice. "This tastes so good. I'm so starving. I could eat just a raw egg, without cooking it."

"I so know what you mean," echoed Tara. "I'm like an animal right now."

"Totally," Sara agreed.

Kesha was on her fourth butter cookie by the time Steven and Madison loped into the room. Kesha held out the jar. Both readily accepted.

The inside of the house was ghostly and dark. It had a lived-in smell—not bad, necessarily, but as if many, many people had recently called it home. The light from the sunset made the windows on the west side glisten and gleam.

The girls settled in to eat, but after just a few cookies, Steven left to explore the second floor. After a few minutes, he returned with two flashlights and a prescription bottle. He tossed a light to Kesha, and the bottle to Madison.

"Painkillers," he said to her. "Should probably start with just one."

"Okay," Madison said, holding it up to read the label.

"I think I saw a shed on the other side of the house," Steven said. "I'm going to go have a look."

"I'll come, too," Kesha said. She pocketed a few more cookies and followed him outside.

Sure enough, on the other side of the farmhouse was a tiny barn with a gambrel roof. It had a latch on the front with a padlock, but it had not been engaged and simply dangled there. Steven pulled the latch and pried the door open. Inside was some hay, garden tools (mostly rakes), spiders and spider webs, and a rusted, puke-orange 1959 Chevrolet Bel Air. The car took up all of Steven and Kesha's attention. It was almost comically long, and had raised fins just above the taillights. It was so dusty and encrusted with insects that it looked like a part of the barn itself.

"Woo-ee," Steven managed. "Don't see many of them anymore."

"Yeah," said Kesha, easing her way around the side of the enormous automobile. "It looks about a hundred years old. Like something from a museum."

"Clean it up, and it could look mighty fine," Steven said. "Run a sponge over it. Shine up that chrome. It'd look better'n hell."

Kesha only nodded.

Steven tried the passenger's side door. The great metal beast was amusingly ancient. Steven had to depress the handle hard just to get it unlatched, and when he pulled the door it was so heavy he thought for a moment that it might be rusted shut.

"Don't make 'em like this anymore," he pronounced, sliding into the long, shared front seat.

Moments later, Steven had located a set of keys from the glove box. He scooted over behind the driver's seat. Kesha didn't expect anything at all to happen when Steven turned the key. When—against, it seemed, all reason and experience—the great machine roared to life, Kesha jumped an inch and fled from the small barn with her fingers in her ears. Steven put the Chevrolet into reverse and eased it out of the barn, its ancient brakes and rotors squealing all the way. The engine sounded more like a lawnmower than something you'd drive around on the street.

Steven was grinning. Kesha smiled back, but kept her fingers in her ears.

Then something. A sound even above the antediluvian sputter from this relic of old Detroit. A piercing shriek that Kesha heard loud and clear, even with her index fingers stuck deep inside her ear canals. It came once, then came again.

Kesha looked back toward the house. The first thing she saw was that a cellar door at the side of the house had been opened wide. A bloody trail led up to it and through the door. Then a window at the side of the farmhouse abruptly shattered as the stoneware cookie jar Kesha had been holding just minutes before went flying through it.

Without a second thought, Kesha grabbed a rusty rake from just inside the barn and took off. She bounded up the steps—almost losing her balance on the blood underfoot—and careened through the farmhouse door and into the twilight maze of rooms inside. She heard movement and high-pitched shrieks of alarm. Pottery and plates had been shattered on the floor.

Kesha moved with the rake held high like a medieval weapon, tines out.

"Madison?" she called. "Guys?"

Kesha rounded a corner and stopped. She could now see into the kitchen. Sara and Tara were both slumped face down into the linoleum. There were three other figures in the kitchen with them. One was a giant, hulking man in dirty jeans and a work shirt with sleeves rolled up over enormous arms. The other two figures were smaller, female, and wore short-sleeved dresses that went almost to the ground. All three of them had the look of the undead upon them—colorless skin, milky white eyes, and bodies that moved like horrible automatons rather than humans. Two of the things were bent over the bodies of Sara and Tara, ripping long strips of flesh from the girls' necks and faces. The third thing—the larger one—was sniffing the air like a canine wandering after a far-off scent.

Kesha retreated back into the hallway.

Then a cry came from a different part of the house. It was followed by an: "Oh, shit!" The voice was quite distinctly that of Madison Burleson.

"Madison!" Kesha cried. "Madison, where are you?"

She was answered by approaching footsteps scrambling toward her. Kesha heard something glass fall over and break as Madison bumped into it. The approaching gait had the familiar clump-step, clump-step of someone with an injured ankle. The broken gait got closer, and suddenly Madison burst around the corner of the hallway. She smashed up against Kesha, almost knocking her over.

"For god's sake, run!" Madison shouted.

They ran.

Halfway down the hallway, Kesha detected another set of footsteps behind them, small and scuttling. When they reached the door, Kesha looked back and saw a toddler with pigtails nipping at Madison's heels. Because of Madison's injury, the two seemed almost evenly matched. The child was clearly undead—its face twisted with a bloodthirsty anger no child could muster in life. Blood dripped from its mouth. Human flesh was already under its nails.

Kesha let Madison lope past, then held out the rake in a fixed position like a pikeman facing a cavalry charge. The tiny zombie raced forward with no hesitation, its pigtails flopping wildly. The tines of Kesha's rake curved slightly at the end so the zombie was not impaled, but Kesha hit it in the chest and pushed as hard as she could. The thing went careening back down the hallway on its bottom. Kesha dropped the rake and ran.

Outside the house, Steven was standing next to the idling Chevrolet.

"What's happened?" Steven was asking.

"Get in and drive!" Kesha called.

Steven was confused, but obeyed. Kesha helped Madison into the backseat of the ancient Chevy. She closed the heavy metal door behind them with a loud *clunk*.

"What about Sara and Tara?" Steven asked, looking into the backseat.

Kesha just shook her head no.

"I don't know what happened," Madison said. "Those people, they came out of nowhere."

Kesha looked through the Chevrolet window at the storm cellar. In the dying light, she saw twine on the inside handles of the cellar door. They had locked themselves in, Kesha realized. Perhaps for protection from the roving undead. Or perhaps they were already bitten—already infected—and they had sought to protect others from the monsters they knew they would become. (In either case, they had failed.)

"Jesus Christ," Steven cried. A small girl with a bloody face had opened the door of the house and was charging toward the Chevrolet.

"Drive, Steven," Kesha said.

"Where?" he asked, turning on the ancient headlights. Only one of them worked, and it was very dim.

"North," Kesha told him. "Just go north."

Steven put the car into drive and they bounced across the farmyard on rusted, squeaking shocks. A driveway took them out across the field, running like a rut through tall rows of corn beyond. Eventually, it intersected with a gravel drive. Steven stepped on the gas. After two minutes, the gravel road intersected with Indiana State Road 57.

There was just enough sunlight left for Steven to tell which way was north.

That was the way he went.

★★★

The ancient Chevrolet felt like it might die at any moment.

Steven drove slowly, never edging much beyond thirty miles an hour. They pressed deeper into the all-encompassing black-ness, feeling like a lighthouse on some ancient, lonely shore. The countryside was completely without power. At one point, Kesha thought she glimpsed two bright flashlights bobbing in different directions atop a distant hill. They disappeared as quickly as they had come into view.

Nobody said anything for a long time.

Madison took a cell phone out of her pocket and tried to make a call. It was obvious right away that it was still broken. Even the date and time were no longer functional. After a few moments of frustration, she put the thing away. Madison dug in her pocket and pulled out the prescription pill bottle. She shook out two oblong, white pills and swallowed them without water.

"Where do you think we're headed?" Kesha wondered.

"We have to go to Indianapolis," Madison said. "We have to reach my father. He'll still be at the capitol, probably. With all the horrible people he works with. That fuckslime chief of staff,

and his kiss-ass secretaries . . . and that basketball-playing policeman he sends to do his dirty work . . . and—"

"James Nolan?" Kesha interjected.

"That's right," Madison answered. "How do you know
about him?"

Kesha slowly realized that in recalling her adventures to
Madison—and the late Sara and Tara—she had not described her
rescuer beyond saying he was a police officer.

"Umm, everybody knows he works for your dad," Kesha
lied. "He's James Nolan. He's famous."

"I guess," Madison said distantly.

Then a thought appeared to occur to the governor's daughter. She perked up a bit.

"Do you want to know a secret about James Nolan?" Madison asked. "Something that only, like, three people and my dad
know?"

"Um, okay," Kesha said. "But how do *you* know it?"

Madison frowned as if this quibble was off-putting.

"Look, do you want to know the secret or not?" Madison
asked.

Kesha nodded.

Madison looked up to the front seat where Steven sat
behind the wheel. Then she leaned into Kesha's ear and whispered, placing her fingers over her mouth to eliminate even the
chance of Steven reading her lips. As Madison spoke, Kesha's
jaw dropped.

"No way . . . " Kesha found herself saying as Madison with-
drew back to her side of the seat.

"You don't have to believe me," she said with a self-satisfied smile. "But it's still true."

"Jesus," said Kesha. "That's just horrible."

"Now do you see why we have to get to Indianapolis?" Madison asked her. "Now do you see why I have to stop my father?"

"Yeah," Kesha said, dumbstruck, staring into the back of the seat in front of her. "I think I do."

22

Inside his tiny office in a dark corner of the capitol building, Doug Huggins read by candlelight. He had discovered a cache of taper candles in a back dining room. Though certainly a fire risk—especially in the cramped confines of his paper-filled office—Huggins thought them preferable to running down the power on his remaining flashlights. Since the generators had failed, the damn things had become like gold. So had batteries.

Turning each page as quietly as he could, Huggins pored through the document from Burundi Petroleum that he had found in the governor's waste basket. ("Document" was hardly adequate, thought Huggins. The damn thing was close to *War and Peace*.) Huggins's flipping of pages was frequent, because his policy as a reader was to skip ahead whenever he didn't understand something. It was increasingly clear that most of the massive document was going to fall into that category.

Still, between the scientific jargon he did not understand, and the lawyerly posturing he also did not understand, Huggins began to get a deep and horrible *gist*.

And it was so, so much worse than he had expected.

Sure, Huggins knew about the governor's deals with BP. Every Hoosier governor made them. Yet Huggins had been under the impression that in his dialogues with BP, Burleson had chosen to err on the side of protecting his state. The side of caution. Burleson had spoken of special protocols that could eliminate contamination if it ever occurred. If a disaster resulted in the release of pollutants into Hoosiers' drinking water.

Yet the thick document in his hands postulated another reality entirely.

What had happened was not complicated. With Hank Burleson's blessing, BP had begun intentionally introducing a new chemical in their refineries up in Whiting. Trace elements of the chemical would make their way into the drinking water that flowed down through the rest of the state. BP didn't want to say what it was—or even give it a name—and the amount that showed up when you turned on the tap was very small. Parts per trillion. Tiny, tiny bits. What were the side effects of these tiny bits? BP thought probably nothing. So did their lawyers. However, even if there *were* to be negative effects—to Indiana's flora or fauna or, God forbid, populace—BP had a contingency plan. Lab tests had shown that the introduction of a few natural phytochemicals could categorically make the new compound inert. Flooding Indiana's waterways with a few truckloads of phytochemicals would erase all traces of this new mystery compound almost instantly. However, it would also render the state's water supply practically useless to BP for refining purposes.

Burundi Petroleum's case to Burleson had been simple. In a few years, our scientists will know exactly what this stuff is and how it works. They'll also know about all the possible side effects . . . which will probably be nothing. But what we know now is that it *does* work in our refining process—boosting productivity and profits—and we want to keep using it. What we'll do is keep trucks full of these phytochemicals at the ready just in case anything happens. Does that sound good to you? Because if it doesn't, we can always move our refineries over to Michigan or to any number of states down on the Gulf Coast that are hurting for jobs and investment right now. And you can be the governor who built a state's entire persona around being friendly to business, and then couldn't hold on to the biggest company he had.

So Burleson had said yes. By all means, yes. Keep using your new chemical. To his way of thinking, Indiana was just being an early adopter. BP knew what it was doing. It had lots of smart scientists in charge of this. There weren't going to be cows giving green milk and babies born with three heads. Maybe a few people who were gonna get cancer anyway would get it a little faster. (They were probably smokers, anyhow.) Besides, in five or ten years, every refinery in the country was going to be using this new chemical. Hell, getting refineries in Indiana to use it first would be a feather in the governor's cap, especially when he was evaluated *at a national level.* It showed he talked the talk and walked the walk when it came to letting businesses grow in an unfettered marketplace, and so on.

But now that Huggins could read the details for himself, it was clear that the oil company had made several notable omissions in their initial dialogue with the governor. First of all, it was clear that the side effects were not unknown. They *were* known. And they were horrible. Skin cells coming back to life in labs. Bits of flesh on Petri dishes twitching or even *crawling out of the dish.* Unexplainable movement in all sorts of dead tissue. (It had been concealed beneath layers and layers of doublespeak and lawyering, but there were some things that you just couldn't hide with a technical term. Dead skin strips inching around like inchworms was one of them.)

The only real unknown for BP involved the consistency of the "events" in question. Most of the time, dead tissue did *not* reanimate, even if you soaked it in gallons of this new compound for months. The reanimation was only taking place in very rare cases, and usually just for a few seconds. Out of nowhere, a tiny pocket of human skin cells in a huge sample cluster would start doing the Electric Slide for no discernible reason. Then, as soon as the researchers rushed over to take a look, it would stop as quickly as it had started.

All of this did not give Huggins confidence that the phyto-chemicals would do anything at all to render the mystery compound inert. What if it just made it take longer for the effects to show up? Conclusive tests had never been performed. Huggins couldn't believe that BP thought their ER-19 protocol could definitively make things okay again.

Or, more accurately, like things had never happened at all.

For, as Huggins wound his way toward the end of the document, it seemed clearer and clearer that the document said nothing existed. No agreements. No compound. No nothing. It was as if the heavy manuscript Huggins clutched in his arms insisted that, legally speaking, he felt no weight at all. In the eyes of the law, any release of phytochemicals—while authorized 100 percent by the governor—would not be connected to the new, unnamed compound that had just been described for hundreds of pages. The governor was giving BP the right to flood the water supply at points all around the state with truckloads of these antidotes, without acknowledging that they were an antidote for anything. BP was held liable for nothing. And yet the state had authorized them to do everything. (Really, "everything" was the word. The phytochemicals were the tip of the iceberg. The document seemed to say that if BP found it necessary to do anything else to the waterways, it could now do so. Total freedom. Zero accountability.)

Suddenly, the door to Huggins's office was thrown open. The resulting breeze blew out the desk of candles quite entirely. Instinctively, Huggins covered the purloined manuscript with his hands.

The figure in the doorway was not the governor. It was a police officer with bags under his eyes whom Huggins had never seen before. The man was young. Probably. (As the crisis wore on, it was harder and harder to determine anybody's age. Being up for days could add years to your timeline.)

"Mister Huggins?" said the sleepy officer.

"Yes?" Huggins said, still covering the pages on his desk like a teenager caught with a Playboy.

"Some of the security team said I should get you," the young man said. "There's something going on outside that you need to see."

After locking the manuscript in his desk, Huggins followed the young officer down the hallway and out the front entrance of the capitol building. The moment Huggins sucked in his first breath of early-evening air, he could tell something was wrong.

"The fires . . . have they gotten *closer*?" Huggins asked the officer.

They smelled like they were just down the block. Huggins thought that maybe—despite the already warm night—he could feel their added heat in the atmosphere.

"I think so, yes," the officer said, unsure of himself.

Huggins looked around for someone who could give solid answers.

There were police, military, and other staffers standing on the street directly in front of the capitol building. All of them were looking south. Huggins joined them.

Although the darkness of the buildings around them was utter and complete, Huggins saw great ripples of red-orange fire glinting off the polished windows of structures to the south. There was also a constant roar. A long, low bass note like the noise before a game in a football stadium. A *full* football stadium.

"Are those . . . zombies down there?" Huggins asked in mounting terror.

The officer shook his head.

"Mostly no," he said. "Mostly, it's just people."

"*People?*" Huggins said, as if it made no sense. "What on earth are people doing here?"

The young policeman shrugged.

Huggins took another look south down Capitol Avenue, toward the fires and the distant roar. People. That sound was people. Why had they gathered here? What were they hoping for?

Huggins scratched his head.

"Well . . . is this what I was supposed to see?" Huggins asked the officer.

The officer shrugged and said, "I *guess* so."

Huggins was not satisfied.

"Who told you to come get me?" Huggins demanded.

"Deputy Chief Jones did," the officer answered. "Actually, he didn't say to get you. He said to get Governor Burleson. But we couldn't find him, so then he said to get you."

"And where is Deputy Chief Jones?" Huggins pressed.

The officer did not respond, but gestured down the avenue toward the noise and firelight beyond the Green Zone.

Huggins strode across the street to where a group of police officers with chevrons on their shoulders huddled confidentially at the entrance to a parking garage. Nobody was the deputy chief, and they too pointed him south. Huggins drifted down Capitol Avenue, walking in the very middle of the street. This, coupled with the nearby municipal vehicles, gave him the feeling of being in some sort of strange parade.

Huggins reached an elevated walkway above the street connecting the Indiana Convention Center to a shopping mall. The National Guard had selected this as the southernmost border of the Green Zone. Several soldiers with sniper rifles huddled in the darkness atop the elevated walkway, and several more stood directly underneath it. A fire truck, a pair of military Humvees, and several personnel carriers had been parked just past that, blocking off the street. On the near side of this barricade were other assorted soldiers, government staffers, and city workers, each armed with precious flashlights. Several IMPD police cars were also parked nearby.

Huggins approached the most important-looking group of people, and from them selected a heavyset black man in an IMPD uniform.

"Deputy Chief Jones?" Huggins tried.

The man looked at Huggins and nodded. Huggins had not turned on his flashlight and was harder to see. The man hit him in the face with a bright blue beam.

"Ah, Chief of Staff Huggins," the deputy police chief said. "Where is the governor?"

"I have no idea where he is," Huggins said.

Another uniformed police officer stepped forward and shouted: "We need to speak to the governor, and we need to speak to him *now!*"

Huggins put up his hands.

"Whoa," Huggins said. "What's going on here?"

"What's going on here?" said the deputy chief. "We've got what looks like half the city massed on the other side of the Green Zone—here, and at about five other points all around downtown."

"Why?" Huggins said. "What do they want?"

"I have no damn idea," said the deputy chief. "Maybe they just came downtown to cause trouble. Maybe they want the lights back on and the hospitals up and running again. Maybe they want your boss to *do his damn job.*"

"Are they being violent?" Huggins asked. "I see fires."

"Not so far," the deputy chief said cautiously. "Those fires are for light and heat. But that could change at any moment. If these people lose their heads and charge, there's not a damn thing we can do. Even if the governor ordered us to shoot them, I don't think we have that many bullets between us."

It hit Huggins that they might be on the verge of something very terrible and very imminent. In an instant, he was no longer in the lone outpost of safety, waiting for the rest of the countryside to slough off its zombies and come back to civilization . . . instead, he was vulnerable. Some enormous, idiot animal was sleeping just outside his gates. And if he—someone, anyone— made the wrong move, the beast was liable to get angry.

"I think I understand the situation . . ." Huggins said with mounting dread. "I'll go get the governor."

"Just be sure you get *somebody*," said the deputy chief, and turned his attention back toward the mass of people south of the Green Zone.

Huggins took off running toward the capitol building as fast as he could.

23

The nondescript one-story bar that served as the headquarters of the Inlaws Motorcycle Club was located at the ass-end of Southeastern Avenue on the south side of Indianapolis. Under normal circumstances, to reach it most expeditiously from south of the city, a commuter would head north on State Road 37, then jog east for a spell on I-465, and then finally turn onto Southeastern Avenue.

But no part of this was normal.

As Nolan and Drextel clung to the back-fat of different bikers seated in front of them, both men noticed that the convoy of Harleys was taking an approach to the city that seemed more than a bit indirect. As they neared County Line Road, the bikers turned onto side streets where modest homes on modest lots alternated with farms and cornfields. It was so eerily, blisteringly dark that Nolan was only able to assure himself of their location via the odd street sign glimpsed in a headlight's glare.

Though technically residential, these streets were hilly and wild, and the convoy of bikers moved across them like an iridescent metal caterpillar. Again and again, Nolan's gut told him they couldn't be this close to the city. He could still see stars. This felt like cornfields downstate. But again and again, familiar buildings and landmarks loomed into view and proved his gut wrong. This was the place.

Except it wasn't.

Lit only by the moon, the city looked dead. Like the grave marker you might erect on the ruins of a previous civilization. This was a monument. A remembrance. The ghost of a Midwestern metropolis that once had been. Not the town that Nolan knew.

As the bikes penetrated deeper and deeper into Indianapolis, Nolan noted that the darkened windows and doorways around them were alive with movement. Furtive movement, but movement. Then, before long, the furtiveness seemed to fade. Nolan started seeing pedestrians out on the open streets. Lots of pedestrians. Had they come here from other parts of the state, seeking sanctuary and safety (or at least electrical outlets with power in them)? And what had they found? This dead dark city where the residents skulked in shadows.

The bikers drove on. One of the winding back roads finally went underneath I-465 and intersected with Southeastern Avenue. The bikers turned and headed into the city, toward downtown. They passed modest blue-collar homes with well-kept lawns where residents—most of them armed—milled about and chatted in the starlight. When the bikers came into view (or, Nolan considered, earshot; for people heard them long before they saw them), these residents waved, gave a thumbs-up, or even lifted their guns into the air. One woman in a ratty housecoat actually burst into applause.

Were these bikers pillars of their community, Nolan wondered? Did they help residents along Southeastern Avenue locate lost dogs and sell Girl Scout cookies? Probably not, Nolan thought. Probably they were just bikers who mostly drank and fought and fucked, and sometimes moved a little meth around. No, the locals were cheering just because the bikers still existed. All the other entities and institutions had fallen away under the stress of this situation. Yet the bikers had survived. They were maybe the one familiar thing that had endured. Their organization, such as it was, had continued to function. They were what was left.

The bikers pulled to a halt in front of the wretched, unmarked tavern that served as their headquarters. Candles flickered in the grimy windows, and people milled about inside. A long row of Harleys was parked in front. Nolan's group pulled up and made it longer.

Nolan was exhausted, hungry, and had bugs in his teeth, but other than this was basically fine. Drextel said nothing, but appeared to be likewise no worse for wear.

Somewhat disconcertingly, Nolan realized that he was the center of attention. (Many of the bikers were as round as they were tall. Spherical, or at least ovoid, men who lived their lives close to the ground. Nolan stuck out above them like a sore thumb. A very tall sore thumb. And then there was the recognition. He could see it on their faces. There was something else too. Something more than just seeing a celebrity. Something like hope.)

Nolan and Drextel were ushered into the squalid bar. Someone had nailed a rotting zombie's head to the door, with a long coffin nail right through the forehead. Despite himself, Nolan smiled at this.

Inside, the headquarters of the Inlaws revealed itself to be smoky and serious. There was a long wooden bar, a pool table, and a number of chairs and tables that did not match. The walls were decorated with posters of hot rods and girls that nobody had bothered to frame. The bikers were obviously using whatever candles they could find to light the place. Many of the flames that flickered on every flat surface (except the floor) arose from scented candles. For Nolan, it was like walking into a perfume store.

The head bikers huddled in the back of the bar, talking in low tones. Nolan was offered a lukewarm beer, which he declined. After a few minutes, Nolan began to see gestures in his direction from out of the huddle. It was clear that he was the lone topic of conversation.

"What do you wanna do?" Drextel said out of the corner of his mouth, sidling up beside Nolan.

"I don't like being anyone's hostage," Nolan said quietly. "We'll see what happens. At the very least, I'll make sure they let you go."

"You kidding?" the bookish editor replied. "Whatever happens, I'm stickin' with you . . . at least until we get back to my neighborhood."

Nolan nodded to indicate he understood.

The huddle of bikers at the back seemed to have concluded their immediate business. They adjourned in all directions, and a number headed straight to Nolan. The police sergeant let an unflinching scowl come to his face, one he usually reserved for the arrest of a particularly unsavory character.

The round leader of the biker gang stepped up to Nolan, staring hard into his eyes. Nolan returned the stare.

"Mister Nolan," the biker said. "We need some words with you."

"That's good, because I need to have some words with *you*. Where do you people get off kidnapping me? Or kidnapping my friend Drextel, for that matter? Do you know what we were doing down in those woods? In the middle of all of this shit, Drextel's daughter is missing. I know her. She's a good girl. She's scared right now, and the only thing she wants is to get back to her father. And now you've brought him up here to Indy, a hundred miles from her."

The biker, confident and untouchable, stared up into Nolan's eyes without flinching.

"I don't know what you expect me to do for you," Nolan continued. "I don't know if you think I can make your little gang important because I used to play basketball, but that doesn't matter. There are bigger problems in this state right now."

"I know that, son," the biker said. (Despite himself, Nolan smiled at this; he had not been addressed as "son" for many years.) "That's why we need you."

Nolan wrinkled his brow and tilted his head to the side.

"What are you talking about?"

"How long you been downstate, son?" the biker said.

"Since it started," Nolan told the biker. "Since yesterday afternoon. I think I was one of the first people to see the zombies when they started coming up. I was in a cave."

"Well, let me fill you the fuck in on what's happening up here," said the biker. "This city is halfway to hell. These things—walkers, zombies, whatever you call 'em—they've been massing into big groups that you can't stop. You wouldn't believe how deadly they can be in a herd. You see one or two? You can run away, sure. But you wander into the middle of a group of three hundred? There's no getting out. Everywhere you run, you run into a zombie. Before you know it you're exhausted, and then they move in and rip you apart. I've seen it."

"So?" said Nolan, "What does that have to do with . . ."

"Listen," said the biker, raising his hands to silence the tall policeman. "You're not hearing me. These groups—these *battalions* of zombies—they're massing in the countryside and heading into the cities. They're attracted to people. I don't know how or why, but they are. Maybe they can smell us on the wind. They know where Indy is, and they're headed here."

Nolan opened his mouth a little, but did not speak. He wondered—if the things *were* headed toward Indiana's capital city—why on earth the bikers had taken him there.

"The government has made a safe zone down on the circle," the biker continued. "They have guns and tanks and hummers and everything. Totally secure."

"That's great," Nolan said. "So swallow your pride, leave your guns at home, and get down there."

The biker shook his head.

"You don't understand," the biker said. "They're not letting anybody in."

"What?" Nolan said. "That can't be right. Maybe they just turned away some of your men because you look a little rough around the edges. You've gotta be used to that . . ."

The biker's stare was unwavering. In his ten years on the force, Nolan had learned to recognize cues that could indicate when someone was probably lying. The biker did not show any of them.

"I didn't believe it till I saw it myself," the biker said. "They've got people camped out all around downtown. Women and children. People have come into the city to get away from the zombies. But now the zombies are coming, too."

"And the Army's doing nothing?" Nolan said. "I can't believe that."

"It's not the Army, exactly," the biker said. "Maybe a few National Guard reservists. But they've got downtown sealed off. I watched them turn away doctors. Honest-to-God doctors in scrubs with stethoscopes around their fuckin' necks."

Nolan studied the man's face. How did this mad tale have such a ring of truth? Did the biker's unkempt beard and broken blood vessels conceal the tells that might otherwise betray a liar? Yet Nolan did not doubt him. Even if he were lying, he at least *believed* he was telling the truth.

"If that's the case," Nolan said, speaking slowly, "I'd like to go and see it for myself."

The biker smiled, revealing a set of glistening white dentures.

"I was hoping you'd say that."

24

The Chevrolet Bel Air slowly crept north along State Road 37. Steven kept it near the shoulder, just in case someone came barreling up behind them doing the limit. He needn't have worried.

The highway was dark and still. Most of the cars and trucks they encountered were empty, abandoned by the side of the road. Steven carefully circumvented these, staring hard into the windows and windshields. The people inside were never alive.

The operational cars were usually off at a distance. It seemed they took pains to keep it that way. At this point in the game— whatever the game was—running into strangers was a roll of the dice. When one car sighted another, they usually moved away to avoid a meeting. Steven did this, too.

Green signs by the side of the road soon announced the approach of Indianapolis. Thirty miles to go. Then fifteen. Unbelievably, it appeared they actually might make it. (The ancient Chevy's gas gauge showed the tank half full, but it had not moved since they had started their journey.) It was closing on ten in the evening by the time they reached the city limits.

"It's not there!" Madison cried.

Madison had been silent for most of the ride, knocked out by the pills she'd swallowed. Kesha thought she needed the rest. Fleeing the zombies in the farmhouse where Sara and Tara had died had not done her ankle any favors. It was now swelled to near-grapefruit proportions.

"The city's not there," Madison reiterated.

"It's just dark," Kesha told her. "All the lights are out, so we can't see it. It's an optical illusion."

Madison sat up and stared through the dusty windshield as if she could not quite believe her eyes.

"It's like the whole city just fell into a giant pit," Madison said.

"Yeah, but Kesha's right; it didn't," Steven said. "You're just not used to seeing it dark. Nobody is."

The Chevy crept into the strange, lightless netherworld that used to be Indianapolis. Now and then they passed a landmark that was familiar to Kesha, but the effect was hardly comforting. She'd wanted to return to the city and find her father, yet this wasn't the place she had imagined in her mind. This was another Indianapolis. An alternate Indianapolis. Where the streets were dark, you smelled fire on the wind, and the atmosphere was ghostly.

They headed north toward the capitol, and began to see other people on the sides of the road. Some kept to the shadows. Others wandered slowly and silently across lawns and sidewalks, apparently unconcerned by the prospect of being detected. Were they humans or zombies—Kesha wondered—or maybe a little of both? In the glow from the Chevy's single, dim headlight it was difficult to tell.

"It's my dad's doing," Madison said icily. "He's fucked the whole place up."

"Maybe it will be better closer to downtown," Kesha said.

"Or worse," Madison returned.

Kesha had trouble picturing how that could be possible. This was a half-empty wasteland with strange men and zombies creeping in the shadows.

Guided by Madison and Kesha, Steven steered the ancient car under 465 and east to Meridian Street. Then they turned north and headed straight for the capitol.

"Just stay on this road," Kesha told him. "Stay on this the whole way."

"Got it," said Steven.

Soon the houses and businesses on the passenger side of the car gave way to a sprawling green field. A small white sign announced the presence of Concordia Cemetery. After several hundred feet, the field became covered with headstones.

"Oh shit," cried Steven. "This can't be good."

Kesha scanned the dark folds of the burying ground, but did not detect any movement.

Madison, who was also looking, said, "I don't see any zombies out there. Is this a *new* cemetery?"

"Maybe the zombies can't get through their coffins," Kesha said. "Or they did but they've wandered away by now."

"Look!" Steven cried. "What's that?"

Kesha looked. There was a small group of human figures near what appeared to be the entrance to the cemetery. They were standing in a half circle.

"Maybe you should pull to the other side of the road," Madison advised. "Just to be—"

Before the governor's daughter could complete her sentence, the Chevrolet began to sputter like an old man out of breath. The engine stopped, started, and stopped again. The coiled springs underneath the seats creaked with every change in velocity. The lone headlight flickered once and went out.

Kesha held her breath for a full ten seconds, willing this to be some temporary hiccup. Steven emitted frustrated sighs as he fumbled with the keys and depressed the gas pedal. Despite his best efforts, the engine would not turn over.

Steven put his head down on the steering wheel for a moment, defeated. Then he turned around to the back seat.

"Can we go the rest of the way on foot?" he asked.

"I guess so," Madison said. "As long as you can still carry me."

"Guys . . . I'm not so worried about that right now," Kesha said.

The car had stopped less than twenty yards from the cemetery gates, where the mysterious crowd still lingered.

Kesha had the two flashlights Steven had found inside the farmhouse. They were now on the seat beside her. Madison grabbed one of them and turned it on.

"Hey!" Kesha said. "What the hell are you doing?"

"It's not like they didn't see us coming . . . and didn't hear this rust-bucket die," Madison said. "Steven, can you open my door and put me on your shoulders again?"

Steven dutifully obeyed. Kesha rolled her eyes and turned on the other flashlight.

As if in answer, a bright white beam appeared from the group standing at the cemetery gates.

"At least we know they're human," Madison said as Steven hoisted her onto his shoulders. "Unless those *things* learned how to use flashlights."

Kesha didn't think they had. When Madison was sufficiently secure atop Steven, they made their way up the shoulder of the road to the cemetery gates. As they neared, more flashlights clicked on. The beams probed Kesha first, then lingered on Madison and Steven. Kesha pointed her own flashlight at the ground.

"Hello there," Kesha called, giving a wave she hoped looked friendly.

"Pssst, hey," Madison whispered. "Don't tell them who I am."

"What?" Kesha said.

"Just don't," Madison snapped.

Kesha thought Madison was being silly, but decided to comply.

The group in front of the gates looked like hunters—some old, some middle-aged, and some almost as young as Kesha. Each held a rifle and a flashlight. More than a few had donned blaze-orange hats and vests. They looked absolutely exhausted. Some leaned on their guns for support, or against each other. One lolled against the cemetery fence in full catnap mode.

Kesha smelled smoke and, beneath it, something foul, like burning nylon. Inside the gates of the cemetery was a giant pile of dead zombies, each carefully shot through the forehead. The pile had been set on fire some time ago, but the bodies had not burned very well. They needed gasoline to do it right, Kesha thought. But it had become too precious a commodity to waste on the undead. Now the pile smoldered in fits and starts.

"Howdy," said a man from the group. He had long white muttonchop sideburns and a barrel-chest, like an old-time boxer.

"Hi," said Kesha. "Are you guys keeping the graveyard safe?"

"Trying to," said one of the young men closer to Kesha's age. "When they come up, we put them back in the ground. Haven't been as many as we thought there'd be. We think they're alive in their graves, but they can't break through the coffins. At least most of them can't."

"Is she hurt?" Muttonchops asked, probing Madison's swollen ankle with his flashlight beam.

"I'm fine; it's just twisted," Madison called back, hiding her face behind Steven's head.

"Looks broken from here," the man replied. His tone said that Madison could lie if she wanted, but it wouldn't change the condition of her ankle.

"Y'all are headed up to the capitol?" the younger man asked. He had peach fuzz on his upper lip and a Beatles haircut that didn't suit him, but Kesha couldn't help thinking that he might have looked handsome after a bath and a good night's sleep.

"Um, yeah," Kesha said cautiously. "Actually, we *are*."

"Don't act surprised," Muttonchops said with a grin. "Half the people in the state seem to have got that notion. Don't worry; you're close. It's not more than three miles up the road. You'll start seeing the campfires soon."

"Campfires?" Kesha asked.

"Oh, you'll see," Muttonchops said with a toothy smile.

"Okay," Kesha answered warily.

"Y'all heard any news?" asked the younger man with the peach fuzz. "About, you know . . . everything?"

"No," Kesha said. "We're coming from the southern part of the state. It's crazy down there. Zombies. People looting and killing."

The hunters nodded grimly.

"Did you see any, like, Army soldiers or anything?" the young man asked hopefully.

Kesha shook her head no.

"Kesha, we should get moving," Madison called from Steven's shoulders. She was still doing her best to keep her face in the shadows.

"Yeah, we should," Kesha said to the hunters. "You be careful out here."

"Ha!" Muttonchops said. "*You* be careful."

"What does that mean?" Steven asked.

Muttonchops paused to consider his words before speaking.

"There's trouble brewing up that road, son. Something's gonna happen. That many people? You mark my words."

Kesha nodded, and their trio moved off toward the capitol.

After less than ten minutes, they began to encounter other refugees. People who had traveled here on purpose, perhaps like them. There were families in RVs and campers. Some had pitched tents in green spaces and on lawns. Others still were sitting on lawn chairs and blankets.

Almost everyone seemed to have started a small fire. Flashlight batteries were at a premium, as was gasoline. But Indianapolis was largely a wooded city, and Hoosiers remembered their campfire training from Boy Scouts and Girl Scouts. Everywhere Kesha, Steven, and Madison went, people were making little fires out of whatever wood was available. Carefully crafted topiary had been sacrificed to the cause. Neatly planted rows of trees had been uprooted from expensive-looking subdivision landscaping and thrown into fires. It was a little cooler than it had been during the day, but most people were not using the campfires for heat. It was light they so desperately desired.

As Kesha pulled closer to the capitol building, the camps on the ground got so thick she could hardly walk without stepping on someone or something.

"This is like at Conner Prairie when they have the Fourth of July fireworks and the symphony plays," Madison said. "People just cover every square inch."

Despite what the hunters had said, the multitude assembled here did not look particularly alarmed. People were cooking hot dogs on sticks and chatting. More than a few were sharing cases of warm beer. There were guns everywhere, sure, but no one seemed to be angling to use them.

"This isn't so bad," Steven observed. "I don't know what those dudes at the graveyard were so worried about."

Yet no sooner were the words out of his mouth than the tone of the crowd began to change. And Kesha saw why.

As they closed on the capitol and the network of hotels, convention centers, and office buildings surrounding it, the way forward terminated. A makeshift barrier had been erected. It was composed of fire trucks, police cars, and National Guard vehicles. Yet beyond the barriers were flashlights, headlights, and other illumination that might have come from generators. Perched atop the barriers were armed guards with M-16 rifles.

"So *this* is where all the police are," Kesha observed.

They drew closer, and it became apparent why the police and National Guard were on watch. The genial campground underfoot petered out and was replaced by men and women who looked ready to riot. They faced the barricade wordlessly and seemed to be waiting for something. Their faces showed an eerie mix of resolution and desperation. Some held bricks or bats. Guns were brandished openly. In the mix, Kesha saw automatic rifles that looked superior to anything the National Guard troops held. One man even wore a bandolier of grenades.

Suddenly, a questionable-looking man in camouflage pants and a muddy IU sweatshirt grabbed Kesha by the shoulder as she slunk past.

"Get back from here," he said. "This is no place for kids."

"Is there another way through?" Kesha asked.

The man shook his head.

"They're all like this," he answered. "All the streets around the circle are blocked off."

"And they won't let people in?" Madison asked from atop Steven's shoulders.

The man frowned.

"No, they won't," he said.

"Why are you guys out here with guns and stuff?" Kesha asked.

"Because they're not doing *anything*," the man replied. "People here are dying. Old folks don't have their medicine. We don't have power or light. Everyone's going to run out of food in a few days. Meanwhile, they won't even give us any information. We haven't heard squat."

Madison shot Kesha a look that said "You see what I mean?"

"You kids need to go back the way you came," the man concluded. "It's not safe here."

The teenagers began to back away. Madison whispered into Steven's ear.

"Take me over to the sidewalk, then take me all the way up to the barricade. It'll be like working the side of the lines at Disney World."

"Okay," Steven whispered back.

Steven took the lead and picked his way through the militarized crowd. Eventually, he found a sidewalk underfoot and followed it north toward the barrier. Kesha followed close, and tried to think of ways they could look less like teenagers. She turned off her flashlight and held it low so that casual onlookers might think it was a gun. She also kept her head down.

Steven's progress along the edge of the street was looking good. The dark office buildings and parking structures beside them loomed overhead like the ebon walls of a mountain range. Kesha could not remember seeing downtown so crowded. It was like when they shut off part of the circle for a summer rock festival, but instead of jockeying their way toward Styx or REO Speedwagon, these Hoosiers were clamoring toward vengeance.

Steven reached the front of the crowd with no trouble. Soon, there was only one man between him and the barricade. This guy was all leather and bandannas and piercings. A sawn-off shotgun dangled almost playfully from his fingers. He stood with his back to Steven, staring down the National Guard troops who were using an armored personnel carrier as cover.

In the space between the two sides, a heartbreaking scene was playing out.

A gentle-looking, overweight man in khakis and a golf shirt was down on one knee in front of the barricade. From behind, he almost looked like a suitor proposing. In his arms was a very old woman who could not have weighed more than ninety pounds. She was apparently dead, or near to it. The man was crying.

"She needs her medication," the man was saying. "She needs her dialysis! This is my mother! Do you hear me? My mother!"

The National Guard and police did not appear unmoved, but they said nothing.

"You have to let us through," the man said. "You *have* to help us."

There was no response from behind the barricade.

Someone a few feet behind Kesha shouted: "Let us in, you stupid bastards!"

Another shouted: "Look what you're doing! Look!"

The soldiers and police did not move. After a few minutes, members of the crowd stepped forward and helped the kneeling man back to his feet. He still held his unconscious mother in his arms as he meekly reentered their angry folds.

"Jesus," said Kesha.

"Come on," Madison said, clicking her heels against Steven's sides as if he were a horse. "Take me up there."

Steven looked doubtfully at the armed men and women on the barricade, then trotted forward. Kesha followed.

Steven came to a halt in front of a National Guard soldier—a man of about twenty-two with pale skin, short hair, and a large wart on the side of his nose—and waited for Madison to speak. The soldier looked the trio over with a frown. His eyes lit on Madison's destroyed ankle, but he did not look impressed. Kesha remembered that this was a soldier who had just turned away a man's dying mother. A teen with a foot injury probably didn't even register.

"Excuse me," Madison began, "but you have to let me through."

Madison's voice had abruptly changed. Despite the unpleasantness of their situation, it made Kesha crack a smile. The governor's daughter had summoned fifteen years of privilege and entitlement and oodles of money, and distilled it down to the iciest tone of voice Kesha had ever heard. It was—in its own way—a powerful accomplishment. Kesha wondered if it would be effective.

The national guard soldier did not immediately respond.

"My name is Madison Burleson. Hank Burleson is my father. I need to see him right now. Your job is to make that happen as quickly as possible."

The soldier did not move.

"If you ask anybody, they will tell you that my father is looking for me."

The soldier sighed. He took a few steps to his left, to where another guardsman leaned against the armored personnel carrier.

"Do you know anything about a *Madison* Burleson?" the soldier asked his colleague. The other soldier said that no, he didn't.

Incredulous, Madison sharpened the point of her moneyed accent as far as it would go. It was now close to a parody of British aristocracy.

"I am *the daughter of the Governor of Indiana.* You will take me to see him this very mom—"

"And I'm the president's nephew!" the soldier shot back. "Haw, haw, haw."

The other troops were in need of a good laugh, and they all guffawed in Madison's face.

"The governor's daughter," said one of them. "*That's* a new one."

"Look, missy, I don't care who you think you are," said the soldier with the wart. "My orders are to not let anybody through the barricade. So that's what I'm gonna do. Not let anybody through the barricade. Is that too complicated for you?"

Kesha guessed that the soldier was not from Indianapolis. This accent was straight bumpkin, right out of the cornfields. A more cultured recruit might have picked up on the cues that said Madison was telling the truth. On this son of the soil, her charms were lost entirely.

"You have to let me through," Madison tried one final time. The soldier looked her square in the eye.

"That may be so," he said. "But I'm still not going to. Now move back."

And the soldier raised his M-16 a little. Not as though he was planning to fire, but enough to say that he might give Steven a poke with it.

Kesha could tell Madison was scandalized. She had told them who she was. She had used an upper-upper-upper-class accent. She had done all of the things that had always worked. And yet it had *not* worked. Her head sagged in defeat as Steven backed away from the barricade and they reentered the mob.

"C'mon," Kesha whispered to Madison. "We'll try another street with a different checkpoint. I'm sure somewhere there's a guard or a police officer who'll recognize you."

"Yeah," Madison said slowly. "Okay."

Kesha realized Madison was crying.

Kesha made eye contact with Steven. She gave him a look to say buck up, they would solve this. But Steven looked pretty defeated, too. Kesha remembered that he was a nomadic carnival worker with no knowledge of this place. This world. He had also been counting on Madison's reputation to resolve things. To create safety and success for them.

But it hadn't, had it?

Still, Kesha knew there could be no giving up. Not when they were so close.

"We can still do this, guys," Kesha added. "We'll walk around and try the next barricade. C'mon. Follow me."

Kesha led the way through the roiling crowd. Downcast and disheartened, Steven and Madison followed after.

25

The governor was asleep in his office, in a chair positioned just beneath the campaign banner on his wall. Or so it first appeared to Doug Huggins.

The office was almost completely dark, though the shades had been pulled back and all the windows opened. The emergency vehicles and conflagrations outside cast some light into the expansive chamber, but not into every corner. The chair that contained the slumbering body of the state's highest executive remained cloaked in shadow.

Huggins crept closer to the chair, wondering if he should address the governor directly or simply clear his throat. Then the smell of expensively cured tobacco hit him, and the cherry on the governor's cigar suddenly glowed in the darkness like a bright red eye.

"She's dead, Huggins," the governor said from behind the curling smoke.

Who was, Huggins wondered . . . ? Burleson's daughter? Had word arrived of her demise? But no. The governor did not sound displeased enough. The governor loved his daughter. Actually, truly loved her. It could not be as bad as that.

His wife then?

"So . . . do you want to be mayor of Indianapolis?" Burleson said coolly.

"What?" Huggins said. "What do you mean? Who is dead, exactly?"

"Mayor Brown is dead," the governor said, taking another puff on his Cuban. "She turned into one of those *things*. Her own security detail had to put her out of her misery. Apparently, a bite from those zombies can change you into one of them. Horrible, Huggins. Just horrible. I guess it was the one that jumped her down by the circle."

"My god, are you okay?" Huggins cried. "I mean, you hit that thing with your hands so many times. It could easily have broken the skin."

"Relax," said Burleson. "I've spent the last hour examining myself with a flashlight. I didn't get cut anywhere. And I feel just fine."

"That's a relief," Huggins said.

"Yes it is, Mister Mayor. Yes it is."

"Why are you calling me that?" Huggins said. "There are I-don't-know-how-many members of the city council who are next in line for that job."

"And I don't see that a damn one of them has shown up for work!" the governor responded, rising to his feet. "If it makes you feel more comfortable, we'll just call you 'acting mayor' for the time being."

"Really, I don't know," Huggins said. "You don't even officially have the power to . . . to . . ."

"Stop with the hemming and hawing," said the governor. With his free hand, he made the sign of the cross twice over Huggins's face. Huggins swallowed hard.

"There," said Burleson. "It's done. Now what did you want to see me about?"

The city's new acting mayor took a moment to collect himself. This was all happening so fast.

"Um . . . yes . . . the barricades outside, Mister Governor . . ." Burleson had another puff.

"The barricades. Yes. What about them?"

"There are people outside of them," Huggins said. "Lots and lots of people. They're setting things on fire. They have guns. And they want to come inside."

"We *need* the barricades," Burleson said. "Just one bite, Huggins! Think of what happened to your predecessor!"

"Yes, but the people . . . they've come here from all over the state. I think they just want help."

"They will figure it out for themselves," the governor said. "Hoosiers are resourceful. Whatever it is, they always handle it."

"Yes," said Huggins. "There are also reports of zombies forming groups in the countryside. Out in the fields where there's nobody to put them down? Big groups. If one of them headed toward the city. . . ? Maybe we'd need to bring everyone inside the Green Zone."

"Are you crazy?" Burleson said. "There's no room. You know that."

"Well then . . . " Huggins said carefully. "Then maybe we need to . . . ask for a little bit of assistance?"

The governor took another puff and stared into Huggins's face, just visible in the reflected light of the vehicles outside. How he hated Huggins and his nitpicking worries.

"Huggins, you're about to make me regret appointing you mayor," Burleson said.

"Acting mayor," Huggins reminded him.

"This *will* blow over," Burleson said. "Believe it or not, we will get through this. The sun will rise tomorrow, and a new day will come. These people outside the Green Zone will get tired of protesting and go back home. Protesters always do."

"If they don't break though the barricades in the middle of the night," Huggins interjected.

Burleson was unmoved.

"This will be over soon," the governor said. "If one or two people—insane people, criminals probably—get shot storming a police barricade, then what can you do? Will it be a tragedy? Certainly. But this is a crisis situation. You've got to expect a little shit to hit the fan, and a few bodies to hit the floor. And when everybody calms down and the power comes back on and people head back to their homes and start numbing themselves with television . . . probably just a few hours from now . . . well. Do you want me remembered as the chicken little who went screaming scared into his satellite phone?"

"We could still fix it—I'm just saying," Huggins interrupted.

"*Or* . . . " Burleson continued. "Do you want me to be remembered as the governor who kept order? Who kept *law* and order?"

Huggins had, many times, advised Governor Burleson that running as a law-and-order candidate would be effective for him at the national level. Now the governor was throwing these words back into Huggins's face.

"I just . . . " Huggins stammered, suddenly feeling like a teenager told he could not have something he desperately wanted. "If you'd only come out to the barricades and take a look . . ."

There was a sudden and loud knock at the door to the governor's office.

"Mister Governor?" called a guard. "There are military and trucks approaching. I think we're being invaded."

In the darkness, Huggins smiled hopefully. Had the federal government taken the initiative and sent assistance unbidden?

"Naw," said the governor. "It ain't an invasion. It's just BP."

A few moments later, Governor Burleson and Acting Mayor Huggins were standing on the steps of the capitol building and watching as three eighteen-wheelers—flanked by as many armored cars—pulled up to the curb. Each vehicle was emblazoned with the Burundi Petroleum logo. John Dawkins—the BP Indiana Jones—waved perfunctorily at Burleson from the window of one of the armored cars.

"What is this?" Huggins asked.

"Trucks of phytochemicals, brought down from Whiting," Burleson answered.

They watched as the truckers disconnected their cabs from their trailers. Then, with no further ceremony, the cabs and armored cars made their way back through the checkpoint heading north on Meridian Street. Outside the armed barricade, the confused crowds parted to let the convoy through. (This might have been because the armored cars had cowcatchers.)

"This is the stuff we add to the water supply," the governor explained. "Every city in the state will get at least one truck."

"But . . . you don't have access to the water system from the state capitol building," Huggins pointed out.

"That's right," Burleson said. "We'll have to wait for these . . . chuckleheads that have us surrounded to head back to their homes. Then we can have the chemicals taken to the various aquifer input points. Badda bing, badda boom—the next time somebody tests our drinking water? No zombie juice. Damn things must have been an act of God, amirite?"

The governor was pleased. He elbowed Huggins jocularly in the ribs.

"But how do we get the people to disperse?" Huggins pressed. "What if they don't want to leave? What if they stay?"

The governor gave Huggins a look to indicate the mayor was killing what remained of his buzz.

"If they don't want to move, then we'll get some damn armored cars with cowcatchers like BP has," Burleson said in an isn't-it-obvious tone. "This is no problem at all."

They stood there a moment longer, looking at the giant green trucks full of chemicals. The police, National Guard, and others within the Green Zone regarded the trucks curiously.

The governor smiled. He seemed content.

Huggins reminded himself that he was now an officeholder. Perhaps, in this connection, he should keep up appearances. Somewhat reluctantly, he too allowed himself to smile. Burleson noticed this.

"There you go," the governor observed. "See? It's not so hard."

Huggins had to agree. It was not hard at all.

26

The round leader of the bikers had introduced himself as Big Red. To Nolan, this was a bit of a puzzle, as nothing about the man was very red. (Big, however, was amply covered.)

Big Red took a small detachment of bikers—along with Nolan and Drextel—and drove up Southeastern Avenue to the heart of the city. It was difficult to hear much above the roar of the engines, but Nolan could smell improvised campfires on the wind. Big Red did not say exactly where they were going.

After just a few minutes, they began to pass other travelers heading down toward the circle. People who had strapped their belongings to the tops of their cars. People on foot with backpacks. It had the feeling of a pilgrimage. One lit entirely by candles and flashlights.

The bikers neared downtown and the traffic became quite thick. Nolan thought of the handful of times he'd worked major events downtown. The place had the feeling of a rock concert, or maybe that time they'd hosted the Super Bowl.

Near the heart of the city, bikers veered off into a string of back alleyways. Nolan was not familiar with this part of downtown, and was soon disoriented. Big Red pulled his entourage to a stop next to a string of dumpsters at the service entrance to a hotel. He got off his hog and fished a large ring of jangly keys from his leather jacket. He flipped through until he found the right one, then used it to open the service door.

"How did you get a key to this place?" Nolan asked. The bikers merely chuckled. They turned on their flashlights and followed Big Red inside.

They were in a dingy service area. It was full of carts holding unwashed room service dishes, plastic tubs full of water that had once been ice, and racks full of silverware. There were also cases of wine in cardboard containers, and stacks of glassware in plastic crates. The bikers touched none of it. Instead, they conducted Nolan and Drextel through a grungy metal door. Beyond it was a stairwell that started going up and never seemed to stop. They began to climb.

The bikers—there were four in total, counting Big Red— performed impressively, Nolan thought. They were panting to beat the band, sure, but their giant guts seemed no substantial impediment. The bikers climbed just as quickly as Nolan. Drextel managed, too.

At the top of the staircase was a metal door with a "Fire Escape Alarm Will Sound" sign. Big Red paid it no mind and pushed through. Nolan, Drextel, and the bikers stepped out onto the hotel roof, many stories above the city.

The scene before him took Nolan's breath away. The architecture of downtown Indianapolis spread out beneath them, dark and broken-looking. The spaces between the buildings were teeming with people. Rivers of flame and flashlight-beam seemed to spill out from the city's center. Yet beyond these human rivers—at the very core of Indianapolis—were blocks that had been cordoned off.

"You prob'ly don't need me to explain this . . . " Big Red began. "But I'm gonna do it anyway."

"There must be a million people down there," Nolan said.

Big Red nodded.

"Like every street festival you ever saw, times ten," Drextel added. He was looking too, but kept his distance from the side of the building. Nolan guessed the bookish man was afraid of heights.

"Why is the city center barricaded like that?" Nolan asked, stepping to the very edge of the building—so close the tips of his shoes extended over the edge. "What's happening?"

Big Red explained that the dark area at the city's core—the area that encompassed the state capitol, the Soldiers and Sailors Monument, and the City-County Building—had been cordoned off hours ago. It was full of police and soldiers. According to Big Red's sources, they'd initially erected the checkpoints just to keep zombies out. Before long they'd stopped letting anybody inside, alive *or* dead. At the same time, people across the state started heading for the capitol. Some people did this because they figured Indianapolis would be the first to regain power and basic services, but most people were fleeing from the zombies that were gathering in the countryside.

"We've ridden across half the state in the last twelve hours," interjected one of the other bikers. "The things we've seen there, you wouldn't damn believe. Whole towns—whole towns!—eaten alive. Zombies get together out in the cornfields where you can't see it happening. The corn is like camouflage for them.

They collect in there. Then all of a sudden they come out of the corn next to some little flyspeck town—and there are a thousand of them, and they come from all directions—and they eat everybody. The whole town."

Nolan nodded seriously.

"Listen," Big Red said. "This here's the important part. And move back from the damn ledge, wouldja? Yer makin' me nervous."

Nolan smiled and complied.

"The Inlaws have what you might call 'relationships' with other bikers across the Midwest," Big Red said.

"Yes, you transport drugs with them," Nolan said. "But go on."

"Well now, I suppose maybe we do . . . come to think of it," the biker said with a grin. "But what we did today—while you were dicking around in the woods—was connect with our brothers in other states. First we went over to Cincinnati. Then we went down to Louisville. And do you know what we saw? We saw tanks and planes and Army soldiers—real Army. We saw Air Force, Marines, Navy. Like that."

"You saw the Navy in Cincinnati?" Nolan asked skeptically.

"They were out on the river," one of the bikers insisted.

"But you don't see that down here, do you?" said Big Red.

Nolan agreed that he did not.

"So what does that tell you?" the biker asked.

Nolan thought. If the bikers were being honest, he had to admit he had no good answer.

"Maybe those other cities are more important than Indy?" Nolan tried. "Or maybe there's a waiting list, and the Army will get to us tomorrow."

"I don't think so," said Big Red.

"Then what?" Nolan asked.

Big Red looked around at the other bikers, and they laughed as though the answer could not have been more obvious.

"What?" said Nolan.

"Well . . . Hank Burleson, o'course," Big Red said after the laughter had died. A late summer wind whipped across the roof of the hotel as the words left the biker's lips.

"James," Drextel said. "Maybe you ought to tell these men what you were doing down south today."

Big Red looked back and forth between them.

"I thought y'all said you were looking for your daughter," Big Red said to Drextel.

"We were," said Drextel. "But first . . . James, you tell 'em."

Nolan hesitated for a moment. He was not completely sure why. He had never hesitated to say he did jobs for the governor. Heck, it was a source of pride. It opened doors and impressed women. And yet now a strange knot came to his stomach. It took him a few moments to fight it off.

"I'm a police officer," Nolan began. "My title is Special Sergeant. During the day I work narcotics. East side."

"You know Nathan Dazey?" asked one of the bikers.

"Who doesn't?" Nolan replied with a smile. "But the reason the word 'special' is in my title is that I also do stuff for the governor when he calls. Odd jobs. Stuff he wants to keep quiet. Things like that."

"Hell, you work for the damn governor?" one of the bikers said. He lunged forward and raised his fists like he wanted to punch somebody. Nolan tried to gauge how high the stout biker would have to jump to connect with his jaw.

"Hold on!" Big Red said to his compatriot. The other biker lowered his fists, but still stared bullets into Nolan.

"Yeah, I work for him," Nolan said. "So what?"

Big Red stroked his beard, thinking.

"We have a plan," Big Red said. "See the barricades down there? People have been pushing up against them and getting pushed back all night. As more people flow into the city, it's just going to get worse. People are gonna get hurt. Or killed. A cop or a National Guard is gonna get nervous and start shooting."

"But what can you do?" Nolan asked.

"It's not what *we* can do," Big Red said. "It's what *you* can do."

Nolan did not understand, and said as much.

"Why do you think we picked you up?" Big Red asked. "Why do you think we brought you to Indianapolis?"

"I don't know," Nolan said honestly. "You're basketball fans?"

Big Red chuckled.

"What I am is a grizzled ol' biker man," Big Red said. "At least that's how people see me. And that's sure as hell how the guards and police on those barricades would see me. But you're a different matter."

Nolan was silent.

"Somebody needs to diffuse this situation," Big Red said. "Someone needs to tell those National Guard troops to set down their guns and let the people through. Then get to the governor and tell him he needs to do whatever they're doing down in Ohio and Kentucky . . . and not *this!*"

Big Red gestured down at the center of Indianapolis with a single violent poke. Nolan could imagine him gouging an eye out in a bar fight with that kind of move.

"If we go to those barricades looking like we do, we'll be the first ones that get shot," Big Red continued, looking around at his brethren. "But if James Nolan did it? Well, I'd sure as hell listen to him."

Nolan was not convinced.

"Whatever your politics are, I think the governor's a reasonable man. He's helped me a lot over the years. If things got truly hairy, I'm sure he'd do something."

Big Red shook his head.

"I don't know if you can see it from here," Big Red said, "but let's give it a shot . . ."

Nolan was not following.

The bikers walked Nolan to the far side of the skyscraper roof. They faced away from the downtown scene, toward the fields and farms south of the city.

"I'll be goddamned," said Big Red.

"What?" Nolan said.

"I thought for sure it'd be impossible to see in the moonlight . . . but there you go," Big Red answered cryptically.

"Huh?" Nolan said. "I still don't see—"

But then he did.

Big Red was looking at two blobs of grey/black on the very cusp of the horizon. On a night with electric light or cloud cover, they would have been impossible to discern. But the only artificial illumination came from tiny campfires, and the full moon blazed away above. Nolan couldn't believe his eyes.

"Just in case you can't put two and two together, those are enormous groups of zombies," Big Red said wryly. "They're the ones I've been telling you about. The ones that form up out in the countryside. They meet other groups and join up. Then they do it again, and again."

"Jesus," Nolan said. "There must be thousands. Tens of thousands."

"Yup," Big Red allowed. "And they're headed this way."

Nolan tried to figure out how close to Indy the zombie groups might be. He recalled his high school physics and tried to gauge the height of the building and divide it by . . . but no. He was coming up empty. All he knew was that if they could be seen at night with the naked eye from a building downtown—even a very tall one—they could not be *that* far from Indianapolis.

"Give those two groups an hour to meet and join up, and there'll be nothing left for them to do except head up here," Big Red continued.

"How long do you think we have?" said Nolan.

"That's the only good news," Big Red allowed. "Damn things are slow, especially in groups. We've got hours until they get here. Until morning, at least."

For Nolan it was only a small consolation. He could see how it would happen, clear as day. The zombies would come up from the south, entering the city quietly and slowly. Nobody would hear them approaching. The refugees would be asleep. Then the zombies would suddenly be *there*. Blocking every road out of the city. Many of the refugees camping near the capitol would be pinned between the zombies and the barricades. All the agitators with weapons had pressed toward the Green Zone, so the ones in back would be unarmed families, elderly folks, and children. They would be the first to see the zombies, and the first to be eaten.

"Okay," Nolan said, turning away from the southern edge of the building.

"Okay, what?" said Big Red.

"I'll do it," Nolan said.

27

For most of the night, Kesha, Steven, and Madison made a long, slow circuit of the Green Zone. At every checkpoint, the story was the same. The National Guard troops seemed not to recognize Madison, or they simply didn't care.

Some checkpoints were quieter. Most of the guards at these were drowsing, but the one or two still awake would tell Madison to "move along" or "get back from the barricade" before she'd had time to explain herself. Other checkpoints were teeming with drama. People trying to charge the barricade. People throwing rocks and bricks and shitty diapers from screaming babies. People crying bloody murder at the tops of their lungs. These rowdy entrances were even more challenging; Steven found it difficult to carry Madison forward safely. (He was concerned that if he were knocked over, she might be unable to stand and get trampled.) Often, Madison found herself pleading her case to a National Guard soldier at an extreme end of a barricade. The soldier was invariably distracted by flying debris, and usually unable to hear her above the din of the angry crowd.

After several exhausting hours, Kesha realized to her dismay that they had made a complete tour of the Green Zone exterior. They were standing back in front of the southernmost barricade where they had started. The troopers manning it were still wide-awake, and still formidable-looking.

"I . . . I think I need to take a little rest," Madison said softly.

"That's a good idea," Steven said. "My dogs are seriously barking."

They picked their way back through the crowd, away from the Green Zone.

"Maybe a new shift of guards will take over in a few hours," Kesha said. "Maybe the new ones will recognize you, Madison."

Madison managed a barely audible, "I hope so."

They wandered a few blocks south and settled to the ground in an empty green space beside an office building. The building had a coffee shop on the first floor. The door had been forced open by looters. All the coffee and baked goods were long gone, but people still went inside to use the restrooms.

Steven gingerly lowered himself to his knees, and Kesha helped Madison to the ground. They reclined on the green lawn and looked up at the sky. Kesha had never seen so many stars at night above the city. It was like an astronomer's map of the Milky Way.

Then a voice said, "Would you like some water?"

Kesha sat up on her elbows and looked around.

Next to them on the green space was a woman with two young children. They had pitched a little pup tent, under which the two boys slept. The woman—athletic with long red hair, perhaps forty—was offering Kesha a metal canteen.

"It's okay," the woman assured her. "Distilled."

Kesha looked over at Madison and Steven, who appeared to have already fallen asleep.

Kesha nodded, crawled over to the neighbor, and accepted the canteen.

"Thank you," Kesha said, drinking deeply. "We've been walking for a long time."

"You look like it," the woman said. "Where y'all coming from?"

"We . . . uh . . . southern Indiana, I guess you'd say."

"Us too," the woman said. "We're from Santa Claus."

It took Kesha a moment to remember that this was a city in the southwestern part of the state.

"That's a long way," Kesha observed.

The red-haired woman agreed.

"We took the Oldsmobile as far as it would go. Ran out of gas up near Bloomington. They weren't selling any, and I was out of money. We walked most of the rest of the way. Some folks gave us rides here and there."

"I know how that goes," Kesha said.

"You're all so young," the woman observed. "Why, you can't be out of school yet."

"I'm a sophomore," Kesha allowed. "Go to school here in town."

"My lands!" the woman said. "Where are your parents?"

Kesha looked over at her sleeping compatriots for a moment.

"I'm trying to find my dad," Kesha said. "He's somewhere in Indy, I think. My mom, I don't know. She hasn't got along with us for a while. That girl there, Madison, she's trying to get to her dad, too. He's past the barricade. I don't know if Steven has a father. His mom was in the wrong place at the wrong time this morning . . . "

Kesha felt silent. The woman took her hand.

"This sort of thing, it makes you feel blessed just to be alive," the red-haired woman said. "For the last two months I've been trying to find a new job. I'm sick of waitressing, but there's no good jobs left in Spencer County that I know of. I did factory work for a while. Didn't like it. Plastic bits from the presses would burn my arms. Then I worked at a hotel, but it closed down. We been behind in bills. Maxed my credit card and then some. Bank fees ate the rest. Shawn and Daniel have been such troopers. Don't complain every time we have to move when I can't pay the rent, even though it breaks my heart a little bit."

The woman took the canteen back from Kesha and had a sip. Then she offered it once more. Kesha politely waved it off.

"I've been praying on things in the last twenty-four hours," the woman said. "More than usual, I guess . . . And I wondered if all the shit—pardon my language—that we've gone through since their daddy left us . . . Maybe it was all to get us ready for this moment. All the others were just small moves to get us ready for a big one. For *this*. You know?"

Kesha did not know what to say. She was not used to adults sharing their problems with her. It made her feel more adult herself, in a way. It also felt a little weird and dirty, like the forces that separated adults from children and teenagers had broken down. (These were strange times indeed. You could see the stars right above the buildings downtown, and adults almost three times your age wanted to talk about their problems with you.)

Kesha wondered if she should ask the nice woman follow-up questions, or simply remain silent. (How did adults do this?

What was the protocol?) Kesha could not imagine what it would be like to try to support two kids on her own, much less to deal with them in a zombie outbreak.

"I . . ." Kesha faltered. "I'm really impressed you did all that with two kids."

The words felt stupid coming out of her mouth, but she could not help her candor. She was exhausted, hungry, scared, and unsure what the coming hours had in store. It didn't feel like a time to beat around the bush.

"Shucks," the woman told her. "It wasn't that hard to get here. You did it, too."

"I don't mean that," Kesha said. "I mean . . . two kids and no partner. Wow."

The red-haired woman smiled gently.

"Aww, honey," she said, adopting an almost avuncular tone. "That ain't nothin'. That's life."

Kesha smiled.

"Do you want a granola bar?" the woman asked. "I think we have one left."

"No, thank you," Kesha said. "I think I should go rest my eyes for a while."

"Good thinking," said the red-haired woman. "Night-night."

The greeting struck Kesha like a blow to the chest. Was it not what her own father said to her at the end of each evening?

"Night-night," Kesha managed, feeling for all the world like she might suddenly start crying.

Kesha crawled back to her position next to Madison and Steven. She turned onto her back, supported by her elbows, and listened to the din of the crowds at the barricade. She decided the responsible thing to do would be to sleep in shifts. There might be people in this crowd who weren't as nice as the red-haired lady. Maybe she would keep a lookout until Steven woke up.

With this conviction firmly in place, Kesha laid back on the grass and looked up at the stars. Her eyes became itchy, and she allowed herself longer and longer blinks to clear them. Before she realized what was happening, she had fallen asleep.

28

As the first rays of morning sunshine found their way into his office, Hank Burleson remained sprawled across his leather couch, dreaming deeply.

It was the old dream. The Always-Dream. The Dream of Dreams.

The governor stood on the steps of the United States Capitol Building, and with both houses of congress, his mother, and his high school wrestling coach looking on, he was sworn in as President of the United States. He looked out at the cheering crowds and waved. He breathed in the frosty morning breeze blowing off the Potomac.

Yet this morning, the dream was burnished by exciting new details. Burleson had won the presidency in a special recall election. The voters had demanded it after seeing the way he had helmed the State of Indiana during the great zombie outbreak. His simple, efficient, and—above all—self-reliant Hoosier leadership had been a model for the nation. The populace had screamed: "That man must lead us!" And so he had. And so he did.

It was as Burleson entered the apex of his dream—the final flourish of the inauguration speech, followed by a quick romp in the Lincoln Bedroom with his favorite mistress before an evening of grand balls held in his honor—that the crowd at the barricade outside his window began to cheer.

For a moment, this mixed with the cheers of the audience in his dream, and the governor did not awaken. Then came the undeniable *clomp-clomp-clomp* of Doug Huggins running down the hallway toward his office. Now the dream died entirely as Huggins burst through his doors and cried, "Mister Governor!"

Burleson irritably scratched himself and sat up on the couch. Huggins stood at the entrance to the office, out of breath and alarmed-looking. It was already light outside. Burleson wondered how long he'd been asleep.

"Governor, there's something happening at the south barricade," Huggins cried. "Listen! You can hear it from here . . ."

Burleson put a hand to his ear. By gum, the acting mayor was right. Cheers, whoops, and hollers were coming from the Green Zone barricade just south of the capitol. Burleson's mind went to the darkest possibility he could imagine.

"It's not the Feds, is it?" he asked, throwing his feet onto the floor. Burleson pictured a parade of headline-stealing Army troops—perhaps brought up from Kentucky or Tennessee—cruising up the ass-end of Indianapolis to the capitol.

"I think you better come see," Huggins said.

"Fuck you," Burleson shot back, still only half-awake. "I'm the goddamn governor. You tell me what it is, and I'll tell you if I need to 'come see.'"

"It's James Nolan," Huggins said. "He's . . ."

The governor leapt to his feet.

"James Nolan!?" he cried. "Does he have my daughter? Is she safe?"

"He . . . I . . ." Huggins stammered. "I don't know if Madison is with him. He appears to be . . . well . . . giving a speech."

A beat passed. Then two. The governor looked around the room, trying to make sense of what he was hearing.

"Why in the Sam Hill is he doing *that*?" Burleson boomed.

Burleson got moving. He built up steam and brushed past Huggins like a charging bull. (The acting mayor jumped aside to avoid being gored.) Burleson rocketed out of his office and down to the steps leading out of the capitol. A few moments later, he was standing in the street.

It was true!

As the governor jogged south, he saw that both the troops and protesters had turned their attention to a giant man standing atop an armored personnel carrier smack in the middle of the barricade. Without a doubt, that man was James Nolan. He gestured dramatically with his giant arms. He seemed to be addressing the crowd on both sides of the barrier. He was not using a microphone or any form of amplification, so the crowd had grown hushed in order to hear. Yet occasionally he said something they liked, and the silence gave way to cheers of encouragement.

Burleson found himself next to a group of uniformed police officers to the side of the barrier. Burleson quickly located the one with the most stripes on his sleeve, and grabbed him hard by the shoulder.

"Hey!" cried the officer. Then he saw who was gripping him and saluted.

"Oh," said the policeman. "Mister Governor."

"What's happening here?" Burleson cried. "What is this?"

"Um . . . " the police officer hesitated. "A few minutes ago, a group of bikers pulled up to the barricade. We thought they were here to start trouble. They're called the Inlaws, run meth and stolen goods on the southeast side."

"I don't care about a bike gang," Burleson barked. "What is James Nolan doing?"

"They brought him with 'em," the police officer explained. "When people saw Nolan, they started to cheer. I mean . . . it's James Nolan! People still love him. Pretty soon, it was like a little parade was happening."

"Nolan works for *me!*" the governor snarled. "He's mine! Everyone in the department knows that! Why didn't you send him through?"

"He didn't want to go through," the policeman said. "He told us he wanted to say something. Then he got up on the barricade."

"What?" Burleson said.

The policeman shrugged, and pointed up toward Nolan's perch atop the personnel carrier.

Burleson began to pick his way closer to Nolan. As he did so, he listened.

"I've seen what these things can do, and I'm betting so have most of you," Nolan was saying. "One-on-one, they're not so dangerous. You can usually run away. But as a group, they can surround you, and you've got no chance. With a *big* group, you probably need machine guns and bombs. The kind of things these soldiers have here."

Was Nolan giving some kind of Zombie 101 lecture? Who had told him to do that?

"This group I've seen heading north, it's got to be in the thousands—maybe the tens of thousands," Nolan continued. "A few hours ago, they were close enough to see from the top of a tall building. By now, they're probably inside the city limits."

A worried murmur ran through the crowd.

"You're a big group out here," Nolan said, addressing the people standing outside the barrier. "But I'm confident we'll be able to fit everyone inside the Green Zone. Especially people who are unarmed, handicapped, or not equipped to fight."

What was *this* bullshit? The governor growled like an angry dog and pushed his way forward through the crowd. When someone stood in his way, he elbowed them hard in the side.

"Now . . . you know me," Nolan continued. "You know who I am."

"We sure do!" someone from the crowd called. A couple of other folks hooted in approval.

"I'm not perfect by any means," Nolan said. "But I like to think you can trust me. I'm asking you to trust me now. I also know many of you on the *inside* of this barricade. We've worked alongside each other for ten years. I follow orders, too. I've followed orders as a police officer, and as a basketball player. I understand that orders are important. But sometimes you get the opportunity for a fast break that can win the game. When that happens, nobody wants you to stop and set up the play. They want you to take it to the hoop."

Several cheers rang out. Nolan put a hand up to stay the applause. Those shouting were soon quieted by others in the crowd, as it became clear that Nolan still had more to say.

"I think we just got the ball at half court, and the other team is underneath the wrong basket," Nolan said. "But I can't do this fast break myself. I need your help. We can save all the people here. We can save everyone. But I need your help to do it."

The governor was now close enough to see across the barricade to the street beyond, swelled far as the eye could see with refugees. To his horror, Burleson found that people on *both* sides of the barricade wore the same expression. They were entranced. They were beaming. They were lapping it up.

And why not? In a time of strife and confusion, this handsome, familiar face—that they had cheered for years—had suddenly appeared out of nowhere. And instead of telling them to shut up, disperse, and go away, he was rallying them to a common purpose.

It was disgusting.

Evidently, Nolan—his best man—had gone rogue. Perhaps even gone insane. (These had been trying times indeed. The governor reflected that he might have asked too much of his favorite policeman.) Yet whatever the cause of Nolan's insanity, the upshot of its effects remained.

The governor's most stalwart servant was now standing on top of a government vehicle like a common, scruffy-faced protester, encouraging troops to abandon their posts, and telling them to flood the Green Zone with the unwashed gamin gathered just beyond.

The governor knew what he had to do . . . .

29

Nolan was terrified.

He'd read somewhere that public speaking was a fear greater than death for most people. In this moment, that felt about right.

It seemed that the entire population of the state was now arrayed before him. The people lining the streets of downtown Indianapolis stretched as far as the eye could see. Compounding his tension, to the other side of him were rows of men and women with guns—a few he knew, yet most were total strangers. Nolan had no idea what orders they'd been given about who to shoot and who not to shoot, but a man standing atop the barricade calling for sedition against their standing orders sure seemed like a good candidate to get popped.

Nolan was risking everything that he had, and he knew it.

From his earliest days of basketball stardom, Nolan had been acutely aware that he was a rare fish that swam in an even rarer slipstream—the sort of slipstream that only happened when all the city fathers (and mothers) smiled upon you. His entire adult life, he had been a star. And not just any star. He was the *kind* of star that people in power liked. That politicians and corporate CEOs wanted to be seen with. That advertisers wanted to hold their products. So doors had been opened for him. Opportunities had always been provided. And his failures—such as they were—had always been hushed-up as much as possible.

To challenge the city fathers publicly was to risk throwing this away. To leave the slipstream and swim under his own power, whatever that might be. He was risking it all.

Some part of Nolan's brain had whispered that his plan would never work. That the National Guard troops would see him approaching with the bikers and shoot him where he stood (or at least tell him to shove off).

Instead, it had been like the old days. Nolan had removed his sunglasses (which helped keep folks from recognizing him). He had shouted his own name to the skinny kids in the Indiana National Guard uniforms working the barricade. And he had seen the wonder in their eyes. They knew him. Or at least knew *of* him. The crowd had seen it too. Their cheers and cries of recognition had become a force. A power. Something you could almost feel in a tactile way. He had become who he once was. Who, perhaps, he always had been . . . and yet never had been. Moments later, the troops at the barricade had helped him up on the barrier and told him to say what he had to say.

Now he had reached the end of his speech, and he'd be damned if it didn't look like it was going to work. The crowd of refugees seemed to understand that nonviolent entry was their shared goal. The soldiers and police did not look like they were going to stop anybody who wanted to walk between the tangle of vehicles that formed the barricade. The snipers on the walkway above had set down their guns; they sat on the edge of the roof, their legs dangling from the overhang, leaning in to get a closer view of Nolan.

To one side of the barricade, the Inlaws stood with their arms crossed. Big Red, who hunkered beside a nervous-looking Drextel Washington, gave Nolan a thumbs-up.

Then—just as it seemed the soldiers would part and the crowd begin filing peacefully into the Green Zone—there came a loud scuffling sound at the rear of the personnel carrier.

A familiar voice said, "Little help?"

Nolan turned back toward the capitol and saw the governor of Indiana trying to pull himself onto the carrier. After a moment's hesitation, Nolan extended two giant arms and pulled Burleson up next to him.

The crowd—most of whom had not seen hide nor hair of the governor since the start of the outbreak—burst into applause. Before Nolan realized what was happening, the governor grabbed one of Nolan's hands and held it up like they were politicians at a rally.

"Don't worry, James!" the governor said from out of the side of his mouth. "It's all under control."

Nolan looked over to the Inlaws. Big Red telegraphed concern. What was this treachery? What had happened?

For his part, Nolan hoped that his words had convinced the governor to remove the barricades. Perhaps Burleson would say that it had been his *own* idea to remove them. (The governor often took credit for things that people liked, whether or not he'd had any part in them. That would be okay. Nolan understood that his boss liked the limelight. For all of Burleson's flaws, Nolan could not bring himself to feel any real ire toward the man. Perhaps he sometimes made choices that Nolan himself would not have made, but he still seemed to try to do his best for the state. And he had done so much for Nolan in the past . . .)

"Thank you, James!" the governor boomed as the crowd finally quieted. "Thank you very much for your concern and your care. This man is a true hero of the state. A treasure! A Sagamore of the Wabash, if ever there was one!"

The governor indicated Nolan with a broad gesture, and the crowd applauded once more.

"Now, we're all doing our best in a *very* difficult situation," Burleson said. "Very difficult. I know that the hardest thing right now is communication. I know I miss my cell phone, just like y'all do."

There was a little polite laughter.

"But here's the thing . . ." the governor began.

Suddenly, Nolan saw a familiar face push her way to the front of the barricade. He pivoted and looked more closely. It was Kesha Washington! She was still alive, and in Indianapolis somehow! Emerging from the crowd behind her was Steven Hipwell, the carnival worker with the burned leg. And on his shoulders sat a familiar-looking young woman with a broken ankle.

Nolan waved down at Kesha. She enthusiastically waved back. Nolan pointed over toward where Kesha's father stood beside the biker gang. Kesha's eyes found her father, and her face lit up with delight.

Beside Nolan, the governor continued to speak. So in shock was Nolan that it took him a moment to begin following the governor's words.

"The thing my friend James doesn't know is that I sent the National Guard to take care of those zombies a few hours ago. I'm pleased to report that the threat has been entirely eliminated. Entirely! From what I hear, it was a hard go. But our brave men and women were up to the challenge. The group of zombies James is talking about was destroyed before the sun was up this morning."

The audience sat in silence for a moment. It was good news . . . but a bit anticlimactic. They began to applaud—not like they had for Nolan; this was more of a polite patter.

"Thanks for all your efforts, kid," Burleson said to Nolan under the applause. "Leave it to my top man to find the same threat I did. Well done."

"Some bikers pointed it out to me," Nolan said. "Did you *really* have all those zombies taken care of in the last couple of hours? I was down on Southeastern before, and I didn't hear gunshots or anything."

"Totally taken care of, champ," the governor said. "You can rest easy."

He put his hand on Nolan's towering shoulder.

Nolan smiled weakly. It all left him with a strange, empty feeling. Could it be that simple? Could the governor possibly be right?

But of course he was. He was the governor of the damn state. Of course he was, thought Nolan.

He was always right.

30

Kesha stood at the front of the crowd and looked over at her father. Improbably, the slight, bookish man was framed by a pack of mean-looking bikers. They seemed to regard him almost as one of their own.

Kesha did not stop to wonder what had brought him here. Her lone, ecstatic thought was that her father was alive and nearby. She'd been so afraid she would never see him again. And yet here he was. Apparently safe and sound, and with some burly new friends.

Her father did not yet see her. Kesha wanted to cry out, but did not want to interrupt the governor. Or Nolan. *Nolan!* What was he doing here? Standing on the barricade making some sort of speech about zombies south of the city? Zombies that had, according to the governor, now been eliminated. It was all so fantastic. All so unexpected.

It also dawned on Kesha that Madison was now within a few feet of her father. Whatever she had needed to do—or to *stop* him from doing—now, presumably, could happen.

Kesha felt she might swoon from the incredibleness of it all (that, and the lack of food and sleep). Then she heard Madison's voice like ice in her ear.

"He's *lying!*"

"What?" Kesha said.

"My dad is *lying*," Madison said. "Whatever his basketball-playing policeman just said about zombies heading for the city; it's still *true*."

Kesha ripped her eyes from her father and looked back up at the improvised stage where the governor stood next to Nolan. All at once, she knew that Madison was right. The governor was saying something about the National Guard having eliminated a zombie threat south of the city. Next, he started explaining why the barricades needed to stay up as a security measure.

Kesha saw Nolan nodding as if he agreed. But he'd just been saying something to the contrary. He'd said that zombies *were* headed this way, and that people needed to come *inside* of the barricade.

"I can tell when my dad is lying," Madison said. "I've watched him do it for years."

Kesha looked back at Nolan. He was still nodding along. Whenever the governor stopped for applause, he leaned in and joked with Nolan.

Kesha took a step forward, then stopped. What was she about to do?

Here she was—back in Indianapolis, where she had always wanted to be. Her father was fifty feet away. She was surrounded by people and there were a bunch of Army men with guns. For the moment she appeared to be safe. Wasn't this what she had been working toward the whole time?

Yet something told her that this was not success. That she still needed to act. That James Nolan was a good man . . . but a good man who did not know the truth.

Kesha took another step forward, then another.

She cupped her hands to her mouth and shouted, "James!"

Nolan saw her and waved, a goofy smile on his face.

A National Guard soldier stepped up to keep Kesha away from the personnel carrier.

"Let her through," called Nolan. "It's all right."

The National Guard soldier looked surprised and backed away from Kesha. Nolan's word was law in this situation. Better than law.

Kesha scuttled up to the personnel carrier. James knelt down to speak with her.

"Kesha!" he said. "You got here! I'm so glad! I ran into your father at the cabin. He's over there with Big Red."

"James, listen . . ." Kesha cried. "The governor is lying. He's not telling you the truth. That's his daughter, Madison, over there on Steven's shoulders. She knows."

"This just keeps getting better," Nolan said.

"Yeah," Kesha said. "But listen to me. Burleson's not telling the truth."

Kesha watched as Nolan looked over to where the governor was still bloviating. Kesha realized that Nolan was afraid Burleson would hear her.

"Why would you say that?" Nolan said.

"Those zombies south of the city? They're still coming. The governor didn't do anything about it. He's lying."

Nolan contorted his face as though he smelled a bad smell. He shook his head. Kesha understood instantly. Something in Nolan did not want to believe.

Nolan looked back at the governor and shifted his weight like he might stand back up. But Kesha had come this far. It was time to go for broke.

"You were never in that car!" Kesha screamed as loud as she could.

For the first time, the governor appeared to notice the teenage girl at the foot of their improvised stage. A number of soldiers were looking at her as well. But she was only looking up at Nolan.

The giant policeman's face seemed to lose all expression.

Nolan said, "What?"

"You were never in that car," Kesha said more quietly. "That night that the accident happened when you were in college? You were a pedestrian. You were walking down the side of the road. The car hit you as it ran into the tree."

Nolan knit his brow.

"But . . . no. I was in the car."

"Do you *remember* being in the car?" Kesha asked.

She realized that the governor had stopped speaking, and was now staring directly at her.

"I . . ." Nolan stammered. "No. I mean, none of us did. We all had memory loss. The doctors said that was normal. I *was* in the car."

"How do you know?" Kesha asked. "Was it because the mayor of Muncie, Hank Burleson, told you so? Or the police chief appointed by the mayor? Or maybe the policemen who reported to the police chief?"

"I was in the car," Nolan said again. "You're wrong, Kesha."

"Young lady, please step away from the barricade," Burleson barked.

He got a guardsman's attention and pointed to Kesha as if to say, "Deal with that."

The guardsman stepped forward and began to push at Kesha with the butt of his gun.

"No!" shouted Nolan. "Leave her alone!"

The guardsman looked back and forth between the governor and the giant policeman. Then he stepped back from the teenager.

"I was in the car," Nolan said to Kesha. "Where did you get the idea that I wasn't? Where is this coming from?"

"*She got it from me!*"

Kesha saw Madison urging her gangly steed forward. Madison had screamed the words like a battle cry. Burleson was agog and aghast.

"Madison!" the governor cried. "You're . . . you're . . ."

"Not going to take your bullshit anymore!" Madison shouted.

"What?" Burleson said.

"I've heard my father talking about the accident for years, and I know the truth!" Madison called.

"Madison . . . be quiet!" the governor hissed, suddenly remembering that he was in front of a crowd.

The governor took a step across the improvised stage toward his daughter. Without turning his head, Nolan extended an arm to the governor's chest, stopping him mid-stride.

Everyone on both sides of the barrier was listening now. Nobody moved.

Madison opened her mouth to speak, but Kesha cast a look that said: "No. He needs to hear this from me."

"You were never in the car," Kesha repeated. "Three other boys were. You knew them, but you hadn't been out with them

that night. They hit you when they went off the road. Afterwards, it became clear that nobody would have a solid memory
of what had happened. The mayor saw a chance to take advantage of the situation. If you were just a pedestrian who got hit,
then you were worth nothing to him. A sad story. But if you had
been *driving*, and then he *covered that up* . . . then he had made
a powerful friend for life. A friend who would be famous and
popular throughout Indiana. So he told you that *you* had been
driving the car . . . but he would hide the truth. He would tell
the press you had been a passenger. His police force would back
him up and alter the evidence accordingly, he said. You thought
Burleson was taking an enormous risk on your behalf. In fact, he
was only taking advantage of you. Making you something that
would serve him in the future."

"Be quiet, whoever you are!" Burleson roared. He pushed
hard against Nolan's arm, but it was like a ten-year-old rushing
an adult.

"You know it's true, Dad!" Madison shouted up at the
improvised stage. "I've heard you brag about it on the phone
when you're drunk! Don't lie!"

Kesha could see the gears turning inside Nolan's head. She
could also see that this was very, very painful for him. Nolan was
a good man. He wanted to believe the best about people. That
was the essence of who he was.

"Listen, you're still a good person," Kesha said—feeling as
though her words were entirely out of bounds for a teenager, but
going for it anyway. "In the last day and a half I've seen you do . . .
amazing things. Brave things. Things most people could never do.

It's just . . . sometimes you could stand to be a little more cynical, you know?"

Nolan nodded.

And it might have stopped there, had Madison Burleson been in a better mood. But the most popular girl in the state missed her nice, soft, memory foam bed, missed her menagerie of stuffed animals, and, above all, missed her mother. Her neglected, mistreated, trophy wife of a mother who had been driven into the arms of the gardener, and then the tennis coach, and then a series of others . . . by this man on the stage next to Nolan. Madison wanted her mommy, and fresh clothes, and a good night's sleep on a *bed*. And—true to Burleson form—she was ready to spew hot fury over anyone who denied her what she *wanted*.

"You also talk about the stuff in the water!" Madison cried. "I know about that, too! Tell them about that!"

From her perch atop Steven's shoulders, Madison could see all the way to the capitol building. There were three giant tankers with Burundi Petroleum logos parked right in front of it.

"See, right there!" Madison said, pointing wildly. "Why are there BP trucks in front of your office? Explain that!"

Suddenly, Nolan reared up and turned to the governor. The consternation and discomfort were still all over his face, but there was something else, too. To Kesha, it looked like something inside the giant man was awakening.

"The water!" Nolan cried, pointing a meaty finger at the governor's chest. "A new mystery chemical making dead flesh move around. That was *you*?"

"It's him and BP," Madison called. "He lets them do any-thing they want. That's all he cares about . . . keeping BP happy."

Nolan turned and looked down the street to the capitol building. He saw the BP trucks, clear as day. Then he turned back to the governor.

"What did you do?" Nolan cried, gripping the governor by the front of his jacket.

Burleson, alarmed, writhed like a fish pulled out of the water. In a few seconds, he had twisted out of his jacket entirely. Nolan was left holding the empty garment, which he threw to the ground.

Burleson retreated to the far edge of the personnel carrier. He looked into the faces of the crowd. They were utterly enraptured by the drama unfolding before them. Burleson looked back at the police and soldiers. Nobody was springing to his aid. Nobody was stepping between him and James Nolan. Their faces made it clear. He was on his own.

"How *dare* you!" Burleson cried.

His voice was deep and theatrical. Despite his circumstances, he was able to summon a powerful tone. It made his audience think of fathers, and coaches, and priests, and, yes, sometimes presidents. Though ruffled and unjacketed, he was not dimin-ished. His voice reminded everyone that they were dealing with an arch-politician. With a master.

"I have done everything for you," Burleson boomed toward Nolan. Kesha could see the sting hit Nolan's face almost like a blow.

Burleson turned toward the crowd.

"And I have done everything for *you*."

Burleson looked out into the sea of faces before him, silently, for a long time . . . almost as though he were daring them to speak.

"I have given my life to the service of this state," Burleson continued. "Everything I have done, I have done for Indiana. For its people. For you."

Burleson strode to the front of the personnel carrier, ready to work the stage.

"Our state is not perfect," Burleson said. "No place is perfect. We have not achieved an *ideal* condition. But do you remember what it *used* to be like here? Think about how far we've come. When I took over, we were a triple-A franchise at best. Now we're in the big leagues! I brought you the Super Bowl. Hell, I brought you a Super Bowl championship! I brought you the NCAA. I brought company after company after company. And yes, one of those companies was BP! I'm not ashamed to say it! I brought you jobs! I brought as many jobs as I could. I will admit to that today, tomorrow, and with my dying breath. You can put it on my tombstone. I did everything I could to bring Indiana jobs!"

The crowd began to applaud. Mostly just a few confused golf-claps, but it was a start.

Burleson turned to Nolan. And Kesha. And Steven and Madison.

Kesha could see the hate rising within him.

"What did you have before me? What would you have without me? People like *this* . . . "

Burleson pointed at Nolan and the trio of teenagers.

"*These* sorts of people . . . you know the ones . . . they want to tell you that what I'm doing is wrong. They want to criticize everything. To Monday morning quarterback. These sort of people should stay out of Indiana. All they do is find something to complain about."

Burleson turned back to the crowd.

"What would y'all have without me? Without the things I've done? Think about it . . . what would you have?"

Suddenly, Kesha found herself climbing onto the side of the personnel carrier. She pulled herself up until she was next to Nolan. Then she faced the governor.

"The best people in the world!" Kesha screamed—looking first at the governor, then up at Nolan, then out to the crowd beyond. "Don't you see that? You have the best people in the world. *That's* what you have. You've told Hoosiers for so long that the only good thing about their state is that it has jobs. They've started to believe it. But it has more than jobs. It has the best people in the world."

"Young lady!" the governor interjected. He took a menacing step toward Kesha, but Nolan stepped between them. He stared down at Burleson, crossed his arms, and shook his head no.

"It has the best people in the world," Kesha said again, looking out at her father, then—miraculously—finding the red-haired lady with two children who had offered her water the night before. "Don't you see that?"

The governor narrowed his eyes at Kesha.

"Young lady, don't 'the best people in the world' deserve jobs?" Burleson barked from the other side of Nolan.

"They deserve to be protected from zombies," Kesha said. "*That's* what they deserve."

Suddenly, there was a commotion at the side of the stage. A member of the Inlaws biker gang had pushed his way up to Big Red. He was speaking excitedly into Big Red's ear, and gesturing down the street.

Big Red nodded. Then he looked up at Nolan and slowly mouthed, "Meridian and I-70."

"The zombies are inside the city," Nolan announced to the crowd.

They were more than inside the city. They were closing on downtown.

"Listen to me!" Nolan added. "We don't have much time left."

31

If Burleson had had time to properly reflect on the situation, he would have been sickened by the indignity of it all. Forced to defend his actions publicly to a teenager and dumb-jock policeman who did odd jobs for him. While standing on top of an Army truck, for god's sake! The indignity! The sheer indignity!

Yet Burleson, blessedly, had only an instant to think, and so largely dismissed these dark ruminations altogether.

If people thought a big group of zombies was coming, they would want inside the Green Zone. Then they would want protection and food that Burleson could not possibly provide. Soon they would *demand* these things. It would look like chaos. Hell, it might actually *be* chaos. It would be apparent to everyone that Indiana needed help. Then the dreaded F-word. Federal assistance. And then all his efforts would have been for naught. The dream would die.

No.

These people *must* disperse. They must go home. They must handle the zombies on their own—handle their problems without complaining, like Hoosiers always had!

The electricity would come back on soon; it had to. Then the Internet. Then the television stations. It would all return. And everyone would go home and sheepishly wonder what they had all been so upset about.

Burleson knew that everything ended. Earthquakes eventually stopped their shaking. Tidal waves receded. Hurricanes dissipated into tropical storms, and then into thunderstorms, and then into drizzle.

This would be over soon, Burleson's brain screamed. And when people around the country turned their televisions back on, they needed to see—they *must* see—a state that had handled things. That had had no breakdown of order. That had got on just fine.

And if these people—these horrible . . . *citizens*—would just leave the barricades, then it *would* all be fine.

But James Nolan—that Judas!—stood in his way.

Perhaps Burleson had underestimated the burly policeman. It was fun to keep a pit bull on a leash—made you feel like a big man, sure—but now that dog had turned cur. Turned on its master. So it was time to pull the choke chain . . . or maybe just put him down forever.

The situation hung on the edge of a knife. Where was Huggins? Where was his support staff? The governor felt naked. Alone in the world up on that improvised stage.

Burleson wracked his brain for something to promise Nolan. Something to bribe him with. But what was left? The giant seemed incorruptible. Beyond reason. (It came down to the same thing.)

Then a miracle.

Then something astounding.

An offering from the universe that seemed to tell Burleson that God was still on his side.

"I don't know who's in charge right now," Nolan was saying. "But it's not this man next to me. An army of zombies is inside the city. Thousands of them are headed this way, and they want to eat us. It doesn't matter who's sitting in the governor's mansion. What matters is saving lives. We need to get everybody outside the barricades *inside*. We need that to happen right now."

Nolan drew his heavy Ruger revolver. Then—miracle from on high!—he turned it around in his hand and held it by the barrel, offering it to the crowd.

"I'm not threatening anybody," Nolan said. "I'm not telling anybody what to do. I'm *asking* you—all of you—to do the right thing. There's one bullet left in my gun. Anybody who wants it can come take it. I'm not going to stop you."

Burleson smiled.

If you wanted to be royalty, sometimes you had to kill a king. But if you were *already* royalty . . . and you wanted to *stay* royalty . . . well, sometimes you had to kill a usurper.

Burleson moved without hesitation, without thought, and most certainly without compunction—leaping across the stage in one fluid movement. Nolan was looking out into the crowd. The crowd was looking at Nolan. Only the black girl—what had Nolan called her, Keesha?—opened her mouth in alarm as he careened forward.

Burleson gripped the weighty revolver with both hands and wrested it from Nolan's fingers in a single deft motion. Burleson stepped back and raised the gun at the giant policeman. Nolan did not cower or raise his hands to defend himself. He merely looked confused.

"*I* am in control here!" Burleson barked. "I am in control!" And he pulled the trigger.

The gun thundered. It seemed to Burleson that the thunder did not stop, but went on and on. The recoil from the weapon bruised his hands, but he was feeling no pain. He was too pleased with the result.

Burleson had blasted a hole in the giant man's side. A huge, gaping wound that began to spill healthy red blood almost immediately. Nolan gripped his abdomen, went weak in the knees, and fell forward off the personnel carrier to the concrete below.

Kesha screamed. Madison screamed. The rows and rows of refugees in front of Burleson screamed or staggered backwards.

The governor looked down at the gun in his hands. He threw it to the ground.

The scene plunged into anarchy. The guardsmen and police drew their weapons, but were unsure at whom to point them. The biker gang appeared especially alarmed. A few of them took handguns out of their belts. The crowd began to roil like an angry, boiling soup. People ran in every direction. They ran forward. They ran backwards. They ran into other people and knocked them down.

Burleson felt eerily calm. He had killed the usurper. The Judas was gone. The weed had been picked from the orderly garden. Now he only needed to reassert control.

"I am the governor of Indiana!" Burleson shouted above the uproar. "We have entered a state of martial law! I need everyone to remain calm and follow orders. I will tell you what to do!"

The crowd did not respond. There was still too much confusion for anyone to hear him.

The sound of the Ruger continued to echo in the governor's ears. He looked down and saw Nolan curled like a sleeping baby on the ground. Several people had run to his aid. Burleson's daughter stared on in horror, still atop the shoulders of a lanky boy. (That would be the next step, the governor thought. He must win her back. But all her seditious words . . . he had lost her and not even known. He must be more attentive to his family in the days to come. Or, at least, to the family members he cared about.)

"Arrest her," Burleson called to the police behind him. He pointed to the black girl holding her hands to her mouth in horror.

The policemen acted as though they could not hear. Burleson himself could not hear. The crowd was yelling. All was chaos. And the report from that giant revolver . . . it had faded to a distant din, but Burleson could *still* hear it ringing. Damn him if he couldn't. Maybe he needed to get his ears checked when all this was over.

"People, please . . . " Burleson tried, addressing the crowd in a gentler tone. "You must listen to me. I know what is best."

The bikers to the side were now all holding weapons—some of them held several. They pointed their guns and knives toward the governor. To his glee, the governor saw that the National Guard and police now had targets. They took aim at the bikers.

Yes! *This* was what he needed—Burleson realized. Chaos. Utter and total chaos. And violence! A large shootout would be optimal . . . as long as Burleson survived it. No official record was being kept of these events. No notes were being taken. And he didn't see a single video camera anywhere. Who was to say what had happened, or what people would remember? It would be rumor and hearsay. *All* of it. There had been some shooting, sure. A big shootout. And yeah, the governor had apparently shot a guy, but so had a lot of people. Maybe the governor had been defending himself. It had been hard to see.

Yes, the governor thought. By seeding a few careful rumors over the next few days, he could make it look like self-defense. Hadn't Nolan been holding a gun . . . and pointing it at the governor? Or at the crowd? Perhaps the governor had saved lives. Hell, he'd come out of this looking like a hero. Which, of course he was. Of course he was. . . .

Burleson glared back and forth between the grizzled bikers and the nervous guardsmen, waiting for one of them to shoot. Willing them to shoot. Using his mind to call forth the carnage and death that would wash his sins clean (or, at the very least, hide them in a tidal wave of blood).

Then something happened.

People began to look up.

At first—through hubris, habit, or simply bad perspective—the governor thought they might be looking at him. He was still standing atop the carrier, after all. Yet on closer inspection . . . no. They were looking *past* him, up into the sky. The din from the Ruger that had never left his ears grew louder, then louder still.

Confused, Burleson also turned and surveyed the heavens.

An armada was waiting.

The sky behind the capitol building was full of helicopters with American flags on their sides. There must have been fifty or more. Burleson was no military man, but even he recognized the large variety they presented. There were transport helicopters, observation helicopters, and ones that were clearly designed for kicking ass—with two big Gatling guns on either side and missiles mounted underneath.

As Burleson watched in confusion, the unarmed copters began to hover in the air above the Green Zone. A few of them descended as though they might touch down. The armed helicopters, however, continued straight south, over the assembled crowd, and down into the city's south side.

Almost immediately, they began to fire their weapons. In instants, it was a war zone. The rapid-fire *ka-chunk-ka-chunk-ka-chunk* of the Gatling guns mixed with the *skreeeeeee* of missiles being launched. Then the deafening explosions began to ripple across the city. Glass windowpanes in nearby buildings shattered. The carrier on which the governor stood shook with each new explosion. Great plumes of smoke and fire erupted up into the morning sky. Wood and building materials and dirt and body parts rained down. Very old body parts. (At one point, the governor ducked to the side as a human hand, black with rot, careened past him like a Frisbee.)

The armed helicopters gradually moved south, farther away from the center of the city. They continued to fire their weapons, yet it soon became sporadic. The rain of debris stopped. The governor looked behind him, up toward the capitol building.

The largest helicopter he had ever seen had just landed on the open street just south of the capitol. Its giant twin blades slowly stopped rotating and came to a halt. Uniformed, armed soldiers were emerging from its giant belly. A small Jeep drove out. Some of these fresh soldiers were already speaking with the exhausted police and National Guard troops. Burleson saw Huggins talking to a group of soldiers and gesturing emphatically down the street to the barricade. A senior-looking soldier in military fatigues and a beret looked at Burleson's position and nodded.

For the moment, the crowd had quieted. Burleson climbed off the personnel carrier and headed back toward the capitol at a trot. He had to make this right. He had to explain himself. He had to do . . . something.

All around the city, the helicopters continued to descend. Some of them bore Red Cross markings on their bellies. Were they bringing medicine and food? Why? Burleson had not asked for either. He had the situation under control!

The lawn of the capitol was crowded with fresh soldiers. Helicopters were landing everywhere they could fit. Burleson approached the senior-looking military man in the beret. He extended his hand in greeting. It was still sore from firing the Ruger.

"Governor Burleson?" asked the man in the beret.

"That's me," Burleson said, shaking his hand.

"Brigadier General Arthur Belden," the soldier said. (Burleson realized the beret had a star on it.) We've been trying to get in touch with you for almost twenty-four hours. Do you still have your emergency phone?"

"It wasn't needed," Burleson announced proudly. "We have not required—nor have we asked for—*any* assistance from the federal government. We are perfectly capable of handling the situation ourselves."

"Yeah . . ." General Belden began. "That's what we thought, too. At first. But our satellite imaging started picking up this giant mass of undead heading toward your capital city. Thousands of them. It looked like you'd created a refugee camp right in the spot where the zombies were headed. We kept waiting for you to do something. We were taking bets on whether or not you had a plan, actually. I was with those who thought you did. I'm a Hoosier myself, y'see. Guess I was wrong on that one . . ."

The general narrowed his eyes at Burleson. Then he peered down the street to where the crowd stood watching the helicopters perform mop-up.

"We could tell you'd cordoned off a safe zone by the capitol," the general continued. "That was good. We were just waiting for you to let the people inside. But you didn't. There came a point when we'd be too late to help. So we had to roll out. Good thing we did, huh?"

"*Entirely unnecessary,*" Burleson retorted. "We had the matter well in hand!"

"Uh-huh," the general said skeptically.

"We did not ask for federal assistance," Burleson stammered. "The record will show this!"

"Uh-huh," the general said again.

Then he turned toward the three BP tankers parked at the steps of the capitol building.

"What's that?" the general asked jocularly. "Your personal heating oil, maybe?"

Burleson raised a finger and opened his mouth to speak. Suddenly, Huggins burst forward through a nearby crowd of soldiers.

"I've already told them, Hank," Huggins said, blubbering, crying. "The jig is up. I've told them about the compounds you let BP put into the water. I've told them about what the report said it could do. That it could reanimate dead tissue. I've told them everything!"

Burleson was aghast. Another Judas! Was no man loyal?

Burleson prepared himself for the worst—whatever that was—but the general in the beret was smiling. He was smiling like it was a joke. A joke!

"Yeah . . ." the general began. "So I guess I ought to tell you that this outbreak is happening all over the world . . . not just in states that sell their waterways to BP."

"What?" Burleson and Huggins said at exactly the same time.

"Yeah, we don't know *exactly* what's causing the bodies to get back up again," the general said in a relaxed tone. "Some astronomers are saying it could be dust from the tail of a comet. I've heard other theories too. Crazy stuff. But the point is, it's nothing you all did in Indiana."

Burleson and Huggins looked at each other.

"I don't doubt what you're saying," the general quickly added, turning to Huggins. "You say you put stuff in the water your citizens drink that makes dead things twitch. I believe you.

But it isn't the culprit. The dead are rising from Manhattan to Moscow to Melbourne. The outbreak is global."

There was a commotion behind Burleson. The general and his men were evidently distracted by something. Their faces showed confusion and alarm.

The governor turned.

The crowd had made it through the barricade and was coming up the street. They were moving slowly. In horror, Burleson realized that this was because they were carrying the giant body of James Nolan with them. They held him at their fore like the masthead on a ship. More horrible still, Nolan did not appear to be completely dead. He still clutched his abdomen, and his eyes were open. On one side of him was the governor's own daughter, riding piggyback. To his other was a very angry-looking black girl.

"Well good God-damn . . . that's James Nolan," the general said. The military formality fell away from his voice. In a trice, he was just a Hoosier again. A citizen. A basketball fan.

"That man shot him!" the black girl screamed, pointing straight at Burleson.

"He did!" Madison shouted. "My dad. The governor. That man right there. We're all witnesses."

A newly arrived Army medic came running forward to examine Nolan's wound.

General Belden turned to the governor with an iron-clad expression that asked: "Is this true?"

"Self-defense!" Burleson said. "I was . . . protecting the state. Protecting my citizens. That man was sowing sedition. He proposed a breakdown of law and order. You understand about order, general. You see that I had no other choice . . ."

A beat passed. The general said nothing.

A few paces off, the medic said, "This man needs surgery right away. He should be airlifted."

General Belden stuck a finger in the air and twirled it, as if to say: "Make it so."

Another medic advanced and helped shoulder Nolan's massive bulk. Together, they began to move him toward a waiting helicopter. The crowd seemed reluctant to let him go. Some people were not even properly supporting him, just eager to touch him with a finger or two.

Nolan groaned and allowed the transfer to happen. Then he looked back and nodded to the crowd. It was time for them to let him go.

As the medics began to ease Nolan toward the helicopter—looking for all the world like trainers helping an injured baller off the court—General Belden strode over.

"Son?" the general said to Nolan.

Nolan looked up, his face contorted. The huge man was evidently in great pain. He opened his mouth to speak, but nothing came out. He had given all that he had to give.

General Belden nodded and made the spinning motion with his finger again. Nolan's head fell to his chest. The straining medics hurried away. The general marched back to Burleson.

"Mister Governor," Belden said. "I think you'd better come with me."

"Of course," Burleson said firmly. "Now that the federal government *is* here—unbidden, of course—I suppose we should coordinate efforts . . ."

"Uh-*huh*," the general said. "Right this way, Governor."

Burleson straightened his shirt and slicked down his hair. Then he followed the general across the verdant capitol lawn to where the helicopter was waiting.

This was not the end, the governor assured himself. It was only the end of the beginning.

Epilogue

Kesha Washington stood at the front of the social studies classroom. She wore her best dress, and even a little makeup. In the autumn that came to Indiana two years after the outbreak, her small private school had finally reopened.

Things had changed.

Before, Kesha had been a misfit, nervous about keeping her grades high enough to retain her scholarship. Now she was one of the school's star students. In fact, the school had contacted her father to *ensure* that she would be returning when they reopened. A full scholarship for the rest of her time was now guaranteed (whatever her grades or disciplinary history might be). After that, a full ride for an in-state college was more or less assured. Kesha Washington had become one of the most famous people in the state.

Kesha had agreed to return. Her one request—perhaps it had been closer to a demand, Kesha would allow, if pressed—was that Madison Burleson (now bereft of money and title) be allowed to finish school with her. All three remaining years, without tuition or fees. And that an orphan named Steven Hipwell be admitted as an incoming junior, with similar conditions.

On this particular morning—as the school formally restarted once more—there was an electricity in the air. It was as if the state itself were restarting. After two hard years, things were finally getting back to normal. The zombies had been cleared from all major cities, and from most of the countryside. Agriculture was operating smoothly again. Commerce was largely unhindered. Military law had been rendered unnecessary, and so rescinded. There were jury trials again.

This was also a special morning, because the class had a visiting guest. The newspaper photographers gathered at the back of the room attested to his importance. (Some of the photographers were also in the employ of the school. The images captured today would be prominently featured in admissions brochures for years to come.) The special guest was James Nolan, commissioner of the IMPD.

Nolan, who had already made a few introductory remarks, stood at the side of the classroom while Kesha finished her report on the history of Indiana's role in the "Z-Day" outbreak. The class stared up at her with something like awe. (Except for Madison, the faces were entirely new. The original sophomore class had been completely decimated.)

"In conclusion . . ." Kesha read from the pages stacked on the podium in front of her. "The Z-Day outbreak in Indiana was important because Indiana had a different challenge than any other state during the crisis. Indiana showed that even if a leader became unfit to govern, the people could work together to peacefully remove him and preserve the interests of the state and its citizens. Thank you."

Kesha knew that this was, of course, ridiculous.

The idea that she could sum up what Z-Day had meant to everyone in the state was a fantasy. There were six million Hoosiers and six million stories. Some were tales of heroism. Others were of murder or neglect or craven fear. What about those? Summing up what had happened was beyond anybody's power. Yet, as Kesha had slowly realized, it had to be done. And because of who she was, it would now be expected of her.

Kesha looked up from the podium. The beaming social studies teacher standing near the door applauded with all her might. So did the principal, and several other members of administration who'd dropped in for this class. The seated students applauded too. At the back of the room, the cameras clicked and flashed.

Kesha smiled weakly. She was still growing accustomed to the attention. As the applause continued to ring out, she looked over at the tall, uniformed police commissioner standing in the corner. He applauded, too.

It was because of Nolan, of course, that Kesha's role in the events leading to the downfall of Governor Burleson had been recognized. Nolan was already a hero. Accordingly, the media had wanted to make the events on the barricade a singlehanded achievement, as if he had been operating alone. Yet Nolan had insisted—again and again—that it was only through the intercession of a brave high school student that he had found the strength to do what he had done.

After the incarceration of Burleson, the record concerning Nolan's accident in college had been reopened. There was still no hard evidence for what had happened, but in the court of popular opinion Nolan had been exonerated. The cries for his promotion to commissioner had come soon thereafter.

Nolan looked over at Kesha and smiled. He was proud of her. He hoped she would go far, and that all of this to-do would be only the beginning for her.

After Kesha's presentation concluded, she gave Nolan a quick tour of the prep school (with photographers and administrators in tow). The damage sustained in the first days of the outbreak had been completely repaired. The school had been restored to its former glory, and then some. Carpeting, windows, and guardrails were all shiny and new.

Kesha concluded the tour at the entrance to the school. An IMPD SUV with an officer behind the wheel was waiting for Nolan. The photographers took a final set of photos of Nolan, Kesha, and the principal of the school standing together.

"Thanks again, Mister Commissioner," the principal said. "Kesha, I'll see you back in class."

"Sure thing, Principal Armitage," Kesha called. "I just need to have a quick word with James."

"Oh . . ." said the principal. "Of course, Kesha. Take as long as you need."

The principal headed back inside the school. The photographers wandered away to the parking lot, chatting and sometimes shaking hands. In moments, Kesha and Nolan were quite alone underneath the fragrant trees that framed the entrance to the school.

They looked at one another for a long beat, smiling. And then Kesha laughed.

"I'm sorry," she said. "I'm not even sure what I'm laughing at. This is just so strange."

"It *is* pretty weird," Nolan allowed.

"Thank you again for everything," Kesha said. "I never know what to say."

"Are you kidding?" Nolan said. "Thank *you*. None of this would have been possible without you. I'd still be working for Burleson and . . . you know . . . the entire state would be a whole lot shittier."

Then they both laughed a little.

"You look like you're doing well," Nolan said.

"I'm old for a sophomore now," Kesha said. "We all are. We missed two years of school. It's weird."

"I think that'll work itself out," Nolan told her. "When you're older, nobody will even notice it."

"I suppose," Kesha said. "I'll do my best."

"You'll do more than that," Nolan said.

He looked at his watch.

"You have to go," Kesha said.

"I kinda do," he told her. "You take care, kid. I'll catch you around."

Kesha nodded, and watched as Nolan climbed into the passenger seat of the SUV. Then she turned back toward the school—that was now somehow hers in a very real sense—and walked back through the doors.

"Pull over," Nolan said to the patrolman in the driver's seat.

"Hmm?" the driver said as if he had not quite heard correctly.

"Right here," Nolan said.

"Commissioner, we're already late."

"This will only take a second," Nolan said.

The SUV crawled to a halt in front of a nondescript subdivision along College Avenue. The nearest home had a real estate company sign on the lawn. Part of the legend read—"Fixer-upper's dream! Minimal zombie damage!" Nolan got out of the SUV and strode up the walkway to the dilapidated dwelling. He raised a hand and hailed the scruffy-looking man sitting on the front porch smoking a cigarette.

"James!" Nathan Dazey cried. "James Nolan?! Is that really you?"

Nolan could hardly believe his eyes. Dazey was like a cockroach. The whole state could go to hell, and somehow he'd survive.

"Me in the flesh," Nolan said.

"You never used to wear a uniform. And when you did, it didn't have that many gold trinkets on it."

"Times change," Nolan said with a smile. "How you doin'? It's been a couple of years."

"I been, you know, survivin'," Dazey said. "Gettin' by. Looking out for zombies."

"There haven't been any for a while," Nolan said. "Not in the cities, at least."

"Yeah, I suppose," Dazey said, drawing on his cigarette. "Never can be too careful, though."

Nolan grinned.

"Are you squatting here?" Nolan asked.

"For now I am," Dazey said, looking away. "For a while there, the livin' was good. Empty houses everywhere. Empty stores. Things just there for the takin'. A man like me could live like a king."

"I'll bet," Nolan said. "But times are changing again, buddy. This house is gonna belong to somebody soon. Maybe a family. A lot of people still need a place to stay."

"Yeah . . ." Dazey allowed. "I suppose so."

"Why don't you let me give you a lift somewhere?" Nolan said.

A mischievous smile crossed Dazey's face.

"Anywhere on the east side, right?" Dazey asked. "Just like old times?"

"Anywhere you like," Nolan said to the scruffy man. "We can go anywhere at all."

"A New Indiana."

Hank Burleson looked down at the heading on the photocopied pamphlet as the guard thrust it through the bars of his dingy cell.

"What the fuck is this?" Burleson growled.

The meaty guard smiled through crooked teeth.

"Orientation brochure," said the guard. "Tells you all about how the world has changed since Z-Day. State says we have to give one to anybody who might get paroled. You got your first review board hearing coming up next week."

Inmate #2345723 of the Marion County Hospital for the Criminally Insane ripped the pamphlet away from the guard with great ferocity. The guard's smile widened.

"Not that I give you much of a chance," the guard said. "In fact, you're the last person I expect to see get out of here. Ever. But you should still read the brochure. It's supposed to familiarize you with the way things are on the outside now."

Burleson was no longer listening. He retreated to the bunk at the back of his cell and began to read the pamphlet.

Because of recent events, the world outside this hospital may look somewhat different from the one you left when you were admitted.

No shit, Burleson thought.

The outbreak of undead approximately twenty-four months ago has created substantial changes to the state's infrastructure, commerce, government, and culture. When you re-enter society, you will probably become aware of these changes.

No shit again, Burleson thought. Who the fuck had written this? Who was this for? He knew many of his fellow inmates were feeble-minded, but this was ridiculous.

Many of these changes are positive.

That stopped Burleson cold.
He frowned down at the page in his hand.
What on earth . . . ? Was this someone's idea of a joke?
Ever intrepid, he read on.

Some of the changes you are likely to notice include:

- *Increased citizen engagement in the political process*
- *Increased openness in government*
- *Increased social connection among community members*
- *Bartering of goods and services*
- *Decreased use of gasoline and personal cars*
- *Increased use of public transportation and alternative energy (solar power, wind power)*
- *Increased access to city services*
- *New connections between farmers and consumers ("farm to table")*
- *Renewed partnerships between Indiana and other states in the region*

- *A stronger sense of state and national pride*
- *Sharing*
- *Cooperation*

Burleson put down the pamphlet. He could read no further. This was not his Indiana. This was not anything.

He wanted no part of it.

"Guard!" Burleson cried. "Guard, come here!"

A few minutes later, the attendant trundled down the grim hallway to Burleson's cell.

"What?"

"Here," Burleson said, shoving the pamphlet back through the bars. "I don't want it."

"You have to take it," the guard informed him.

"No," Burleson said. "I don't want to."

"If you don't take it, you can't go to your review board hearing."

"Then I'm not going," Burleson barked.

He threw the pamphlet through the bars where it settled at the man's feet. The guard looked down at the pamphlet, then up at Burleson.

"Are you *sure*?" the guard said. (His tone indicated he might be dealing with a six–year-old who'd just insisted he didn't need to use the restroom before a long car trip.)

Burleson retreated to his bunk and sat down with his arms crossed. He stared straight ahead. He was very, very still.

"Yeah," Burleson said.

"You're *sure*?" the guard repeated.

Burleson looked at the guard and nodded.

"There's nothing out there that I want."

The guard shrugged, picked up the offending pamphlet, and shuffled back down the hallway. Burleson listened to him plodding away, his steps growing softer and softer. Soon there was nothing to hear at all.

Burleson was alone in the silence.